# The Republic
# of
# Broken Places

**A Radical Rootless Cosmopolitan Culture
Maccabi-Punk
Judeo-Futurist
Alternate History
of the
Unnervingly Imminent Tomorrow**

## Peter Ullian

**Swamp Angel Press**

**Judeo-Futurist Dystopian Lit

# Dedication

To my wife and kids, for everything.

To Donna Minkowitz and Lit Lit, for a place to imagine.

To Stanza Books, for the books and inspiration.

# Table of Contents

# Author's Note:

The city in which the Horwitz family resides bears similarities to Cleveland, Ohio, but I have managed to avoid mentioning the name of that great metropolis in this narrative because I have taken a few liberties with geography and street names.

"The world breaks everyone and afterward many are strong at the broken places. But those that will not break it kills. It kills the very good and the very gentle and the very brave impartially. If you are none of these you can be sure it will kill you too but there will be no special hurry."

— Ernest Hemingway, *A Farewell to Arms*

# Part One: On the Continent of Broken Places

**Seven years after the Collapse**
**Eight weeks before Operation Supreme Flood for America**
**Eight weeks before the Fall of Eden**
**In the Sovereign Republic of North America**

# Chapter One

"There goes Anne Frank," Polly Horwitz said. "No big surprise. Anne Frank always goes into the fire."

"Why are they burning Jack London?" Manny Horwitz asked. "He wasn't Jewish."

"No, but they don't like sled dogs."

"That's not true," Manny said. His sister was always being caustic.

"You think White nationalists *do* like sled dogs?" Polly asked.

"I don't think it's the sled dogs, is what I'm saying," Manny explained.

"Of course, it's not the sled dogs," Polly said. "It's the socialism."

Manny hadn't known Jack London was a socialist. His twin sister Polly had always been the smart one. She'd learned her Torah portion six months before their still upcoming co-B'nai Mitzvah, which was now just a few more weeks away – assuming the government didn't close the synagogues before then.

The only thing Manny had read of Jack London was "To Light a Fire" for some kind of state test thing. He wondered if the book burners knew Jack London was on the state tests.

The book burners stood across the park from them, their bonfire surrounded by banners proclaiming, "Down with ZOG" and "Resist the Zionist Occupied Government

Entity" and "Jews Will Not Replace Us" and "No Zionists in Government – We Serve ONE Nation" and "There is Only One Solution, White Christian Revolution" and "Blood and Soil" and "Just Say No to Cultural Marxism" and "No More Jewish Wars" and "No White Lives for Jews" and "Make America White Again" and "Zionist Occupied Government = Terrorism" and "End Jewish Terror" and "Zios Aren't Worth Dying For" and "The Patriot Front Will Reclaim America" and "*Judenrät*, You Can't Hide, You Commit White Genocide" and "Forward for a New American Nation State" and "American by Blood" and "The Way to Victory is White Solidarity" and "Our Nation, Our Duty" and "The Holocaust is an Anti-White Lie" and "Ban the ADL" and "From Sea to Shining Sea, White America Will Be Free" and "Every Aspect of Mass Immigration, Pornography, Abortion, Gun Control, the Media, and Child Sacrifice is Jewish" and "End the New World Order -- Globalize the White Christian Uprising" and "Every Violent Act Against Jews is an Act of Freedom Fighters" and "Jewish Dollars Fund Cultural Marxist Ideas" and "Not Our People, Not Our Problem" and "White Lives Matter" and "Zios Don't Care About You" and "Diversity = White Genocide" and "ZOG = White Genocide" and "Jews = White Genocide" and "The Zionist Entity = White Genocide" and "We Must Secure the Existence of Our People and a Future for White Children" and "Refugees Not Welcome" and "White Power" and "Hail to the White Race" and "End Jewish Control of Banks, Media, and Politicians" and "Free America from Jewish Supremacy" and "Action, Refusal, Resistance -- By Any Means Necessary" and "Resistance is Justified when America is Occupied."

"What do they mean by 'resistance,' again?" Manny asked.

"Dude, using the blood of Christian babies to make our Matzoh almost always leads to resistance," Polly said.

"I never liked the taste of Christian baby blood in Matzoh anyway," Manny said. "Too salty."

"If it weren't for salt, Jewish food would have no taste whatsoever."

"So, I'm confused about something: are Jews White or not-White now?" Manny asked. "I've lost track."

"To the Swastika Right we're not White," Polly said. "Never have been to them. But to the naked eye, you're about as White as it gets. If the Nazis knew someone as White as you were actually a Jew-boy, their heads would probably explode."

"There goes Proust into the fire," Manny said, as the book burners began to throw one volume after another of *Remembrance of Things Past* into the conflagration.

"I approve of that one, actually," Polly said.

"You haven't read Proust," Manny said.

"I have too," Polly said.

"You are a big fat liar," Manny said.

"I'm not fat," Polly said. In truth, they were both tall and gangly.

"But you *are* a liar," Manny insisted.

"*You* are," Polly said.

"At least I don't pretend to have read Proust."

"I'm not pretending," Polly said. "I have."

"What, like a page?" Manny asked.

"Like a whole chapter."

"Ok. How was it?"

"It was so boring!" Polly exclaimed.

"So that makes you the Proust expert."

"More than you," Polly said.

"Proust wasn't Jewish, though, right?" Manny said, turning his focus back on the book bonfire, which was by now quite large and blazingly robust, fueled by Proust's prodigious literary output.

"He was baptized, but his mom was Jewish," Polly explained. "That's why he made such degenerate art."

"Do you think they'll raid the museums and start burning the degenerate paintings?" Manny asked. He found the possibility alarming. He knew nothing about art in particular, but he imagined some art neo-Nazis and Christian Nationalists deemed degenerate might be kind of sexy and he'd have liked a chance to look at it before it got completely immolated in White supremacist infernos.

"The museums have already taken the degenerate art off the walls and put it into storage," Polly said.

"So, that'll make it easy to find when they decide to burn it all," Manny said, despairingly. "They'll just look in their storage room under 'D' for 'degenerate'."

"I think they're too greedy to burn it," Polly said. "That shit is priceless. I think they'll probably sell it for cash. Maybe overseas. Or maybe to the Cooperative Commonwealth of Pacifica. They love degenerate art in the CCP."

"Miri says they don't love Jews in the Commonwealth, particularly, though," Manny said. Miri was their oldest brother Frenchy's wife. She was originally from California, which was now part of the CCP, which encompassed California and the Pacific Northwest. "They only tolerate their 'approved' Jews."

"What are 'approved' Jews?" Polly asked.

"I'm not sure," Manny admitted. "Secular, queer, anti-Zionist, anarchist, intersectional, vegan Jews, I think. You know — like you."

"Shut up!" Polly cried. "I am *not* vegan. I'm not particularly secular, either."

"You basically are," Manny said.

"*You* are!"

"But I admit I am."

"We're about to become B'nai Mitzvahs!" Polly said. "How secular is that?"

"But you're just doing that to please Mom and Dad."

"Mom and Dad aren't around anymore, in case you haven't noticed," Polly said, irritably and a little sadly. Their parents had both been "disappeared" by the government of the Sovereign Republic of North America, which encompassed most of the Rust Belt, about a year ago and hadn't been heard from since.

"I have noticed," Manny said, sadly. "And that's *why* you want to please them. If they were still around, you'd just want to piss them off."

Polly was silent as she thought that over and realized Manny might be right.

"We go to services twice a month and light Shabbat candles every Friday night," Polly said. "That's not Orthodox, but that's not exactly secular, either."

"We don't keep kosher."

"Just because the Horwitz family recognizes the awesomeness of pork fried rice and bacon does not make us secular!"

"It's secular-ish," Manny said.

"It's iconoclastic," Polly said. "There's a difference."

"We celebrate Christmas and Easter!"

"We celebrate Thanksgiving, too," Polly said. "That doesn't make us Pilgrims! We celebrate Arbor Day! That doesn't make us trees! We celebrate the 4th of July! That doesn't make us land-owning delegates to the Continental Congress wearing powdered wigs! And I'm not *anti*-Zionist either! I am *post*-Zionist."

"I am a *synthetic* Zionist," Manny said, irreverently.

"What's a 'synthetic' Zionist?" Polly said. She had never heard the term, and it was rare that her brother knew something she did not.

"I'm not totally sure," Manny said. "I think it's Zionism for robots."

"So, if the Cooperative Commonwealth only approves of secular, queer, anti-Zionist, anarchist, intersectional, vegan Jews, who are the approved Jews in the Free

Republic of the Southwest?" Polly asked.

"I guess the kind who can ride broncos while quoting Ayn Rand," Manny said.

"What about in the United Democratic States of America?" Polly asked. The UDS of A was all that was left of the old USA, mostly clustered in the Northeast corridor between North Carolina and Maine and extending to Western Pennsylvania. It was run out of New York and New Jersey now that DC and Arlington had been reduced to radioactive ash.

"They don't approve of any Jews," Manny said. "But they don't make any laws against them either."

"What about in the Great Plains Agricultural Federation?"

"They approve of Jews who are farmers," Manny said. "But not Jews who are bankers."

"How about in the Western Mountain Federation?

"They approve of Jews who are cowboys, but not Jews who are lawyers."

"And the Utah Nation of Latter-Day Saints?" Polly asked.

"They approve of us once they've posthumously converted us."

"And what about in the White Christian Confederacy of the Nazarene Nation?"

"They only approve of one kind of Jew," Manny said. "The dead kind."

"What about converts?"

"They approve of converts, too," Manny said. "After they kill them."

Polly thought that over, and it didn't make her feel very good.

"Well, anyway, the Cooperative Commonwealth definitely loves 'degenerate' art, if not so much the Jews who created it," Polly said, finally, being caustic again. "Proust was gay, so I'm guessing they probably love him."

"*You're* gay," Manny said.

"*You* are," Polly said.

"But you *really* are," Manny said.

"I'm a semi-secular, iconoclastically practicing, pan-sexual, post-Zionist, anarchist-inclined, intersectional, carnivorous Jew," Polly said. "So, I'm modestly degenerate. But don't tell the book burners. They might throw *me* on the fire."

She meant it to be a joke, but both of them stood there for a moment by the giant "Free Stamp" sculpture in Willard Park, watching the books burn and wondering if the book burners by the Pulaski Square Cannon Monument, a very long cannon erected in honor of Revolutionary War hero Casimir Pulaski, across Lakeside Avenue from the American Legion Hall on one side and with City Hall behind them, actually would throw Polly on the fire if they knew she were a bi-sexual pubescent Jew.

"Speaking of queer Jews," Polly said, as next into the fire went Tony Kushner's *Angels in America,* both *Millennium Approaches* and *Perestroika.*

"Well, that's shitty," Manny said, irritably. "I love that play."

Neither of them had ever seen a production, of course, because of censorship laws that had been in effect since they were young, but the Horwitz family library still had a tattered copy from the Before Times.

Polly and Manny watched sadly as *This Book is Gay, Portnoy's Complaint, Not All Boys Are Blue, The Hate You Give, The Fixer, The Perks of Being a Wallflower, The Complete Maus: A Survivor's Tale, The Bluest Eye, Number the Stars, The Night Trilogy, Life in a Nazi Concentration Camp, Hitler's Final Solution, Survival in Auschwitz, The Painted Bird, Herzog, Black White and Jewish: Autobiography of a Shifting Self, Suite Française, Bee Season, The Arc of a Covenant: The United States*

*Israel and the Fate of the Jewish People, Call Me By Your Name, Life Goes On, The Oppermans, The Passenger, The English Teacher, The Reader, Israel: A Simple Guide to the Most Misunderstood Country on Earth, Gender Queer, The Splendid and the Vile, The Storyteller, Sophie's Choice, The Freedom Writers Diary, Slaughterhouse-Five, Twelve Years a Slave, The Handmaid's Tale, Mayim's Vegan Table: More Than 100 Great-Tasting and Healthy Recipes from My Family to Yours, Paradise Lost, I Know Why The Caged Bird Sings, The Plot Against America, The Tin Drum, All the Rivers, To Kill a Mockingbird, Catcher in the Rye, The Adventures of Huckleberry Finn, One Flew Over the Cuckoo's Nest, Animal Farm, The Scarlet Letter, 1984, Fahrenheit 451, Lord of the Flies, Battle Cry, Exodus, The Naked and the Dead,* and *Catch-22* were all tossed into the flames.

"Those fucking right-wing Swastika Hamasniks," Polly said. "Burning books that not one of them had even read, or has the talent to read, much less to write."

"How can they be Hamasniks?" Manny said. "Don't they hate Palestinians, too?"

"They hate all non-Whites and non-Christians, including Palestinians," Polly agreed. "But Hamas hates Palestinians and Jews in equal measure, so the Swastika Right finds common cause with them. Hamas basically exists to stack up Jewish bodies on one side and Palestinian bodies on the other and then see who has the bigger pile. The Swastika Right is hoping they'll wipe out most Jews and Palestinians, and then the White Christian Nationalists can sweep in and finish the job."

"Are there left-wing Hamasniks?" Manny asked.

"Definitely."

"What's the difference?"

"A left-wing Hamasnik has a paraglider screensaver," Polly explained. "A right-wing Hamasnik can't spell the word 'paraglider'."

"So, we have the Hamasnik Paraglider Left on one side, and the Hamasnik Swastika Right on the other," Manny said.

"Don't forget about the Hamasnik Silent Majority in the middle."

"How can they be Hamasniks if they're in the middle?" Manny asked.

"Well, they don't want to kill Jews or Muslims personally, but they don't particularly care if someone else does it for them."

"That's what qualifies as the middle?"

"These days, yeah, pretty much," Polly said.

"Are the Hamasnik Silent Majority into paragliders or swastikas?"

"No one knows," Polly said. "They never say. They're *silent.*"

When the Arden edition of the complete works of Shakespeare went into the bonfire, Polly said, "Let's get out of here. I can't stand to watch anymore. It's a total sacrilege. Besides, that Neanderthal is staring at us."

From across the park, there was indeed a nasty-looking man with an overhanging brow giving them the stink eye.

Instinctively, Manny reached below his throat, checking to make sure his Magen David necklace was hidden under his shirt, as it had always been since the rise in Jew-hate began after the establishment of the Sovereign Republic. His fingers closed around empty air; his necklace was properly hidden. He glanced at Polly; his sister's necklace was hidden as well.

"Neanderthals were actually quite smart, it turns out," Manny murmured distractedly and nervously.

"Tell it to that guy giving us the stink eye," Polly said.

"How does he even know we're Jewish?" Manny whispered.

"*Jewdar,*" Polly said. "All Hamasnik Swastika Right-

Wingers have it."

Polly tugged on Manny's arm and the two of them hurried down Rock n' Roll Boulevard to the bus stop at the corner of Lakeside Avenue, hoping to catch a bus home to Balfour Court in Coventry Village in the Heights.

# Chapter Two

So far, Julius Horwitz thought, the job interview was going pretty well.

"Well, I must say, your college grades are terrific," the HR woman, Cecily Simpson, said. "And your writing samples are first rate."

"Thank you," Julius said. "I'm a hard worker."

"You must be," Simpson said. "It can't have been easy. Particularly . . ."

She trailed off.

"You mean the campus exclusion thing?" Julius said, cautiously.

"You had to take your last year of classes online, is that correct?" Simpson asked.

"I guess they didn't want Jewish students in the same classrooms as everyone else or something," Julius admitted. He was now feeling uneasy about where this was going. Cecily Simpson appeared kind and sympathetic, but . . . one never knew. "They said it was a safety issue."

"After the campus riots, is that correct?"

"I suppose."

"That must have been very difficult," she said.

"It wasn't ideal."

"I can only imagine," Cecily Simpson said. "One group blaming you for White genocide, another for colonial settler Zionist genocide, and the other . . ."

She trailed off.

"For killing Jesus?" Julius offered.

Cecily Simpson nodded sadly. "I want you to know that I do not in any way blame you personally for the death of our Lord and Savior, Jesus Christ," she said.

Julius felt his heart drop to his stomach. He pursed his lips. "Well, I mean, I barely knew the guy," he said.

Simpson looked at him in bewilderment for a moment. Then she smiled. "Oh, that was a joke."

"Such as it was," Julius said. "I hope I didn't offend."

"No, not at all," Simpson said. "I myself know Jesus quite well. Not in the way you mean, of course. Which raises the question . . . would you like to . . . ?"

"Like to what?"

"Know Jesus?"

Julius held his breath for a moment. "Does he work here?"

"There's that Jewish humor again," Simpson said with a tolerant smile. "But I'm very serious. If you'd like to know Jesus, I can help."

Julius frowned. "Is that a requirement of employment?"

"No, no, not at all," Simpson said. "But you know . . ."

She trailed off again.

"I know . . .?" Julius said, trying to prod her to be forthright.

"All that 'Jews will not replace us' business," Simpson said, softly, as if not to be overheard. "I mean, it's inevitable that if you take a job here, some people are going to question whom you replaced."

"Are you thinking of firing someone and giving me their job?"

"No, no, of course not," Simpson said. "That's not what I mean."

"But you're saying if you give me the job, someone will wonder ...?"

"Yes," Simpson said. "Someone will wonder."

Julius sighed, more audibly than he had intended. "Can we just say out loud what it is they will wonder, just so I don't have to wonder what it is they'll wonder?"

"They'll wonder who the White person is we did not hire in order to hire you," Simpson said . . . forthrightly, for the first time.

Julius held up his hand and looked at it. "I'm not White enough?"

"Well, of course, I recognize that racial categories are social constructs," Simpson said. "But as far as the law in the Sovereign Republic of North America sees it, no. You're not."

Julius was impressed Cecily Simpson knew concepts like "social construct." He nodded with a resigned understanding. "It's a little hard to keep up," he said. "My great-great grandparents were not considered White by most White Americans when they came over from the Pale. Then my parents, in the Before Times, were considered *too* White and privileged to be categorized as an oppressed minority, even when hate groups shot up their synagogue and painted swastikas on the windows of their place of business and threw Molotov cocktails at them when they were marching in a peaceful protest. Now Jews are *not* White again. It's enough to give you whiplash."

"It must be quite confusing. But, of course, if you knew Jesus . . ." Simpson said, hopefully.

"I could become 'White' again?"

Simpson nodded hopefully. "Certainly, more white than you are now," she said.

Julius frowned. "Would it help me get the job?"

Simpson shrugged. "Well, in the Sovereign Republic, Jewishness is not a strictly religious category. Unlike the White Confederacy, we're not a theocracy. Under the law, Jewishness is more of a racial, ethnic, cosmopolitan, globalist, Culturally Marxist, tribal, ethno-nationalist, Zionist, or Zionist-adjacent or, if you prefer, *socially constructed* category. So, under the law, even if you convert, you'd still be considered a Jew. But, you know, there aren't actually any laws against hiring Jewish employees. It's just that it's . . ."

She trailed off.

"Frowned upon?" Julius offered.

Simpson nodded, sadly. "And if you convert, it might be less . . ." She trailed off again.

"Frowned upon?"

"At least in this place of business," Simpson said. "Yes."

Julius took a deep breath. "Well, this is a big decision. Do you have a pamphlet or something?"

Simpson smiled and opened a desk drawer, from which she produced a pamphlet. She handed it to Julius. The print on the front said something about how the conversion from sinner to Christian was like a caterpillar becoming a butterfly. Julius's head swam with images from the book *The Hungry, Hungry Caterpillar*. Julius wondered if *The Hungry, Hungry Caterpillar* had been tossed on any bonfires, recently. He recalled that Eric Carle's book *Draw Me a Star* had been, for its depiction of a naked man and woman.

Julius looked at Cecily Simpson and smiled as he slipped the pamphlet into his inside suit coat pocket. "Thank you for this," he said. "I will look it over and give it the utmost consideration."

Cecily Simpson smiled back. "I'm so glad to hear it," she said. She looked over some papers. "I assume you have no objections to signing the oath affirming you have no dual loyalties?"

"I have no dual loyalties, and I'll sign a document attesting to it," Julius affirmed, although it irked him that only Jewish people were required by law to sign such an oath as a condition of employment.

"And you have no objection to signing the standard denunciation of the Zionist ideology and its practice of White genocide, government occupation, and ethno-supremacist settler colonialism?"

This brought Julius up short. "Is that a thing, now?"

Cecily Simpson looked both a little surprised and a little embarrassed. "Well, that's where the dual loyalty business comes in."

Julius frowned. "So, when they ask for a denunciation of Zionism, do they mean Political Zionism, Practical Zionism, Synthetic Zionism, Labor Zionism, Liberal Zionism, Revisionist Zionism, Religious Zionism, Revolutionary Zionism, or Reform Zionism?"

The list had apparently left Cecily Simpson bewildered. "Honestly," she admitted, "I have no idea."

"Well, if I can take the text of the denunciation home with me, I'd be happy to look it over," Julius said. "I'm sure it will be fine."

He did not believe for a second that anything would be fine, perhaps ever again.

Cecily Simpson smiled and handed him another sheet of paper. "We'll let you know our decision by the end of the week," she said, cheerily.

# Chapter Three

Milton Horwitz walked through the high school hallway avoiding eye contact with his fellow students.

This was something he rarely did. He was an athlete, and much admired. He usually walked these halls with confidence and a little bit of swagger. Even the anti-Semites usually steered clear of him. Although Milton – or "Miltie" as he was known -- knew he was a pussycat at heart, he was a head taller and quite a bit more muscular than most of his classmates. He'd never been in a proper fight, but most of them didn't know that. His father had taught all of the family self-defense skills, but because of his size and athleticism, Miltie hoped he'd never have to use them.

Although his last name was a dead giveaway, Miltie never admitted to anyone that he was Jewish. He never actually said he *wasn't* Jewish, exactly, either. When people asked, he told them not every "Horwitz" was a Jew, and that his name came from the Bohemian town of Hořovice, in the Czech Republic.

This was true, as far as it went.

Of course, the kids from families who had known the Horwitz family since the Before Times all knew that he was Jewish. But no one had ever contradicted him – at least not to his face.

Today, rumors were flying around the hallways that after the end of the semester, Jews would be formally expelled from all Sovereign Republic public schools, and Jews would have to create their own schools in the government-designated Jewish neighborhoods without state assistance or taxpayer money. Everyone Miltie passed looked at him, some sympathetically, some sadly, some contemptuously.

Miltie was beginning to wonder if maybe his caginess about his last name hadn't been as convincing as he'd hoped.

At lunch, Miltie sat with members of his team, as he usually did.

"Did you hear about the *Jewspulsion?*" Robbie Dale, the star quarterback, asked him, as Miltie toyed disinterestedly with his Salisbury steak and a plastic spork.

That's what the kids were calling it now, Miltie thought. The *Jewspulsion.* He supposed that was the kind of thing that passed for clever. His heart kicked up a gear, slamming against his ribcage.

Miltie forced himself to make eye contact with Robbie, to appear confident and strong and unafraid and unaffected by the news of the day. "You think it's true?" he asked, his voice level. He was grateful he'd been able to contain the quaver and tightness he felt rising in his throat.

Robbie shrugged. "Who knows?" he said. "There's rumors like this every year."

"Hope they don't expel you just because of your name, Horwitz," linebacker "Sloppy" Joe Long said.

"Hope they don't expel you because of your dumb-assery, Joe," Miltie shot back with fake bravado.

The rest of the team laughed heartily. Sloppy Joe was universally regarded as the stupidest kid on the team, although he wasn't a bad linebacker.

Robbie laughed as well, but with his eyes locked on

Miltie's. He had a knowing expression on his face.

Did Robbie know? Miltie wondered.

And if he knew, what did he know?

"Hey, who is that hot chick coming our way?" said "Moose" Milford, the halfback.

Moose liked to pretend to be a jerk, but he was actually not a bad guy. It was a running joke that whenever Miltie's twin sister, Bertie, showed up, Moose would make an inappropriate comment, because he knew it annoyed Miltie. But everyone on the team actually adored Bertie and treated her like a sister – even Moose. They all agreed she was a beauty, and they all respected that -- to them anyway -- she was off limits.

Bertie slid onto the bench beside Miltie and immediately took the spork from his hand and cut his Salisbury steak in half. Then she began shoveling bites into her own mouth. Miltie's teammates laughed. Bertie was renowned amongst them for her ability to eat like a pig and never put on weight. This was possibly because she was on the cross country and women's lacrosse teams as well as the star of the school dance company and just burned everything off.

"I *am* a hot chick, Moose," Bertie said with her mouth full. "The humidity outside is over seventy-five percent today."

Moose's face flushed. "I didn't know you heard me, Bertie," Moose said, embarrassed.

"You don't have an indoor voice, Moose," Bertie said. "Everyone heard you."

Moose's face flushed a deeper red, which Miltie had not thought possible.

"Eat your protein," Bertie said, holding up the spork for Miltie, upon which was skewered a chunk of Salisbury steak. "You've got practice today."

"It's a good thing you've got your sister to mother you, Miltie," Robbie Dale said. "Or else I'd have to do it."

Their mother had packed a lunch for all eight of her children every day until the government had "disappeared" her and their father a year ago. His sister-in-law Miri had offered to do the same, but Miltie couldn't bear it; that's when he started eating school lunches.

Which he hated.

To make his sister happy, he took the spork from her hand and fed himself.

"When you're done with that, let's go outside before class starts and have a smoke," Bertie said.

Everyone knew she was joking. Neither athlete smoked. But they also knew Bertie wanted to talk to her brother alone, and they knew to respect that.

They all adored Bertie, but they were all a little afraid of her, too.

# Chapter Four

As Julius left the old Citizens Building on Euclid, he slipped the Christian pamphlet and the Zionist denunciation pledge out of his suit coat pocket and dropped them in a trash can on the curb.

He was feeling at loose ends. When he'd started college, even with the Sovereign Republic of North America by then already firmly in power, no one doubted a young man of his talents would be able to get a good job *somewhere*. Antisemitism had become fashionable again – maybe it had never truly gone *out* of fashion -- but not everyone was yet a shameless Jew-hater.

Now, as a new graduate, he was finding all the doors slammed in his face. People were now either all proud Jew-haters, or, more commonly, wanted to avoid invoking the wrath of the Jew-haters. Since job discrimination on the basis of religion and ethnicity was now socially acceptable and there were no laws against it, that left a young man like Julius out in the cold.

What was he supposed to do with his fancy degree? Work in the Horwitz music store like his big brother Frenchy? Take up underground bare-knuckled boxing like his brother Lenny?

Maybe he could teach in one of the new schools being set up for Jewish children, since the rumor was that all the Jewish kids were just about to be expelled from the public K-12 schools. They must need teachers, he thought. But how much did a job like that pay? How much *could* it pay? Probably not enough for him to move out of the Horwitz family home on Balfour Court.

It was an inauspicious way for a young man to get his start in the world.

Julius passed Schönberg's Delicatessen on East 8th Street. Plywood boarded up its broken windows and charred interior.

It had been firebombed just a few nights previously. Authorities said it was a "spontaneous" demonstration, but reports indicated that the cops had passively stood by and watched as the one-hundred-year-old family business, indisputably the best Jewish deli in the downtown business district -- had burned to the ground.

Didn't these wannabe Nazis like to eat? What was wrong with them?

On the plywood that covered the broken window, someone had spray painted in red "Jews, go back home."

This was supposed to *be* our home, Julius thought. Where do they think we should go "back" to?

Next to the admonition to return to a nonexistent place, the vandal had painted a backward swastika.

The idiots couldn't even get their own swastikas right.

Julius continued down the street. He caught a glimpse of himself in a store window and stopped to examine his face. He had grown a mustache recently to try to make himself look older and give himself more *gravitas.* Now, he thought, the mustache just made him look more Jewish. With his glasses on, he realized, it made him look discomfortingly like a baby-faced Groucho Marx – for whom his parents had named him. His parents had named all eight of their kids after members of the Marx Brothers' family.

His parents were completely insane.

He missed them terribly.

A few doors down, he slipped into the Pepper Pot

Diner.

There were still no actual laws on the books restricting restaurants – yet. And he liked their pea soup. Besides he had once dated the waitress there.

Inside, the diner felt warm and inviting, with the smell of bacon and fries permeating the air. Julius took a seat at the counter and flipped open a menu.

"Why're you looking at the menu, Jules?" a familiar voice asked him from behind the counter. "Don't you always order the same thing?"

Julius looked up at Riley – the girl he had dated in high school. She had worked at the Pepper Pot even then, after school. Her parents owned the joint. She was a hard-working kid who had paid her way through community college with the cash she earned from tips.

"You know me so well," Julius said. "You'd almost think we went to school together, or something."

Riley laughed and wiped down the counter with a rag. "Seltzer with a lime, half a BLT on rye toast light on the mayo, a pickle and Cole slaw, and a cup of split pea soup."

Julius closed the menu. "How'd you know?"

Riley called the order to the kitchen behind her and filled a soda glass at the fountain, placing it in front of him on a paper napkin. She squeezed the lime into it herself, unwrapped the straw from its wrapper, and plopped it into the glass. "*L'chaim*," she said.

That was a bold thing for Riley to say. While there was no law against saying it, it was likely to offend someone. Judging by the turned heads in the diner, it had offended – or at least surprised -- a few of her customers.

Riley was not a Jewish girl. She was Catholic. An Irish Catholic girl with bouncy, curly auburn hair, a round face, red lips, big white teeth, and blue eyes that gleamed with delight under the florescent lights of the diner.

Like most Jewish boys, Julius had a thing for Catholic girls.

Although he also had a thing for Jewish girls.

Come to think of it, he pretty much just had a thing for girls.

In this regard, Julius took after Lenny, the second oldest Horwitz brother. The oldest, Simon, who went by the nickname "Frenchy," only had a thing for *one* girl – Miriam, or "Miri," as she was affectionately called. Frenchy and Miri had met one July at the family's annual summer retreat at the Eden Hollow Health and Nature Outdoor Recreation Association Family Bungalow Community when they were both sixteen. Nine years later, they were now happily married – or as happily as a Jewish couple could be in the Sovereign Republic, given current conditions.

Julius still had a thing for Riley, and he thought maybe she still had a thing for him. But he knew that was all over. He could never again be with a gentile girl – at least not without significant legal peril. That actually *was* against the law, now. Even Jewish/non-Jewish marriages from the Before Times had been invalidated by court order.

This had not been the case when they were both still in high school.

A lot had changed since then.

The cook put a plate on the counter in the window to the kitchen. Riley brought the plate to Julius.

In culinary matters as well as romantic ones, it was not Julius's preference to keep kosher. He took a bite of his BLT.

It was delicious, as he knew it would be – crunchy, savory, neither dry nor greasy. The rush of protein surged through his body and made him feel invincible.

Riley leaned into him and whispered. "Listen, have

you guys come up with an exit strategy? After they burned down Schönberg's, it's anyone's guess where this thing is gonna go."

"Where do you think we should escape to?" Julius mumbled, as he gulped a spoonful of his soup.

It was also delicious.

"Well, the best place would be the United Democratic States of America, but they've shut the doors to refuges. The Nazarene Confederacy is obviously out. The Free Republic of the Southwest is supposed to be all live and let live libertarian, but they hate immigrants of all kinds from all places, especially non-White ones, and, in case you haven't heard, you're not White anymore."

"I heard," Julius said.

"They also grant big-time latitude to localities to run their own affairs, even if that means discriminating against Jews or anyone else. The Great Plains and Mountain states don't have anti-Jewish laws, but things are a little Wild, Wild West-y out there, right now, if you ask me," Riley continued. "I mean, you'd be free to live as you please, but if any of those Posse Comitatus, Christian Identity, American Patriot, Constitutional Militia wingding whack-a-doodle nutjobs out there have a problem with y'all, no one is going to stand in their way. But isn't Miri originally from the Cooperative Commonwealth?"

"She is," Julius admitted, taking a bite of his pickle. "Back from when they used to call it California and the Pacific Northwest."

"You look like Groucho with that pickle in your hand and your glasses and mustache," Riley giggled.

"Too Jewish?" Julius whispered.

"Not too Jewish for me," Riley said. She scanned the patrons in the diner. "But, yeah. My advice: lose the mustache. And go West, young man."

"Where will I get my BLTs?" Julius asked.

Riley leaned in again and whispered. "The talk is all the restaurants are going to be restricted, soon. Most public places, actually. Parks, public transportation, theatres, malls, multiplexes. You name it. I was you, I'd get out of Dodge now instead of later."

"But I'd miss you, Riley," Julius whispered.

Riley smiled sadly. "I'd miss you, too, Jules," she said. "But I'll miss you more if you're dead."

That was a blunt assessment. It brought Julius up short. He took a bite of his BLT and chewed so he could think before he said anything more.

"Riley," a patron called. "Stop kibbitzing with that kike and top off my coffee."

Riley spun towards the customer, a powerful looking man in a work shirt and boots who was sitting down the counter from Julius. "He's not a kike, Tucker, he's a customer, and that's more than you're gonna be if you talk to me or my patrons like that again, we clear?"

Tucker raised his thick eyebrows in surprise. "Never took you for a Zio-lover, Riley."

"Never took you for a fuckhead, Tucker," Riley replied. "Oh, no, wait, I did take you for a fuckhead because you are one. You don't even know the word 'kibbitzing' is Yiddish, do you? That means it's a Jewish word. If it wasn't for Jewish words to fill out your vocabulary, you'd still be grunting like a caveman, you fucking troglodyte. Get out of my restaurant, needle dick. This is a place of business, not your private club for assholery."

"You're taking *his* side over mine?" the man named Tucker said, sounding both plaintive and peevish, as if it had never occurred to him that Riley might think him an asshole.

"Get out of my place or I'll stab you in the eye with this fork," Riley told him, picking up a fork from the counter.

Riley's dad, a man of about fifty, had come from

behind the register and was standing at her side. "Riley," he whispered. "You can't treat our customers this way."

"*Tucker* can't treat our customers this way," Riley said, pointing an accusing fork at the man named Tucker.

Her dad looked at Julius. "Julius, you'd better leave," he said, not without sympathy.

Julius stood up.

Riley turned to Julius. "Don't you dare!" she shouted.

"It's Ok," Julius said, putting some money on the counter.

"No charge, just leave, please," her dad said, softly, in a voice tinged with empathy and regret.

"Sit back down," Riley commanded.

Julius sat back down. He was more scared of Riley than of her dad – or of Tucker, for that matter.

Riley turned again to Tucker, pointing at the door. "Out."

"I'm leaving," Tucker said, pulling out some cash.

"Forget about the bill," Riley's dad said.

"Just go," Riley said.

Julius stared at his pea soup as Tucker walked passed him. He heard the bell on the door tinkle as the man presumably left.

A customer asked for more coffee, and Riley went to fill his cup. Her dad leaned down to Julius. "Just finish your meal and leave, Ok?" he whispered. "Make some excuse that you have to be somewhere. No charge. I know this is not your fault, Julius. But I can't have this kind of scene in my place of business. And I can't risk anyone doing to my place what they did to Schönberg's. Or doing something worse to my daughter. I know you understand me, Julius."

"I understand," Julius said hoarsely, and hurried to finish his soup. It felt oddly lukewarm and pasty, as if all the goodness in it had been suddenly leached out.

# Chapter Five

Standing in the shadow of the school building gymnasium, watching a pick-up basketball game, Bertie asked, "do you think the *Jewspulsion* rumors are true this year?"

"I think so, yeah, probably," Miltie said. "It feels like that's a bullet we've dodged one too many times for the rumors not to be true this time."

Bertie nodded, lost in thought. "Do they even have a list?" she wondered aloud. "I mean, how do they know our name isn't actually Bohemian Czech?"

"I'm sure they have a list somewhere," Miltie said. "Or they'll put one together soon enough." Miltie stared at the basketball game for a few moments. "Bertie? Are you scared?"

Bertie looked at her twin brother like he was crazy. "Of course, I'm scared. I'm always scared. I'd be a moron not to be scared."

"You never act scared."

"That's how I manage being scared," Bertie said. "By not acting scared."

"Fake it 'till you make it?"

"More like muddle through until it's over, but yeah, basically."

"I'm scared too," Miltie admitted. "All the time. And not just about the *Jewspulsion.* I'm scared about another thing, too."

Bertie waited, patiently. She knew Miltie wanted to say something important, and she didn't want to press him. "What else are you scared of, Miltie?" she asked.

"Can you keep a secret?"

"You know I can."

"Promise not to tell anyone?" he asked. "Even family?"

"Pinky promise," she said, and held up her pinky finger.

Miltie smiled and locked his pinky with hers. He looked into her eyes and leaned in closer.

"I'm gay," he whispered.

Bertie held his gaze a moment longer, and then burst into laughter.

Miltie pulled away, hurt. "I'm serious."

"I know you're serious, Miltie," Bertie said through her laughter. "I already know you're gay."

"Quiet!" Miltie said.

Bertie lowered her voice. "Miltie," she said, softly. "I know you're gay. I've always known."

"What?" Miltie said. "How? I've never even been with another boy."

"A twin sister knows these things."

Miltie stared off into the distance. "Huh," he grunted.

He immediately began to worry who else knew.

"If they take me away, do you think they'll put a yellow star or a pink triangle on me?" Miltie said.

Bertie stopped laughing. "Jesus, Miltie, don't talk like that."

"I'm just saying."

"Your secret is safe with me." Bertie said. "Although I think everyone in the family already knows."

"How can they already know?" Miltie exclaimed.

"Well, you've never shown any interest in girls."

"I've never shown any interest in liver and onions, either," Miltie said. "That doesn't make me vegan."

Bertie laughed again. "You're clever for a jock," she

said.

"A gay Jewish jock," he whispered.

"It takes all kinds, Miltie."

Miltie looked at his sister, an eyebrow raised. "Does it?" he said. "Tell that to the people who are about to *Jewspel* us."

Bertie gave her brother a hug.

What else could she do?

# Chapter Six

"Why were you watching those thugs burn books?" Frenchy demanded of the twins.

The twins looked at each other sheepishly.

"We were looking for reading recommendations," Polly said.

"Is everything a joke to you?" Frenchy said.

Polly realized her oldest brother was really angry. This puzzled her. She'd done much worse things in her opinion, and he hadn't been this angry.

"We passed it on our way home," Manny said, softly.

"You passed it on your way home from the Rock n' Roll museum, where you went while skipping school," Frenchy said. "Have I got that right so far?"

Manny pursed his lips like he was trying to keep something down. "Um, pretty much, yeah."

They stood in the living room of the Horwitz house on Balfour Court, a leafy cull-de-sac within walking distance of Coventry Road, where their great grandfather had opened the first of the family's record and music shops. The store was now the only one that remained of the three family stores that once thrived in the metropolitan area, the others having been forced to close because they were not located in Jewish-designated areas.

The Horwitz home was a large foursquare in the classic Prairie style, with a brick veneer, hipped dormers, overhanging eaves, and a long, wide front porch. The interior was all their parents' style. The siblings had made no major changes since their parents' disappearance. The walls were hung with vintage instruments, paintings by local artists, and photographs of classic rock and jazz musicians.

"They burned down Schönberg's the other day, did you know that?" Frenchy said.

"The deli?" Polly asked.

"No, the composer," Frenchy said. "Yes, the deli, what do you think?"

Polly hadn't known this. "Why would they do that?" Polly said. "Everybody loves pastrami."

"They did that because the Schönbergs are Jews," Frenchy said. "Don't you get that? It doesn't matter what you do. It doesn't matter what you say. It doesn't matter where you are. It doesn't matter how great your pastrami is. They are out to get us because we are Jews. Don't make a target of yourself. It's hard enough to keep you guys safe as it is. Go to your rooms."

"We're not toddlers," Polly said. "Don't treat us like toddlers."

"I'll stop treating you like toddlers when you stop behaving like toddlers. Go to your rooms and practice your Torah portions."

"Simon," Polly said. She called her oldest brother by his proper name, Simon, when she was trying to be serious.

"Go," Frenchy said. "Now."

"You're not my dad!" Polly cried.

"Now!" Frenchy repeated, firmly.

"Oh my God!" Polly said, turning on her heel and running up the stairs to her room. The slamming of her bedroom door reverberated through the house.

Frenchy looked at Manny, who stood there uncertainly. "Well?"

Manny followed his twin sister up the stairs.

## Chapter Seven

Frenchy flopped down on the couch and put his feet up on the coffee table and his head back. He could hear Polly upstairs in her room, screaming into her pillow.

He could relate. He considered removing one of the couch cushions and screaming into it himself. More than anything, right now he wanted to scream.

His wife Miri came into the room, holding steaming hot tea in two huge mugs in front of her big, round belly, swollen in the sixth month of pregnancy. Her mug had the logo for the Rock n' Roll Museum on it. His had the local public radio station logo upon it. Of course, the radio station had been appropriated by the Sovereign Republic and now only broadcast government-approved content. The Rock n' Roll Museum was still operating, but it was Frenchy's understanding that the authorities had forced it to undergo a thorough redesign to better reflect the Sovereign Republic's ideology.

Both mugs were from the Before Times.

Miri's cell phone timer went off, indicating the tea (Yorkshire, his favorite, for him, decaffeinated Darjeeling for her) had steeped for exactly five minutes. She removed the tea bags and placed them on a saucer and handed the public radio mug to Frenchy.

"You're a goddess," Frenchy said.

"I know," Miri said. "But thanks for noticing."

Frenchy sipped his tea. It was hot and strong and

bracing.

"Did I fuck that up?" he asked Miri.

Frenchy assisted Miri as she lowered herself onto the couch beside him.

"I don't think so," Miri said. "I think they needed to hear it."

"I hate adulting," Frenchy said. They were both only twenty-five and hadn't expected to take responsibility for all of the Horwitz siblings when they'd married two years before. But after Frenchy's parents disappeared a year later – or were more likely "*disappeared*" by the government – that responsibility had fallen on Frenchy as the eldest sibling. He'd also had to take over running his dad's three record and music shops, which had been in the family since his great-grandfather opened them – although now there was only one left, as the Republic had pulled their licenses to operate the two that were located in non-Jewish neighborhoods.

Miri had stood by him throughout – much more so than he'd ever thought to ask of her – especially given that she could have returned to her own parents in the Cooperative Commonwealth any time she'd wanted to.

"Is it time to come up with an exit strategy?" Miri asked, casually, between sips of her Darjeeling.

They'd asked the question dozens of times but had always concluded "not yet."

Now, Frenchy wasn't so certain.

"Do you think the Commonwealth will give us asylum?" Frenchy asked. Miri was originally from the CCP, back when it was still just California and the Pacific Northwest, and still part of the original United States of America, the battered remnants of which were now located in the Northeast Corridor, plus South Florida, Puerto Rico, and the US Virgin Islands.

"They have to take me back," Miri said. "It's the law. And they'll have to take you as my husband. And if our kid is born there, that'll give us a further foothold."

"What about the other seven of us?" Frenchy asked. Frenchy had seven other siblings: Lenny, Julius, Artie, Miltie, Bertie, Manny, and Polly. Their parents had married young, stayed busy, loved each other very much, and didn't practice birth control.

"Well, obviously, we're not going to leave them behind," Miri said. "But the Commonwealth claims they have an open-door policy for refugees."

"Will they consider us refugees?"

"Do you want me to make an appointment with the consulate?"

Frenchy sipped his tea and considered. "Not yet," he said. "We don't want to arouse suspicion. We've got to have everything in place before we set those wheels in motion."

"Let's not wait too long, though," Miri said. "You know the story about how my great-great grandfather didn't want to lose his law practice in Amsterdam and ended up having to hide in a barn from the Nazis for the duration of the war."

"Yeah," Frenchy said softly. "I remember."

"And, you know, the longer we wait, the more complicated it's going to be. They say not to travel in the last thirty days of pregnancy. And if we wait until the baby is born? I mean, that's going to be even more complicated. Oh!" She grabbed Frenchy's hand and put it on her belly. "Your kid has an opinion about this, I guess."

Frenchy felt his child squirm and kick inside his wife's tummy for a moment, and just for a second, all the troubles faded away – until they were replaced by the fear and dread of considering what kind of a world they were bringing their child into.

Polly screamed again into her pillow from her upstairs bedroom.

"I'll talk to her," Miri said.

"Would you?" Frenchy said. "She hates me."

Miri smiled. She kissed him on the mouth. Her lips were soft and lovely. Her eyes, as ever, were the most glorious violet eyes Frenchy had ever seen. "She doesn't hate you, Frenchy. Don't you know anything? People only get *that* angry with the people they love."

# Chapter Eight

Miri knocked on Polly's door and waited a moment for Polly's invitation to enter. Receiving permission, she opened the door, and found Polly with her face in her pillow, screaming.

"You're going to hurt your throat if you keep doing that," Miri said.

With her face in her pillow, Polly mumbled, "I don't care."

"You'll wreck your singing voice," Miri said.

"I have a terrible singing voice," Polly said, still into the pillow. She sounded muffled and far away, but Miri could hear the stuffy nose from the crying through which she spoke.

"You know that's not true," Miri said. In reality, the entire Horwitz family were accomplished musicians, and good singers, although Artie was the only one pursuing a degree at the Institute of Music.

Miri sat down heavily on the edge of Polly's bed, grabbing a box of tissues from the nightstand in anticipation of their imminent use. Sure enough, Polly held out her hand for a tissue. Her face was still in the pillow, but she must have seen Miri grab the box out of the corner of her eye.

Miri handed her several tissues and Polly sat up and blew her nose. She held out her hand for more tissues. Miri handed them to her. Polly blew her nose again, and then wiped tears from her eyes and her cheeks.

"Your brother just wants to protect you," Miri said.

"I'm not a baby," Polly said.

"No," Miri agreed. "But you're still a kid."

"Not after my Bat Mitzvah," Polly insisted.

"Being a Bat Mitzvah isn't going to protect you from the book burners, Polly," Miri said. "And just like Frenchy tries to protect you, you need to protect Manny."

"Why do I have to protect Manny?" Polly cried. "We're the same age and he's bigger than me."

"But you're more adventurous," Miri said. "And these are dangerous times to be adventurous."

"What does that have to do with Manny?"

"Your twin brother adores you, Polly. He'll follow you wherever you go. And if you get into trouble, he'll get into trouble too."

"He can run faster than me," Polly said. "He can get away."

"Manny would never leave you behind, Polly, you know that," Miri said, sternly. "He'd put himself between you and danger even if he knew there was nothing more he could do about it than give *you* a chance to get away."

"Manny's not that brave," Poly said.

"No, he's not," Miri agreed. "But he loves you *that* much."

Polly sniffled. "I would never leave Manny behind."

"So, then you'll both get hurt – or worse. Why tempt it?"

Polly was silent for a few moments, contemplating. She blew her nose again. Her face was flushed and glistening, and her nose was red. From the walls of her room, the faces of Emma Goldman, Rosa Luxembourg, Patti Smith, Josephine Baker, Angela Davis, Simone de Beauvoir, Golda Meir, Emma Lazarus, Gertrude Stein, Gloria Steinem, Barbra Streisand, Susan Sontag, Anne Frank, Hedy Lamarr, Lauren Bacall, Fanny Brice, Carly

Simon, Carole King, Big Mama Thornton, Laura Nyro, Amy Winehouse, the Bangles, the Runaways, and the members of the Slits from the cover of their album *Cut* all stared down at them from large posters that covered every surface.

"We went to the Rock n' Roll Museum today," Polly murmured.

"I know," Miri said. "You skipped school."

"The rumor is that Jews are going to be restricted from museums soon, so we thought we should go there one last time."

"How was it?" Miri asked.

"It sucked!" Polly exclaimed. "The government removed all the Black, Jewish, Latin, LGBTQ, First Nation, sexy, and leftist artists! No Clash, no Bowie, no Dylan, no Elton, no Jimi, no Bad Brains, no James Brown, no Iggy, no Robbie Robertson, no Link Wray, no Santana, no The Brats, no Blondie, no PJ Harvey, no Joan Armatrading, no Tracy Chapman, no Melissa Etheridge, no Slits, no Liz Phair! No Patti Smith, no . . . basically, no anyone good."

"No Black, Jewish, Latin, LGBTQ, First Nation, sexy, or leftist artists?" Miri said in astonishment. "What's left?"

"Well, they had a really expansive exhibit on the Bay City Rollers," Polly said, grimly. "You know, Mom and Dad used to take all of us to the Rock n' Roll Museum annually. It was like a religious pilgrimage. We used to spend hours in the listening booths with the pre-rock n' roll blues artists, listening to these scratchy old recordings from the 1920s. And then after we'd spent hours going through the place, when we left, Dad would say, 'this is our religion, kids, and that is our temple. As much as Torah and Talmud and the East Side Reform Synagogue and the sunshine and the air and the sky and the moonglow and the Eden Hollow Health and Nature

Outdoor Recreation Association Family Bungalow Community and the Marx Brothers and Charlie Chaplin, rock n' roll is the Horwitz religion, because it is the *American* religion. We can hear the hungry masses yearning to be free in Earl Palmer's backbeat and the licks of Chuck Berry and the syncopated rhythm of Bo Diddley and the howl of Little Richard and the boogie-ficated, countryfied croon of Elvis Presley and the nasal roar of Bob Dylan and Jimi Hendrix's screaming guitar and Clarence Clemmons's soaring saxophone.' Or something like that. And even though I thought he was crazy and silly and corny as hell, I also thought everything he said was true. Like, *gospel* true. Like *Five Books of Moses* true. By which I mean, maybe not all *literally* true, but *emotionally* true. And now the America my dad loved and worshipped and claimed as ours as much as anyone else's is all gone and snatched away from us and shattered into scattered shabby republics on a continent of broken places."

Miri nodded, thoughtfully. "You've been studying those PSAT words."

"Fat lot of good it'll do me," Polly pouted. "I'm sure Jews will be excluded from standardized testing soon enough."

"Thank the God of Small Miracles for that," Miri said. "Every cloud and everything."

"Do you believe in God, Miri?" Polly asked with sudden urgency. "I don't mean the God of Small Miracles, I mean the God of Big-Ass Miracles, the creator of the universe and the tablets on Sinai kind of thing."

"Sure," Miri said. "Why not? Do you?"

"Sure," Polly said. "I believe in God. I just think God is a fucking psycho."

Miri laughed despite herself. "Well, no one said God was perfect."

"Are you sure about that? I thought someone did."

"All powerful, maybe. Not perfect."

"If God's so all powerful, why did He let them take Mom and Dad away from us?" Polly said, a sob in her voice. "Couldn't an all-powerful deity do something to stop *that*? I mean, I don't expect God to clear up my acne or give me bigger boobs or get Suzie Landsberg to ask me to Middle School Prom and kiss me on the lips behind the bandstand or make learning calculus less fucking shitty, but couldn't a God of Big-Ass miracles have just done that *one* thing?"

Miri put her arm around Polly's shoulders. Polly was all cried out, but she laid her head on Miri's bosom.

"God didn't do that to Mom and Dad," Miri said. "*People* did. I guess we see God or the absence of God in people, and what people do or don't do. So, when people don't do the right thing . . . that's on them."

"So how come almost nobody does the right thing anymore?" Polly mumbled into her chest.

"That's above my paygrade, sweetheart," Miri said.

"Well, whose paygrade, is it?" Polly said. "I want to write a sternly worded email."

"If I find out, I'll share the address," Miri said.

After a moment, Polly said softly, "you know Dad used to write angry letters all the time. To politicians, corporations, newspapers, anyone who pissed him off. That's probably why they took Mom and Dad away. They probably had a file somewhere filled with all of Dad's letters." She took her head from Miri's chest and looked at her with wide, watery eyes. "Do you think they're still alive, Miri? Do you think we'll ever see them again?"

Miri felt like a hole had opened up in her chest. "I don't know, sweetheart," she whispered. "I'm sorry, but I just don't."

Polly sighed unhappily and rested her head on Miri's big belly. "Mom and Dad were completely batshit crazy," she said. "They named every one of us after a member of the Marx Brothers family. And as if that's not weird enough, they named their first born 'Simon,' which is the name of the Marx Brothers' father – which means they intended to keep going until they had enough kids to name after Groucho, Chico, Harpo, Zeppo, Gummo, and Manfred *and* their sister! How crazy is that? And Dad loved it that our last name, Horwitz, was the actual real last name of Moe, Curly, and Shemp Howard from the Three Stooges. My parents were both fucking nuts. I sure do miss them."

After a few moments, Miri asked, "would it help if I got Frenchy to make tacos tonight?" Miri asked.

"With cheese?" Polly asked. The Horwitz family, although semi-regular synagogue attendees, did not *usually* keep kosher . . . but sometimes Frenchy got weird about things.

Miri nodded. "Definitely with cheese."

Polly sniffled. "It wouldn't hurt," she replied

Miri held her and stroked her hair.

There wasn't much else she could do.

"Oh!" Polly said. She lifted her head and looked at Miri's tummy. "My niece or nephew has an opinion about tacos, I think."

Miri smiled, lifted up her shirt, took Miri's hand in hers, and placed it on her bare belly. Together, they felt the baby move inside her.

"Do you worry about bringing a kid into this world?" Polly asked.

Miri nodded, sadly. "Every minute of every day," she admitted, her hand on Polly's. She looked at her sister-in-law and smiled. "But with you for an aunt, I think our kid will be all right."

Polly's eyes filled with water. She leaned down and kissed Miri's undulating belly.

"Don't worry, kid," she said to Miri's tummy, *sotto voce.* "I'm going to be the best auntie ever."

# Chapter Nine

In the showers after football practice, Sloppy Joe pointed at Miltie's crotch and said, "Hey, Miltie, I hope they don't check your dick when they decide who to *Jewspel*."

Sloppy Joe was conspicuously not circumcised.

Miltie thought wistfully about the Eden Hollow family Jewish summer camp where all the guys were circumcised, and this was never an issue in the locker room or showers.

"A quarter of the guys on the team are circumcised, you moron," Robbie said to Joe. "Seventy percent of American men our parents' age are circumcised, and about twenty-five percent of males our age are also circumcised." Matter-of-factly, he pointed to his own crotch. "*I'm* circumcised. Are you saying I'm a Jew?"

Sloppy Joe looked embarrassed. "I'm not saying that, Robbie," he mumbled.

"What are you saying?"

"My dad says the reason so many Americans are circumcised is because after World War Two, there was a Zio doctor plot to circumcise all American boys so that in the future, no one would be able to tell who was a Jew and who was not a Jew just by looking at their wieners."

"Is that what your dad says, Sloppy?" Robbie said. "Why don't they just check the horns then?"

Sloppy's eyes widened. "What horns?" he said.

"The one's Jews have on their heads," Robbie said.

"I thought that was just superstition," Sloppy said. He looked at Miltie. "Show him your horns, Miltie."

"I don't have any horns," Miltie mumbled. He was embarrassed by the whole thing. He knew Robbie was trying to help, but Miltie felt he was just making it worse.

"Show him," Robbie insisted.

Miltie parted his wet hair in several places to show his scalp.

"See that?" Robbie said. "No horns." Robbie parted his own hair and displayed his scalp to Sloppy. "No horns here, either." Robbie pointed at his own *schmekel* and then at Miltie's. "Circumcised," he said. He pointed to his head and then at Miltie's. "No horns. Not Jewish. Got it?"

"Ok, Robbie," Sloppy murmured. "I was just joking, anyway."

"If you're going to joke, try to be a little bit funny," Robbie said.

That was when they heard Coach McCurdy call for everyone to gather in the locker room because he had an announcement to make.

## Chapter Ten

Some of the girls on the lacrosse team grabbed towels when Coach Lindsey called them out of the shower, but Bertie just stood in the entrance to the showers, not anticipating the announcement was going to take that long. Beside her stood Adah Loeb, also without her towel. A puddle of water formed at their feet as the coach addressed them.

By the time Coach Lindsey was finished, Bertie wished she had grabbed a towel, and also that she was not standing next to Adah, who wore a conspicuous Magen David around her neck, because everyone was looking at them.

Bertie and her brother Miltie didn't wear their Magen David necklaces anymore even under their shirts so they wouldn't have to hide them every time they changed before or after practice. But Adah was the only girl on the lacrosse team – the only girl Bertie knew anywhere – who wore hers. Although it wasn't against the law to wear it, half the team wouldn't speak to her, and a few periodically tried to assault her with lacrosse sticks. If it hadn't been for the roughly one-third of the team who repeatedly stood by her and came to her defense -- not so much because she was Jewish but because she was a teammate -- she'd have probably been hospitalized at some point.

Right now, Adah's star was the only thing she wore,

standing beside Bertie, the little silver hexagram hanging at her throat like a beacon, calling everyone's attention to it, and to her – and to Bertie, making Bertie feel even more naked – and more Jewish -- than she was already, like those eyes on them were flaying off her skin – like one of the martyrs you read about on Yom Kippur -- and looking inside.

Coach Lindsey took off her baseball cap and scratched her head. "Ok, there's no way to say this delicately, so I'm going to say it direct," she said. "You've probably all heard rumors floating around, and it's my job – although I didn't ask for it – to confirm what parts of those rumors are true. And here it is – none of the Jewish students in the Republic are going to be allowed to enroll in public school after this academic year. In the fall, they're all going to have to finish their education somewhere else. Don't ask me where – that's above my paygrade. And that's not all I have to report. After today, no Jewish students will be allowed to participate on any sports teams. That means all your teammates of the Jewish faith or ethnicity will no longer be playing by your side."

About a quarter of the team let out a cheer.

Bertie found this shocking – and alarming. She felt a cold fist wrap around her heart. She knew some of her teammates were anti-Semites, of course.

She just hadn't known how gung-ho they were about it.

About a third of the team – including Robina Delahunt, the team captain -- quickly shouted down those who cheered.

"You shut it with that cheerleader fuckery!" Coach Lindsey thundered. She was older than God and twice as authoritative. Everyone accordingly shut it with their cheerleader fuckery. "I don't know who among you are Jews and who among you aren't, but I guess at tomorrow's practice we'll know all right, because someone's got a list and they sure as hell are determined to use it! But until then, everyone in this room is your teammate and God damnit you will treat them as such or you're gonna have to deal with me! On this team, there's no difference between Jew and gentile, Black and White, Asian or Caucasian, indigenous or non-indigenous, tinker, tailor, beggar girl, thief! We got one religion here, and that's lacrosse! We got one creed here, and that's teamwork! On this team, you are all the same no matter what the government wants to say about it! Now hit the showers and go on home. And those of you we won't see here tomorrow – it's been my honor being your coach. You have made me proud. It will break my heart when you're no longer with us on that field."

With that, she turned on her heel and walked out of the locker room.

About a third of the team applauded the coach as she left. The rest were smart enough to shut it with their cheerleader fuckery.

Bertie felt all kinds of emotions she could barely comprehend welling up inside her. She went back to the shower and turned on the spray and put her face under it, to hide her tears.

She heard the shower beside her and saw Adah there with her Magen David hanging at her throat sparkling in the cascade of water like a pebble in a stream.

Without looking at her, Adah leaned into her. "There's a protest tonight about the expulsion order outside the district school administrative building," she said. "Bring Miltie."

"Will only the Jewish students be there?" Bertie asked, her voice hoarse and raw.

Now Adah did look at her. "Only way to find out is to show up," she said, before putting her own face into the spray.

## Chapter Eleven

The underground bare-knuckle fighting venue was not actually underground -- it was in a disused garage.

Julius helped Lenny warm up by going a few practice rounds with him. Julius wore boxing gloves, and Lenny promised to hit his bare knuckles against only the gloves, and not against Julius.

Lenny's bare knuckles against the gloves were quite forceful enough, Julius thought. Their dad had taught all of the Horwitz children to fight at the local gym, learning boxing, Taekwondo, and Krav Maga, and, as was inevitable after the end of the Before Times, they had all needed to defend themselves in street brawls from time to time. But none of them had taken to it like Lenny, who had excelled in pugilism when he served with Frenchy in the war that erupted upon the fracturing of the USA. Lenny probably would have made a career out of it if Jews hadn't been banned from professional sports. As it was, Lenny still managed to make pretty good coin in the illegal bare-knuckle circuit – although even here he hid his Jewish identity by pretending to be Italian, fighting under the moniker "Chico the Amico."

It was not lost on Julius, of course, that his brother was named "Leonard," the real name of the Marx Brother who had also been known professionally as "Chico."

Julius didn't mind warming up with Lenny, despite the pounding of Lenny's fists into his hands, which reverberated into his bone marrow throughout his body and shuddered his brain inside his skull.

It was serving as Lenny's bucket man he hated.

This was usually Artie's job, but Artie was busy practicing for his upcoming harp recital at the Institute of Music, the semesters of which ran several weeks longer than the school from which Julius had recently graduated. Jews hadn't even been expelled from campus at the Institute – probably because it's hard to practice remotely with other musicians -- although they *had* been expelled from the dorms.

Julius hated having to close up wounds and open up swollen eyes and wipe blood from his brother's face. It wasn't the blood that bothered him. It was the beatings Lenny took in the ring. The blood Julius could see and wipe away. It was the possible injuries inside his brother's battered body that gave him *shpilkes*.

"Fighting isn't only about how well you can throw a punch," their father had told them. "It's about how well you can take one."

Julius worried Lenny had taken that lesson a little bit too much to heart.

"What's the first lesson of street fighting?" Lenny drilled him as they sparred.

"Take out the opposing team's leader, first," Julius replied. "That will leave the rest of them confused and uncertain, which will give you a chance either to sucker punch or run, or both, before they have a chance to recover."

"And what if it's just you and one other guy?"

"Fight him with what he doesn't have," Julius said. "If he's big and slow, hit him fast and let him tire himself out throwing punches that don't connect. If he's small and fast, hit him early, hit him hard."

"What if he's big and fast?" Lenny asked.

"Then fight dirty," Julius replied. "Scratch, bite,

gouge, kick him in the balls."

"What if none of that works?"

"Grab a brick."

"What if there's no brick?"

"Run like hell."

"Good kid," Lenny said, and the bell rang for round one.

Lenny spent most of round one sizing up his opponent and letting the man tire himself out by throwing punches that didn't connect. His opponent was a head taller than Lenny, a brutish gladiatorial pugilist with male pattern baldness, huge arms, and a surprisingly soft stomach, who went by "'Malcolm Maclean the Malice Machine." Maclean had reddish whisps of hair and fair skin that flushed redder than his hair every time he threw a punch. But the formidability of those arms, thick as telephone poles, could not be denied.

Lenny, in contrast, was a squat fireplug – but he could move.

Lenny let his opponent come to him. Maclean charged, punching wildly. Lenny dodged, weaved, ducked, and sidestepped. Maclean almost lost his footing more than once as his blows connected only with air.

By the end of the round, the crowd was restless and turning on Lenny for ducking instead of fighting.

Round two, Lenny allowed Maclean to land a few punches, satisfying the audience's bloodlust while testing out his opponent's hitting power. Lenny knew how to take a punch, but it looked to Julius like the force of Maclean's blows exceeded Lenny's expectations. He saw Lenny's eyes go glassy as he stumbled shakily backward after Maclean landed a cross on Lenny's temple.

At the bell, Julius had to close up a cut above Lenny's left eye. He applied a cold towel to the wound, then an epinephrine-soaked cotton swab. He put Avitene into the cut to coagulate the blood, and then applied Vaseline to the area.

"Don't stop the fight," Lenny grunted.

Julius looked at Lenny. "Do you think I have a reason to throw in the towel?" Julius asked.

"Just don't," Lenny barked. "Not under any circumstances. I know what I'm doing. I got a strategy."

"Are you hurt, Lenny?" Julius asked. "Did you get hurt more than I can see?"

"Under no fucking circumstances are you to stop this fucking fight, Jules," Lenny said as the bell rang, and he sprang to his feet.

As Lenny charged into the ring, Julius noticed him listing almost imperceptibly to his right side. He must have taken a shot to the torso and was still feeling it. Julius worried he had a cracked rib.

Despite the tilt, Lenny came out from his corner fast and ferocious. Maclean had longer arms and could have kept Lenny away if Maclean were a better fighter and Lenny a worse one; as things were, Lenny ducked beneath his opponent's reach, came in close, and hit Maclean repeatedly with a flurry of blows to his ribcage – maybe getting even with him, Julius thought.

Julius saw Maclean wince and knew he'd been hurt – how hurt, it was too early to tell. Maclean stumbled back and put his arm to his side, protecting it, leaving the left side of his head undefended. Lenny pressed this momentary advantage, landing a front hook into Maclean's jaw that snapped his opponent's head to one side and sent a wad of bloody saliva flying from his mouth and across the garage's concrete floor.

The crowd cheered and booed in roughly equal measure.

For the next few rounds, Lenny went hard at Maclean's ribcage, and when Maclean left his face unprotected to guard his torso, Lenny landed blow after blow into his jaw and temple. But Maclean kept hitting Lenny above the eyes, trying to open up that wound.

As Julius closed up the wound again between rounds seven and eight, he told his brother, "if he opens up this wound again, I'm throwing in the towel."

"Don't you fucking dare," Lenny grunted, and Julius could tell he was in pain.

"Then finish it, Len," Julius said, pleading. "Finish it before he finishes you."

When the bell rang, Lenny ran right up to Maclean and right into Maclean's left jab. The blow snapped Lenny's head back and momentarily lifted him off his feet. Blood flew from his mouth. Julius was certain the fight was over.

But somehow Lenny landed back on his feet and managed to steady himself, and when Maclean came in to finish him off, Lenny dodged and Maclean hit air, throwing himself off balance.

Lenny landed a rear hook into Maclean's temple.

Maclean staggered, and when he straightened himself, he was still disoriented. Lenny followed up with a gut punch that doubled Maclean over.

Then Lenny delivered a haymaker in the form of an uppercut right into Maclean's jaw. The blow straightened Maclean's torso and sent him off his feet.

Maclean came down on his back and stayed there.

The crowd erupted. Both anger and celebration rocked the garage walls.

A lot of people had made money on Lenny that night.

A lot of people had lost money, too.

The ref held Lenny's arm up and declared him winner.

Lenny smiled. His mouth was filled with blood. The wound above his eye was open, the eye swollen shut.

Julius thought his brother had never looked happier.

# Chapter Twelve

There was no proper locker room in the garage, but there was a former break room in the back where Julius patched up his brother as best he could.

"You should see a doctor about those ribs," Julius said.

"They don't allow Jews into public hospitals anymore," Lenny said, his voice slurred through swollen lips.

"I think we might be able to find a Jewish doctor somewhere in the greater metropolitan area to take a look at you," Julius said.

Lenny chuckled, then grimaced. "Don't make me laugh, you shitweasel," he said.

"I'm serious," Julius said. "Let me take you to Doc Cooperman."

"Coop's asleep by now."

"I'll wake him up."

"I'll see him tomorrow."

"You're a fucking moron, you know that?"

"What can I say?" Lenny shrugged, then winced. "It's my nature."

"Said the scorpion to the frog. Let me at least wrap up your ribs."

"Go for it," Lenny said.

As Julius wrapped up Lenny's torso, the fight promoter, Harry "Hooligan" Hoolihan, whom everyone called "Hoolie," came in with Lenny's winnings.

"Hell of a fight tonight, champ," he said, handing Lenny a wad of cash.

Lenny flapped the cash around in the air. "This is light," he said.

"Why don't you count it first before you make accusations, Chico?" he said.

"I don't need to count it because A) everyone knows you're a goniff and B) you owe me a third of the house and I seen the size of the house out there and this ain't a third."

"A third after expenses, kid," Hoolie said.

"Fuck your expenses, you owe me a third," Lenny said. "You rearrange our deal, I'll rearrange your face."

"I got guys out there working for me, Chico," Hoolie said, calmly. "You wanna take on half a dozen guys in the state you're in?"

"Only half a dozen?" Lenny said. He pointed to Julius. "That's four for me, two for Jules here. I thought you were serious for a second there, Hoolie. Call for reinforcements or give me my winnings."

Hoolie sighed, looking at Lenny, looking at Julius, as if trying to decide if the two of them could take his six guys.

Julius was the bookish type, but even back during the Before Times, the rising antisemitism was so precipitous in the metro area that a Jewish boy couldn't get through the day if he didn't learn how to fight. So, Julius learned how to fight. His dad taught his kids to fight properly, and Lenny taught him to fight dirty. Julius felt fairly confident he could take on one guy if he had to. Two? Probably not. But he wasn't going to let on about that, so he fixed a hard expression on his face and glared at Hoolie.

Hoolie grunted, spat on the floor, peeled off more bills, and handed them to Lenny. Lenny looked them over and seemed satisfied.

"Don't come back here," Hoolie said as he opened the door.

"The fuck I won't," Lenny said. "I'm your biggest draw and you know it."

## Chapter Thirteen

Artie had just finished practicing with the Third Year Jazz Ensemble at the Music Institute.

They were going to perform Alice Coltrane's complete compositions from the album *Journey to Satchidananda,* a complex series of modal constructions and bass ostinatos, and one of the few jazz landmarks to feature the harp – Artie's instrument – as a central musical component.

While his dad worshipped rock n' roll as a kind of irreligious spiritual lodestar, his mother was a jazz devotee, and took particular pleasure in listening to the rare but remarkable jazz harpists. Her music collection started with Dorothy Ashby and Corky Hale from the 1950s and continued right on through the history of jazz harp in the Before Times with artists like Brandee Younger and Edmar Castañeda.

What his mother said she loved so much about jazz harp was that the instrument wasn't inherently well-suited to jazz, so the creativity it took to play jazz on the harp brought out some of the most unique sounds in the genre. Artie had thrilled at that idea and took up the jazz harp with gusto. Although still only a college student, he was by now probably already the best jazz harpist in this part of the continent. But of course, there hadn't really been many new jazz harpists in this region since the foundation of the Sovereign Republic.

It had not been lost on Artie that his parents had named him for the Marx Brother, Arthur, who had been known professionally as "Harpo" and was himself an accomplished harpist. He sometimes wondered if his mother had introduced him to jazz harp for that reason.

Artie had loved every album his mother had introduced him to, but the one he really went completely animal crackers over was Alice Coltrane's *Journey to Satchidananda*. Alice Coltrane, saxophonist John Coltrane's widow, had been an accomplished jazz multi-instrumentalist, and on *Satchidananda* her instrument had been the harp.

Neither jazz nor the harp had ever sounded quite like this.

Listening to the album had been an almost religious experience for Artie, and he was not surprised to later learn that Alice Coltrane's inspiration for the music was her spiritual journey with Swami Satchidananda Saraswati. Although Artie had studied Saraswati's teachings as part of his fanboy enthusiastic research into the album, he was not an adherent of the Swami's spiritual particulars, per se – he was still a Jew, and always would be whether he wanted it or not, it was so deeply ingrained in who he was. But Artie felt the spirituality contained in the music of *Journey to Satchidananda*, as with the other landmarks of the "spiritual jazz" movement, including John Coltrane's *A Love Supreme*, transcended theological specificity.

Artie, who was only a junior, felt that this upcoming performance of *Journey to Satchidananda* was easily the culmination of his musical education thus far, and he often wondered if his senior recital next year could possibly top it.

He said farewell to his fellow musicians as they packed up their instruments following rehearsal. The institute's Third Year Jazz Ensemble was one of the last inter-racial musical groups in the city, and that was only tolerated because they were merely a college group who played in educational settings rather than commercial ones. It saddened Artie to think that once they all graduated, they'd probably never be allowed to play together professionally – at least, not until things changed.

If things ever changed.

Artie was the last one out of the theatre and was just loading his harp onto the dolly when he noticed Dean Jennings standing in the wings, as if waiting for him.

"Artie," she said. "Got a minute?"

"Sure," Artie said, tipping the dolly back to its resting position.

Jennings approached him and cleared her throat. "There's no easy way to say this –" she began.

Artie felt panic seize his chest. "Is my family Ok?" he asked, his voice quavering. "Is everyone in my family Ok?"

Artie took out his phone and started scrolling through messages and missed calls to see if he'd overlooked any.

The Dean looked startled. "What? Oh, no, it's nothing like that," she said. "They're all fine as far as I know."

"Oh," Artie said, putting his phone back in his pocket. "Ok." He cleared his throat. "It can't be that bad, then."

"The trustees have voted to cancel the recital, Artie," she said, sheepishly.

"What?" Artie said, in disbelief. "*Our* recital? The Third Year Jazz Ensemble recital? Why?"

"Well, you know," the Dean said vaguely. "The issue of the propriety of inter-racial ensembles and also some concerns about CRT."

"CRT?"

"CRT is illegal now, as I'm sure you know."

"It's music without lyrics," Artie said. "How does Critical Race Theory play into it?"

"Jazz is being eliminated from the curriculum," the Dean said. "There's a feeling we need to concentrate more on Western canon."

"Jazz has been around for over a hundred years, Dean Jennings," Artie said softly. "It *is* canon."

"It's out of my hands, Artie."

"So . . . I'm supposed to switch to classical harp my senior year?"

"Well, I'm afraid there's more, Artie," Dean Jennings said.

Artie couldn't imagine what more there could be, but at this point, he didn't want to guess.

"Don't keep me in suspense," he said.

"You won't be enrolled next year," Dean Jennings said. "The trustees voted to expel all non-White and LGBTQ+ - identifying students."

Artie felt his head spin. He screwed up his face. "Since I'm not LGBTQ+, are you saying I'm not White? Just so I'm clear, Jews aren't White again? Is that official?"

"Artie -- "

"Because, when my family came over in the late 19th century, we were definitely not considered White. But then *my* generation, they told us that Jews weren't entitled to anti-discrimination intersectional inclusion, because we're emblematic of White privilege and Ashkenormativity and have a colonial oppressor mentality. But, just so I'm clear, now we're *not* White again?"

"I don't make the rules, Artie," the Dean said, sadly.

"No Black, Jewish, Asian, LGBTQ+, or Latino musicians?" Artie said. "No contemporary classical ensemble will ever have another Yo-Yo Ma, Itzhak Pearlman, Sharon Isbin, Wynton Marsalis, CN Lester, or Martha Argerich? You know how much that's gonna suck, right?"

"We'll consider the rehearsal tonight as the fulfillment of everyone's recital requirements for the semester, so everyone in the ensemble will have full credit through junior year to transfer elsewhere," Dean Jennings said.

"Transfer *where* elsewhere, Dean Jennings?" Artie said. "Any suggestions? Any music colleges in the Republic you know of that are still accepting non-White students?"

Dean Jennings just sighed. "I wish you the best of luck, Artie. You're a very talented musician. I wish there was more I could do about that than just say it."

Then she turned and walked away.

Artie thought about his fellow members of the Third Year Jazz Ensemble and wondered how many of them knew about this. He imagined Dean Jennings would talk to each of them individually – each of the 'non-White" and LGBTQ+ members of the ensemble, that is -- violinist Alison Woo, bassist Soledad Ortega, pianist Sinatra Folsom, guitarist Najem Ahmaro, percussionist Jex Florentine, saxophonist Deb Moreno, clarinetist Roger Jenkins, and flautist Genesis Ondolo.

What would they do when they found out?

Probably the same thing he was doing – pack up their instruments and go home.

What else was there to do?

## Chapter Fourteen

"Are you a real Italian, Chico the Amico?" the woman asked.

Lenny looked her over. He recognized her from the featured "girl fight" earlier in the evening. She had won her match, and her face looked just as beaten up as Lenny's – and yet, somehow, strangely alluring.

Lenny usually went for the more girlish types – willowy petite blondes he could lift off their feet with one arm. But, man, oh man there was something about this girl, he thought. Her cheekbones were sharp as razors, her skin a swarthy olive, her shoulders broad, her bare arms and legs roped with sinews of muscle. Her hair was black and cut short to her scalp. Was she Native American, he wondered?

There were rumors Native Americans were all soon going to be deported back to the rez.

What was her fight name? He remembered – "Maggie the Cat Fighter." He liked the literary reference to *Cat on a Hot Tin Roof.* He doubted anyone else in the garage got the reference, except of course for Julius – who now stood beside Lenny, uncomfortably.

"I'm as Italian as you are feline," Lenny said.

Maggie – if that was her real name – tossed her head back and laughed. Everything about her had been hard-core until that moment. But her laugh was full of joy and delight. It was throaty and hoarse, like her speaking voice, but while everything else about her said "keep away" her laughter felt like an invitation.

"I'm Maggie," she said.

So that *was* her real name. "I'm Lenny," he said. "That's my brother, Groucho."

Julius scowled. "I'm Julius," he said. "No one ever called me 'Groucho' until today."

Maggie and Julius shook hands, and then Maggie turned her attention back to Lenny. Her attention made Lenny feel like he was the center of the world. He liked that feeling. It was a talent, he knew, that some people possessed to make others feel like they were the center of the world when they talked to them. It didn't necessarily mean they were interested in you beyond conversation.

But it didn't necessarily mean they weren't.

"Congrats on your win, tonight," Maggie said.

"You too," Lenny said. "They try to stiff you on your cut?"

"Don't they always?" Maggie said.

"What's your take supposed to be?"

"A quarter of the door. They tried to get away with something closer to fifteen percent."

"I hope you didn't stand for that."

"I got it up to about twenty percent, I think, but I still got robbed."

"I get a third," Lenny said. "That's sexist you only get a quarter."

"You're the draw," Maggie said.

"Seeing you fight in your sports bra and spandex shorts, I kinda doubt that," Lenny said. He saw Jules shake his head at his brother's audacity. Jules didn't like the way Lenny behaved – but Jules rarely got laid.

Maggie smiled. "I thought my fighting prowess was the draw."

"That too," Lenny said.

"You got chops yourself," Maggie said. "It looked like

you got hurt in the ring, though."

"You should see the other guy."

"I've seen the other guy," Maggie said. "He left on a stretcher. Even so, you gonna be Ok?"

"Nothing a bottle of aspirin and a pint of Jack can't cure."

Maggie smiled. "Doctor's orders?"

"Best medicine money can buy," Lenny said.

Their eyes locked. Her eyes were dark, almost black. He liked looking into them.

"You know what?" Lenny asked.

"I don't know what," Maggie said. "Why don't you tell me?"

"I'd really like to *schtup* you," Lenny said.

Julius put his face in his hands and shook his head in dismay.

This was a line that Chico Marx, according to legend, had tried on Tallulah Bankhead back in the day, although reputedly Chico had used the Anglo-Saxon F-word instead of the Yiddish equivalent. And, reportedly, it had worked for Chico. Lenny was fond of using the Yiddish version of the line himself. It didn't always work.

But often enough, it did.

Maggie grinned. "And so, you shall, you sweet old-fashioned boy," she said.

This had been, reputedly, Bankhead's reply to Chico. So, Maggie knew some Hollywood lore, herself.

Lenny was liking this woman more and more.

"I've got a bottle of Advil and another of Jameson back in my place," Maggie said. "Will that substitute for aspirin and Jack?"

Lenny handed Julius his gym bag, which contained not only gym stuff, but his winnings. "Bring this straight home and give it right to Frenchy," he said. "Don't fuck around."

"Lenny . . . " Jules protested.

Lenny bent down and took the Colt Cobra snub-nosed revolver from his ankle holster, handing it to Jules. "Anyone tries to take that bag from you, you use this. Remember, it's a thirty-eight, not a twenty-two girlie pistol like the ones we used when Dad taught us how to shoot. It's got a kick."

"Lenny don't be fucking crazy here," Jules said.

Lenny slapped him on the back. "No worries, kid," Lenny said. "I got faith in you."

Lenny turned back to Maggie. "Lead the way, Princess Pugilist."

"Oh, I like that," Maggie said. "Maybe I'll change my fight name."

As they walked away arm in arm, Jules called after them, "leave that wrapping on your torso, Lenny. I don't care what you do with your pants, but do not remove that wrapping."

Without turning around, Lenny gave his brother a jaunty wave over his shoulder.

## Chapter Fifteen

There were about a hundred people at the protest, which Miltie thought was not too bad.

Even more comforting, about three quarters of the attendees were non-Jews – at least people he assumed to be non-Jews, insofar as they had never identified themselves as Jews, and Miltie thought he knew at least casually most of his Jewish classmates, even if that was an identity most kids kept to themselves in school these days.

Except of course for Adah Loeb, who stood there proudly with a home-made sign that read "Un-Restrict Our School" chanting with the crowd "No expulsion, no hate, we won't capitulate!"

Miltie's twin sister Bertie stood beside Adah, with her own handmade sign that read "Hell No, Jews Won't Go" and chanting along with Adah and the crowd.

Both girls wore their Magen Davids conspicuously outside their shirts.

There was also a counter protest across the street with about twenty people. Cars kept pulling up and more people joined the counter-protestors, armed with identical printed signs that read "Jews, Jews, You Must Flee, Our Republic Will Be Free!"

Well, that's pretty unambiguous, Miltie thought.

The counter-protesters were chanting "Zio Traitors You Can't Hide, You Commit White Genocide!"

That was a pretty alarming sentiment as well.

There was a handful of television news reporters and camera people set up on the sidewalk. This created a certain amount of peril for the protestors since the government would have easy access to their identities through the footage. No one seemed dissuaded, however. Maybe they calculated this particular protest wasn't significant enough to warrant government scrutiny and retaliation.

The cops were there, too, parked at a street corner, watching the goings on with casual interest. It wasn't clear to Miltie that the cops could be bothered to intervene if the counter-protestors got violent, and it was less clear to him whose side they would take if they did.

"I thought I'd find you here," said a voice behind him.

Miltie turned to find Robbie and Moose standing there with grins on their faces. Robbie held a homemade sign that read "No Hate, No Fear, Jewish Students Welcome Here" and Moose held up one that read "Education is a Right, Not Just for Those They Say are White."

"I didn't think I'd find you guys here," Miltie admitted.

"Why not?" Robbie said. "You don't think jocks can be social justice warriors?"

"I don't think anyone can be a social justice warrior, not in this climate," Miltie said.

"Look around," Robbie said. "There's at least a hundred social justice warriors standing up for you and your sister."

"What do you mean standing up for me and my sister?" Miltie asked, defensively.

"Come on, Miltie. I know you're Jewish. We all do. We don't care." He pointed to the school district building across Miramar Boulevard. "I just wish *they* didn't."

Miltie pointed to the counter-protestors. "Right now, I just wish *they* didn't."

Robbie grinned. "Don't worry. Half the team is here.

They try anything, we'll give them a beat-down they won't forget."

"I'm actually just here to flirt with your sister," Moose said, and began to weave his way through the crowd toward Bertie and Adah.

"Don't worry," Robbie said. "He's really here to flirt with Adah."

Miltie nodded and watched Moose sidle in between Bertie and Adah. "You know, it would be illegal for them to actually hook up," he said.

"Who said anything about hooking up?" Robbie laughed. "Adah's gay."

Miltie looked at Robbie, one eyebrow raised. "That's illegal, too."

"Only if you get caught."

"Does Moose know?" Miltie asked.

Robbie looked at Moose as he tried flirting with Adah, who reacted with polite indifference. "I think he's about to find out."

"Thanks for being here."

"Wouldn't miss it," Robbie said. "You know, you and I have something in common."

"Something other than football?"

"We have something in common with Adah, actually," Robbie said.

Miltie felt his heart skip a beat. "You're not Jewish, right?"

"No," Robbie said. "Not that."

Miltie furrowed his brow. "You're not a lesbian, right?"

Robbie laughed. "No, not exactly."

Robbie looked into Miltie's eyes. Miltie almost turned away. The look was so intimate, it made him uncomfortable. He forced himself to meet it.

He'd never noticed how warm Robbie's eyes were.

For a moment, Miltie seemed to lose track of time. All he could see were those eyes. His heart pounded like it was about to explode.

Then he felt Robbie's hands cupping the back of his neck and gently pulling Miltie towards him while Robbie leaned into Miltie.

Their lips touched.

Miltie almost recoiled at the sudden unexpectedness of it. But he restrained himself and then managed to relax into it.

And then they were kissing.

And there were tongues involved.

And Miltie felt an electric tingle surge through his body from his head to his toes, with particular emphasis in his loins.

He put his hand gently to the side of Robbie's face, and they continued to kiss, which became more protracted and elaborate as the moments ticked by.

That was when the first of the tear gas canisters landed nearby and clattered on the ground.

# Chapter Sixteen

Almost every building in the neighborhood was as abandoned as the garage where the fights were held and walking down these empty streets with a gym bag of money on his shoulder made Julius very nervous. It didn't help that most of the streetlights were broken, either.

Julius reached an alley off Canal Road just as he thought he heard footsteps echoing in the vacant street behind him. He looked around but didn't see anything; everything was shadow and darkness, surrounded by empty, boarded up warehouses.

He knew if he ducked through this alley, he could get home faster. But it was also an alley. . . even darker and more shadowy than Canal Road.

Still, keeping to this deserted stretch of Canal Road didn't seem to offer much more in the way of protection than the alley, so he might as well go for speed.

Julius turned down the alley and adjusted the gym bag strap on his shoulder. He put his hand inside his jacket pocket and closed his fingers around the pistol's grip.

He was about halfway through the alley – equidistant from his arrival to his destination – when he heard the tinkle of broken glass behind him.

Julius was not surprised when he saw the man standing in the shadows. What little moonlight entered the alley from above glinted off the jagged edges of a broken bottle clutched by the neck in the man's hand.

Julius *was* surprised, however, to discover the man was not a thug from the garage but that guy Tucker from the diner – the one whom Riley had threatened to stab in the eye with a fork.

"What the fuck are you doing here?" Julius asked.

"I'm here to get a piece of you," Tucker said.

"A pound of flesh?" Julius replied.

"What?" Tucker said.

"I'm just wondering the size of the piece you want to get, and see if we can cut to the chase, so to speak."

"Is everything a fucking joke to you?"

"Not everything," Julius said. "Just you."

"We'll see how funny you feel when I get through with you."

"Not half as funny as you look right now," Julius said. "Did you really follow me here from the diner? Haven't you got anything better to do with your time? Wait, don't answer that. On second thought, I'd rather not know what you do with your time. It probably has something to do with beer, trucks, and *schtupping* your cousin, am I right? Or do you prefer to *schtup* sheep?"

Tucker's face reddened and he took a step toward him.

Julius removed the pistol from his jacket and fired.

The bullet shattered what was left of the bottle in Tucker's hand.

Tucker looked down at the glass neck, all that remained of the bottle. The *blam* of the pistol reverberated in the alley and in Julius's ears, which were ringing.

"The next one will go in your gut," Julius said, speaking loudly to compensate for the ringing in his ears which he presumed Tucker was also experiencing. "Actually, I don't know where the next one will go. Your guess is as good as mine. The first one was supposed to go in your foot."

Tucker dropped the neck of the bottle and ran. The neck of the bottle shattered and tinkled on the pavement.

Julius fired a shot in the air to encourage Tucker's progress. Tucker picked up speed when he heard the shot and ran faster out of the alley, disappearing around the corner.

"I didn't know you were such a good shot," Riley said, appearing out of the inky black across the alley.

Julius nearly jumped out of his skin and recognized her voice just in time to stop himself from raising the pistol and firing a round.

"I'm not such a good shot," Julius said, feeling his heart slamming into his ribcage. "But I'm good enough to put one in your chest when you appear out of nowhere in the dark. Didn't anyone ever tell you it's impolite to sneak up on an armed man, even if he is a short Jew who looks like Groucho Marx?"

"You told me your dad taught you how to shoot," Riley said.

"That doesn't mean I'm any good at it. Why did you follow Tucker to Industrial Valley?"

"I didn't follow Tucker," Riley said. "I followed you."

"Why on Earth would you do that?"

Riley smiled and walked up to him. When she reached him, she didn't stop. She pressed herself right into him and she kissed him on the mouth.

Julius liked to tell himself that he was nobody's fool.

Here was his chance to prove it.

He kissed her back.

What else was there to do?

# Chapter Seventeen

Bertie could tell her brother Frenchy was not happy.

"For fuck's sake," Frenchy said. "I can smell the tear gas on your clothes and hair from here. My eyes are watering."

"*We* didn't fire the tear gas canisters," Bertie said, she thought sensibly.

"Didn't it occur to you something like this was going to happen?" Frenchy asked. "You're lucky you didn't get your heads bashed in. And it was on television? Do you have any idea the kind of trouble this can bring?"

"Dad always said to stand up for what's right," Bertie said.

"And where did that get him, Bertie?" Frenchy said.

Bertie looked at Miltie. Miltie looked back at Bertie and mouthed the words "shut the fuck up, Bertie."

"Why doesn't anyone get how precarious things are for us right now?" Frenchy asked. "Go upstairs and get showered right now, both of you. Wash your hair to try to get that stink out. Leave your clothes on the bathroom floor. We'll see if we can wash the smell out or if we have to burn them. In twenty minutes, you both better be down here clean and not smelling like tear gas."

"I'm taking the full twenty minutes," Bertie said.

"I'm gay," Miltie blurted out.

Bertie was surprised at Miltie, but also not so

surprised. She knew Miltie wanted to get this off his chest.

Frenchy looked at Miltie for a moment. "And?" he said.

"I just wanted you to know," he said.

"I know," Frenchy said. "We all know. Just be careful. Be discrete. Don't get caught. Do you need me to explain how to use a condom?"

"No!" Miltie cried. "God, I just wanted everyone to know."

"Great," Frenchy said. "You can announce it to everyone in your family who already knows at dinner. I'm making tacos. Hurry up and get showered so we don't have to smell your tear gas while we're eating. Move it. Go."

# Chapter Eighteen

Polly was pogo dancing around her room listening through her earbuds to Annette Ezekiel Kogan of the klezmer-rock band Golem singing "Odessa" from their album *Homesick Songs.*

When the music stopped, she heard the tinkle of Artie's harp coming from the backyard. She took out her earbuds and listened to her brother play.

The song was "Gloria," Patti Smith's hybrid of "Gloria in Excelsis Deo" and the Van Morrison tune of the same name, that begins with the unforgettable lyric "Jesus died for somebody's sins but not mine."

Sounded about right to her.

Polly snuck outside and, under the night sky, observed unseen as her brother's fingers moved deftly across the strings of his harp. He could play anything on that instrument, she thought, and make it sound like it was composed to be played on the harp. His hands were like a kind of poetry as they plucked those strings.

Polly looked up at the sky. Most streetlamps were out by this time of night as a cost-saving measure, and blackout restrictions were still in effect since the Sovereign Republic was still technically in a state of war with the White Christian Confederacy of the Nazarene Nation, even though the fighting had stopped two years ago. Without the light pollution, the bright spray of stars swirling across the inky sky was breathtaking, and a fitting visual accompaniment to Artie's musical finesse.

When the song ended, Polly burst into tears, still looking at the stars.

After a moment, Artie was beside her, his arm around her shoulders, holding her tight.

"How can things like the harp and the stars and Patti Smith and Van Morrison be so beautiful when everything else is so shit?" Polly blubbered.

Artie shrugged. "Maybe the beauty is to show us that everything doesn't have to be shit?" he suggested, tentatively.

"Then why do people make everything shit when we know we can make things beautiful instead?"

Artie considered. "Well, maybe the shit is to better help us appreciate the beauty?" he said.

Polly sniffled. "That's the stupidest thing I've ever heard," she said.

Artie handed her a tissue and Polly daubed her eyes. Together they looked at the sky.

After a moment, Manny walked out. Seeing his siblings looking up, he turned his gaze to the stars as well, wondering if there was a meteor shower.

Julius entered the backyard from the side gate. He looked at his siblings for a moment, then looked up to try to figure out what it was they were looking at.

Miri came out on the back porch with a bottle of Perrier in one hand, the other on her swollen tummy. She surveyed the scene, then joined in the star gazing.

Frenchy poked his head out the back door. "Anyone seen Lenny?" he asked.

"He had a date," Julius said. "With a cat on a hot tin roof."

"Ok," Frenchy said, knowing better than to press for details. "Well, there's two more Horwitz siblings inside who only smell a little bit like tear gas sitting at the dining room table and Miltie has a big announcement to make. Who wants tacos?"

Still looking at the sky, Artie, Manny, Julius, Miri, and Polly all raised their hands in affirmation.

# Part Two: Summer in Eden

87

**Nine years earlier**

**Two years before the Collapse**
**Nine years before Operation Supreme Flood for America**
**Nine years before the Fall of Eden**

# From the Journal of Simon "Frenchy" Horwitz, Aged 16:

## June 30

### Eden Hollow Health and Nature Outdoor Recreation Association Family Bungalow Community

Today I met the girl I am going to marry.

I know, I know, I just met her, and I'm only 16, how could I possibly know?

But I know.

Seriously.

I know.

I just do.

I should back up again and tell you something about the place where we met, which is the place where my family and I have spent every summer of our lives since I was born – the Eden Hollow Health and Nature Outdoor Recreation Association Family Bungalow Community.

Eden Hollow is sort of like one of those bungalow summer communities they used to have in the Catskills in New York, except in Ohio.

It's also a Yiddish-speaking community.

That means everyone at Eden Hollow speaks Yiddish.

Eden Hollow was founded in 1917 by Yiddish-speaking anarchist refugees from the Lower East Side – including my great-great grandfather, Moishe Horwitz. They originally set up in New Jersey, but eventually moved to the location where it's been for over a century, in the countryside in Northeast Ohio, about forty minutes (depending on traffic) from Coventry Village, which is an artsy-fartsy neighborhood in the greater metropolitan area with a diverse population and a long Jewish history where my family lives and where Dad has one of his record and musical instrument shops. He owns three of them. The first was established in Coventry Village by my great-grandfather, and we still live in his house in nearby Balfour Court.

Today, Eden Hollow is a lot less "anarchist" -- it's really pretty bougie but tilting a little bit more towards the hippy-dippy, boho side of bougie.

It's still one hundred percent Yiddish-speaking, though.

We are, I think, one of the only fully Yiddish speaking communities in the world that isn't orthodox or Hassidic or something like that. We look pretty much just like any other bougie summer community. Guys mostly wear shorts and usually go shirtless, weather permitting, which it does most of the summer. Girls mostly wear shorts, crop tops, cut-off tank tops, or bikini tops. Lots of us wear our bathing suits under our shorts so we can go swimming at the lake any time we want to. Along with footwear, sometimes a hat, and sunscreen, that's mostly it. The *Haredim*, some of whom live in year-round Yiddish-speaking communities, would never be caught dead wearing what we wear – or barely wear – at Eden Hollow.

In this regard, we look almost exactly like any other group of Americans enjoying the summer . . . . except for one thing:

Most of us wear our Magen Davids around our necks. Not everyone. But a lot of us.

Most of us don't wear our Magen Davids openly outside of Eden Hollow, since antisemitism is becoming fashionable again and those little Jewish stars make us targets. But here in Eden Hollow, antisemitism is definitely not in fashion. Because most of us are Jewish.

You don't technically have to be Jewish to be a member of Eden Hollow, but since we're a Yiddish-speaking summer community, most of us are. There aren't a lot of Yiddish-speakers anywhere these days, but among the few that have kept up the tradition, almost all of them are

Jews. Among the Eden Hollow members, almost none of us speak Yiddish in our daily lives during the rest of the year – like I said, none of us are Hasidim or Haredim or anything like that -- but we all speak Yiddish here in Eden Hollow all summer long. Chances are, if you find a Yiddish-speaker, they're probably Jewish, and if you find a Yiddish-speaker at Eden Hollow, they are probably Jewish members of Eden Hollow.

It's nice to be in a place all summer where people can not only speak Yiddish but wear a Magen David without fear or having to endure insults or just uncomfortable situations or conversations.

If you're a dude, the same is true about your foreskin, which most dudes in Eden Hallow parted with eight days after they were born. Almost every guy at Eden Hollow is circumcised. In my parents' generation, something like seventy percent of American dudes were circumcised, but by the time I was born, that number had dropped to about twenty-five percent. Jews only make up about two and a half percent of Americans, so that means, even today, most circumcised dudes are actually not Jewish. But as a circumcised Jewish dude, I can attest that you get a lot of antisemitic comments about your wiener in high school locker rooms and such. Some uncut dudes will even comment on your circumcised wiener when you're standing next to each other at a urinal, which seems to me extremely weird, but I guess to anti-Semites is completely normal behavior.

Being circumcised puts a target on your back . . . or a target on your *schmekel*, anyway. It can lead to uncomfortable situations where you either have to pretend you're not Jewish, or admit that you are, both of which are potentially precarious circumstances in this day and age.

Although the cabins and bungalows at Eden Hollow have their own showers, there are men's and women's changing rooms and showers at the lake where we go swimming, and, unlike the locker rooms at school and the

Y and the gym, you never have to endure those uncomfortable moments of dudes asking if you are Jewish and you have to decide if you want to tell the truth or not, because at Eden Hollow, almost everyone wears a Magen David without shame and every dude has an unselfconsciously circumcised wiener just like yours (or mine, anyway).

This is an incredibly refreshing and affirming thing, for me, at least, and, as far as I can tell, for every other dude at Eden Hollow.

I'm pretty sure Eden Hollow is the only non-orthodox Yiddish-speaking summer bungalow community in America, and probably in the entire world. So, literally people from every Yiddish-speaking secular, Reform, Conservative, Reconstructionist (or any other Jewish subset that isn't Haredim) on Earth visits for the summer. This is, admittedly, an extremely marginal community. But it exists. And there's enough of us to fill this campground with about two hundred and fifty people, mostly families, every summer.

Anyway, the girl I'm going to marry was proudly and without shame wearing her Magen David when I met her on the lakeside beach.

She was also wearing a tasteful two-piece bathing suit, a string, halter-top triangle bikini that showed just as much of her as it possibly could without showing *too much*. It was decorated with images of the *Hamsa,* which is an image of a hand (often referred to as "Miriam's hand") with an eye in the palm. It's a Jewish symbol to ward off evil.

I was shirtless, wearing my swimming trunks with the words "Jewish American Heritage Month" printed across the crotch and also across the butt, and an American flag on one leg and a Star of David on the other.

I was also wearing my Magen David around my neck. And sunscreen, of course. My mom is very strict about that.

Maybe the girl was, too. Wearing sunscreen, I mean. I'm not sure. But her skin did not look like it was getting burned by the sun, so I think probably she was.

Anyway, sunscreen or not, this girl is the prettiest girl I have ever seen in my life, which as I said has been 16 years so far, which, OK, isn't that long, but I've been lucky enough to see a lot of pretty girls, and pretty women, in those 16 years -- including a lot of ones in attractively revealing swimwear that reveals as much as it possibly can without revealing *too much* -- so I think I know what I'm talking about.

But it's not how pretty she is that lets me know we're going to be married.

I don't need to marry the prettiest girl in the world. That's never been my ambition.

I just want to marry the *right* girl.

Which she is.

And also, the prettiest one.

So, I guess I kind of won the jackpot of life or something.

Ok, so, what happened is this:

My family arrived, as we usually do, a few days before the 4th of July weekend. During the 4th of July weekend, Eden Hollow is packed with members and their guests. As lifetime members, and as long-time board members, my parents are always part of the crew that helps get the grounds in shape for the summer kick off.

Anyway, I'm part of a huge freakin' family – and that's just the immediate one, to say nothing of cousins and stuff. I'm the oldest. Next is Lenny, who is fifteen. He's a hothead, a brawler, and a lover – he's spent more time with girls than I have, and I have a one-year head start on him. I don't know if he's still a virgin – I mean he's only fifteen – but he sure spends a lot of time with girls of the opposite sex. And I'm not exactly reticent in that department myself.

Julius is the smart one in the family, although in truth, we're all pretty freakin' smart. But he's a little smarter. He's eleven, and he gets smarter every day. It's a little scary how smart he's getting. If he were Skynet or something, I'd be, like, "pull the plug now!"

Of course, he's not a computer, he's my brother, so that's out of the question.

Artie is ten, and he's already a musical prodigy. He plays a million instruments, but his main one is the harp. The jazz harp, no less. I don't know any other ten-year-old kids who play harp, much less jazz harp. Except for Artie. Everyone in the family plays an instrument and sings well, even the little ones. We're all musical. Our dad owns three record and musical instruments shops, after all. But Artie is definitely next level.

Miltie and Bertie are fraternal twins, and they are six. They are really cute, and total terrors, rivaled only by the littlest siblings in the Horwitz brood, Polly and Manny, who are also fraternal twins. They are three. They are also totally cute, and unlike Miltie and Bertie, not merely *total* terrors, but total *holy* terrors.

Anyway, so what happened: around mid-day today we got to our bungalow, which we own. Most of the members of the Eden Hollow community own their own cabins or bungalows on the grounds, although there are a few rooms in the lodge and a few small cabins that are rented out to members or guests of members or prospective members. Our cabin-slash-bungalow (we use the term interchangeably, I'm not really sure what's the technical distinction between the two) is rustic and big. It's actually pretty cool – filled with books and a vintage stereo system with an old-fashioned turntable and a great collection old-fashioned vinyl records extensively covering the genres of, as Chuck Berry would have put it, "rock, rhythm, and jazz." My dad has never stopped carrying actual vinyl records in his stores, so we have an extensive collection.

The cabin is filled with overstuffed chairs and couches,

and, get this ---it's got internet, but no TV. I mean, it's got a tv *screen*, but that's only hooked up so we can watch movies on discs. No streamers! Mom and Dad, you may not be surprised to know, have an extensive disc collection of every movie genre but, like the dweebs they proudly are, it leans heavily to old-fashioned classics, often in black and white, especially comedies. The Horwitz siblings were raised on Chaplin, Keaton, Lloyd, Laurel and Hardy, the Three Stooges, screwball comedies, and the Marx Brothers.

Also, in case you were wondering why all our names sound so old-fashioned and frankly weird, it's because Mom and Dad named each of us for someone in the Marx Brother family. Every single one of them, including the sister and the parents. The real names, not the stage names, of course. "Julius" was Groucho's real name, for example.

Dad is also extraordinarily fond of the Three Stooges – Mom admittedly a little less so – and is bizarrely proud of the fact that our last name, Horwitz, is the real last name of Stooges Moe, Curly, and Shemp.

So, anyway, as soon as Dad put the car in park, the rug-rats – who are every kid but Lenny and me – went rushing for the front door, discarding their clothes on the lawn as they went, leaving it to Mom and me to pick them up as we followed, and Dad and Lenny to get the bags.

Inside, the kids rushed around the place like the little ankle-biting demons that they are, bouncing on the furniture, crashing into each other, laughing like little naked hyenas. The rest of us wrangled them into their swimsuits, and then changed into our own like civilized humans, and, once all our clothes were neatly folded and put away and the bags had been schlepped to the right rooms, Mom made us all sandwiches and we all sat at our big wooden picnic table on the back patio like the perfectly nuclear family we are.

There's something about the food your parents make

for you that is so way better than the food anyone else makes for you, I think. It's not that the food itself is actually different. I think it's a chemical reaction of parental love interacting with the culinary ingredients. I guess families with shitty parents who resent feeding their kids have shittier meals than the Horwitz's do.

This afternoon, Mom made us grilled cheese sandwiches. No special ingredients. Good cheese but not super fancy cheese or anything like that. The same grilled cheese sandwiches people make the world over.

Only ours were infinitely better.

Because our mom made them.


After lunch, Mom and Dad sent me and Lenny to the lakeside beach at Eden Hollow with the rug rats, so Mom and Dad could meet with some committee or other and start getting the grounds in shape for the 4th of July weekend.

The beach is a good place because you don't have to come up with things to constantly amuse the ankle biters. But it's also a bad place because you have to make sure none of them drown. All of the Horwitz siblings know how to swim, even the three-year-old twins . . . but they're still only three. Three-year-olds will get into trouble if you look away for even a second, even going so far as to drown themselves just out of spite in order to get you into trouble with your parents.

What Lenny and I ended up doing is this: I stood about knee deep in the water and the little kids took turns running up to me and I grabbed them up and tossed them as far as I could into deeper water, where Lenny waited to pull them to the surface, so they didn't drown. The little urchins loved it. Their squeals of laughter echoed across the lake.

Julius and Artie felt they were too old for this game, which was good, because they're not as small as their siblings, and while I can easily pick them up and toss them a mile, I'd get a lot more tired a lot more quickly doing that with them. Jules and Artie had both brought their ukuleles to the beach, fortunately, and they went off and started playing and making up songs for some girls their age further down the beach.

Artie's ten and doesn't even have pubes yet. Jules is eleven, and just barely does. The girls were about the same ages and were completely goo-goo-eyed over my little brothers. Of course, none of them even knew what to do about it at their age. But those two boys sure know how to put on the charm. I think they'll be a lot of trouble when their balls drop and they're old enough to know what to do about it.

Sort of like Lenny is now.

Me, I've never been that much trouble. I'm the oldest, and with so many younger ragamuffins in the brood, I've always had to be the responsible one. I have a – I think – healthy interest in girls, but I've always been discriminating. Lenny teases me about that. He says, as good looking as I am – people do tell me I'm a good-looking young man, tall and broad-shouldered, lean and muscular, with an adequately put-together face that even I don't flinch from when I catch a glimpse of it in the bathroom mirror – that I could have any girl I want.

Maybe so, but I've never wanted just *any* girl.

I've only wanted *this* girl – the girl I met today and whom I will one day marry.

Only I didn't know that until I met her just today.

Besides, Lenny, will snog anything that moves – and, despite that he's built like a squat fireplug, anything that moves always seems to want to snog him back.

Anyway, I'd been doing this game of tossing the progenies for about half an hour, and, while I'm in really good shape, my arms were starting to burn with fatigue. I'd just scooped up little Polly when I looked up.

I don't know why I looked up.

I just did.

Maybe I sensed someone was there, standing a few feet away on the sandy beach. Maybe I had a sense someone was looking at me.

In any case, I looked up.

And there she was.

The most beautiful girl I've ever seen.

She's got dark, curly hair, and big violet eyes. She looks a little like young Elizabeth Taylor (I told you Mom and Dad make us watch all the old movies).

She was looking at me, with just a trace of a smile on her lips. Like she kinda liked what she was looking at. She was standing with her arms folded beneath her bosom and her weight on her back foot and her front leg was bent at the knee, and she looked absolutely perfect this way.

And of course, her Magen David dangled below her neck and between her breasts and in addition to swimwear she wore sandals and maybe sunscreen, I can't say for sure, but her skin was glistening in the sun, so maybe, yeah.

I won't go into anatomical detail about how great she looked in her two piece, which she wore as comfortably as most people wear their favorite t-shirt, except without the actual t-shirt, but I will say everything about her was expertly positioned and balanced and proportioned like a really thoughtful and beneficent deity had awakened the day after He rested on the seventh day and realized He had one more thing to do, maybe the most important thing of all, and He spent that eighth day sculpting out of clay (or whatever it is *Hashem* sculpts beautiful girls out of) the most perfect girl I have ever laid my eyes on, or ever will.

I've seen a lot of girls, spending every summer of my life swimming with them in Eden Hollow. And I can appreciate them in all their variety. But everything about this girl was just *Goldilocks* – not too this, not too that.

In other words, just perfect.

But having said that – it was her eyes which got me, not

her body – which is no shade on her body, which is impeccable.

But those violet eyes.

And that light spray of freckles across her nose.

And those bouncy, flouncy ringlets of dark hair that framed her perfectly symmetrical face.

Man, I wish you could have seen her so you'd know, because I can't really describe her well enough to do her justice. But she is spectacular. Every part of her. In every way.

"Looks like you've got your hands full," she said. She said it in Yiddish, of course. What she said was: "*es kukt vi ir hot deyn hent ful.*"

Her Yiddish was as perfect as her violet eyes and freckled nose and dark curly hair on her head that seemed to have a mind of its own and as perfect as every other part of all the rest of her.

Growing up in Eden Hollow, one does get a lot less judgy about bodies and a lot more judgy about Yiddish.

But in her case, both were flawless.

"I do," I admitted, not taking my eyes off her. I said this in Yiddish, of course.

Basically, almost everything anyone says when I'm writing about Eden Hollow will be in Yiddish, unless I tell you otherwise. Just as everyone in Eden Hollow is just barely dressed unless I tell you otherwise. You should just assume that to be the case in all situations. If they're not speaking Yiddish or not wearing just shorts or swimwear, then it's worth mentioning. Otherwise, take it for granted that they are.

But I'm just going to go ahead and translate everything for you into English, instead of going back and forth, because I don't know if anyone reading this – if anyone ever does, or if I ever want anyone to, come to think of it – actually speaks Yiddish.

"I'm Miriam," she said.

"I'm Simon," I said. "People call me 'Frenchy'." I lifted

Polly up higher. "This is Polly."

"Throw me, Frenchy," Polly said.

"Say hi, Polly," I said.

"Hi, Miriam," Polly said, looking at Miriam. "You look pretty."

Polly by the way, also said this in Yiddish. Even at three, she's fluent, like her twin brother Manny.

"Thank you," Miriam said, her face reddening slightly, as if she didn't know she's pretty. I'm telling you, if I hadn't already recognized that I wanted to marry her, I would have right then seeing her blush. "You're very pretty, too."

"Thank you," Polly said. "You have pretty eyes."

"Thank you. So do you."

"And you have pretty boobies."

Miriam blushed a deeper red and I fell more deeply in love with her. "Why, thank you Polly," she said, laughing.

Polly turned back to me. "Throw me, Frenchy," she said, in Yiddish: "*varfn mir*, Frenchy."

"I'll leave you to it, then," Miriam said, and turned and walked away from me.

"Throw me," Polly said.

But I didn't throw Polly, not yet.

Instead, I watched Miriam as she walked away from me.

I just stood there and watched her, stupidly.

It was the best thing ever. Just watching her.

Not because she was beautiful and moved beautifully and her *tushie* was as incredible as the rest of her -- although that certainly didn't hurt.

It was the best thing ever because it was *her*.

Then Lenny was beside me.

"Oh my God, do you see the *tuchus* on that girl?" Lenny said.

"Shut up Lenny," I said, without taking my eyes off Miriam as she walked away from me. "You're talking about the girl I'm going to marry."

"Throw me!" Polly demanded.

So, I threw Polly into the deeper water and Lenny scurried to retrieve her.

## July 1

Yesterday was a red-letter day.

Today was even redder.

The day started out as all days do at Eden Hollow in the summer, with an outdoor yoga session on the Great Lawn led by my mom.

Not everyone at Eden Hollow attends these daily yoga sessions but a lot of the members do.

The entire Horwitz brigade was there, as well as about two dozen others.

Including Miriam.

"Hi," Miriam said, as she took the mat in front of me. "Simon, right?"

"You can call me 'Frenchy'," I said, and my voice came out in a hoarse croak, my throat suddenly dry.

Everything about her was just as beautiful as yesterday as she stood in front of me wearing a sports bra and skintight yoga shorts, but it was those eyes I couldn't stop looking into. Those violet eyes. We were physically closer now than we had been at the beach, and those eyes just swallowed me up from this proximity.

"Miriam," she said. "People call me Miri."

"Hi, Miri," I said, stupidly.

"Do you have plans later?" she asked.

"Yes," I blurted out without thinking.

I had no plans, but for some reason I didn't want Miri to think I was a complete slacker.

"Oh?" she said. "Because I was thinking of going to the archery range."

"Those are my plans, too," I lied.

"Great," she said. "We can go together."

"Good," I said. "I don't like doing archery alone."

"I've hardly ever done archery."

"Ok," I said. "I can teach you."

"Would you?" she said, hopefully.

Are you freakin' kidding me? I thought. Would I? Asbso-freakin-lutely I would.

"It's a date," I said, immediately regretting using the word "date."

Miri's smile widened. "It's a date," she said, happily.

Then she turned her back to me and toward my mother as the yoga session began.

I endeavored to be mindful of my position in regard to Miri and not to take undue advantage of my viewpoint to see things at a level of intimacy that I had not earned.

Even so, I'm not gonna lie – when she struck the "warrior" poses (Virabhadrasana I, II) and the "reverse warrior" pose (Viparita Virabhadrasana), as well as the Garland pose (Malasana), the Pyramid pose (Parsvottanasana), the Tree pose (Vrksasana), the low lunge, the Cobra pose (Bhujangasana), the Knees, Chest, and Chin pose (Ashtanga Namaskara), the Bridge pose (Setu Bandha Sarvangasana), the Balasana pose, and the Adho Mukha Svanasana, I was captivated by the beauty, power, and grace of her figure.

And when she struck the Standing Forward Bend pose (Uttanasana) I had to look away for fear of becoming undone.

I was shirtless and wearing snug men's yoga shorts and should I have become undone, it would have been immediately obvious to everyone.

But for God's sake, I mean, I'm only human.

Afterwards, Miri said to me, "you want to introduce me to your parents?"

"No," I said. "I really don't."

She frowned. "Why not?"

"They'll just embarrass me."

She laughed. "They seem all right."

"They're not, believe me," I said. "They're insane."

This seemed to delight her. Her violet eyes sparkled.

"Everybody thinks their parents are insane."

"Mine *really* are. Besides, if we don't get out of here, they'll conscript us both to babysit for the ankle biters."

"Ok, Frenchy," Miri said. "Lead the way."

I put my hand chastely on Miri's arm – one of the things I'd like to think I've learned in my sixteen years is how to properly touch a girl in her summer clothes while avoiding inappropriate physical contact – and led her away from the yoga mats and sweaty bodies and to the archery range.

"How does your mom look so good?" Miri asked.

"Yoga, I guess," I answered. I was somewhat aware that my mom looked as good or better than most moms of my friends, and I was secretly a little proud of that.

"*Namaste*, all right," Miri said. "Hasn't your mom pushed out like a million kids?"

"I've lost count," I said. "But I think it's eight."

"Was she just basically pregnant for a decade?"

"Yeah, pretty much," I said. "The last set of twins were my Bar Mitzvah present."

"I bet you would have preferred the Norton Anthology of Jewish American Literature."

"I got that too," I said. "I'm very spoiled."

"So did I," Miri said. "How much have you read?"

"I only read the Phillip Roth parts," I admitted. "They weren't nearly as dirty as advertised."

"I read the whole thing," she said.

I looked at her. She looked back at me. She smiled. Her eyes sparkled. I got lost in those sparkly violet eyes again. I also got lost in the rest of her, which for a moment captivated my attention as well. I quickly returned my focus back to the trail in front of us. "Did you really read the whole thing?" I asked. "You must be a glutton for punishment."

"I like to read," she said.

"I like to read, too," I said. "But I like books that taste good, not books that are good for you."

She laughed. I was falling in love with that laugh as much as with the rest of her. It had a trill of joy in it that made my heart bounce and made me feel like the center of her world. Which was exactly where I wanted to be.

"Ok, what are the books you think taste good?" she asked.

"Well, for my Bar Mitzvah I also got the *Big Book of Jewish Humor*, and the books *Why a Duck?, Harpo Speaks, Groucho and Me, The Groucho Letters,* and *Memoirs of a Mangy Lover.* I read all of those."

"That's a lot of Marx Brothers," Miri said, sounding a little concerned.

"Yeah," I said. "My great-great-grandfather Moishe, who co-founded Eden Hollow when it was called Freedom Hill and was located in New Jersey, was a die-hard anarchist. But today, the Horwitz family are all card-carrying Marxists."

She laughed at that, too, throwing her head back and letting the delight of her laughter fill the summer air. This was more generosity than my lame joke deserved, but much appreciated even so.

"So, is it true they call you Frenchy because you're so good at French kissing?" she asked.

This brought me up short and I looked at her and saw a mischievous glint in her eye. This was the first time I'd seen evidence of this aspect of her personality.

I liked it immediately.

"Who told you that?" I asked.

"That's what the girls are saying."

"Which girls?"

"The ones our age in Eden Hollow," she said. "The ones presumably you've Frenched kissed before."

"Well, that's flattering," I said, feeling my face flush with heat. "But, no, it's not true. My dad has called me 'Frenchy' since I was a toddler, because I'm named for Simon Marx, the father of the Marx Brothers, who was from France and nicknamed 'Frenchy'."

"So, you're not good at French kissing?" she asked, with mock innocence.

I shrugged. "Well," I said. "I didn't say *that.*"

And again, she gave me that infectious laugh of hers. And if I could have, I'd have stepped into that laughter floating in the air and lived inside of the bubble of her delight forever.

Miri had never done archery before, so I helped her figure out how to nock an arrow, pull back a bowstring, and whatnot. This required a certain physical closeness. Another thing I've learned to do in such situations of intimate propinquity is to lean into physical contact with your upper body but putting some space between your lower body and the lower body of the other person. This helps avoid accidental bumping together of your embarrassing parts, such as *schmekel* into *tush*, or vice versa.

But that didn't prevent me from inhaling the scent of Miri's hair – she used a strawberry shampoo – or the sunscreen on her skin (which smelled like coconut). Nor did it prevent me from noticing how smooth the skin on her shoulders was as it touched my chest, or from noticing the muscularity of her arms as I guided her in pulling back the bowstring. I felt tingles all over my body as I did this and had to make a conscious effort to restrain myself so as not to allow myself to become ridiculous.

"Your heart is pounding against my back," Miri whispered.

The breath caught in my throat.

"Archery is very exciting," I said.

She let the arrow fly and it actually hit the target this time, although not particularly close to the bull's eye. Even so, this pleased her tremendously. She jumped up and down and cheered. I guess I don't need to go into detail about how this made me feel as I watched her doing this.

She turned to me, smiling, and then suddenly stopped

smiling, and looked at me with a serious expression, as if she was thinking about something.

I thought she might kiss me or slap me, I wasn't sure which, but then a volley of gunfire erupted in the morning air, and she started.

"Jesus!" she shouted. "What was that?"

"We have a shooting range," I said.

"We have a shooting range?"

"We sure do," I confirmed. "Want to try it?"

On our way to the shooting range, I asked her where she's from.

"I grew up at the Glen River Family Nature Ranch in California," she said. "It's a planned community and it looks a lot like Eden Hollow, with more palm and citrus trees. It's a community of year-round residents – a small town, basically. My parents are college professors, so they commuted to work every day and I went to school in the nearby town. It's warm and sunny all year long, so every day was like summer in Ohio."

"I guess with global warming, maybe we'll be able to move into Eden Hollow full time one day," I said.

"Every cloud, right?" she said. "Anyway, we just recently moved to Northeast Ohio because my parents are going to be teaching at the state university. I like Eden Hollow, but I'm going to miss not being able to enjoy weather like this year-round."

"We live in the greater metro area," I said. "A lot of the members here do as well – mostly what they call the First Ring Suburbs, some the Second Ring, and a few in the city proper. There's a lot you can do in Northeast Ohio in the fall, winter, and spring. Metroparks has seven-hundred-foot chutes for tobogganing, and we've got ice skating rinks, snowshoeing trails, and there's even downhill skiing and at resorts nearby. In the spring and fall there's hiking and pickup basketball, softball, ultimate frisbee, flag football, and volleyball. And who knows? Maybe we can arrange social gatherings with the Eden Hollow kids during the winter months or something. Rosa's parents have an indoor pool."

Miri smiled at me with a smile that felt like she had jabbed me in the heart in the best possible way.

"Will you teach me to ice skate?" she asked.

OhMyGod, was she kidding?

"You bet I will," I promised.

She gave me a hug and I hoped I wouldn't die before I could teach her ice skating.

"What's it like where you grew up?" I asked because I had to say something before I died.

"Well, we weren't founded by Yiddish-speaking anarchists or anything like that. I learned Yiddish at home. This is the first time I've been part of a Yiddish speaking community, actually."

"Your Yiddish is perfect," I said.

"Well, thank you," she said. "I'm just getting to the point where I don't have to translate every word in my head before I speak it."

"Were there any other Jews in Glen River?"

"Oh, sure," Miri said. "Few Yiddish speakers, but we have a large Jewish membership. Otherwise, Glen River is pretty much like here but less humid and drier. It's a desert climate. But the neighborhood looks like just any other Southern California cul-de-sac, you know, with Spanish colonial houses and the like."

"Any brothers or sisters?"

"Just me," she said. "I'm an only child."

"I'm envious," I said.

"You can't fool me," she said. "I saw you with your little siblings. You love them to pieces."

"Maybe so," I said. "But that doesn't mean I'm not envious."

Dad had made sure that Lenny and I knew how to fight and shoot. He intended to do the same with the younger

Horwitz brood when they were old enough.

Miri, on the other hand, had never even picked up a gun much less fired one. It was kind of fun teaching her how to do so, in no small part because it again necessitated a certain amount of physical intimacy – although of course once again I was scrupulous in avoiding contact between my naughty bits and her intimacies.

Even so, I stood behind her, my chest against her shoulders, my arms on hers, her hands in mine, as I helped her steady the .22 target pistol.

"Remember," I said. "Squeeze, don't jerk."

"You're talking about the pistol, right?" she said.

I was a little shocked by her remark.

Delighted, but a little shocked.

I didn't know how to respond, so I just said, "Ok. When you're ready, squeeze. The trigger, I mean."

She fired, jerking the trigger instead of squeezing. The recoil jolted the pistol in her hand and pushed her shoulders back harder into my chest. Which felt kind of really good and made me a little proud that I was standing there to cushion the recoil.

"Oh my God!" she cried. "It just leaped in my hand. It's like the thing has a life of its own."

"That's a good way to think about it," I said. "Guns are serious business. Ready to try again?"

By the time we finished target practice, Miri was really into it – if no better at hitting the target.

"Come to my cabin for lunch," she said. "I want you to meet my parents."

That sounded promising, I thought.

"Are they crazy?" I asked.

"Batshit," she admitted. "Maybe not as crazy as yours . . but I'm not totally sure of that."

I self-consciously touched my chest. "I don't have a shirt," I said.

She gently put her fingertips on my pecs, and my heart

kicked up a notch.

"You don't need one," she said.

As we walked to her family's cabin, Miri slipped her hand into mine . . . which made my heart race like a little bird's. Her hands were soft, and her fingers intertwined with mine like we were meant to fit together this way.

I was a little nervous about whether or not her parents would see it this way.

Her parents were reading the newspaper when we arrived at their cabin, still hand in hand. Nervously, my fingers twitched, wondering if I should let go. But Miri only clamped her hand more tightly around mine.

Her mom and dad were sitting at the round patio table in back of the cabin, with the sections of both *The New York Times* and *The Plain Dealer* spread out, and a pot of tea between them. They both rose to their feet when they saw us and smiled at us as we neared with indulgently pleased expressions on their faces.

Her father was a little on the short and stout side, with a big belly, broad shoulders and chest, a receding hairline, a pair of glasses on the end of his nose, and an impressively bushy and professorial beard. His hair was dark and streaked with gray, and he had a jovial face with rosy apples of cheeks above his beard below twinkling brown eyes, all of which put me in mind of a Jewish Santa Claus. The only thing he wore other than his glasses were cargo pants, a pair of sandals, and his watch. He was shirtless, and unashamed at his Buddha belly.

Her mother was a real beauty. You could tell where Miri got it from. She had the same deep violet eyes of her daughter, and the same dark ringlets of hair, only hers were streaked with gray. She was a head taller than her husband. Other than her Magen David and a pair of flip flops, she wore a halter top and shorts, and a silver chain around her middle that hung below her belly-button.

I guessed they were about the same age as my parents,

mid-forties.

"Esther, Schlomo, this is Simon Horwitz," Miri said. "You can call him 'Frenchy.' Frenchy, these are my parents, Esther and Schlomo Bernstein."

Miri held tight to my left hand, but I thrust out my right and gave each of them a firm handshake, starting with Esther so I wouldn't seem sexist.

"Call me Tessie," Esther said as I shook her hand.

"Call me Moe," Schlomo said. "Like Moe Howard from the Three Stooges."

"Pleased to meet you both," I said. "You know, Moe, Curly, and Shemp's real last name was Horwitz."

"I did know that," Moe said. "Tessie, did you know that?"

"I did not know that," Tessie said.

"Miri, did you know that?"

"I knew that after Frenchy told me," Miri said.

"Are you a fan of the Three Stooges, Frenchy?" Moe asked.

"I'm more of a Marx Brothers guy, myself," I said. "But I'm a big fan of Iggy and the Stooges."

Moe seemed impressed and looked me over from head to toe as if seeing me for the first time. "Say, Miri, this young man's got some pretty good taste in music." He looked at his daughter. "And also, good taste in girls, if I do say so myself." He looked back at me. "And I don't mind the cut of his jib, either."

I wasn't certain exactly what he meant, since all I wore was shorts, but I felt myself blush anyway.

Tessie ran her hands through my hair. "Where do you get these gold highlights in your dark hair?" she asked. "They're like straw woven into strands of gold."

"Like in Rumpelstiltskin," Miri chuckled. "Tessie, stop pawing Frenchy."

Tessie took her fingers out of my hair. "I do apologize," she said.

"No worries," I said. "In the winter, those strands are

red. In the summer, they turn to gold."

"Why, that sounds just like a fairy tale. Miri, wherever did you find this handsome young man?"

"I fished him out of the lake," Miri said. "Why don't we sit down so you guys can stop scrutinizing Frenchy's abs?"

I *really* blushed at that, but her parents just laughed.

I'm told I do have nice abs.

"We're just admiring the cut of his jib, Miri," Moe said.

"And we're not looking at his abs, dear," Tessie said.

"Why not?" Miri said. "I am."

This remark was greeted with gales of laughter from her parents, and a wave of heat flushing in my face.

Miri was turning out to be a much sassier girl than I realized.

This did not disappoint me in the least.

We sat down, Tessie asked me if I wanted tea, I said yes please, cleared my throat, and asked, "so, Tessie and Moe, what are you guys professors of?"

"Literature for me, history for Tessie," Moe said. "Speaking of which, what's your favorite book?"

"You mean, other than *The Groucho Letters*?"

Moe chuckled. "Let's start with novels."

I tried to think of an impressive answer, but I decided just to be honest.

"*Billy Bathgate* by E.L. Doctorow," I said.

Moe raised an eyebrow. "That's a surprising and delightful answer for a young man, Frenchy. Why not *Ragtime*?"

"*Ragtime*'s on the list, too," I said.

"What about Vonnegut?" Moe asked. "Every intellectual your age goes through a Vonnegut phase."

"I don't know about intellectual, sir," I said. "But *Slaughterhouse-Five* and *Bluebeard* are probably in my top ten."

"*Bluebeard*? What appeal does a book about a fictional minor abstract expressionist have to a young man like you?"

"Well," I began – and spoiler alert here, although really, it's revealed early in the book – "here's this guy that spends a life making paintings that are well-regarded and hung in museums and then, in middle age, the paint on the canvases all peels off because of the chemical compositions of oils and his entire life's work just turns to dust all at once."

"Yes?" Moe said, expectantly.

"Well," I said, "That's kinda like life, sometimes, isn't it?"

"Your boyfriend is a hard-nosed realist, Miri," Tessie said, not without a note of approval in her voice. "That could stand you both in good stead if he doesn't spiral into cynicism."

Miri neither confirmed nor denied I was her boyfriend. We hadn't even kissed, yet, after all.

But she did take my arm and pull it to her and give it a squeeze and rested her cheek on my shoulder.

"Isn't he delicious?" she said.

To paraphrase Peter Gabriel, my heart went *boom.*

By the way, Peter Gabriel is not Jewish, but the bassist on all his solo albums, Tony Levin, certainly is.

## July 2

This morning, Miri and I snuck away after yoga and went to the lakeside beach.

There was almost no one there but the lifeguard when we arrived, so we splashed and swam out to the swimming platform and dove off and swam back to shore and did that all over again until we got tired, and then we slathered ourselves with sunscreen and laid out on our towels in the sun.

And, yes, Miri asked me to put sunscreen on her back and shoulders, and she did the same for me . . . and it was amazing.

We were lying side by side on our bellies and Miri said, "are you embarrassed to introduce me to your parents?"

"Yes," I said. "I'm embarrassed of my parents."

"Not of me?"

"Are you kidding me?" I said.

"Well, how should I know?"

"I told you my parents are insane."

"You've met *my* parents. Are yours that much more insane than mine?"

I shrugged. "Well, maybe not that much more insane," I said.

Miri laughed and then someone landed on my back.

"Gotcha!" said my cousin Rosa as she slipped her arms under my arms and locked her fingers behind my neck and lay down flat on my back, pinning me to the towel.

Remember when I said about learning how to interact with people in their summer clothes without your intimacies and theirs making inappropriate and unintended contact?

Well, my cousin Rosa never figured that part out. Or figured out anything else when it comes to proper boundaries, for that matter.

Not that she has any kind of inappropriate intent or

anything gross like that. It's just that she doesn't perceive anything awkward when intimate bits and other people's body parts make contact.

So, that's why now she was lying on my back, straddling my butt, her bikini-clad chest pressed into my shoulder blades, and she was kissing my cheek even as she held me tightly in a headlock.

Miri looked at us with both eyebrows raised and an expression that seemed to suggest she was trying to stifle her laughter.

"Miri, I'd like you to meet my cousin, Rosa Lieberman," I said. "She's almost as embarrassing as my parents."

Rosa released me and raised herself up but remained sitting on my butt. She stuck out her hand to Miri. "You're the girl," she said. "The Horwitzes told me all about you."

Miri took Rosa's hand. "What did they tell you?"

"Well, Polly said you have pretty boobies and Lenny says you have a really nice *tushie*," Rosa said. "That's about it since they haven't actually met you. Well, except for Polly." She scrutinized Miri for a moment. "I can see they were correct in their assessments."

As you might have noticed, Rosa has no filter.

"When did you get here, Rosa?" I asked, still pinned beneath her as she continued to sit on my butt.

"Just now," she said. "Hey, there's a volleyball game about to start down the beach with some of the kids our age."

"You need to get off my butt, first," I said.

Rosa stood up. I did, too. I turned and looked at her.

Rosa looked like the hot mess she was, but she was a sweet and silly person, if a little too much to take sometimes. She had wild red hair that could never be tamed and a spray of freckles across her nose, cheeks, and shoulders. She had fair skin, but with repeated applications of sunscreen she usually managed to avoid burning and her skin instead turned a light honey-tone by summer's end. She was cute but she didn't care if she was cute or not. She made absolutely no effort to please anyone or fit in with anyone. As a result, she had a wide circle of friends because she didn't demand anyone be anything other than what they were, and she never tried to be anything but what she was, and most people eventually accepted the same of her. Her closest friends were mostly misfits and screwballs like her, but Rosa made them feel as important as anyone, and she would tolerate no disdain directed towards them from the "cool kids," and they loved her for it. They were about as loyal as friends can be. She and her family summered with us at Eden Hollow every year. She was my age, so I had known her basically for the entirety of both our lives.

Rosa gave me a big kiss and hugged me hard. I hugged her back just as hard because I knew if I didn't, she'd never let go.

Then she gave Miri a hug that was just as intense, and a wet sloppy kiss on her cheek. Miri, to her credit, hugged her back with equal enthusiasm, after recovering from her initial surprise.

"Gosh, you are a cutie," Rosa said, looking her over.

I turned to Miri. "You want to play volleyball?" I asked.

"Sure," she said. "I'm like Tigger. I like to bounce."

I really enjoyed playing volleyball, watching Miri as she leaped into the air and spiked the ball. She was good at it, a natural athlete.

Except for sprinting, at which she excelled, Rosa was a terrible athlete. But she played with such joy and enthusiasm that no one cared.

The other players consisted mostly of regulars our age or around our age, and a few new kids of some new members. Miri knew a few of them, and I introduced her to the rest, and Rosa introduced us both to the new kids, whom Rosa had already befriended. One good thing about Rosa's lack of boundaries was that she never hesitated to make a new friend. All of the players were either her old friends, her close friends, or her new friends. Rosa never met a person she couldn't befriend.

After the game, the twelve of us all went for a swim together, and then we all lay out on our towels in the sun. Most of us reapplied our sunscreen. I got to attend to Miri's back and shoulders again, and it was just as awesome as the first time. Rosa demanded both Miri and I slather sunscreen on her back and shoulders, and, of course, we complied, because you don't say no to Rosa unless you absolutely have to.

"You know what?" I said to Miri we lay there on the towels in the sun. I was feeling warm and at peace with the world.

"No, I don't know what," Miri said. "You want to tell me?"

"If Rosa didn't scare you away, I think it's time for you to meet my parents."

Miri nodded. "What can I bring?"

"Just yourself."

"What should I wear?"

"Just yourself."

"You want me naked?" she asked, coyly.

My heart slammed. "You will make a great impression no matter what you wear, or don't," I stammered, my mind filled with images of Miri showing up to shabbat dinner wearing nothing but the glory *Hashem* gave her. "Wear whatever you want. Just be you."

Miri nodded, thoughtfully. "I can do that," she said, with a smile.

## July 3

So, tonight, I finally had Miri over to break bread with the Horwitz family.

She arrived looking more splendid that ever. She wore no make-up, just shorts and a plunge flyaway halter top that tied below her bosom, revealing shoulders, cleavage, and midriff – a bold choice which she somehow managed to make look almost formal and unexpectedly demure, I suppose due to the naturalness and unaffectedness with which she does, and wears, everything. She had done something with her hair and accessorized it with a flower behind her ear. She accessorized her body with a belly chain that hung just below her navel, like the one her mom wore, and an anklet as well as a more elegant and fancy pair of sandals than her usual. She also wore a pair of *Hamsa* earrings.

It was amazing how stylish she looked with just those simple frills.

She was so beautiful that everybody just sort of stopped short for a moment when she arrived. We were all out back, setting the patio table for shabbat dinner.

Dad approached her with his hand outstretched. Dad is tall, fit, and handsome, with a trim beard speckled with gray. He's one of those people who appears classy and commanding even when shirtless, like he could preside over a board meeting in his swimsuit as authoritatively as in a three-piece suit. It's only when you get to know him a bit that you realize what a total goofball he is.

"Miri, welcome to the Horwitz family estate," Dad said. He was dressed in neatly pressed shorts and a short sleeve button down shirt, open at the collar. "I am very pleased to meet you."

"Very pleased to meet you as well, Mr. Horwitz," Miri said.

"Call me Sol," Dad said. "Short for Solomon. This is my

wife, Jennie."

Mom squeezed in and gave Miri an affectionately generous and unrestrained embrace and a kiss on both cheeks. Mom wore shorts and a short sleeve blouse. "My dear, you look absolutely lovely," she said. "Thank you for joining us."

"Thank you for having me," Miri said, blushing charmingly.

"Give me some of that," Lenny said, elbowing his way in. He wore jean shorts and no shirt.

"Shake hands only, Len," I said, quietly but firmly.

Lenny does not respect authority, but he respected the tone of my voice. He extended his hand and Miri took it.

"Miss Bernstein, it is a pleasure to welcome you to our shabbat table," Lenny said, acutely vigilant to be on his best behavior, lest he incur my wrath.

Lenny is the brawler in the family; I am not.

That doesn't mean I can't flatten him.

Julius and Artie, both good Jewish menschy boys, approached with arms extended and politely shook hands and welcomed Miri. They wore shorts and t-shirts. Artie's t-shirt had a picture of Harpo Marx. Jules's had a picture of Groucho.

The ankle biters, on the other hand, ran to her with extravagant embraces. They had been wrangled out of their swimsuits and also wore shorts and t-shirts.

When it was Polly's turn, she leaped into Miri's arms.

As Miri held Polly aloft, she looked with delight at my littlest sister. Polly kissed Miri's face and said, "I'm glad you like Frenchy. Somebody has to."

This remark was met with tornados of laughter from my ever-supportive family.

When it came time to light the shabbat candles and say the prayers, my mom asked Miri if she wanted to do the honors.

Initially, this pissed me off. After all, just because Miri

is Jewish doesn't mean she knows the words and the songs and feels comfortable leading prayers on Friday night. I felt this was putting her on the spot. I wondered if this was some kind of test – although that idea mystified me because my parents, for all their quirks, are not the kind of people who engage in subterfuge. They are always pretty direct and out there about things. They are not sneaky.

And also, while they are very Jewish, they are very much adamantly their own kind of very Jewish. We go to temple either on Friday night or Saturday morning usually at least twice a month, and of course major holidays; we celebrate B'nai Mitzvahs and weddings with our Jewish co-congregants; and we cry at Jewish funerals with them as well. We revel in Jewish culture, particularly Jewish-American culture (like the Marx Brothers). But we don't keep kosher, we practice non-western traditions like yoga and meditation, and in the summers, we practice our Judaism and speak Yiddish at Eden Hollow, a formerly anarchist community the founding members of which were likely all atheists. I don't think my parents would have a problem if any of us married a non-Jew, although they might feel a twinge of regret if their grandchildren weren't raised in the faith. On the other hand, I think they'd be perfectly fine if their grandkids were raised, for example, *both* Jewish and Catholic, or Lutheran, or Buddhist, or Hindi. People say you can't do that, you have to choose. But I think my dad would say, "who says you have to choose? *Hashem*? He never told *me* we have to choose, and if it says that in some ancient text written by men trying to understand the will of God while asserting social control over the rest of us, well, that lacks ultimate authority in our book. So, we'll be our own kind of Jew, thank you very much."

So, why were they putting Miri on the spot?

But, as it turned out, Miri was just as comfortable – and just as good at – leading Shabbat prayers in her summer clothes as anything else I had seen her do – except of course for archery and target shooting.

She lit the candles, covered her eyes with her hands, and sang the prayers in Hebrew, which translate more or less as: "Blessed are You, G-d, our L-rd, King of the Universe, Who has sanctified us with His commandments and instructed us to kindle the Shabbat lights."

Then she led us in singing "Shalom Aleichem," as we stood around the table, in Hebrew. The English translation is (more or less): "May peace come to you, angels of service, angels of G-d on high, who come from the King of all kings, the Holy One, Blessed is He. Bless us with peace, angels of peace, angels of G-d on high, who come from the King of all kings, the Holy One, Blessed is He."

Then she went around the table and recited the blessing of the children again in Hebrew. For the boys, it translates (more or less) as:

"May the L-rd make you like Ephraim and Menashe. May G-d bless you and protect you. May G-d shine His light on you and be gracious to you. May G-d show you favor and grant you peace."

And for the girls:

"May the L-rd make you like Sarah, Rebecca, Rachel, and Leah. May G-d bless you and protect you. May G-d shine His light on you and be gracious to you. May G-d show you favor and grant You peace."

Then she led us in the Kiddush, again in Hebrew, roughly translated as:

"And it was evening, and it was morning, the sixth day. And the heaven and the earth and everything in them were completed. And on the seventh day the L-rd finished His work which He had done; and He abstained on the seventh day from all His work which He had done. And the L-rd blessed the seventh day and He sanctified it, because on it He abstained from all His work which He had created. Your attention, my masters, rabbis, and teachers: Blessed are You, G-d, our L-rd, King of the Universe, Who creates the fruit of the vine. (Amen)

"Blessed are you, G-d, our L-rd, King of the Universe, who has sanctified us through His commandments and was pleased with us, and [therefore] He gave us His holy Shabbat, lovingly and willingly, as a heritage, a reminder of the work of Creation. Because it is the first of the holy days, a reminder of the exodus from Egypt. Because You have chosen us and sanctified us above all the nations, and You have given us Your holy Shabbat, lovingly and willingly, as a heritage. Blessed are you, G-d, who sanctifies the Shabbat. (Amen)"

Then she led us in the ritual washing of hands (in Hebrew, of course, translated more or less) as:

"Blessed are you G-d, our L-rd, King of the Universe, Who sanctified us with His commandments and commanded us on the washing of hands. (Amen)."

Then she held together the two loaves of challah we had put on the table and sang (in Hebrew):

"Blessed are You, G-d, our L-rd, King of the Universe, Who brings forth bread from the earth (Amen)."

Miri sang with an absolutely angelic voice, but not an ethereal one – more of an earthy one. Kind of like a Jewish Beyoncé.

And then we broke the challah into pieces, and we all ate it, and dinner was served.

There was something both beautiful and spiritual watching Miri lead shabbat dinner prayers, her natural physical beauty an earthly counterpart to the spiritual beauty of the moment. I felt my head spin with the power of the experience, and I was reminded not for the first time, that the power of Eden Hollow was that it allowed us, the spiritual descendants of anarchist-Yiddishers, to be our most pure and unadorned and unashamed Jewish selves free from the outside world's judgement and attempted subjugation.

Miri sat down next to me again as Mom served the brisket.

She smiled at me shyly.

"How was I?" she whispered.

I had no words.

So, I kissed her.

Just a peck on the cheek.

But it was our first kiss.

## July 4

The 4th of July at Eden Hollow is traditionally a big-ass hootenanny.

We all gather on the Great Lawn that slopes down to the beach, and we cook and eat and sing and play music and there's face painting and games and races and such.

The Horwitz family are all musicians, and so we all play along with the hootenanny's klezmer-flavored traditional and labor-movement folk songs. Dad plays banjo. Mom plays clarinet. I play concertina. Lenny plays piano. Artie plays harp. Julius plays guitar. Bertie plays hammered dulcimer. Miltie plays violin. Polly and Manny play percussion instruments like shakers and maracas (they're only three, for Pete's sake).

And Miri, it turns out, plays viola, and quite beautifully. Also, a beautiful girl like Miri wearing only cut-off jeans and a *Hamsa*-print bikini top and playing klezmer viola is far more captivating than should reasonably be allowed by law.

After music and eating and dancing and singing and playing the ring toss and winning a giant stuffed panda for Miri, it was almost time for the fireworks over the lake.

"You want to watch them from my secret spot?" I whispered into Miri's ear.

"You have a secret spot?" Miri said, excitedly. "Lead the way."

So, I took her hand and we slipped away from the crowd and walked along a path among some trees and then up to the top of what's called Frog Hill because of the pond at the top which is filled with frogs.

We stood up there listening to the frogs as they croaked and then the first hiss and boom of the first fireworks erupting over the lake, and Miri watched enraptured at the pyrotechnic display on the water.

I was enraptured to – but I was watching the colors of the fireworks as they painted Miri's beautiful skin.

Miri looked at me with a big smile after a particularly impressive explosive display and saw me looking at her instead of the fireworks. She stopped smiling and a serious expression came over her face. She seemed to be thinking hard, as if trying to make a decision.

Then she went to me, and she kissed me.

On the mouth.

And I kissed her back.

And I wrapped my arms around her, and she wrapped her arms around me. And we kissed some more. And her lips were soft and kissable and there were tongues involved.

"Are you sure you didn't get your nickname because of your kissing?" she whispered in my ear, breathlessly.

She pulled me tightly to her and our bodies pressed together, and I kissed, and she kissed. I was already shirtless, and then her bikini top dropped off and then we both were shirtless. My hands ran up and down her flesh, and hers ran up and down mine. I kissed her mouth, and I kissed her neck, and I kissed her shoulders.

I felt myself becoming aroused.

I started to pull away.

"No, don't," she whispered. "It's Ok."

And she pulled me more tightly to her. And I kissed her mouth and her neck and her shoulders. And she kissed my chest. We unbuttoned one another's shorts and they dropped to our ankles. We kicked them off our feet. We gazed upon one another in our mutual nakedness, and then we held each other tightly. Our hands caressed and our lips kissed each other all over, in all those intimate places a boy like me does not touch or kiss a girl like her unless she invites him to and a girl like her does not touch or kiss a boy like me unless she really wants to.

I held her tightly in my arms and I was really enflamed by now, pressing into her.

"Is this, Ok?" I asked, softly, as booms erupted over the lake and our skin was bathed in colored light.

"Just keep kissing me," she said.

And so, I did.

# Part Three: Iceberg

**Two years later**

**One day before the Collapse**
**Seven years before Operation Supreme Flood for America**
**Seven years before the Fall of Eden**

# From the Journal of Simon "Frenchy" Horwitz, Aged 18:

## July 3

### Eden Hollow Health and Nature Outdoor Recreation Association Family Bungalow Community

In a few weeks, I am going to marry the girl I met two summers ago at Eden Hollow.

See? I told you so.

We lost our virginity that night two years ago, on July 4. Miri and me. Together. With each other. On top of Frog Hill. With the booms of the fireworks and the croaks of the frogs.

And now, two years later, we are getting married, just like I knew we would.

I meant to keep up with this journal, but looking it over, I realize I haven't made an entry since that summer two years ago.

So, what's happened since?

Well, that summer was spectacular. Miri and I spent most of it together. We got to know each other really well – sexually, sure, but in every other way, too -- and the more we got to know each other, the more I fell in love with her.

And I guess she fell in love with me, too, because when I asked her to marry me – after we had both turned eighteen a couple of months ago – she said yes.

In the meantime, Miri took to winter sports like a bagel takes to cream cheese. She was particularly good at snowboarding, I guess because she had some experience surfing out in California. She also had some experience roller blading, and she also excelled at ice skating, which she loved.

She was terrible at downhill skiing, but that didn't stop her. Every tumble she took sent her into gales of laughter and left her undauntedly resolute for the next one. She hated snowshoeing, but she loved cross country skiing.

I hate cross country skiing, but cross-country skiing with Miri, I hated it a lot less.

When Miri and I suggested to Rosa that she invite kids our age from Eden Hollow to her house for indoor pool parties over the winter, she immediately expressed enthusiasm. At the first gathering, however, she made a proposal that surprised everyone.

Rosa explained she had done a deep dive into the history of Eden Hollow, and discovered that, originally, when it was located in New Jersey in 1917, it was not only an anarchist, Yiddish speaking community, but an *anarcho-naturist* Yiddish-speaking *vegan* community. Not everyone understood that terminology, so Rosa explained it.

What it meant was that in addition to speaking Yiddish and in general being anarchic, the original members also ate vegan food and lived as naturists – which means they all went completely naked all of the time, at least while at Eden Hollow.

As far as I know, this would have made them the first – and quite possibly the only – Yiddish speaking naked community in history.

Rosa had actually printed out her research on the history of Eden Hollow, and her conclusion seemed pretty irrefutable.

Rosa went on to propose, in honor of the original founding members of Eden Hollow, that we renew the anarcho-naturist tradition and meet weekly at her house for naked pool parties and vegan snacks. We would meet every Sunday afternoon when her parents could reliably be counted on to be out of the house for their weekly Yiddish book club at the JCC, which was just as reliably followed by Mahjong.

Miri immediately expressed enthusiasm for the idea. She was from California, after all, where I guess they do this kind of thing.

Some of the kids our age bailed immediately, but about a dozen of us stuck around. We began to meet every Sunday. The vegan snacks were mostly terrible, but the nakedness quickly became as normal to us as speaking Yiddish and provided a refreshingly cathartic sense of connection and even mindfulness. It wasn't a hedonistic or unseemly experience. It was just about *being* – something it was harder and harder to do outside of Eden Hollow and Rosa's pool.

For me, personally, I found it somewhat affirming having to hide neither my Magen David nor my circumcised *schmekel* among a group of peers with whom I could converse in the language of my forebearers.

Rosa dubbed us the "Eden Hollow Anarcho-Naturist Youth Brigade."

The Eden Hollow Anarcho-Naturist Youth Brigade got to be so normal that members began to bring their younger siblings. Pretty soon, the entire Horwitz clan of siblings – Polly, Manny, Bertie, Miltie, Artie, Julius, Lenny, me, and Miri – joined the brigade for these Sunday naked pool gatherings. We never had been, after all, an exactly traditional family. I think, had we told them, our parents would have probably approved – I'm certain they did the same kind of thing when they were young bohos -- although we all would have been mortified if they had ever suggested they join us with all of the other Eden Hollow parents to turn our Sunday afternoon pool events into family occasions.

Come to think of it, that's probably why we never

told them.

So, that's how we spend the fall, winter, and spring.

In addition to winter sports, Miri and I have been able to spend a lot of time together these past two years. She also lives in the same neighborhood, Coventry Village, and we go to the same school, and also attend the same synagogue.

So, we really do see a lot of each other – and even more of each other when the Anarcho-Naturist Youth Brigade meets at Rosa's house Sunday afternoons.

Spending so much time with Miri is the absolute best.

It's been idyllic – or, it would have been, if it hadn't been for all the bad news online and on TV lately. Some people are saying the US is on the brink of another civil war, although I think that's a little alarmist. Some people say the semi-autonomous regional federations of states that were instituted a few years ago are on the verge of declaring themselves independent republics. I kind of doubt they would *all* do that. . . but maybe some of them would – most likely, the Bible Belt states people are calling "The New Confederacy" and maybe the Southwestern states, Texas, Arizona, and Oklahoma, which people are calling an anti-immigration libertarian wet dream.

I can't see the midwestern post-industrial states, where we live, or the plains states next door or the Pacific states where Miri's from actually breaking away like that. Maybe the mountain states would. They like being all ruggedly individualistic and all that.

I mean, I *guess* it's possible. I guess *anything* is possible.

There's also been an even sharper rise in antisemitism than before, which has been pretty stressful. It's mostly been vandalism and graffiti and online shit, dumbass things like that, but there's also been an uptick in assaults. Most Jewish kids I know didn't wear their Magen David outside their shirts before, and now hardly *any* of them do anymore. A lot of them don't wear their Magen Davids even *inside* their shirts anymore. You run the risk of getting it from all sides if anyone catches sight of your Star of David – right-wing fanatics think you're an agent of the Zionist Occupied Government and radical leftists think you're an agent of the Zionist Entity, which is what they call Israel, I guess. Some people have even removed the mezuzahs from their doors. The Horwitz family hasn't, though – even after someone painted a swastika on our local synagogue (a backwards swastika, of course – the Jew haters never seem to know the proper orientation of the Nazi swastika). Someone even shot out the windows at our shul, although fortunately no one was there at the time.

That's partly why we decided to have our wedding at Eden Hollow – it's isolated, gated, surrounded by high privacy walls, hard to find, and relatively safe.

Plus, it's where we met.

Plus, it's more fun to do things outdoors, especially on a nice summer day – including get married.

My dad got one of those on-line ordinations that authorizes him to perform a legal wedding ceremony. We're going to do all the bells and whistles for a real Jewish wedding – the chuppah, etc. That won't make it a real Jewish wedding under official Jewish law, but like I've said, my parents have never hesitated to do things their own way. And the same, it turns out, is true of Miri's parents.

I guess we're kind of made for each other.

A bigger issue for my folks and hers was that both sets of parents were worried that we are too young to marry. But we reassured them by proving to them we had a plan.

We'd both been accepted at the state university in the city. We decided we'd both attend, to stay close to home – and avoid being far away when travel is such a pain and things are so uncertain. We'd live in married student housing. We'd be scrupulous about using birth control so we could both graduate on time and not have a kid until we can support ourselves. When I graduate, I'll start working with Dad, helping to run his record and musical instrument stores, which are called "Rock, Rhythm, and Jazz Roadhouse: A Record and Instrument Emporium." We have one on Coventry Road, one by the Music Institute, and one near the Rock n' Roll Museum by the waterfront.

Miri isn't certain yet about her next move after university. Maybe she'll pursue graduate studies. Maybe she'll get a job.

Or maybe we'll start our family.

I don't think it was so much the solidity of our plan – although it wasn't bad as far as it went – that convinced them. I think it was more the realization that if we were going to go so far as to come up with a plan, such as it was, we were pretty much unstoppable in our intentions, and since we didn't really require their approval – since we're both eighteen -- they might as well approve.

## July 4

Today was the best day ever – until it wasn't.

The day started off like every other July 4th hootenanny at Eden Hollow, with music, food, face painting, games, the whole nine yards. The Horwitz family and Miri played our instruments – the youngest twins are now five and have both graduated to ukulele – and we all had a grand old time.

When it was almost time for the fireworks, I took Miri's hands in mine and we walked along the path to the top of Frog Hill, where we had made love under the flash and boom of the pyrotechnics and to the accompaniment of the frogs two years earlier – and the following year as well. We watched the fireworks for a while, and then, just like two years ago and last year, Miri turned to me and saw me watching her, the colorful lights illuminating her skin, and we kissed, and we sank to the ground – this time on the towel we had the foresight to bring with us.

Two years ago, we had grass stains on our butts by the time we came down off the hill. We made sure to bring towels the next year, and this one.

We also had a small bag with us this time in which we carried our towels, sunscreen, water bottles, and cellphones.

Obviously, it was night, so we didn't need the sunscreen just now. And while neither one of us usually walked around with our cellphones at Eden Hollow, we were both anxiously awaiting confirmation we had been approved for married student housing, so we'd kept our cellphones close by, just in case, even though it was the 4th of July, and we probably wouldn't hear anything until the holiday weekend was over.

As it turned out, the phone would come in handy, but for all the wrong reasons.

*(the next part is written in present tense because even as I write it now, it just feels that way:)*
For the moment, though, we lie on the towel while the fireworks boom overhead and illuminate our bodies in flashes of colored light. We kiss each other as our clothes, almost of their own accord, drop off our bodies. I kiss her mouth, and then her shoulders and her neck. Then I move down her body.

I am lost and I am found, and I am undone, and I am hers, as I have been since I met her, now and forever.

A massive firework explodes above, quaking the ground beneath us, tendrils of purple, blue, white, and red light snaking through the sky. It's followed by a series of powerful multicolored blasts of flare and percussion in the firmament.

I won't go into detail about our love making, but I will say, we give the pyrotechnics a run for their money. I think we shake the earth more than they do.

Finally, we are satiated, and we are spent, and we lie down on the towel together, and I hold her in my arms in the spooning position, and she turns her face to me, and we kiss.

That's when our cell phones in our bag begin to screech like a klaxon.

Neither one of us have ever heard our phones make that sound before, and so we are both immediately alarmed.

We fish for our phones and look at the screens. We've both received the same message.

The United States of America has collapsed seemingly from one moment to the next, balkanized into multiple independent republics, each of varying degrees of shittiness. The one we find ourselves in is called the Sovereign Republic of North America, stretching from the Ohio to the Missouri rivers, and from the Great Lakes down through Kentucky.

It all seems very sudden, but the notifications on our phones proclaim this was a long time coming, that plans have been in place for years, and that the recent regional problems and instability was just the tip of the iceberg that led to this.

As if this isn't all disturbing enough, the next notification is even worse.

Every able-bodied man and woman from the age of seventeen to thirty-five is ordered to report for military duty at 9 am the following morning.

There's even a link you can click to find the "intake" office nearest to you.

Because we are now at war.

# Part Four: The Ballad of the Gefilte Grunts

**Two days after the Collapse**
**Seven years before Operation Supreme Flood for America**
**Seven years before the Fall of Eden**

# From the Journal of Simon "Frenchy" Horwitz, Aged 18:

## July 5

Every iceberg needs a *Titanic* in order to sink its ship.

This particular iceberg needed its own *Titanic* in order to sink the ship of state.

As the hours went by, more notifications popped up on our phones, and the pieces began to fall into place.

Moments before the crackup of the USA, likely while Miri and I were together atop the hill entwined in erotic splendor and the rest of the Eden Hollow Health and Nature Outdoor Recreation Association Family Bungalow Community members were by the lake watching the Fourth of July fireworks – in fact, seemingly timed to coincide with firework displays all over the Eastern Seaboard -- a series of nuclear explosions took out most of the federal government, leaving DC and Arlington in cinders and killing the president and everyone in the line of presidential succession, from the vice president to the secretary of homeland security, as well as most of the cabinet deputies and assistant secretaries, and all of the Supreme Court. Most of congress was taken out as well, either in the DC explosions, or in targeted assassinations at 4th of July events in their home districts.

The ragged, random remnants of the government, those who survived, immediately conferred, and issued emergency declarations. These were promptly ignored by the states, which years ago had been organized into several semi-autonomous regional authorities in an effort to diffuse some of the successionist sentiment that had been building steadily throughout the country for several decades.

Some claimed the seemingly random government survivors were not so random and had secretly engineered a coup.

Others said these federal survivors simply lacked constitutional authority to take control, since none of them were actually in the line of succession.

Others suspected a competing regional authority other than their own was behind the whole thing, in an effort to create an excuse to break away from the central government and dismantle the republic.

In any case, no one trusted anyone, so even those regional authorities that didn't originally want to declare independence did so anyway, in order to avoid being subjugated by someone else's regional authority.

This all happened within a very short amount of time before those of us too far away to hear the explosions back in DC – or perhaps only far enough away to mistake them for fireworks – knew anything was amiss.

But everything was amiss.

Everything.


It's the wee hours of the morning. Miri and I were supposed to be married in a few hours. Instead, we'll be reporting for duty. If we go through with the wedding before we report, the war will be our honeymoon, I guess.

## July 6

Yesterday, we arrived at the forward operating base, somewhere south of Saint Louis. There was no basic training, because the war is already on and everything is full speed ahead, with the White Christian Confederacy of the Nazarene Nation rapidly pushing their way north from the part of the country that used to be called "the Bible Belt" into the Sovereign Republic of North America, which basically is the part of the country that used to be called "the Rust Belt," from the Great Lakes through Kentucky and Missouri, and from the Ohio River in the East to the Missouri River in the West.

So, it's the Bible Belt versus the Rust Belt, basically.

None of the splinter republics have an air force, because when the US collapsed most of the war planes were flown to the new United Democratic States of America, which is basically most of the Northeast corridor from North Carolina to Maine and contains the remnants of the US government we all used to call our own, now haphazardly housed in New York and New Jersey since DC was burned to a crisp. I guess that transfer of war planes is a good thing, at least insofar as the enemy can't bomb us from the air unless they want to push explosives out of Piper Cubs or something.

Which, come to think of it, could be a possibility.

There's a lot of military bases in the South, so the Nazarenes, pushing up from Tennessee into Kentucky and from Arkansas into Missouri, have a lot of weapons and equipment and are gaining ground rapidly.

It's not clear to me what is the White Christian Confederacy's end game. Are they going to push all the way up through Michigan if they can, and join up with our backwoods militias up there? Hopefully not, because the Sovereign Republic is counting on those militias to supplement our National Guards and our newly hobbled together Republic Defense Force to defend us in the South.

Our plan, to the degree I understand it, is to shore up the Sovereign Republic forces outside St Louis and Louisville and try to stop the enemy's advance there.

We're outnumbered and outgunned. That's where this massive call up comes in. They gave us weapons and a uniform and put us right on a bus waiting outside the intake center. Ten hours later, we disembarked at our forward operating base.

There's nothing standard issue about any of our gear. Our uniforms are Dickies and Carhartt work clothes from Wal Mart shelves with private's stripes sewn on the sleeves. Our weapons are appropriated from gun stores.

We are well armed even so. In case you haven't heard, there's more guns in America than people, so it was easy enough to find sufficient weaponry for all of us. But we've all got different guns – Ruger, Browning, Springfield, Remington, Savage long guns; Beretta, Smith & Wesson, Sig Sauer, Glock semi-automatic pistols; Heritage, Colt, and Taurus revolvers. I personally have a Smith & Wesson semi-auto pistol and a Savage semi-auto rifle.

I just hope with no standardized weaponry they have enough of the different required ammunition for all of us and all of our guns.

Most of us from the Eden Hollow Health and Nature Outdoor Recreation Association Family Bungalow Community are actually pretty good with firearms. Even though Eden Hollow is a very hippy-dippy kind of place, many of us excel at target practice, thanks to our shooting range.

Of course, they tell me shooting targets is not the same as shooting people, and I am inclined to believe them.

Most of us have no particular loyalty to the Sovereign Republic of North America . . . which didn't even exist until a few days ago. But I guess most of us can unite in our revulsion at what life under our neighbor to the south would be like, who seem to be fashioning themselves into a kind of Christian Nationalist Taliban/Hamas.

Lenny and I both know how to shoot and how to fight. Lenny is an amateur boxer, and Eden Hollow also has Krav Maga classes. Rosa, perhaps surprisingly, is also really good at shooting and self-defense. And in the two years since we met, Miri has gotten pretty good at it, too.

But of course, none of us have ever faced anyone in combat, nor ever fired a weapon at another human being. Lenny and I are the only ones in our group from Eden Hollow who have even had our share of schoolyard and street brawls. And Lenny a lot more than me.

Everything seems very haphazard around here at the base, which they are calling "Camp Farty-Four," which is, I guess, a joke on what the locals call nearby Route 44 -- "Route Farty-Four." They've got us sleeping on cots in tents, one tent per squad, and eating in the cafeteria under another big tent that serves everyone on base. Showers are outdoors and they're just a platform with pipes overhead and shower spigots attached to the pipes. There's no walls for the showers, not even canvas ones, and no roof. There's no gender segregation in the showers, either, or in any of the other arrangements. We eat, sleep, shit, and shower together. This has less to do with any notions of gender equity, I think, and more to do with everyone just being thrown together quickly and without any particular consideration. They want us to fulfill our role as cannon fodder to soften up the enemy for the Michigan backwoods militias to come in after us and kill some Nazarenes – unless the militias join up with the Nazarenes, instead. The jury is still out on that.

They seem to have randomly assembled the squads based on who showed up at the intake center at the same time. In addition to me, Lenny, Rosa, and Miri, we've got the siblings Richie and Deb Lipschitz from Eden Hollow. The rest of our squad consists of Privates Samuel "Sully" Sullivan, Hank Günther, Roy Scott, Cody Knox, Luke

Gossett, Benson Tiller, Angela "Angie" Chen, Trisha Vikram, and Ruby Hopper. Our corporal is Miguel "Mike" Hernandez, and our Sergeant is Gillian "Gillie" Gilroy. Gillie and Mike are the only two with military experience, fighting in some of those Middle Eastern wars a few years back. The rest of us are between 17 and 21 years old. Mike is Hispanic, Gillie and Ruby are black. Angie is East Asian. Trisha is South Asian. Sully, Roy, Cody, Luke, Ben, and Hank are all various shades of White.

By happenstance, roughly a third of the squad, those of us who arrived together at the intake center closest to Eden Hollow, are Jewish. Despite the rise in antisemitism, Eden Hollow's membership has actually grown in recent years, as more and more places around the country started becoming "restricted" again. We've even had to hire more Yiddish language teachers for new members who aren't so fluent – or not fluent at all.

There were more Jews of fighting age from Eden Hollow at the intake center, but they all were assigned elsewhere. My guess is that none of the recruiters wanted a fully Jewish squad, so they spread us around.

Anyway, all the squads here at base have nicknames, and they call us the Disco Biscuit Squad. I have no idea why. "Disco Biscuit" was a 1970s slang for quaaludes.

Maybe they think we're all on drugs.

Maybe if we were, this whole thing would be a little less shitty.

Miri and I decided to postpone the wedding. We could have done something quick before we left Eden Hollow, but we decided instead to tie the knot once the war is over, and we can do it nice.

Assuming we are both still alive once the war is over.

Whenever that may be.

## July 7

Today they issued us our dog tags. They have letters stamped on them designating our religion, to assist in proper burial if -- or when -- the need should arise. P is for Protestant. C is for Catholic. M is for Muslim. H is for Hindi. O is for other, which includes agnostics and atheists, as well as, I imagine, Deists, Druids, Wiccans, Buddhists, and anyone else you can think of.

J, naturally, is for Jew.

This was a little bit concerning since the Nazarenes are already well-known for their vicious antisemitism.

"We might as well wear our Magen Davids openly, I guess," Lenny said, once the dog tags had been issued. "There doesn't seem to be any point in being coy about it."

We spent the rest of the day filling sandbags and using them to shore up the perimeter and the machine gun nests set at regular intervals along it. By the end of the day, we were all hot and sweaty and dirty.

And so, we hit the showers.

"Hey, gentlemen, where's your foreskins?" asked Hank "Gunner" Günther, standing under the showers across from the Jews in the squad.

The Jews were all showering on one side, the gentiles on the other. I don't think this was intentional, but it seemed to serve Gunner's purpose which was becoming apparent.

The Jewish men were all circumcised.

As it happened, the non-Jewish men on the other side of the shower all still possessed their foreskins.

It probably didn't help that all of us on the Jewish side, male and female both, also wore our Magen David's around our necks. If it hadn't been for our dog tags giving us away, we might not have done so on base, but the "J" on the tags was only slightly less prominent than that Star of David around our necks. Or the missing foreskins at the end of our wieners, for the Jewish males among us.

None of us from Eden Hollow seemed particularly uncomfortable with the showering situation. We had all been at Rosa's anarcho-naturist pool parties, for one thing.

But more importantly, I think we were more worried about killing or being killed than being naked.

Personally, I found it far more mortifying to shit next to someone of the opposite sex than to shower next to them.

In any case, as far as I could tell, none of the Disco Biscuit gentiles using the shower facilities, male or female, were particularly concerned about their gender-inclusive nature, either. What they *did* seem concerned about – or at least what Gunner seemed concerned about – was the missing foreskins of me and my male coreligionists.

Gunner nodded to Sullivan, who was showering beside him. "You ever seen so many circumcisions in one place, Sully?"

"You leave me out of this," Sully grumbled. He didn't seem happy with Gunner.

Roy, Cody, Luke, and Ben showered nearby, and observed the interaction warily but without obvious partiality towards either side. I figured they were waiting to see how it played out.

Ruby, Trisha, and Angie stood a little further away from the rest of us, and they looked on the proceedings with concern, but didn't seem to want to get involved.

I couldn't blame them.

Mike and Gillie were nowhere to be found. Maybe NCOs had different shower facilities. I wasn't sure.

"Why are you looking at my wanger?" Lenny asked Gunner.

"Tell me, Horwitz, you ever miss it?" Gunner asked.

"Your wanger?" Lenny asked. "How can I, with you

waving it around in front of me?"

"I mean your foreskin," Gunner said.

"You mean that thing that makes your *schmekel* look like it's wearing a wrinkly old turtleneck?" Lenny asked. "Based on the evidence, no, I don't miss it at all."

"Funny guy," Gunner said. "I heard that's a characteristic of your people."

"What people are those, Gunner?" Lenny said, aggressively. "You want to make yourself plain? Or you want me to shove this bar of soap down your throat? On second thought, given your fascination with my wanger, maybe it's not the soap you want me to shove down your throat."

Gunner's face turned red. "You better not be implying what I think you're implying," he said.

"I'm not *implying* anything," Lenny said. "I'm saying it outright. You want me to go over there and demonstrate?"

Lenny took a step towards Gunner. I put a restraining hand on his shoulder.

Lenny has broad and strong shoulders. He's short but built like a tank. His biceps are like telephone poles.

Even so, I'm his big brother, and I'm not so frail, either. When Lenny feels my hand on his shoulder, he takes a pause.

"I got a perfect name for you," Gunner said. He scanned the Disco Biscuit Jews. "For all of you Zios."

"Gunner, 'Zio' is a racist slur popularized by KKK Grand Dragon David Duke back in the day, conflating all Jews and all Zionists to provide plausible deniability so that people can pretend when they say it, they mean 'Zionist' and don't really mean 'Jew,' which is of course exactly what they *do* mean," Rosa said. "I just thought you should know, although I do not expect you to care."

"I got a better term, anyway," Gunner said. "Just came up with it."

"Don't keep us in suspense," Miri said.

"I'm gonna call y'all the 'Gefilte Grunts'," Gunner said.

We all took a moment to let that sink in.

"That's the most awesome name ever," Rosa remarked, brightly, beaming joyfully. Her normally wild and frizzy red hair was now shorn close to her scalp, the same haircut we had all received. But somehow on her, it continued to look untamed. "I'm gonna have that stitched on my uniform."

## July 8

We got word this morning of an upcoming musical festival outside St Louis. It's called *Jewess-palooza*, and it's a festival of all-female cover bands of Jewish or Jewish-adjacent music artists. So, we've got Schmaim, which is a Haim cover band; the Velveeta Underwear and Nicolette, an all-female Velvet Underground and Nico cover band; Sweater-Skinny, a Sleater-Kinney cover band; Riley Smiley, a Rilo Kiley cover band; the Roberta Zimmerman Experience, which is an all-female Bob Dylan/Jimi Hendrix cover band (Hendrix wasn't Jewish, but he did record the best Bob Dylan cover ever, "All Along the Watchtower"); Birdies on a Wire, an all-female Leonard Cohen cover band; the Rock n' Roll Animaniacs, an all-female post-Velvets Lou Reed cover band; the Blitzkrieg Teenyboppers, an all-female Ramones cover band; The Rag Mamas, an all-female The Band cover band (Robbie Robertson was both Jewish and Indigenous American); The Barenaked Bros, an all-female Barenaked Ladies cover band; The Beastly Girls, an all-female Beastie Boys cover band; the Holly Holies, an all-female Neil Diamond cover band; Walk Like Egyptians, a Bangles/Suzanna Hoffs cover band; the Rock n' Roll All Nighters, an all-female Kiss cover band; Sirens of Swing, an all-female Dire Straits cover band; Three Cool Kittens, an all-female Lieber-Stoller cover band; Biters of Reality, a Lisa Loeb cover band; Excitable Girls, an all-female Warren Zevon cover band; the Tendaberries, a Laura Nyro cover band; and Bang My Gong, an all-female T. Rex cover band.

"No, you can't go to the Jewess-palooza Music Festival," Sergeant Gillie told me.

"Why not?" I asked.

"Why not? There's a war on."

"Where?" I asked, pointing south. We hadn't seen any

action.

"Are you impatient to get your war on?"

"I'm impatient for the war to be over and to get back home," I said.

"Give it time," Gillie said. "And be careful what you wish for."

"The only thing I wish for right now is to go to Jewess-palooza."

"You're needed here," Gillie said. "We all are. When the fighting comes, you'll see."

Later in the barracks, Lenny and Gunner both showed up with bruised faces, blackened eyes, swollen lips, and bloodied noses.

"You two get into it?" I asked.

"You should see the other guy," Lenny said.

I looked at Gunner. "I'm looking at the other guy."

Lenny handed me a wad of cash. "Hold onto this for me," he said.

"You fought for money?" I asked.

"If I'm going to get my face pounded, I might as well get paid for it," he said.

"You won?"

"By decision," Lenny said. He stared at Gunner. "His head's too thick to win by KO."

"How much?" I asked.

"Two hundred and fifty."

I looked over Lenny's face.

"It wasn't worth it," I said.

Lenny smiled through swollen lips. At least his teeth looked all intact.

"It ain't about the money," he said. "It's about smashing Gunner in the face."

"You got lucky this time," Gunner growled.

"Any time you want to test your luck again, go for it," Lenny said.

Gunner grumbled something inaudible and put an

icepack to his mouth.

## July 10

Captain Harlow stopped by our barracks this morning and demanded we all attend church services on Sunday.

"Disco Biscuit Squad has the worst attendance record for religious services in Camp 44," Harlow said.

This was the first time I realized our camp wasn't officially called "Camp Farty-Four."

"We haven't even been here a week, sir," Sergeant Gillie said.

"It's still the worst," Harlow said.

"The thing is, sir," Gillie said. "Horwitz, Horwitz, Bernstein, Lieberman, Lipschitz, and Lipschitz are all Jewish. Hernandez and Sullivan are Catholic. Vikram is Hindu. Chen is Buddhist. Hopper is Rastafarian. Scott is an atheist, Knox is Zoroastrian, Gossett is Swedenborgian, Tiller is Rosicrucian, and Günther is *Wotansvolk*."

Harlow stared at Gillie, his face getting redder and redder, trying to decide if she was putting him on, and none too happy even if she wasn't.

"What religious persuasion are you, Sergeant Gilroy?"

"I'm a Deist, sir," Gillie said.

"I don't know what that is," Harlow said.

"Neither do most Deists, sir," Gillie said.

"Listen, I don't care a rat's rear end what religion y'all are," Harlow growled. "I want you at services Sunday."

"Respectfully, sir, it's against regs to demand attendance at religious services if none are offered in a soldier's chosen faith."

"I don't give a shit about regs, Sergeant," Harlow said.

"Be that as it may, Captain," Gillie said. "Regs are

regs."

Harlow stood there for a long moment, glowering. Then he turned on his heel and left our barracks.

After a silence, Tiller muttered, "I'm not a Rosicrucian. I don't even know what that is."

Gillie turned back to us. She looked pretty nonchalant for an NCO who had just defied her Captain. "Anyone in Disco Biscuit Squad is free to go to services on Sunday. Or not. As you choose."

With that, she turned and walked out of the tent.

Rosa spoke to Tiller. "I used to want to be a Rosicrucian, Tiller," she said. "If you find a service, I'll go with you."

Tiller's face reddened like he was embarrassed. He lay down on his side and turned his face away.

Miri nudged Rosa. "I think he likes you," she whispered.

"Maybe you can have a Rosicrucian wedding," Lenny suggested.

I turned to Gunner. "Are you really a *Wotansvolk?*" I asked.

*Wotansvolk* is a White supremacist, occult, Nazi-inspired, White revolution, neo-Pagan belief system. It's become a lot more popular and widespread in the last few years than I'd like.

"What's it to you?" Gunner asked, defiantly.

"Same thing me being a Jew is to you, Gunner," I said. "A big fat nothingburger."

"You call White genocide a nothingburger?"

"I call *you* a nothingburger, Gunner."

Gunner took a step toward me, but Sully put a restraining hand on his shoulder.

"Leave it," Sully said. "At least he didn't call you a Rosicrucian."

## July 11

Today, we saw action for the first time.

I'm not sure how I feel about the term "action."

On the one hand, it certainly does involve a lot more action than the tedium of daily life at a forward operating base.

On the other hand, the term makes it feel like it's supposed to be an action movie or something, which it is not – it's a *lot* less fun and satisfying.

It started as I was on my way to perimeter patrol duty. I was waylaid by Lieutenant Eggert, who asked, "why is your shirt unbuttoned and untucked, soldier?"

I was confused. "Sir?" I replied. Eggert was not even my lieutenant, after all.

"Do you think you're at a rave, soldier?"

"Sir, no sir, but if you're offering, I would like to attend Jewess-palooza," I said.

"Is that a joke, soldier?"

"Sir, no sir," I said. "I really would like to attend Jewess-palooza. So would some of my friends if that can be arranged."

"Are you a funny guy, soldier?"

"Sir, no sir."

"Are you under the impression that the armed forces of the Sovereign Republic of North America are suffering from a dearth of humor in the ranks?"

"Well, now that you mention it, sir," I said, "a little bit of levity from time to time wouldn't hurt."

"Are you under the impression that war is a laughing matter, soldier?"

"Sir, no sir, I was just thinking that a laugh now and then might boost morale."

"Are you saying there's something wrong with the morale on this base?"

"Sir, yes sir," I said. "It's not great."

"Are you telling me how to run my base, soldier?"

"Is this *your* base, Lieutenant?"

"Never you mind about that," Eggert said.

"I was just thinking a little entertaining diversion might improve matters, that's all, sir."

"Were you under the impression that the military pays you to think, soldier?"

I guessed that the answer he was looking for was "no."

"Sir, no sir," I said.

"What does the military pay you for, soldier?"

It was a good question.

"To fight and die, sir?" I offered, tentatively.

"To follow orders, soldier!"

"Sir, yes sir that was going to be my next guess," I said.

"Button your shirt and tuck it in, soldier," Eggert demanded. "That's an order."

I buttoned my shirt and tucked it in, as commanded.

"Top button," he said.

"Sir?" I asked.

"Button the top button," he said.

"I have a rather thick neck, sir," I protested.

"Did I ask you for your measurements, soldier?"

"Sir, no sir," I said, "but it would have been nice if the guy who issued me my uniform had." I buttoned my top button, feeling it choke me.

Eggert scanned me up and down, skeptically.

"Dismissed," he said.

I saluted. "Sir, yes sir!" I exclaimed, just as I heard a distant series of booms followed by a whistling overhead.

Eggert looked up, annoyed.

A massive explosion blasted earth into the sky and threw me off my feet and backwards about three yards.

I landed hard on my back and skidded in the dirt, digging a shallow ditch in the soft ground until I came to a stop.

The concussion had knocked the breath out of me. I'd read about explosions shredding people's lungs, and I panicked for a moment as I gasped, trying to force air into my chest and find out if my respiratory system was still intact.

I felt like I'd been punched in my face by a huge fist that had also punched my entire body. My ears were ringing. I was momentarily deafened. I could not hear the distant booms, the whistling overhead, or the explosions on the ground.

But I could *see* them. Great flashes of light, cascades of earth shooting into the sky, coming down in a deluge of dirt.

All around the base.

I looked for Eggert. All I could see of him was his boots, upright, as if he'd been blown right out of them.

I wondered where he was, and if he was badly injured.

I got my answers a moment later when a torrent of meat and blood showered down on me.

I couldn't say for sure it was Eggert.

It looked like chopped sirloin. It could have *been* chopped sirloin. Maybe one of the explosives had hit the mess tent.

Except they didn't serve chopped sirloin in the mess. They served creamed chipped beef – which is not kosher, by the way, but none of us Gefilte Grunts are particularly strict about keeping kosher.

I don't even know where they got the creamed chipped beef. It used to be standard fare in military mess halls decades ago. I guess it still is. Or at least it is in ours.

In any event, this stuff raining down from the sky definitely wasn't creamed chipped beef.

So, it might have been a person.

That didn't mean it was Eggert, necessarily.

But the absence of his body and presence of just his boots indicated that maybe it was.

I finally managed to gulp air into my lungs, which I guessed meant I wasn't dying, and I decided to try to stay that way.

I got to my feet and ran for the perimeter, less out of a desire to defend the base, and more out of a vague sense that the sandbags that surrounded Camp 44 might provide better protection from shrapnel than anywhere else nearby.

As I ran, explosions burst all around. My hearing suddenly returned, and the flash and shock of the detonations were now accompanied by the sound of them as well.

And by the yelling and panic and commands and sometimes the screaming of people.

I preferred the silent version.

I ran and people ran all around me, in all different directions, some with purpose, others without.

I made it to the perimeter and saw an unmanned Browning fifty caliber machine gun surrounded by sandbags. I threw myself into the enclosure of sandbags and lay on my back, hearing the explosions and feeling them convulse the world around me.

I would have preferred to remain on my back out of sight in the nest of sandbags, but two things happened:

The first was a gnawing sense of guilt that I had a duty to man that unmanned fifty cal. I read somewhere that many people who perform heroically during battle do so because they are more afraid of looking shameful in the eyes of their comrades than they are of dying.

The second thing was it occurred to me that if this bombardment was prelude to a ground attack, I'd better do my part to try to prevent it, or the sandbags wouldn't be much help if a Nazarene breached the perimeter and stabbed me in the belly with a bayonet.

Finally, I thought of Miri and Lenny and Rosa and

Deb and Richie, and I realized if I had the opportunity to try to prevent a perimeter breach that could lead to their deaths, I should take it.

So, I got to my feet and manned the fifty cal.

These Brownings were among the few actual military, as opposed to civilian, weapons we had at the base, and they were powerful and fierce. I'd been trained for about five minutes on the thing, but I managed to remember how to use it, more or less.

I could see the enemy troops coming over the hill in the field beyond us. I vaguely remembered something about the range of the fifty cal – about 1800 meters.

I had no idea how to determine distance without technological assistance, but I guesstimated. I aimed and waited.

I could hear bullets flying by me. They say you don't hear the one that gets you, but I sure heard a ton that missed me. They say that's a good thing. I guess it's better than getting struck down by the one that gets you and you don't hear, but it's no day at the races, or night at the opera, or however you want to put it, because it is absolutely terrifying.

When I thought the enemy was close enough – little black dots turning into little gray army people on a canvas of grass and weeds – I began firing.

And the people I was shooting at began to fall.

So now I know what 1800 meters looks like on a battlefield.

And I know what it's like to kill somebody for the first time, from 1800 meters.

I mean, it's not like killing people is actually normal behavior. It's actually pretty aberrant behavior, and not something people should be doing under most circumstances. This is not the Wild West – or at least, it wasn't until recently. I guess it makes sense that at the age of eighteen I hadn't killed anybody.

Yet.

Until today.

I mean, I can't say for certain I killed the people who fell after I fired.

But I think I did.

I'm pretty certain, actually.

The big chunks of them that went flying off their bodies were a pretty clear giveaway. I could see that even from the distance between us, and I'm pretty sure most people die when that happens. They say a fifty cal can take a chunk out of a person the size of a grapefruit. I can't pretend I measured it that closely as I fired, but it certainly looked like I was doing substantial damage to the bodies of human beings 1800 feet or less from me.

It took me two tries before most of the people I was shooting at began to fall as chunks of them went flying. The Browning fifty cal has a tremendous kick, and it rattles your body and brain, and it took a moment or two until I could figure out how to hold it steady and aim true.

But once I figured it out, I got pretty good at it.

I'm not proud of that.

But I prefer it to the alternative.

So, this went on for a while.

I fired. They fired. I heard bullets whiz past my ears. I heard bullets thud into the sandbags surrounding me.

I continued to fire. The enemy continued to fall. Chunks of them went flying off their bodies. Shells continued to whistle overhead. Explosions continued to rock the camp and blast craters in the ground. Between the Browning's recoil and the shells hitting the ground, I was in a constant state of violent vibration.

I wasn't alone, of course. Machine gun nests dotted the perimeter of our camp, and we were all firing at the enemy as they skulked towards us. We had pretty good coverage of the field of battle. There was nowhere a Nazarene could advance without facing the fire from our Brownings.

I figured it was only a matter of time before something – a bullet, an explosion, an enemy soldier breaching the perimeter – got me. I was hoping the enemy would give up before that happened.

I was hoping we wouldn't be the ones to surrender, because I didn't know if the Nazarenes were into taking prisoners, or what they did with them when they took them.

Especially the Jewish ones.

So, I kept firing, they kept falling, and more of them kept coming over the hill. With every wave, they inched closer and closer to the wire.

Then a series of detonations burst behind the hills, fire mushrooming upwards into the sky, and the shells stopped falling on Camp 44.

I was confused, although I didn't have time to be *too* confused. I knew we didn't have an air force. So where did the explosions come from that had taken out the Nazarene's batteries?

In any case, the Nazarene infantry was till creeping towards us, gaining ground slowly and painfully and at great human cost, but gaining, nonetheless. So, I kept firing, hoping to contribute to them gaining a little less, or maybe stop gaining altogether.

Then the advancing enemy disappeared in a surge of flame. The field between the camp and the hills was blasted into the sky, along with the enemy soldiers. I could feel the heat of the explosions on my face, and the concussion knocked me back off my feet.

I guess that's what they call "danger close."

Or maybe it's not. Maybe that's totally normal. If it is, I don't want to be there when a "danger close" bombardment happens.

When the smoke cleared, the field was nothing but charred corpses and upturned dirt, along with pockets of fire still burning. Another round of explosions detonated behind the hills and then into the forest beyond, setting the trees ablaze.

The battle was over. I wasn't sure what was supposed to come next, but I didn't care. I slung my Savage semi-auto rifle over my shoulder, left my post, and headed back to Disco Biscuit Squad's tent.

On the way, I ran into Captain Harlow.

"Why is your collar unbuttoned, soldier?" he demanded.

I reached for my throat and realized that my collar was, indeed, unbuttoned. I had no memory of having unbuttoned it during the battle.

"The rattle of my Browning fifty caliber must have shaken it loose, sir," I said, and turned and walked away from him as quickly as possible. My ears were still ringing, so I ignored the words he shouted at my back. I was afraid if I responded, I'd march right back to him and punch him in the throat.

I did a quick cost benefit analysis and decided the gain would not justify the pain.

I ran into Miri on my way back to our tent. Like me, she was hot and sweaty and dirty and had a look on her face like what had just happened would haunt her forever.

I was so freaking happy to find her alive.

I guess she felt the same way, because without discussing it, we snuck behind a storage container and had the quickest quickie -- and also the best -- that I could have ever imagined.

If I were a poet, I might say that having seen death and faced death, we wanted to affirm life through the union of our bodies.

But if I'm honest, I think it's closer to the truth to say that after our first firefight, we were both desperate for something that would make us feel less shitty.

## July 12

When today began, I was still hopeful we might be given leave to attend Jewess-palooza, which kicked off today.

Be careful what you wish for.

At breakfast, we learned that the explosions that had won the battle for us were made by drones. Apparently, the Sovereign Republic has drones – a lot of them -- if not a proper air force.

That gives us a tactical advantage.

I was glad to hear it.

I'll take any kind of advantage we can get.

Late morning, news began to break that the Jewess-palooza festival, which was being held in the Jefferson County Fairgrounds in nearby Hillsboro, was under attack.

Information was sketchy, but it involved Nazarene troops in uniform riding pick-up trucks, motorcycles, and paragliders, and carrying automatic weapons.

As soon as Gillie heard the news, she ordered us to gear up. But when we went to the motor pool to commandeer some vehicles, we were met by Captain Harlow, who gave us the stern face.

"Stand down, Sergeant," he said.

"No can do, sir," Gillie responded.

"We have not been authorized to intervene," Harlow said.

"All due respect, sir, Disco Biscuit is intervening."

"Stand down, Gilroy."

"We're the closest operating base to the fairgrounds, sir."

"I'm not making a request, Sergeant. I'm giving you an order."

Gillie took a deep breath and let it out, slowly.

"Captain, over a third of my squad are Gefilte Grunts. No way are they gonna sit this one out."

"It's not up for negotiation, Sergeant."

"Captain, it should be all hands-on deck to meet this attack. All I'm asking you for is one squad. One. Don't try to hold us back, sir. You can have me court martialed for insubordination, but you're not stopping me from taking my squad to try to put down this thing. Those are kids at a music festival. We're going, authorization or not. If you want to waste a good NCO like me by jamming me up with a court martial, have at it. But you'll have to wait until we get back."

"I can have the MPs here in a second," Captain Harlow said.

"I'll be out of here in half that time," Gillie said.

The captain screwed up his face and growled in his throat.

"Don't expect any reinforcements, Gilroy," he said. "You get yourselves in a fix, you're on your own."

"Copy that, Captain," Gillie said. She turned back to us. "Saddle up, Disco Biscuit. Cavalry is on the way. And we're the cavalry."


When Disco Biscuit Squad arrived forty-five minutes later outside Jewess-palooza, riding Jeeps instead of horses or even Hum Vees, we found White Christian Confederacy Nazarene soldiers firing into civilian vehicles trying to flee the fairgrounds.

This was the first time I had seen the enemy up close. The Nazarenes were dressed in what looked like modified old Confederacy uniforms – grey with a high collar and a gray cap with a black visor. I assumed they were made of cotton rather than the wool from which the originals were made.

Or maybe they'd been raided from a Halloween costume store.

The Nazarenes were shouting "*Judenrät!* Praise

Jesus!" and "May thousands die in the name of the Christian National Crusade! May thousands die in the name of Christian National Resistance!"

*"Judenrät"* is actually German for "Jewish Council," which were the governing bodies the Nazis set up to allow Jewish ghettos to – supposedly – govern themselves. It was an odd choice of terminology, but I don't think the Nazarenes really knew what it meant.

As we pulled up to the stopped cars and the Nazarene gunmen shooting through the windows I jumped out and fired at the nearest Confederate. The blast from my Savage punched through his skull and out the other side.

That was the first time I'd killed anyone up close.

By the time the day was done, it would prove not to be the last.

Killing someone up close is different than doing the same from far away.

But I didn't really have time to think about that.

We continued on foot. The Nazarenes were so intent on their purpose that they did not at first even notice us. I fired several quick shots, taking down half a dozen of them, one after the other. My squad mates did likewise.

The Nazarenes realized they were being fired upon, and they haphazardly returned fire as they retreated back into the fairgrounds upon which the festival had been held.

Why hadn't the festival been cancelled, I wondered, after yesterday's attack? My guess was that the authorities thought the Jefferson County Fairgrounds were far enough from the front to proceed.

They also probably thought the fighting was over, and we had won.

They also probably thought if the enemy were going to run through our lines, they would have picked a target with more strategic importance than a bunch of kids at a music festival.

I mean, why wouldn't they think that? I thought the same thing.

What no one had yet figured out was just how irrationally and completely the White Christian Confederacy of the Nazarene Nation really, really, really hated Jews.

After today, though, I think everyone will be pretty clear on that.

We entered the festival grounds, and I saw a white van, and a woman lying beside it, her hands on her belly. I went to her, while the rest of the squad fanned out.

The woman was alive but had been shot in the abdomen. She was moaning in pain. I looked inside the van and found a man lying on his back with his eyes wide open. His shirt was covered in blood. I checked for a pulse.

"Is my husband Ok?" the woman on the ground asked me.

"He should make it," I lied.

Her husband was dead.

I heard the screech of car brakes and turned around to see a pick-up truck pull up and about a half dozen Nazarenes pile out of the truck bed.

I grabbed the injured woman by her collar and dragged her around to the far side of the van, firing at the Nazarenes as I went. She cried in pain as I dragged her.

I laid her down with the wheel well for protection, and then I went to the other wheel well and began firing over the hood of the van.

I hit one Nazarene as he was taking aim at me. Another fired an RPG. The RPG sailed over the van. I heard it explode somewhere behind me and felt the force and heat of the concussion slam into my back.

The guy with the RPG reloaded, but I managed to put him down before he fired. The RPG sailed into his own pick-up truck, and the resulting explosion killed all but two of the remaining Nazarenes.

I took aim at the surviving two, but then a fusillade of semi-automatic weapon fire erupted to my right, and I saw

Gillie and Gunner heading towards us, firing at the Nazarenes.

I never thought I'd be glad to see Gunner until that moment.

The two remaining Nazarenes went down, and then I saw something in the sky.

"Look!" I called out, pointing up.

Gillie and Gunner turned to look.

Two dozen Nazarenes on paragliders were sailing over the stadium walls and heading towards us.

They looked sort of like condors, weirdly peaceful soaring there in the sky, wings framed against eggshell blue and white cotton clouds.

Then they started firing their weapons at us.

"Shit," Gunner said, raising his rifle and firing.

We took out at least six of them, but then two more pick-ups pulled up and at least a dozen Nazarenes piled out, weapons raised, yelling at us to surrender.

Sensing the three of us couldn't shoot our way out, Gillie laid her rifle on the ground and raised her hands in surrender. Gunner and I did likewise. Meanwhile, Nazarenes on paragliders were landing inside the stadium and heading out to search for more victims.

"Where are your Jews?" a Nazarene sergeant asked.

"I'm sorry, what?" Gillie said.

"Tell your Jewish soldiers to step forward," the sergeant said. "They'll get a chance to convert."

"A battlefield conversion?" Gillie asked.

"If they want to live," the sergeant said.

"We don't have any Jews," Gillie said. "And we are all Jews."

The sergeant looked at her, perplexed.

Then he raised his rifle, the barrel pointed to her forehead.

I glanced at Gunner. I was afraid he was going to give me away.

Gunner glanced at me. "You think Jews are worth

dying for?" he muttered.

He was telling me not to let Gillie die to protect me.

I stepped forward. "I'm a Jew," I said.

The sergeant lowered his rifle. He fished in his pocket and pulled out a mini bible. He held it toward me.

"On your knees, Zio," he said.

"I'm good here," I said.

"On your knees, Zio, kiss the book, and declare your soul unto Jesus," he said.

"No, thanks," I said. "I'm good."

The sergeant pulled his sidearm with his free hand, thumbed back the hammer, and pointed it at me.

"If you do as I say, you'll be taken prisoner and treated in accordance with the Geneva convention," he said. "If you don't, your blood can fertilize the soil you're standing on right now."

"You don't call it 'Blood and Soil' for nothing, I guess," I said. I knew I was playing with my life, but I figured I was probably dead, anyway, no matter what I did or said.

"Make your choice, Zio," the sergeant said.

"I'll take option number three," I said. I was playing it cool, but my heart was racing.

"There is no option number three," the sergeant said.

"There's always an option number three," I said, although I didn't believe it for a second.

A shot rang out, and the sergeant's head snapped back in a misty spray of blood and brain, and he went down.

Turns out, there actually *was* an option number three.

We hit the dirt as we saw Lenny, Rosa, Miri, Deb, Richie, and two others I didn't know heading towards the Nazarenes, firing their weapons in unison.

The two strangers were in the same tan work-clothes from Wal Mart with stripes stitched on the sleeves that we wore. So, they were Sovereign Republic soldiers. They were a man and a woman. They were both olive-skinned. The woman wore a headscarf.

The Nazarenes started to go down. Gillie and Gunner

and I retrieved our weapons and joined the firefight.

We were still outnumbered, but we managed to put down the Nazarenes in about five minutes. I think the White Christian Confederates, for all their belligerence, were disadvantaged by their zeal for pogroms and battlefield religious conversions, which gave an edge to those of us focused on combat instead of slaughtering civilian music festival attendees.

"This is Omar and Fatima," Lenny said, introducing us to the newcomers, after we had put down the last of this group of Nazarenes. "They're siblings from Michigan. Their squad is called the Dearborn Arabian Knights."

"We didn't choose the name," Fatima said, as she knelt down beside the woman with the belly wound, who was moaning weakly, and began to administer first aid. She carried a small medical kit at her side. In this war, it seemed, the medics had to shoot first and heal later.

"They know we're Jews," Lenny added.

"They're Ok with it," Rosa added.

"As long as you're not Nazarenes," Omar said. "We're good."


With more reinforcements from Dearborn, we quickly spread out and in about an hour, we had taken the fairgrounds. Most of the Nazarenes died fighting. We took about a dozen prisoners.

We found bodies of concert goers hacked to pieces by machetes.

We found a storage room where people had gone to hide, and the Nazarenes had tossed in grenades and killed them all.

We found the bodies of couples bound together with wire and set on fire.

We found young women and teenage girls with their clothes ripped off their bodies.

A forensic team would be needed to know for sure, but it sure looked like they had been sexually violated before they had been killed.

What had started as a celebration of Jewish music and Jewish women had been targeted for exactly that reason.

"I don't know if we're going to win this war with our neighbors to the south," Miri said, "But it's pretty clear that we can't afford to lose."

## July 13

The body count at the festival was estimated at 1200, with two hundred and forty hostages believed to have been kidnapped, possibly to be offered as wives to the most impressively holy warriors of the Nazarene Christian Crusaders, which is what they called their soldiers.

After chow, Gillie gathered the squad for a briefing.

"Please be advised that if your dog tags read anything other than 'P' for your religious designation, it is recommended that you destroy them if you are in immediate danger of being taken prisoner," she informed us. "Word is that the Nazarenes are checking dog tags and forcing what they call 'battlefield conversions' on non-protestant POWs. Those who do not comply are summarily executed. This violates the Geneva convention, but they don't seem super-concerned about that, since their White Christian Nation, or whatever they call it, is the only earthly authority they respect. Let me say something else here. There are reports coming from southern Kentucky that some of our soldiers turned over their Jewish, Muslim, and Catholic fellow citizens to the Nazarenes when captured. I'm going to be as clear as I can about this. That's not going to happen in Disco Biscuit Squad. We are not going to turn on our own. Anyone thinks they can't abide by that, you come speak to me. I'll have you transferred to another squad, no questions asked. But if you stay with Disco Biscuit and you rat out one of our team, I will make it my business to see you pay for that treachery, one way or the other – even if that means putting a bullet in your head myself. 'Are Jews worth dying for?' I heard someone ask that question at the music festival yesterday. Here's the answer. Your squad is worth dying for. Every goddamn one of them, Jewish or otherwise. Don't you forget it."

Later, Lenny, Miri, Rosa, and I huddled together by the latrines.

"Do you think we can trust our squad not to turn us in?" Lenny asked.

"I think Gillie really would kill them if they did," Miri said.

"But what if Gillie is killed in action and the enemy captures the squad?" Lenny asked.

"We've got a Catholic, a Hindu, a Rastafarian," Rosa said. "They'd all be thrown under the bus if someone ratted us out. Who would do that?"

We all looked at each other and we all knew the answer.

"Gunner might," Miri said.

"Gunner might rat out everyone who doesn't have a 'P' on their dog tags," Lenny said.

"But he didn't rat me out at the fairgrounds," I said.

"Yeah," Lenny said. "But Gillie was right there."

"Something he might not do in front of Gillie," Rosa said, "he might do somewhere else."

We were silent for a few moments, thinking it over.

"Should we frag him?" Lenny asked.

I looked at him sharply. "You've been watching too many Vietnam movies," I said.

"We could do it," Lenny said. "Next time we're in a firefight, or there's an attack on the camp. One stray bullet would do the trick, and no one would even think to ask any questions."

It was a sound plan, but I hated it.

Miri, it turned out, hated it even more. "No," she said. "We're not doing that."

"You wouldn't have to do it," Lenny said. "I'd do it."

"That's not who we are," Miri said.

"That's not who *you* are," Lenny said. "I'm an entirely different proposition."

"It's not who you are either, Lenny," Miri said.

"I'm flattered by your faith in my character, Miri,"

Lenny said. "But that's *exactly* who I am."

"You've never done anything like that in your life, Len," I said.

"Everybody's got to start somewhere," Lenny said.

"It's not who you *deserve* to be," Miri insisted. "It's not who your brothers and sisters *deserve you* to be. It's not who your cousin Rosa deserves you to be. And it's not who your future sister-in-law deserves you to be."

Lenny looked at Miri like he was surprised that someone would care so much about what kind of person he was or should be.

"What if he tries to rat us out, though?" Lenny asked.

"Then you can do whatever you want to him," Miri said. "But not until then."

"But by then it might be too late," Lenny said.

"That's a risk we'll have to take," Miri said, firmly.

Lenny nodded, thoughtfully. "Ok, sis," he said. "You deserve to have a brother-in-law you're not ashamed of. I'll try to be that brother-in-law for you."

Miri went to him and embraced him.

It wasn't a casually friendly or merely sisterly hug.

It was a very serious hug. A *thank G-d you chose not to take that turn into total dick-itude for the rest of your life* hug.

And Lenny hugged her back.

And, in a way, I think he was grateful.

He would have willingly sacrificed his soul for the safety of his family and friends.

But I think he appreciated having a compelling reason not to.

# Part Five: Anarchist Summer Nuptials

**Five years later**

**Five years after the Collapse**
**Two years before Operation Supreme Flood for America**
**Two years before the Fall of Eden**

# From the Journal of Simon "Frenchy" Horwitz, Age 23:

## July 4

We are back at Eden Hollow for the first time since the start of the war.

I kept a journal for most of the war, writing most days in a series of composition books, but I lost most of them when we were down in Kentucky pushing the Nazarenes back into their own territory and a mortar shell hit the barracks in our camp. I only managed to save the first few entries. I lost most of my personal belongings in the resulting fire. So did we all.

But at least I didn't lose the people I love.

I was lucky to make it through the war without losing those closest to me: Lenny, Miri, and Rosa.

But we lost everybody else over the course of the war, except for Sergeant Gillie. And, of all people, Gunner, who, unbeknownst to him, came perilously close to being fragged by Lenny.

We lost Cody and Luke in an attack on Camp Forty-Four. We lost Sully and Benson in an action down in southern Missouri. Angie, we lost in an ambush in southern Illinois. Trisha in a firefight in Indiana. Ruby in southern Indiana. We lost Mike and Roy in Tennessee during an ill-conceived effort to push into Nazarene territory.

Günther fought with us until just a few months before the armistice. He never ratted anyone out, even though there were several times the enemy had us surrounded and offered to let the 'P's go if our fellow soldiers turned in the rest of us.

Gunner's fighting days came to an end when we were

in Kentucky fighting off an assault and an enemy soldier dropped a grenade into our foxhole.

Gunner grabbed the grenade and attempted to throw it back. It exploded just as it left his hand.

The blast took off most of his arm to the elbow and scarred the right side of his face, but his effort saved the rest of us.

That was the end of Gunner's war. They evack'ed him, patched him up, and sent him home with a shitty prosthetic. The last I'd heard, he was living in a trailer park in or near Joplin, Missouri.

We lost Richie to a landmine outside of Frankfort soon thereafter. We lost Deb outside of Jefferson City after the armistice to an enemy sniper who hadn't heard the news that the war was over.

Actually, we're all technically still in a state of war. But a cease fire has been declared, the fighting has stopped, and most of the troops have been discharged and sent home.

We had new guys along the way to replace the guys we lost, but by the end, I never bothered to learn their names. The casualty rates in our company were among the highest in our division.

Gillie, Miri, Rosa, and I received a series of battlefield commissions over the course of our military career and finished the war as lieutenants. Harlow informed us we'd have all made captain, but the brass had put a cap on advancement for "non-White" officers. Lieutenant was as far as we could go. Even Harlow, whom I never particularly liked, seem outraged by this.

Not that it mattered much to me. I didn't even want to make lieutenant, much less captain. I had no interest in a military career.

But I had one whether I wanted it or not, at least for the five years of the war.

Lenny kept getting battlefield commissions for conspicuous gallantry and such, but then getting demoted for insubordination. He finished the war as a private, although at least he managed to retain the rank of PFC instead of being busted back down to PV1.

By the time my younger siblings had come of age, new regulations had been put in place barring new Jewish and Muslim recruits from military service. This despite the fact that the Arabian Knight Squadron from Dearborn was one of the most highly decorated units in the war. Those of us already in the military kept on serving, of course. No respite for us. We were grandfathered in, like that was some kind of kindness towards us on the part of the authorities.

I was happy my younger siblings were spared from the dangers and rigors of combat. But I was annoyed that they were denied this on the basis of their ethnicity.

We all came back with scars on our bodies. My left side from my thigh to my chest is pockmarked with shrapnel wounds. Miri has a nasty knot of scar tissue on her right bicep where a bullet struck her clean through; the entry and exit wounds both scarred over. Rosa has a scar at a diagonal across her belly where a Nazarene tried to gut her with a bayonet. The wound was fortunately not deep, but it left its mark. Rosa says that she's grateful it missed her belly button, and that she wasn't stabbed in her ass or her boobs, body parts of which she takes great pride.

Lenny had the worst wounds of our family. A mortar shell blew him out of a machine gun nest. He was in the field hospital for six weeks. In wars of the past, that'd have been his ticket home, but in this war, they patched him up and sent him back to fight with his unit. His upper torso is now splattered with scars, which he has endeavored to conceal with a variety of abstract tattoos.

Tattoos, by the way, are frowned upon but not actually *farbotn* (that's Yiddish for 'forbidden') in most Jewish denominations in case you were wondering. It's a myth, for example, that you can't be buried in most Jewish cemeteries if you have a tattoo.

At least that's what our rabbi says.

Not that Lenny cares where he's buried. He only seems to care whom he's fighting and whom he's *schtupping*. His bare-knuckle boxing career took off in the military, and he has every intention of continuing it in peace time. And every punch he takes and every scar and tattoo on his body only seems to make him more attractive to women, a quality of which he takes full advantage.

Gillie looks the same as ever, except she's only got half of her left arm. The rest of it was ripped to pieces by a Nazarene machine gun. She says she's grateful that she didn't lose the hand she uses to pick her nose, wipe her ass, and punch out her enemies. She's got a gleaming, shiny, high-tech looking prosthetic. It only looks high-tech, though. It doesn't actually do anything but fill the space where her original arm from fingers to elbow used to go.

Someday, I tell myself, I'll write the story of the rest of my war. I can remember most of it pretty vividly. The only trouble I have is that I can't always remember the order of events. It's all kind of a giant blur of boredom, terror, and rage.

I guess I could just write it in the order the events come to me and say fuck all to chronology.

Anyway, the 4th of July hootenanny at Eden Hollow is already underway. Tonight, there will be a lightshow but no fireworks. Too many people around these days with PTSD who might be triggered by giant explosions in the sky.

Miri and I will take in the light show from our special spot atop the hill with the frogs providing the soundtrack now that the fireworks have gone silent. Hopefully, we will make love again, like we did the last time we were at Eden Hollow for Independence Day –

five years ago.

A lot has happened since then. But making love with Miri is still my favorite thing to do.

Hopefully, she still feels the same about me.

176

## July 10

Miri and I finally got married. Five years after we'd originally planned.

As you can imagine, we didn't have much time for intimacy in the military. Or, rather, we had plenty of time for intimacy – eating, sleeping, shitting, and showering together – but not for privacy, as we did these things with our entire squad.

I'm not saying we didn't find moments here and there for carnal embraces in hidden corners of camp or the trenches. But our lives were filled much more with soldiering than love-making.

After we both made lieutenant, we had a little privacy, as each lieutenant had their own private tent to serve as quarters. But we also had less time together, as we were now in charge of our own platoons, and that takes basically all of your free time at least during a war . . . which is the only experience I have of being a lieutenant, having never served in peacetime.

We got married in the gazebo under a chuppah on the Great Lawn with most of the members of the bungalow community and all of the family in attendance. Dad did the service. We used all the traditional Jewish bells and whistles, but Dad's not officially a rabbi, so it's not officially kosher. It is, however, legally binding.

So, we are finally legally married.

The bride wore a cream-colored veil and a matching sleeveless number that wasn't really a gown but was more than a summer dress. I wore a linen suit and comfortable shoes with a good sole so I could break the glass without cutting my feet. The guests wore casual summer wedding attire, a category I hadn't realized existed until my own summer wedding. Gillie wore a strapless number that did not conceal the prosthetic arm strapped to her torso.

One thing I've learned recently is that when you get an all-over suntan, your scars remain white and shine like mementoes of combat etched on your flesh. Going shirtless in the sun this summer, those scars began to gleam like stars in a golden sky. I began to regard them as something of a badge of honor. They weren't pretty, but I'd earned each and every one.

Wearing my linen wedding suit was almost the first time I'd covered them up since arriving at Eden Hollow.

Even so the wedding was perfect, scars and all.


Miri and I have spent the last several days in a small, private cabin on the grounds, making up for lost time.

By which I mean *schtupping* pretty much non-stop.

We're still using birth control, though.

We're both looking forward to spending our lives together, but we're getting worried about what kind of world we're going to be spending it in. We're holding off on starting a family at least for now, until we figure some things out.

We've come back from the war to a republic that has passed laws excluding 'non-Whites' – which includes Jews -- from government, judicial, and university positions. Miri's parents are going back to California for this reason. I've asked Miri if she wants to join them, but she insists on staying with me in the Sovereign Republic. I think this is because she knows how hard it would be for me to leave my siblings behind. And, of course, because I promised to work with Dad at the music and record stores. But it also can't be easy for her or her parents to be so far away from each other, either.

Non-Whites have also been dismissed from secondary school teaching positions. Schools have been segregated in the manner of the old Jim Crow laws in the South. Jews and gentiles are still going to the same schools for now, but we'll see how long that lasts. It is now forbidden to teach the history of the Holocaust or Israel in public school social studies classes.

The government recently passed the Law for the Protection of American Blood and Soil, which prohibits new marriages or sexual relationships between Whites and non-Whites (including Jews). The status of marriages between Whites and non-Whites from before the Collapse is still being debated. Non-Whites are required to register our assets with the government. All passports belonging to Jews have been ordered to be turned in and stamped with a "J" to facilitate identification . . . since I guess you can't always tell by the horns on our heads. Non-Whites have been restricted to designated, government-approved ethnic enclaves. The Horwitz home on Balfour Court in Coventry Village in the Heights has been in the family for generations, and is, luckily for us I guess, already in such a neighborhood. So, at least we don't have to move.

A government campaign against "dual loyalty" has forced those with dual Israeli and Sovereign Republic citizenship to either renounce their Israeli citizenship or face deportation. All Israelis, European Jews, Jews from South America, and Jews from anywhere else in the world who lack dual citizenship have been deported back to their countries of origin – even those who hold Green Cards.

Homosexuality has not yet been officially outlawed, but homosexual "activity" has. So, I guess you can *be* gay, but you can't "act" gay, whatever that means.

A government campaign against "cosmopolitanism" and "globalism" has shut down all Jewish publishers and shuttered all Jewish newspapers, as well as any deemed "Zionist." Jewish journalists from mainstream publications have been dismissed. Jewish military officers in ranks higher than lieutenant have either been dismissed or demoted to lieutenant. Hebrew, Jewish, Israel, antisemitism, and Holocaust studies have been eliminated from universities. Jewish quotas are back at colleges for the first time since, I think, the 1950s. Jewish sororities and fraternities have been closed. Hillel has been banned from all campuses. Visiting Israeli professors have been deported. Any professors identified as "globalist" or "Zionist" have been fired. All Jewish universities have been shuttered.

Any organization deemed Zionist or globalist or culturally Marxist in its philosophy has been accused by the government of perpetuating "White genocide," Zionist domination of media, government, banking, education, and the economy, facilitating mass illegal immigration and crime, and of being the historical oppressors of all real Americans. Such organizations have been banned.

Accordingly, the Anti-Defamation League, the American Jewish Committee, the Association of Reform Zionists of America, the Jewish Council for Public Affairs, the Jewish Federation of North America, the National Council of Jewish Women, the Union of Progressive Zionists, the Hebrew Immigrant Aid Society, Hillel International, Alliance for a New Zionist Vision, American Dental Volunteers for Israel, the American Zionist Council, JStreet, JewBelong, B'nai B'rith International, Birthright Israel, the Conference of Presidents of Major American Jewish Organizations, Creative Community for Peace, Hadassah Women's Zionist Organization of America, Partners for Progressive Israel, United Jewish Appeal, the Zionist Organization of America, and the International Holocaust Remembrance Alliance have all been outlawed in the Sovereign Republic of North America.

It's discouraging to come back from five years fighting a war you didn't start to find the republic you've been fighting for less welcoming than when the war began.

And it wasn't exactly super-welcoming to begin with.

It kind of makes you wonder why we bothered to fight off the White Christian Confederacy of the Nazarene Nation if we were just going to turn around an become a slightly – but only *slightly* – less loathsome version ourselves.

181

# Part Six: Before the Flood

182

**Two years later**
**The present day**

**Seven years after the Collapse**
**Four weeks before Operation Supreme Flood for America**
**Four weeks before the Fall of Eden**

## Chapter Nineteen

Two weeks after the end of the school year, the government closed all synagogues and Jewish Community Centers in the Sovereign Republic.

That same day, the authorities declared all non-Whites and non-Christians were officially reclassified as "de-naturalized non-citizen alien residents of the Republic."

The next day, the Horwitz family packed up their minivan and drove out to Eden Hollow for the summer.

Despite being denaturalized, there were no laws preventing them from doing so.

Yet.

Frenchy wasn't certain they were ever coming back. He didn't want to panic anyone, so he didn't say anything, other than to Miri and Lenny. But things felt bad. Things had been bad for a while, but now they felt worse.

Shutting down the synagogues and revoking citizenship had crossed a red line.

Not that every line previously crossed wasn't also a red line.

But this latest red line clarified something, and not in a good way. It made it clear that the government wasn't going to be satisfied with shutting out Jews from political, social, cultural, and economic life in the republic. They wanted to erase Jewish identity all together. The most optimistic scenario was one in which they left Jewish life to wither away with no Jewish religious or community institutions in which to participate.

The less optimistic view was that the next step would be to seize the assets of Jewish "resident aliens" and shut down their places of business, even within designated Jewish neighborhoods. And after that, the next logical step was deportation, either internally, or externally.

Or worse.

Frenchy didn't want to contemplate the worst-case scenario.

Not yet.

Frenchy and Miri and Lenny secretly packed extra clothes and supplies for everyone and hid them in the back of the van among the luggage and the musical instruments. Just in case they were needed. The musical instruments took up a lot of space, even in their used Ford Transit fifteen-seater, especially Artie's harp. So, it wasn't easy to find the space to tuck away the extra clothes and supplies.

He hoped no one would notice them. He didn't want to cause concern.

But things weren't looking great.

Frenchy wondered if Eden Hollow would be allowed to stay open much longer. It was not officially a Jewish institution, although it did have a primarily Jewish membership, and a Jewish history going back to 1917. Frenchy wondered if it was merely an oversight the authorities hadn't shut it down already. There were no laws against speaking Yiddish, per se, at least not yet, but Eden Hollow, with its Yiddish-speaking membership was exactly the kind of thing that the authorities would deem "cosmopolitanism" or "globalism."

He and Miri had stayed up half the night, finally working out an escape plan. Such as it was. Just as Miri had worried might happen, the avenues for safe departure had suddenly been sharply curtailed.

Arriving at the Horwitz cabin in Eden Hollow, it was easy to pretend things hadn't fallen to shit in the world outside. The sun shone brilliantly, warm and comforting, and a gentle breeze wafted from the lake. The rest of the Horwitz family – every last one of them -- Polly, Manny, Bertie, Miltie, Artie, Jules, and even Lenny – ran into the cabin and bounced around on the furniture like hyenas, as if they were all still the ankle biters they had once been. Then they put on their swimsuits, leaving their clothes scattered throughout the cabin, and ran to the beach.

Miri and Frenchy brought in the luggage and instruments, and picked up the discarded clothes from the floor.

"Ah, youth," Miri said, with better humor in her voice than Frenchy felt in his chest.

After the van had been unloaded, Frenchy and Miri undressed, folded their clothes neatly, and left them on the dresser in the master bedroom – the room that as recently as last summer had been for his parents.

Both naked, Miri regarded her husband with an appreciative eye. She gently ran her fingertips over the scars that flecked his skin from thigh to chest.

"They give you character," she said.

Frenchy smiled and ran his fingertips over Miri's big round belly. He loved looking at his wife, naked, clothed, expectant, or otherwise.

"You look beautiful, Frenchy said. "Pregnancy suits you."

"Shut up," Miri said. "I'm hella *zaftig*."

"More of you to love."

"Shut up. My boobs are swollen, and my ass is

huge."

"Yes," Frenchy said. "In the best possible way."

"Are you saying I have a fat ass?" Miri said, with a frown.

"Yes," Frenchy said. "You have the best fat ass in the world."

Despite herself, Miri smiled, and they kissed.


They threw on their swimsuits – Frenchy a pair of swim trunks decorated with cartoon matzoh balls, Miri a two-piece halter string triangle bikini decorated with tiny Magen Davids that left her big belly bare to the sky – and headed to the lake.

On their way down to the beach, they found Polly, alone on the path, standing and weeping bitter tears. She wore a one-piece with the words "Shalom Bitches" printed across the front.

"Sis?" Frenchy asked, tentatively. "What's wrong?"

Polly howled in despair and threw herself into her brother's arms, burying her face in his chest.

Frenchy put his arms around her and held her tightly. The flesh on her back and shoulders was already warm from the sun. He glanced at Miri, checking to make sure she had the tote bag around her shoulder in which they had brought the sunscreen. He began to worry about the rest of his family, no doubt crisping under the sun without sunscreen as they splashed in the lake or played on the beach.

Miri approached them and gave Polly a hug as well. Polly was now sandwiched between them.

"Why are you sad, sweetie?" Miri asked.

Polly howled her response, but the words were unintelligible through her sobs.

"It's Mom and Dad, isn't it?" Miri asked. Somehow, she had understood.

Polly nodded, her head still in Frenchy's chest.

"Is that it, sis?" Frenchy asked. "The first time we're at Eden Hollow without them?"

Polly nodded more vigorously and howled more loudly.

Frenchy and Miri held her more tightly.

There wasn't much to say about it. Their parents weren't here. There was nothing they could do to change that. And it sucked. There was no way around that.

They held Polly that way for about ten minutes until she cried herself out.

As Polly began to sniffle instead of sob, Miri fished in the bag and produced some tissues.

Miri always comes prepared, Frenchy thought, for anything.

Miri handed the tissues to Polly. Polly blew her nose, and then wiped her eyes.

"Oh, gross," she said, looking at Frenchy. "I got snot all over your chest."

As Miri and Polly began to wipe the snot off his chest with fresh tissues, Frenchy asked "you want some ice cream later?"

"Yes, please," Polly said as she daubed his chest, her voice hoarse from crying.

# Chapter Twenty

When they got to the beach, they found their cousin Rosa already there, throwing a frisbee with Manny, Miltie, and Bertie, while Jules and Artie were chatting up a couple of girls who were sunning themselves on beach towels, and Lenny was showing off his tattoos to a trio of attractive young women who seemed fascinated with each one and wanted to know the story behind them.

Everyone on the beach wore Magen Davids openly on their throats, something you never saw these days anywhere outside of Eden Hollow. A few also wore a *Chai.*

Lenny wore his dog tags as well. So did Frenchy, Miri, and Rosa. Dog tags had become something of a status symbol since the end of the war. But they also sometimes helped deflect the malign intentions of anti-Semites. The Jew-haters didn't particularly respect Jewish veterans, but they usually left them alone, either because they were uncertain as to the social rules about harassing Jewish vets, or because they figured a vet, even a Jewish one, might not prove to be such easy prey.

Additionally, in the second year of the war, all service members' dog tags had been reissued without the religious designation, to make it more difficult for the Nazarenes to identify and execute Jewish, Muslim,

Catholic, Hindu, Buddhist, and other non-Protestant Sovereign Republic soldiers. So, when people saw a Jewish vet wearing dog tags these days, they couldn't know for sure if the vet was also a Jew.

In the outside world, Frenchy, Miri, Lenny, and Rosa wore their dog-tags openly, while they wore their Magen Davids, if they wore them at all, concealed under their shirts.

But here, in Eden Hollow, they wore them both openly and proudly.

Artie and Jules wore matching swim trunks with the words "Nice Jewish Boy" printed in a repeating pattern. Lenny wore a pair of snug swim briefs decorated with Stars of David that left very little of his anatomy to the imagination. Rosa wore a skimpy triangle string bikini with a print designed to make it appear to be made of matzo.

Rosa screeched in delight when she saw Frenchy and Miri and Polly and ran to them, leaping into Frenchy's arms and wrapping her arms and legs around all three of them, showering their faces with kisses.

War had undoubtedly changed her deeply on some level, as it had them all, but it had not given her any better boundaries than she'd had previously.

"I am so glad the Horwitz siblings are finally here!" she shouted. "My lame parents aren't coming this summer."

"Whyever not?" Miri asked.

"Because they are lame!" Rosa shouted. "But, also, because they can't travel here from California anymore."

Like Miri's parents, Rosa's parents had relocated to California during the war, when emigration was still possible. They had always expected Rosa would be able to join them, but it was now very hard to obtain a visa to leave the Republic – undoubtedly made harder by recent developments.

"But now that you are here, everything is Ok again," Rosa added.

"Yes," Frenchy said. "Everything is Ok."

He didn't believe it for a second, but he didn't want to depress anyone.

"Oh my God, Miri, you're huge!" Rosa shouted, as she began to kiss Miri's big belly.

Taking advantage, Miri began slathering sunscreen on Rosa's shoulders while Rosa continued to plant kisses on her belly.

"Cos, a girl as fair as you shouldn't go unprotected in the sun," Miri admonished, gently. "You'll end up a withered prune with skin cancer by the time you're thirty."

"This is why I love your wife so much," Rosa said, standing up straight and giving Miri a smooch on the cheek. "She is a caring nurturer."

Looking about, Frenchy thought that Eden Hollow, always unique, had now become a final refuge for a certain kind of particular Jew. Here was the last place in the Republic, it seemed, where Jews could walk around unashamedly in, literally, their own skin, where Yiddish was spoken freely, Jewish stars worn openly, Jewish-themed swimwear was common, and even circumcised *schmekels* went unabashedly and proudly unconcealed in the men's locker room and showers.

After applying and reapplying sunscreen to the rest of the Horwitz tribe and playing on the beach and in the lake for hours, the family, with Rosa in tow, went to the cabin for the promised ice cream, which they ate on the porch as sunlight dimmed and the light cooled.

"Did you know that God created nine hundred and

seventy-four worlds before this one, but he didn't like them, so he destroyed them and built this one instead?" Polly said suddenly, her mouth full of Chunky Monkey. "At least that's what one of the Talmudic rabbis thought."

"Were you going to talk about that in your d'var Torah?" Miri asked, cautiously. Polly and Manny's B'nai Mitzvahs had been indefinitely postponed when the synagogues were all suddenly shut down.

Polly nodded, her mouth full.

"You would have had such a better d'var Torah than me," Manny said.

"Well, that goes without saying," Polly said.

"Would you guys like to do your B'nai Mitzvahs here in Eden Hollow?" Frenchy asked. "I mean, it wouldn't be official since we don't have a proper Rabbi. But we could do all the bells and whistles."

Polly furrowed her brow. "Would that be kosher?" she asked.

"About as kosher as anything else our family does," Frenchy said.

Polly looked at Manny. "What do you think?"

Manny shrugged. "I feel like B'nai Mitzvahs are stressful enough without doing them outside of a synagogue."

Polly turned back to Frenchy. "Yes," she said. "We definitely want a dual B'nai Mitzvah at Eden Hollow before summer's end."

Manny threw up his hands and rolled his eyes, unsurprised his sister would want to do something once she knew it was outside his comfort zone.

Frenchy shrugged. "I'll see what we can figure out," he said, and ate a spoonful of Chunky Monkey ice cream.

# Chapter Twenty-one

After breakfast, they began the day with yoga. The siblings' mother used to lead these sessions. In her absence, Rosa, herself an experienced yoga enthusiast, led the session instead.

Miri remained surprisingly flexible despite her pregnancy. Frenchy enjoyed watching her do yoga as much as he had the first time.

Afterwards, they all made plans to meet for lunch and went off in their separate directions.

Sitting on the patio back at the cabin, Miri and Frenchy spent a few moments reading emails and texts on their phones.

"So?" Miri asked, anxiously.

"Ownership of the music store and our other non-liquid assets have been officially transferred to Jayson," Frenchy said. "So presumably the government can't seize them. Jayson can liquidate or manage those assets in our absence. Getting the proceeds to us if we liquidate might be tricky, though, depending on where we end up, if we have to pull the trigger on the escape plan."

"And you trust Jayson?"

"As much as I trust anyone outside the family," Frenchy said. "His firm handled the family's legal issues since forever."

"Why didn't the family have a Jewish lawyer?"

"We did," Frenchy said. "But the partners forced him out."

"And you still trust this goyim?" Miri asked.

"He voted against removing our Jewish lawyer," Frenchy said. "I think he's one of the good ones."

Miri nodded. She still had a bad feeling about all of this. "Do you still think the Cooperative Commonwealth is our best bet? We're closer to the United Democratic States of America. We're closer to Canada for that matter."

"They tell me the gates are shut tight against immigrants into the UDS of A," Frenchy said. "And even if we had a boat, it would be too dangerous to cross Lake Erie into Canada, with all the Coast Guard patrols. And the land crossings are all sealed up tight."

"If we take Route 80, we've still got to cross the rest of Ohio, Indiana, Illinois, and Iowa before we cross into the Great Plains Agricultural Federation," Miri said. "Then we've got to make it through Nebraska until we cross into Wyoming and the Western Mountain Federation. Then we jog into the Utah Republic of Latter-Day Saints and then cross the border back into the Mountain Federation through Northern Nevada, and then finally into California, ending up in Sacramento, if we're lucky. And I never thought ending up in Sacramento could be described as lucky."

"Piece of cake," Frenchy said.

"That's five borders to cross without passports," Miri said. "As long as our passports are stamped with a 'J' we can't travel with them."

"Maybe we can figure something out when we get to Council Bluffs."

"You think?" Miri said, doubtfully.

"You have to trust me."

"I do trust you," Miri said. She went to him, sat on

his lap, and embraced him, his strong flesh against hers. Frenchy put his hand on her belly and could feel the baby move inside her. "It's the rest of the world I don't trust."

# Chapter Twenty-two

Lenny was hitting the bags when a woman with sinewy, rippling muscles and snaking, abstract tattoos on her body approached him.

Eden Hollow had a modest little outdoor boxing gym set up in a clearing in the woods, with a boxing ring and a variety of punching bags set up at its perimeter. Lenny was almost always the only one to use it. Occasionally another member would punch a bag for exercise, but literally no one ever took him up on his offer to go a few rounds sparring in the ring.

Then again, Lenny thought, he probably wouldn't take himself up on that offer, either.

She was approaching him as she put on a pair of boxing gloves herself.

"I saw the girls checking out your ink yesterday at the beach," she said.

"Yeah?" Lenny said. "I didn't see you." He looked up and down at her muscular physique approvingly. "And I think I would have noticed."

She smiled, her eyes glittering. "I think you were too busy checking out the girls who were checking out your ink. And your pecs. Both are hard to miss."

"I think that's a compliment?" Lenny said.

The woman scrutinized his body with a discerning eye. "It's not an insult," she said.

Lenny scrutinized her in turn. Her ink snaked up

and down her shoulders, arms, and legs, emerged from her skin-tight workout gym shorts, and meandered across her belly and into and above the sports bra that encased her bosom. He imagined she had a lower back tattoo. He wondered if she had one on her *tush*.

He would like to find out.

"You use the tats to hide your war wounds, right?" she asked.

Lenny was surprised by the question. "Not to hide them," he said. "To turn them into something beautiful."

The girl nodded. "That's poetic," she said. Lenny couldn't tell if she was being sarcastic. She pointed to her own right arm with her gloved left hand. "Same with me."

Lenny could suddenly see the scars her tats concealed. "I guess we have something in common," he said. "Where'd you serve?"

"Kentucky, mostly. You?"

"All over," Lenny said.

She nodded again, understanding. "We have more than the war in common, by the way," she said.

"Yeah?" Lenny asked. "What's that?"

"I'm a pugilist, too," she said. "Not bare-knuckled, though, Chico the Amico."

"You've seen me fight?"

"More than once."

Lenny shook his head, unbelieving. "I think I'd have noticed you," he said.

"Well, you can notice me, now."

"Oh, I do," Lenny said. "I definitely notice you now."

She grinned. "Have you thought about teaching boxing to the members here?"

Lenny screwed up his face. "Do you think anyone would be interested?"

The woman pointed with a gloved hand. "With the

way things are out there?" she asked. "I think so, yeah. I teach Krav Maga."

"Yeah?" Lenny said, excitedly. "I'd like to take your class."

"We meet in the mornings after yoga," she said. "Join us."

"I will," Lenny said. "I'd also like to *schtup* you."

The woman grinned, amused by Lenny's chutzpah.

Most women were put off by it, or worse.

She raised an eyebrow. "You don't even know my name."

"Let me guess," Lenny said. "Abigail."

"Talia," she said.

"I'm Lenny," he said. "Pleased to meet you. I still want to *schtup* you."

"Let's go a few rounds, first, and we'll circle back to that."

"I don't fight women."

"Just *schtup* them, huh? Pretend I'm not a woman.

Lenny gazed at her figure. "I don't think I can do that."

"Try."

"Pretend when we fight or when we *schtup*?"

"Let's see how you handle yourself in the ring, first," she said.

Talia turned to the ring. He watched her climb in.

She did have a lower back tattoo. It looked like barbed wire, in black. Her gym shorts had a circular patch on the butt that read "Secret Jewish Space Laser Corp" – a charmingly sassy enhancement to an already perfect *tush*, he thought.

"Come on, Chico," she said. "Let's see what you're made of."

Lenny shrugged and climbed into the ring after her.

# Chapter Twenty-three

Julius was lying on a beach towel at the edge of the Great Lawn in the shade of the oaks that ringed the perimeter, reading TS. Eliot's *The Waste Land* when he felt something hovering above him

Julius looked up and saw a pretty woman, about his age, with dirty blond hair, looking down at him with a sly smile at the corner of her mouth. She had a long face and a thinly regal Jewish nose. She carried a towel under one arm and a book in her hand. She wore light green shorts, a matching halter top, a pair of sneakers, a straw cowboy-style sunhat with a band of shells, and a Magen David around her neck with a *Chai* and a *Hamsa* attached to the same chain, framing the six-pointed star.

"Tell me, do you think April really is the cruelest month?" the girl asked with a trill of mischief in her voice.

So, she knew poetry, Julius thought. "That's a good question," he replied. He was shirtless, which made him feel slightly naked. He wore cargo pants, and his pockets were filled with small notebooks and pens, which made him feel nerdy. "Lately it feels like every month is the cruelest month."

The girl nodded and gestured to the ground beside him. "May I?" she asked. "I also prefer the shade."

"Please," Julius said. He raised himself into a

sitting position.

He watched as the girl spread her towel beside his. She turned her back to him as she did so. He tried not to enjoy the view from that perspective too much, but he found it difficult not to. She looked very good in those shorts.

Once her towel was properly laid out, she turned back to face him and smiled. She extended her hand. "I'm Adah."

Julius got to his feet and took her hand. He always felt awkward meeting someone for the first time especially if that person was a pretty girl his age. "I'm Julius. Jules. Call me Jules. People call me Jules."

She smiled at him shyly, her cheeks blushing slightly. Julius wasn't sure what he'd done to make her blush. Had he glanced at her bosom for too long? He didn't think so. Maybe it was the intensity with which he refused to look at her body and kept his eyes locked on hers. After all these years, Julius still sometimes got flummoxed about proper etiquette when it came to pretty girls in their summer clothes.

"You can call me Adie," she said as she sat down facing him. "Although I always think there's something funny about nicknames that are the same number of syllables as the original name, don't you?"

"I can just call you Adah, if you like," Julius said.

"No!" Adie cried. "I like Adie. Adah sounds so – 19th century Ellis Island, don't you think?"

"What's wrong with that?" Julius said.

"Nothing's *wrong* with that," Adie said. "But I like Adie."

"So do I," Julius said. "I like Adie a lot."

Adie blushed. "Aren't you the charmer?"

Julius hadn't quite meant it that way, but he'd take it. "Sometimes nicknames are just cute instead of time-savers," Julius said. "That's legit, too."

Adie raised her eyebrows. "You think my nickname is cute?"

"Your nickname's not the only cute thing about you," he replied.

She seemed pleased, but Julius suddenly felt embarrassed. He was being overly bold, and he feared it made him look swaggery, and he was anything but swaggery. He cleared his throat. "What are you reading?" he asked.

She smiled and held the cover of her book for him to read.

The book was *Prufrock and Other Observations*.

Julius chuckled. "You're kidding," he said.

"I kid you not," Adie said, opening her book and idly flipping through pages. "Who would have thought two Jews would both read poetry by such a rude anti-Semite as T.S. Eliot on such a lovely day? Hey, that would be a good name for an indie rock band, don't you think? Two Rude Jews?"

"Are we rude?"

"No, that's the joke," Adie said.

Julius wasn't certain he got the joke, but he didn't care. "Well, I am a guitarist," he said.

Adie raised an eyebrow, delight shimmering in her eyes. "Any good?"

"Pretty good," he said. "Everyone in my family is a pretty dedicated musician, although only my brother Artie is pursuing it professionally. He's a harpist."

"A harpist? Like Harpo Marx?"

"Yes. He's named for Harpo, actually – Arthur."

"I thought Harpo's real name was Adolphe."

"I think he changed it after – well, you know, the other Adolf ruined the name for pretty much everyone else."

"Except for Adolphe Menjou."

Julius's eyes widened in surprise. "You know a lot

of things."

"For a girl?"

"For anyone your age."

"Aren't we the same age?"

"I'm twenty-two."

"I'm twenty-one," Adie said.

"So, you see," Julius said. "I am so much older."

Adie laughed. "If you know such things, why shouldn't I know such things?"

"No reason," Julius admitted. "But literally no one our age knows who Adolphe Menjou was."

Adie smiled. "Except for us."

"Do you know I'm named for Groucho Marx?" Julius blurted out, and immediately felt like a dope.

"I did not know that," Adie said. "Because I just met you. But now I do. And it's good information to have, possibly. Did your parents name all your siblings after Marx Brothers?"

Julius felt his face blush more vigorously, his cheeks radiating heat. "Yes, but I only bring it up because Groucho and T.S. Eliot were pen pals. In fact, it was Eliot who first reached out to Groucho, asking for a signed picture which he put up on his wall."

"Do you think Eliot was less of a Jew-hater by then?"

"I'm not sure if he was," Julius said. "But I think maybe he wanted to be."

Adie pursed her lips and crinkled her nose as she thought that over. Julius thought she looked almost unbearably cute that way.

"Would that more anti-Semites took after later-day T.S. Eliot," Adie said, wistfully. "So, when are we going to debut our indie folk duo?"

"Which indie folk duo is that?"

"Two Rude Jews."

"That's a thing, now?"

"Of course, it is," Adie said. "How could it not be? I play mandolin and fiddle, and I'm a really good singer. Do you sing?"

"A little."

"There's a talent show tonight on the Great Lawn. Let's debut then."

"Tonight?"

"You have other plans?"

"Not a one," Julius admitted.

"It's settled," Adie said. "We're performing. Tonight. As Two Rude Jews. I know *all* the songs. Do you?"

"Most of them," Julius admitted. "When do we practice?"

"No time like the present," Adie said.

"We don't have our instruments."

"We can work on our harmonies. I say we only do songs by Jews or Jewish-adjacent artists. Like Elvis Presley."

"Elvis Presley?"

"Five generations of unbroken matrilineal descent," Adie said. "Even if he wasn't raised in the faith."

"Wow, he was more Jewish than most of the people in shul on Rosh Hashana."

"We'll sing 'Three Corn Patches'," Adie said. "That was written by two Jews, Lieber and Stoller."

"That's an impressively obscure yet tasteful choice," Julius said.

"And we should do a Dylan song, a Leonard Cohen song, and a Bangles song."

"The Bangles were Jewish?"

"Suzanna Hoffs is Jewish," Adie said. "Also, we'll do Alanis Morsette's 'Irony.' And don't tell me you're one of the irony bros. Every example in the song qualifies as situational irony."

"I'm not an irony bro, but is she Jewish?"

"She didn't find out she was ethnically Jewish until

she was in her late twenties, but her family were refugees who were traumatized into living as Christians after surviving the Shoah," Adie said.

"Wow," Julius said. "You know everything."

"Almost everything," Adie agreed. "Also, Jewish artists Sleater-Kinney, Rilo Kiley, and Regina Spektor should be represented in our repertoire."

"Wait, are we doing a whole concert just by ourselves, or taking part in a talent show?"

"Good point," Adie agreed. "You know 'Dance me to the End of Love' by Leonard Cohen?"

Julius nodded. "Words and music, both," he confessed.

 Great!" Adie exclaimed. "Let's get started."

Julius really, really wanted to kiss her.

But he settled for harmonizing with her, instead.

# Chapter Twenty-four

Artie was walking in the shade along Aleksander Zederbaum Trail, one of many nature trails in Eden Hollow named for Yiddish-speaking cultural figures, with his lyre tucked under one arm and a towel under the other, when he heard the bowing of what sounded conspicuously like a *masinko,* the one-stringed Ethiopian fiddle-like instrument, floating through the warm summer air.

He paused for a moment to ascertain the direction from which the sound originated. It seemed to be coming from in front of him, and to the right. He continued on his journey, twigs occasionally crunching under his sneakers. He was shirtless, wearing his Magen David, a pair of blue jean shorts, and his baseball cap. The music got louder as he neared, and then the trees to the right of him opened up into a small clearing where a beautiful, coffee-colored woman sat on a bench, her eyes closed, as she bowed her *masinko.* She had a thin nose and long, dark-rust-colored, braided hair cascading down the right side of her head past her shoulders. She wore shorts, a crop top, sneakers, a Magen David, a bright red ribbon in her hair.

Artie stood there silently watching her for a few moments. He felt guiltily voyeuristic doing so. But he didn't want to interrupt her playing, which he found almost as beautiful as he found her.

Finally, he decided the best and least awkward introduction to his presence would be to play along with her. He draped his towel over his shoulders and began to play his lyre.

It wasn't easy, because the *masinko* is not a Western instrument, and its tuning is a different thing altogether. But Artie was a pretty resourceful musician, and he managed to augment her playing pretty admirably, he thought.

She did not open her eyes when she heard him play. She cocked her head, taking in his sound, and adjusted her own playing just a little to join with his. Artie thought he saw a little smile curl up one side of her mouth.

They played for what seemed like a long time. Their music gently filled the air in the space around them, embracing the clearing and the trail up to the canopy of trees. The atmosphere was warm but temperate because of the shade the trees provided. Artie wondered only half-jokingly if this is what heaven was like.

He looked at the woman playing her *masinko*.

He hoped it was.

When their improvisation came to its natural conclusion, the woman opened her eyes and smiled at him.

"You're the harpist," she said.

This surprised Artie. "Have we met?"

"I've heard about you," she said. "There's not a lot of people who would schlep a full-sized harp with them on summer vacation."

"Well, I carry the lyre for hikes and stuff," he said. "I was worried for a second there. I was pretty sure I'd have remembered you."

She grinned. "Because I'm black?"

"Because you're beautiful," Artie blurted out, immediately regretting it. "I mean, you're playing is beautiful."

She frowned looking vaguely disappointed.

"And the rest of you is too," Artie blurted out, again immediately regretting his choice of words. "By which I mean, you, um, have a beautiful soul."

She laughed. He liked her laugh. "Now I know you're bullshitting."

Artie was embarrassed again and didn't know how to respond, so he said, "I'm Artie."

"I'm Eden," she replied.

"That's an appropriate name," he said.

"Because we're in Eden Hollow?"

"Because you're beautiful," he said, uncertainly. "And it's a beautiful name. Um, and also, the name of this place, so, you know, it fits."

"You're not very good at this, are you?" Eden asked.

"Good at what?"

"Meeting people."

"Terrible, actually," Artie admitted. "In my defense, though, I require constant supervision."

Eden laughed again and her laughter filled the air the way her music had. Artie liked her laughter even more.

"You're Beta Israel?" Artie asked.

"By way of Israel and New York," she said. "How could you tell? Because I'm black?"

"Because you play the *masinko*," Artie said. "And because you're black."

She smiled and patted the bench beside her. "Sit," she said.

Artie went to her, laid the towel down on the bench, and sat upon it, at what he thought was a respectful but not stand-off-ish distance.

Artie wasn't certain what the government rules were regarding an Ethiopian Jew at a place like Eden Hollow. On the one hand, Eden Hollow wasn't officially "Jewish," but since Jews were now segregated from non-Jews, and most Yiddish-speakers were Jewish, Eden Hollow would now effectively have to maintain an entirely Jewish membership. Similarly, Whites and non-Whites were now officially segregated from one another, but since Jews were classified as non-White, there was no reason non-White Jews should be excluded from the summer community. Artie wasn't sure this was what the government intended. It was probably a situation that slipped through the cracks and which they hadn't even considered.

If so, fuck 'em, Artie thought.

"You play beautifully," Artie said.

"So do you."

"I went to the Institute of Music to do it professionally, but I guess there's no more opportunities like that for Jews anymore."

"I only ever did it for family and cultural events," Eden said. "Of which there are fewer and fewer, it seems."

"You should perform at the talent show tonight," Artie said.

Eden shrugged. "It had crossed my mind," she said. "But I'm shy."

"Oh, I don't believe that."

"Why don't you believe that?"

"You seem very nice."

"I didn't say I wasn't nice," she said. "I said I was shy."

"How about if I play with you?" Artie suggested. This struck him as an extraordinarily good idea.

Eden looked contemplative for a moment. "I think I'd like that," she said. "What shall we call ourselves?"

"Artie and Eden?"

"No, we need something catchier."

"Eden and Artie?"

"What are the great musical duos?"

"Sonny and Cher? Hall and Oates?"

"Those not named after themselves."

"The White Stripes. Tenacious D. Daft Punk."

"Pet Shop Boys. Wham."

"Eurythmics," Artie said.

"Tears for Fears."

"Suicide."

"That's depressing," Eden said. "How about Milli Vanilli?"

"Seeley Dan."

"Outkast."

"The Black Keys."

"Oh!" Eden cried. "I've got it! Two Rude Jews! Like Two Live Crew, but more Jewish!"

Artie laughed, and then realized she was serious. "Two Rude Jews? Really?"

"Why not?"

"Are we rude?"

"No, that's the fun part," she said.

Artie looked at her, her dark sparkling eyes and the swoop of her nose and her long neck. He noticed *Hamsa* earrings in her lobes.

"I can't think of any reason why not," Artie said. "What shall we play?"

"You know Leonard Cohen?"

"Of course."

"'Dance Me to the End of Love'?"

"Sure."

"Do you sing?"

"Passably. You?"

"I'm a great singer," Eden said, without false modesty. She picked up her *masinko*. "Let's practice," she said.

Artie smiled and picked up his lyre and began to play the melody.

Eden picked up her bow and joined him.

When they began to sing, Artie thought they sounded like they'd been playing this song together their whole lives long.

# Chapter Twenty-five

Bertie and Miltie swam hard, racing to the swimming platform in the lake, and Bertie won.

Bertie had always been a faster swimmer, which Miltie could not quite figure out, but he figured it had something to do with her lithe and streamlined figure cutting through the water better than his linebacker bulk, even if he could bench press twice her weight.

As it was, she reached the platform and had already pulled herself out and upon it just as his hand touched the edge. He pulled himself out after her, and they lay side by side on the platform, looking at the wide expanse of blue sky dotted with occasional cotton balls of puffy white clouds.

Bertie put out her hand and Miltie took it in his and squeezed it tight.

"Ouch," Bertie said.

"Sorry," Miltie said, and loosened his grip on her fingers. He tried to take his hand away, but she gripped it tightly herself and wouldn't let him go.

The sun felt good on his skin. He wondered how long they could lie here before they'd need to put on another layer of sunscreen. The sunscreen was supposed to be waterproof, but Miltie wasn't entirely certain how waterproof that actually was. He wore a Hannukah-themed pair of swimming trunks decorated with images of Hanukkiahs that went down almost to his knees, but that left a lot of skin to burn if he wasn't careful. Bertie wore a matching Hannukah-themed string bikini, so she had even more exposed skin to potentially cook under the sun.

"Another day in paradise," Bertie said. "Looking at the sky can almost make you forget the state of the world outside of Eden."

Miltie agreed but couldn't think of any words to augment the sentiment, and so he kept silent.

"Do you think we're going to move?" Bertie asked.

"From our house?"

"From the Sovereign Republic. Things are going from worse to worser."

"Where would be move to?"

Bertie sighed. "No one will take us," she agreed. "No one's taking refugees, and no one's taking Jewish refugees, especially."

"It's only a matter of time before they shut down Eden Hollow," Miltie said.

Bertie nodded. "They probably already would have but they just don't know about it."

"This could be our last summer here," Miltie said.

He felt Birdie's hand close yet more tightly around his.

Two figures appeared above them, haloed in the sky by the sun behind their bodies. Miltie could see one was a pretty girl about their age wearing a purple two-piece decorated with prints of dreidels, and the other a boy also about their age – a rather handsome boy their age, Miltie thought.

The handsome young man wore a matching pair of dreidel-print swim briefs that rather handsomely delineated his fulsomely proportioned intimacies right in Miltie's line of sight.

Miltie had no complaints about this.

"Are you guys dancers?" the girl asked. She pointed

to Bertie. "You have a dancer's body."

Bertie continued to lie on her back, one hand shielding her eyes from the sun. "I'm a dancer," she replied. "My brother's just a dumb jock."

"Actually," Miltie said, shielding his own eyes from the sun, "my football coach made all of the team take ballet to improve our balance and overall athleticism. I wouldn't say I'm an accomplished dancer, but I can do a pirouette without falling over."

The boy and girl standing above them looked at one another. Each nodded to the other. Then they turned their attention back to Miltie and Birdie, extending their hands in greeting.

"I'm Danielle," the girl said. "You can call me Danni."

"I'm Alan," the boy said. "You can call me Alan."

Bertie and Miltie got to their feet and took Danni and Alan's hands.

"Not Al?" Miltie asked, shaking Alan's hand. Alan's grip was strong and firm and confident. Miltie liked the feel of his hand in Alan's.

"You can call me Al," Alan said. "But I'll think you're referring to the Paul Simon song."

Miltie smiled. "I'm Milton, but please don't call me 'Milton'," he said. "You can call me Miltie."

"I'm Bertie," Bertie said, shaking Danni's hand. "You can call me Bertie. I have a longer name, but it's completely mortifying, and I'll never tell."

"Our parents named us after the Marx Brothers and their family members," Miltie said. "Their real names, not their stage names."

"Our parents were crazy," Bertie explained.

"Were?" Danni asked. "Did they get un-crazy?"

"They got *disappeared*," Bertie replied.

"Oh," Dannie said.

"Shit," Alan said.

"I'm so sorry," Danni said. "Are they -- ?"

"Alive?" Bertie asked.

"We don't know," Miltie said.

They were silent for a few moments, looking into the eyes of the person standing opposite, feeling the sun shining down on them from above, and letting that unpleasant factoid hang in the air between them. Despite the solemnity of the moment, Miltie couldn't help but appreciate Alan's physique. He was muscular and trim, a male dancer's body. Although Miltie was all muscle, he had a linebacker's body, and he suddenly felt self-conscious about this. He felt thick and clumsy compared to Alan's lithe and graceful figure.

"Our last name is also the real last name of Moe, Curly, and Shemp Howard," Bertie said, breaking the silence.

"Horwitz," Miltie explained.

"The Three Stooges?" Alan said.

"You *would* know that," Danni said.

"My cousin has limited regard for Jewish-American culture," Alan said.

"Shut up!" Danni cried. "I have a ton of regard for Kinky Friedman and Shel Silverstein."

"We should get along famously then," Bertie said, with a grin and a twinkle in her eye that seemed to charm both Danni and Alan.

"We're the Rosenfeld cousins," Alan said.

"Is that your stage name?" Miltie asked.

"Our real name," Danni said. "Our stage name is the Rosenfeld Twins, even though we're really cousins. How do you guys feel about Leonard Cohen?"

"As a poet or as a singer-songwriter?" Miltie asked.

"Both," Alan said.

"Love him," Bertie said.

"Great!" Danni said. "I'm choreographing a number

to 'Dance Me to the End of Love' for the talent show. We're both in it – I dance and choreograph. Alan just dances."

"But I dance beautifully," Alan added.

"My little sister Naomi and Alan's little sister Hannah are in it, too, with Alan and me," Danni said. "They're both Bat Mitzvah brats, but good dancers. Want to be in it with us?"

Miltie wasn't certain he did want to be in it, but he did want to get to know Alan better.

As it happened, Bertie decided the question for both of them. "Do we ever!" she cried. "When do we rehearse?"

"Now would be good, if you're free," Danni said.

"On the swimming platform?" Miltie asked, nervously.

"No, too wobbly," Alan said. "We know a little clearing off one of the trails. Follow us."

With that, Alan and Danni both dove off the swimming platform and headed to the beach.

"They both have really nice *tushies*," Bertie said.

"Shut up," Miltie said.

"I hope Alan's gay," Bertie said. "Maybe you can have your first boyfriend."

"Second," Miltie said.

"One kiss amid the tear gas doesn't count," Bertie said.

"You think about sex too much."

"I think about it exactly the right amount, actually," Bertie said. "You think about it too much because you're still a virgin."

"And you're not?"

Bertie shrugged.

Miltie was astounded. "Really?"

"Why is that so incredible?" Bertie asked. "I'm not a nun."

"I just can't imagine anyone wanting to have sex with you."

"Well, someone did, which is more than you can say for yourself."

"Who?" he demanded.

"I'll never tell," Bertie said, and dove into the water to meet Alan and Danni who were by now already waiting for them on the beach.

# Chapter Twenty-six

Polly and Manny, each wearing shorts, sandals, and sunscreen, Manny shirtless and Polly wearing a canary-yellow billowy crop top, followed the Yehoshua Mordechai Lifshitz Trail until they found their favorite spot, a little glade with a pond called Lilly Pad Lagoon. The croaks of frogs greeted them before the cat tails came into view. The pond itself was a vision of frogs on Lilly pads and box turtles on logs and rocks. Dragonflies flitted about like little World War One bi-plane fighters.

"How come there's never mosquitos here?" Manny asked.

"Because the fish and the frogs eat their larvae," Polly said. "Don't get too close to the water, by the way. A snapper might mistake your tiny wiener for an earthworm."

"More likely a frog will mistake your itty-bitty titties for Lily pads."

Manny watched in perplexity as his sister suddenly crouched down at the water's edge and her arm swiped through the water.

She came up again with a frog clutched in her hand.

"Here, I found you a girlfriend," Polly said.

"Funny," Manny said, not thinking it at all funny.

"Kiss it and it will turn into a princess," Polly said.

"Then you can have a girlfriend."

"I don't want a girlfriend!" Manny said, pushing her hand away.

"A boyfriend, then," Polly said. "Magic frogs can be either one."

"Will you cut it out?"

"The Frog Princess won't even care that your balls haven't dropped or that you barely have pubes, and your weenie is the size of a cocktail sausage."

"Oh my God, you are literally the worst!" Manny shouted.

"I know!" Polly said, renewing her efforts to bring the frog to Manny's lips. "Kiss it!"

"It's bad enough that you have to torture me, but do you have to torture that poor amphibian, too?" Manny cried.

Polly's face transformed from gleeful to thoughtful. She took the frog from Manny's face and looked at it sympathetically. "You're right," she said. "I'm being cruel."

"Yes, you're being very mean to me," Manny said.

"Not to you, dummy," Polly said. "To the frog."

She kissed the frog on its mouth and tossed it back into the pond.

"You are truly the worst," Manny said.

"Yuck," Polly said, wiping her mouth with the back of her wrist. "Frogs taste awful."

"I could have told you that."

"They taste like swamp gas."

"*You* taste like swamp gas."

"Your farts *smell* like swamp gas," Polly countered.

"Your farts smell like Sasquatch poop."

"How do you know what Sasquatch poop smells like?"

"From smelling your farts, of course," Manny said.

"You have literally never smelled my farts."

"I like literally always smell your farts."

"You never smell my farts because I have literally never farted because pretty girls don't fart," Polly insisted.

"That's not true, and even if it was true, you're not a pretty girl."

"You don't believe I have girly parts? They were like literally the first thing you saw out of Mom's birth canal. And you've seen my girly parts at every assembly of the Eden Hollow Anarcho-Naturist Youth Brigade."

During the war years, Bertie had managed to finagle the continued use of Rosa's family's indoor pool on Sundays (when Rosa's parents continued to play Mahjong at the JCC) for the younger set of the Youth Brigade – those not otherwise engaged in military service. Regular Youth Brigade assemblies resumed at Rosa's house once she returned from the war. Although Rosa's parents moved to California when their university jobs were eliminated soon after the war's end, they still owned their house in Coventry Village, and Rosa, who didn't want to leave the neighborhood, lived there in their absence, maintaining the property, and hosting a wide variety of Yiddish-speaking anarcho-naturist events.

The fully reconstituted Youth Brigade, less youthful than it had been before the war, remained Jewish and Yiddish-speaking, but now included a great many participants who wore their dog tags as well as their Magen Davids around their necks.

Many also wore the scars of their military service.

"In the first place, I scrupulously avoid looking at your girly parts *ever,* including at the Youth Brigade assemblies, including when we emerged from Mom's birth canal, for fear of going blind," Manny said. "In the second place, I didn't say you aren't a *girl*. I said you aren't *pretty*."

"Are you queer like me, Manny?"

"Shut up."

"Because otherwise you'd know I'm pretty," Polly said.

"I'm your brother!"

"But aesthetically speaking, it's impossible for you not to recognize how pretty I am."

"Even if I was gay, I'd still know you aren't pretty."

Polly frowned. "Maybe you aren't gay after all," she mused. "Gay people have more aesthetic appreciation for beauty than you do."

"You are too much, Polly."

"Much too pretty, you mean?"

"You're the worst."

"I know!" Polly exclaimed. Then she made a sour face. "Yuck!" she said. "I can still taste the frog."

She turned to her brother and before he could stop her, kissed him on the mouth.

"Gross!" Manny screamed and turned and ran a few feet away before he turned back to make sure his sister was not in pursuit.

Polly was not in fact in pursuit but, rather, was laughing uncontrollably at her brother's discomfort. "You are hilarious!" she cried.

"You are gross!" Manny replied.

He waited a few moments for Polly's laughter to subside. When it did not, he began to laugh as well, despite himself.

Soon, the two siblings were both laughing mercilessly.

When at last the laughter subsided, Polly lay down on the grass. "I have to rest," she said. "That took a lot out of me."

After a moment of regarding his sister lying on the ground, Manny lay beside her.

"You really are a bag of dicks," he said.

This started Polly laughing again. She put her hands on her belly.

"Stop!" she cried. "It hurts!"

Manny sighed. "You really are the worst."

Polly's laughter ebbed. " I know!" she exclaimed, happily.

They lay there for a few moments, side by side, staring at the eggshell blue sky and the puffy white cotton ball clouds.

"That one looks like a cartoon dolphin," Polly said.

Manny looked to where Polly was pointing.

"It actually does," he said, astounded. "I've never seen a cloud look so much like something. Usually, they just vaguely resemble something if you use your imagination."

"That one looks like an elephant," Polly said.

Manny scrutinized the sky. "It looks a little like an elephant," he said. "Not that much."

"Don't you see the trunk?"

"I see the trunk, but it could be anything."

"Not anything," Polly countered. "It's far too extensive to be your teeny tiny weenie, for example."

"Oh my God, how do you sleep at night?" Manny asked.

"Like a baby," Polly said, with a mischievous grin.

"Like a baby farting Sasquatch, more like."

Polly thought that was hilarious and laughed uproariously for a few more minutes before farting thunderously, which only made her laugh more intensely.

"Oh, gross," Manny said, holding his nose.

"That wasn't me!" Polly cried through her laughter.

"You fart like Godzilla after eating a Cheesy Gordita Crunch."

This provoked even more intense laughter on Polly's part.

"It's biologically impossible for pretty girls to fart!" she exclaimed, her face turning red and mirthful tears coming out of her eyes, as more flatulence exploded from her *tush*.

Manny became genuinely fearful Polly would faint from the intensity of her laughter, so he kept quiet, allowing her merriment to finally subside.

Laughter fading, Polly wiped the tears from her cheeks and took her brother's hand in hers. She took a deep breath, and lay there quietly, only occasionally trembling with renewed hilarity of a lesser sort than previously.

After a few more moments of cloud watching and chuckling, Polly said, "are you scared, Manny?"

"Of you?" Manny said. "Yes."

"I'm serious."

"So am I."

"No, I mean it."

"I am genuinely scared of your farts, Polly, yes."

"Shut up I have never farted in my entire life and I'm actually very serious in an existential way."

"You're never serious in a serious way."

"This time I am."

Manny frowned and turned his head to look at his sister. "Afraid of what?"

Polly turned back to look at him. "Of everything."

Manny thought her face looked genuinely worried. "Of girls?" he asked.

"No, I don't mean of girls, or boys, or whatever it is you like."

"I like girls."

"Do you?" Polly asked. "Want me to set you up with one?"

"I absolutely don't want you to set me up with anyone."

Polly looked hurt. "Why not? You don't think I'd

make a good *shadkhn?*"

"I think you'd be the worst matchmaker ever," Manny said. "You'd probably set me up with a psychopath because you'd think it was funny."

Polly smiled. "That would be pretty funny, actually," she said. "I can think of a couple of *meshugene* Bat Mitzvah bitches who would really put you through the wringer."

"Remind me never to ask you to set me up on a date with anybody, ever."

Polly looked at him seriously again. "Have you seen the stuff on social media about Operation Supreme Flood for America?"

"I try to stay off social media when I'm at Eden Hollow," Manny said. "Where would I carry my phone, anyway?"

"You could try your pocket."

"But what about when I'm just wearing swim trunks?"

"Well, when I'm just wearing my swimsuit, I carry my phone between my butt cheeks," Polly said.

"You do not."

"You're right," Polly said. "I carry it up my butthole, actually."

"You're gross."

"You want me to show you?"

"I'd rather die," Manny said. "That would definitely give me PTSD."

"I've still got PTSD from seeing your teeny tiny weenie right out of Mom's birth canal," Polly said. "Made me want to crawl right back inside."

"You're an idiot," Manny said.

"Seriously, though, don't you check your feed when we're back at the cabin?"

"I check my notifications, but I don't doom scroll, if that's what you mean."

Polly sighed. "I doom scroll," she said, sadly. "There's

just so much doom to scroll. Operation Supreme Flood for America is all over the social media feeds.”

“What is it?” Manny asked.

“That’s what’s so scary,” Polly said. “No one seems to know.”

They were silent for a few moments.

“Do you hear that?” Manny said.

Polly listened. “Is that . . . ?”

“Leonard Cohen?”

“I thought he was dead,” Polly said.

“It’s a recording.”

“Where is it coming from?”

Manny listened for a few more moments. Then he got to his feet.

“Let’s find it,” he said.

Manny offered Polly his hand to help her up.

After a moment, Polly took his hand in hers and allowed Manny to help her to her feet.

She stood there for a moment and screwed up her face. “I can still taste the frog,” she said, unhappily.

“You're an idiot,” Manny replied.

Polly turned her back to him and pulled her shorts down, thrusting her bare *tush* in Manny’s direction.

Then she farted thunderously towards her brother.

She pulled up her shorts and turned around to face Manny, a smirk on her face.

“You’re disgusting,” Manny said, holding his nose. “And you fart like King Kong after eating the contents of an Olympic-sized pool filled with pork and beans.”

Polly’s face took on an expression of perplexity.

“Who would fill an Olympic-sized pool with pork and beans?” she asked. “Oh, and by the way? Pretty girls don’t fart.”

# Chapter Twenty-seven

"*We* were going to play 'Dance Me to the End of Love' at the talent show," Artie said.

"*We* were going to play 'Dance Me to the End of Love' at the talent show," Julius said.

"I'm Eden," Eden said, extending her hand.

"I'm Adie," Adie said.

They shook hands and made introductions.

Julius and Adie had followed the sound of Leonard Cohen to a clearing off the Yehoshua Mordechai Lifshitz Trail, where they found Bertie, Miltie, and a pair of kids their age named Alan and Danni, cousins, along with two kids of Bat Mitzvah age, also cousins, little sisters to Alan and Danni (Julius couldn't keep track of which sister belonged to whom) named Hannah and Naomi. They had all been rehearsing a ballet to 'Dance me to the End of Love.' Soon thereafter, Artie and a pretty young woman named Eden had arrived, also following the sound of Leonard Cohen. Artie had his lyre with him, and Eden, a *masinko*. Julius carried his guitar, a vintage pre-war acoustic Gibson L-5, and Adie her mandolin.

"So, what's the problem?" Bertie said.

"We can't have three 'Dance Me to the End of Loves' in the talent show," Artie said.

"Why not?" Bertie asked.

"Because then none of them will be special," Julius said.

"Why don't we ditch the recording and you guys can play and sing while we dance?" Bertie said. She turned to Danni. "Is that Ok?"

Danni smiled. "Live music would be even more awesome," she said.

Artie thought it over. "What do you guys call yourselves?"

"Two Rude Jews," Adie said.

"That's *our* name!" Eden cried, more out of delight than protest.

"Well, we can't both be Two Rude Jews," Julius kvetched. "There's four of us."

"Why don't you call yourselves Two Rude Jews Times Two," Bertie said.

"That's the same as four rude Jews," Manny added, helpfully.

Artie narrowed his eyes. "Maybe that would work?"

"The dance company is called the Rude Jew Revue," Alan said.

"Hannah and I call our duo 'The Bat Mitzvah Brats'," said Naomi. "We sing, dance, and juggle."

"We could call the event the Two Rude Jews Times Two Rude Jew Revue featuring the Bat Mitzvah Brats," Hannah said.

"Who are the Bat Mitzvah Brats?" said Polly's voice from nearby.

Everyone turned to see Polly and Manny entering the clearing.

"Guys, these are the littlest Horwitz siblings, Polly and Manny," Julius said.

"We're not little," Polly said. "We're just not old like our other siblings."

After introductions were made all around, Naomi asked, "can you guys dance?"

"I can," Polly said. "Manny can barely walk."

"Shut up," Manny said.

"We can figure something out," Hannah said. "You guys want to join the Bat Mitzvah Brats?"

"How can *I* join the Bat Mitzvah Brats?" Manny asked. "I'm a Bar Mitzvah bro."

"You can't," Naomi admitted.

"Unless we rename ourselves the B'nai Mitzvah Brats," Hannah said.

"I don't like that as much," Naomi said.

"How about 'the Bat Mitzvah Brats and the Bitchin' Bar Mitzvah Bro'?" Hannah suggested.

"Oh my God, that's perfect!" Naomi exclaimed.

"So, we're the Two Rude Jews Times Two Rude Jew Revue with the Bat Mitzvah Brats and the Bitchin' Bar Mitzvah Bro?" Artie asked.

"Sounds cumbersome," Julius chimed in.

"It sounds perfect," Polly said. "Want to show us the choreography?"

"Do I ever!" Danni said, as the rehearsal commenced.

# Chapter Twenty-eight

At the talent show, there was a pair of rhythmic gymnasts who performed with long ribbons they twirled around, a stand-up comedian, a klezmer band, a folk song trio, a magician, a tap dance brother and sister duo, a tuba quartet, an indie rock/rap trio called "Three Jews and Seven Attitudes," several singer/songwriters who sang and accompanied themselves on guitar or banjo, and a guy who did stupid pet tricks with his dog.

The Two Rude Jews Times Two Rude Jew Revue with the Bat Mitzvah Brats and the Bitchin' Bar Mitzvah Bro was the only live music and original choreography combination.

The performance went perfectly. Miltie mostly stood center stage and lifted the girls when they leaped into his arms, but he didn't drop anyone, or even come close, so he considered that a success. Alan Rosenfeld proved himself an accomplished dancer. He and his cousin Danni did an impressively athletic *pas de deux.* Naomi, Hannah, Polly, and Manny executed their choreography perfectly. Artie, Julius, Eden, and Adie played and sang as if they'd been practicing together for all time.

Their performance was well received, no more enthusiastically than by Frenchy, Miri, Lenny, and Lenny's new girlfriend, Talia, who had tattoos all over her body like Lenny did and who was mad sexy, Polly thought.

In line with Eden Hollow's anarchic origins, there was no winner of the talent show, but instead a generalized appreciation for all the participants.

After the reception that followed the show, the Horwitz siblings, Eden, Adie, Naomi, Hannah, Alan, and Danni all went down to the beach for a dip in the lake to celebrate.

The next day was the Fourth of July. The Hortwitz siblings joined the musicians for the hootenanny, and their new musical friends joined as well. It turned out that Naomi, Hannah, Alan, and Danni were accomplished musicians as well as dancers. Naomi played the dulcimer, Hannah played the dobro, Alan played the clarinet, and Danni played the accordion.

They watched the fireworks that night on the beach. This was the first year since the war in which there were actual fireworks instead of a silent lightshow.

As the sky flashed and exploded above them, Naomi and Polly stood neck deep in the water side by side. When Polly felt Naomi's shoulder touch hers, an electric thrill went through her body. She waited and Naomi did not move her shoulder from hers. Then Naomi put an arm around her waist. Polly felt Naomi's fingers gently stroking her hip.

"It's Ok if you want to kiss me," Naomi said, still looking at the sky.

Polly felt the breath catch in her throat. "What makes you think I want to kiss you?" she asked.

Still looking at the sky, her face lit up by purple and blue fire, Naomi smiled and said, "why wouldn't you want to kiss me?"

"Do you want me to kiss you?" Polly asked.

"If you want me to," Naomi said.

"What do *you* want, Naomi?" Polly asked, a little bit of frustration in her voice.

Naomi turned from the pyrotechnics, still smiling, and leaned into Polly and kissed her on the mouth.

Polly, without hesitating, kissed her back.

Polly felt Naomi's tongue in her mouth. It was not the first time she had kissed a girl, but it was the first time she had *French kissed* a girl. She had known she was pansexual for some time, but most of her snogging had been with boys.

Like the song says, she liked it. Even without the cherry Chapstick.

Before the start of the fireworks, Frenchy and Miri had slipped away to their secret spot.

There, to the accompaniment of frogs and fireworks, they made love. Frenchy regarded his wife as she moved atop him and he moved inside her, her flawless body and swollen belly framed by the flashes of light above, illuminating her flesh in its varied colors. When she threw back her head in climax, he felt his own ardor rise, and he held her with his hands on her hips and emptied himself inside her as the sky exploded into an array of booming webs of sparks that cascaded earthward until extinguished in the darkness.

After the fireworks, the community members held a big drum circle and dance party on the Great Lawn, around a bonfire. It all felt very pagan – in a good way -- all these barely-clothed bodies writhing in the undulant light from the fire, Bertie thought, as she danced with Danni. She liked watching Danni dance. Danni moved with both grace and ease and a complete lack of self-consciousness, not like some trained dancers who were actually terrible at dancing without choreography to guide them. Those dancers always seemed to be repeating choreography they had learned while trying to make it look like something they had just made up – but they always looked fake and awkward.

When Danni wrapped her arms around Bertie's waist and pulled their bodies close and kissed her on the mouth, it felt to Bertie like the most natural and logical thing, even though she'd always thought she was straight and had never wanted to kiss a girl before.

But she definitely wanted to kiss Danni.

And so, she did.

# Chapter Twenty-nine

After yoga the next morning, Julius took Adie out in a rowboat on the lake. They rowed out to a small island in the middle of the lake and around to the far side, where they dropped anchor and lay in the boat in the shade of the pines shielded from Eden Hollow and its members.

Julius strummed his guitar and Adie plucked her mandolin and the two of them sang an improvised duet of the song "Everybody Says I Love You."

"We have to do that one for the next talent show," Adie said.

"Groucho Marx sang that in *Horse Feathers*," Julius said.

"So did Chico," Adie said. "And Harpo played it on the harp."

"Were your parents as crazy as mine?" Julius asked.

"I doubt it," Adie said. "But maybe close."

Julius put his hand on the gunwale and gently rocked the rowboat.

"What are you doing?" Adie asked.

"I'm just wondering if we'll capsize if I try to kiss you," Julius said.

"I think the boat will stay afloat provided I don't object."

"Do you think you will object?"

"There's only one way to find out," Adie said, with a smile.

Julius put the guitar aside and carefully went to Adie in the boat and kissed her.

She did not object.

Instead, she threw her arms around him and kissed him with even greater vigor. They lay down in the bottom of the boat, which rocked precariously.

They began to remove their clothing.

The boat rocked even more precariously.

"If we capsize, we can swim to shore and pick this up where we left off," Adie said as she pulled off her halter top and bit his lower lip.

## Chapter Thirty

Artie and Eden were sitting on the banks of the Isaac Babel Swimming Hole, a wide and deep section of the I.L Peretz creek, in a glade off the Sholem Asch Nature Trail.

They were making a shared playlist of Jewish female singers and bands on their phones, which they had carried in a tote bag along with the towels upon which they now sat, and the picnic lunch they soon intended to devour.

Sunshine dappled the glade through the leaves of the trees that surrounded it, painting their swimsuit-clad bodies with a gentle spray of light, creating a perfect blend of summer shade and heat.

"The Shondes," Eden said.

"Definitely," Artie agreed. "And Haim."

"I like the juxtaposition," she said. "Don't forget Elastica."

"I don't know Elastica," Artie admitted.

"Oh my God, they are excellent," she said. "Mid-90s art punk with spiky guitars but a melodic pop sensibility. Founded by Jewess extraordinaire Justine Frischmann. They only made two albums, which is a crime against humanity."

"I'll see if we can bring it up at the Hague," Artie said.

"Well, I would appreciate it if you could get on

that," Eden said. "Ok, Bangles, Suzanna Hoffs solo, Alanis Morrissette, Sleater-Kinney, and we can include any offshoots bands of Carrie Brownstein like Wild Flag and Excuse 17, and who else?"

"Well, there's some dispute whether or not Courtney Love is part Jewish," Artie said.

Eden's eyes flashed with delight. "Oh, we have to give her the benefit of the doubt, don't you agree?"

"Absolutely," Artie concurred.

"Ok, Hole goes on the list."

"And St. Vincent."

"St. Vincent is Jewish?"

"Well, only twenty percent according to 23AndMe," Artie admitted. "She's eighty percent Irish and was raised Catholic."

"Still, twenty percent ain't chopped liver," Eden said. "St. Vincent goes on the list."

"There's Phranc, the self-described 'All-American Jewish Lesbian Folksinger'," Artie suggested.

"Phranc goes on the playlist, that goes without saying," Eden said.

"Pleasant Gehman of the Screaming Sirens is half-Jewish," Artie said. "But matrilineally."

"Half-Jewish is more Jewish than not-Jewish," Eden said. "Screaming Sirens goes on the list. And don't forget about Screaming Females. Marissa Paternoster is fully Jewish. They go on the list. What about Kira Roessler?"

"Black Flag's bassist?" Artie said. "The name sure sounds Jewish, but I don't know for sure."

"Let's assume she is," Eden said.

"So, if you don't mind my asking . . ." Artie said, hesitantly.

"How does an Ethiopian Jew end up in Eden Hollow?" Eden asked.

"I was going to say, how did you end up learning

Yiddish?"

"From my dad," she said. "He's Ashkenazi. Mom and Dad went back to Israel when the government gave us the ultimatum to renounce Israeli citizenship or be deported."

Artie furrowed his brow. "Why didn't you go with them?"

"Well, I was in college, and I was raised in America – unlike my parents, I barely lived in Israel, mostly only visited. And you know, I foolishly thought things couldn't get worse."

"You're not alone in that," Artie said.

"The one good thing is that as a non-White Jew, I fall between some cracks," she said. "It's totally legal for me to be at Eden Hollow, despite the segregation laws, for example, because even White Jews are no longer officially White."

"Well, I'm glad for that," Artie said. "If you weren't here, I might never have met you."

Eden smiled. Artie looked into her deep, beautiful eyes.

Both their phones lit up with an emergency alert.

"Do you see this?" Artie asked.

"Yeah, I do," Eden said, worriedly.

"What's 'Operation Supreme Flood for America'?"

"I have no idea. Maybe it's something about waterproofing basements?"

"There's no description of the event and no date, but someone keeps sending out these alerts reminding people that it's coming up."

"If these alerts are going out to every phone, it's got to be the government, right?" Eden asked.

"Or at least someone who hacked the government system," Artie said.

Eden sighed. "I don't know which possibility is worse," she said. She looked at the swimming hole.

"Want to go for a swim?"

"Absolutely," Artie said.

Eden got to her feet and walked to the water's edge. Artie watched her walk for a few moments before getting up and joining her.

They stood side by side and looked down at the clear running water. Eden dipped in her toe.

"It's freezing!" she cried.

"Hold my hand," Artie said. "We'll brave it together."

Eden looked up at him and smiled as they clutched hands.

Then Eden stepped to him and stood on her toes and kissed him.

The kissing turned into clutching. And caressing.

"How about we swim later?" she asked, between kisses.

"I'd like that very much," Artie said.

They hurried back to where they had laid down their towels and sank down together upon them.

## Chapter Thirty-one

Miltie and Alan swam out to a little island in the lake and lay side by side on the sand and looked up into blue sky while the sunshine kissed their skin.

"How long have you known you're gay?" Alan asked, innocently.

"Who says I'm gay?" Miltie said, defensively. He was taken aback by the question.

"You're not?"

"Who says I am?"

"I'm sorry if I said something wrong," Alan said. "I just thought you were out."

"I just want to know why you think I'm gay."

"Look, if I made things awkward, I'm sorry," Alan said. "Let's forget I asked."

"I still want to know why you think you know," Miltie insisted.

"Let me ask you this," Alan said. "Do you think *I'm* gay?"

"How would I know?"

"I didn't ask what you *know*," Alan said. "I asked what you *think*."

Miltie turned his eyes from the sky and regarded Alan, who was regarding him – his beautiful blue eyes, his lithe, tightly muscled body . . . to say nothing of his perfectly formed crown jewels clearly outlined by his snug swim briefs, as if chiseled by a Renaissance sculptor. Miltie felt his heart butterfly in his chest even as he felt a tingling in his loins he struggled to contain.

"I *think* you *are* gay," Miltie admitted. "Or in any case, I *hope* that you are."

Alan smiled, and he leaned over to Miltie, and they kissed.

"I hope that was Ok," Alan said.

"I don't know," Miltie said. "I think we need to do it again so I can be certain."


As Manny and Hannah walked along the Jacob Gordin Nature Trail on their way to Lookout Point, Hannah slipped her hand into his.

Manny felt the breath catch in his throat and thought that maybe he was going to faint or possibly die, he wasn't certain. This was all new to him.

"Did you know that President Taft was so big they had to have a special plus-sized bathtub made for him at the White House?" Manny blurted out.

Hannah turned to him with a shy smile and a blush in her round cheeks. Her honey-brown hair swayed in the breeze and framed her sparkling green eyes, and the spray of freckles that danced across her nose.

"I didn't know that," Hannah said. "I knew he got in trouble for a teapot."

"I don't think he was our greatest president," Manny admitted. "But he was from Ohio."

"Who do you think was our greatest president?" Hannah asked.

Manny was liking this girl more and more. "Well, I think we have three presidents in the top tier: Washington, Lincoln, and FDR."

"Good choices," Hannah said. "What are your reasons?"

"Well, I think it's partly a question of the accidents of history," Manny said. "The way I look at it, the greatest three presidents are the ones who helped America through our most dangerous moments. So, Washington, he helped establish the country by keeping us together when we were new and could have fractured like –”

“Like we did during the Collapse?” Hannah asked, seriously.

“Exactly,” Manny said. “So, he’s in the top three. Lincoln guided us through the First Civil War, when we actually did fracture, and brought us back together. And, of course, he ended slavery, which is kind of major.”

Manny thought he sounded pretty smart – almost as smart as Polly.

“That’s convincing,” Hannah said. “What about FDR?”

“Well, he brought the country through both the Great Depression and World War Two, and beat Hitler’s ass, so, he’s up there in the top three.”

“What about turning his back on Jewish refugees, though?” Hannah asked. “What about not bombing the rail track to Auschwitz?”

“Well, he beat Hitler, which was the only way to actually stop the slaughter of the Jews.”

“But he could have saved many more,” Hannah said.

“Well, yes, but no one’s perfect.”

“It’s one thing not to be perfect,” Hannah said. “It’s another to stand aside and let people die.”

“He didn’t stand aside,” Manny countered. “He defeated Hitler.”

“I’m descended from a survivor of the St. Louis,” Hannah said.

“The ship carrying almost a thousand Jewish refugees from Nazi Germany?” Manny asked.

“Turned away at every port – Cuba, Canada, and the United States. A quarter of them ended up dying at the hands of the Nazis after they were forced to return to Europe. FDR could have saved them.”

“I guess FDR was a shitty person in some ways,”

Manny admitted.

Hannah shrugged. "Well, like you said. No one's perfect."

"You are," Manny said.

Hannah stopped walking and turned to look at him. The smile was gone, and her expression was serious.

Manny hoped he hadn't messed things up by saying that. He wanted to kiss her, badly. He just had no idea how to go about it.

He'd never kissed a girl.

"Do you really think I'm perfect?" Hannah asked.

Manny swallowed. "Yes," he said, his voice hoarse and his throat dry.

"I'm not perfect," she said. "My freckles are ugly."

"Your freckles are adorable."

She raised her eyebrows. "Do you really think so?"

"I do."

Hannah suddenly covered the eyebrows she had just raised. "My eyebrows are crazy thick," she said. "Like Groucho Marx."

"I love Groucho Marx," Manny said. "Our parents named us after the entire Marx Brothers family."

Hannah looked worried. "Really?" she said. "You poor thing."

And then they were kissing.

Manny wasn't sure how it happened. He was only sure it was happening.

Her lips were soft, and her tongue tasted like strawberry. Her hair smelled like lavender.

Manny wasn't sure what he was supposed to do, exactly, but he put his arms around her and held her as they kissed. He caressed her back – although he was careful to make sure he didn't touch her too intimately on any part of her that might be too personal.

"You're a good kisser," she whispered, as they stood there, their noses touching.

"Thanks," he whispered. "I'm new at it."
"So am I."
"You're the best kisser," Manny said.
"How do you know if you're new at it?"
"I just do," Manny said.
"You want to kiss some more?"
Manny answered in the affirmative.
And so, they did.

# Chapter Thirty-two

Lenny and Talia were sparring in the boxing ring when Miri appeared at the ropes and said, "you guys have a sec?"

Lenny turned to his sister-in-law – just as Talia threw a haymaker that caught him in the jaw and sent him staggering across the mat until he righted himself, clutching the corner post for stability.

"Shit, I'm sorry," Talia said. "I meant to land a clean KO."

"Ha, you funny," Lenny said, laughing. He shook his head to clear it.

"I'm sorry, I shouldn't have distracted you," Miri said.

"That's Ok, sis," Lenny said, grinning. "I'm always happy to take a punch for you."

This was even more true than it sounded. Lenny could be reckless and impetuous, but he was always ready to put himself between trouble and his family.

"That's quite a hook you got there," Miri told Talia.

"I use it to fight off handy randies like Lenny," Talia said.

"You love my randy handies," Lenny protested.

Talia just grinned.

"Talia, you're a vet, right?" Miri asked, eager to get the conversation off of Lenny's randy handies.

"A veterinarian?" Lenny asked. He turned to Talia. "You never told me that, Tal."

"I'm a large animal veterinarian, Len," she said. "That's what first attracted me to you. I thought you were a patient."

Lenny thought this was hilarious and cackled until he bent over in pain. The laughter seemed to hurt him more than the blow to his face, Miri thought.

"I mean a *veteran*," Miri said, although she knew they both knew what she meant.

Talia smiled and gestured with a gloved hand to the dog tags that hung around her neck, below her collarbone tattoo and beside her Magen David. Then she gestured to the tags that hung around Miri's neck, right beside her own Magen David.

"Same war as you," Talia said.

"Do you guys have a minute?" Miri said. "Frenchy and I are gathering up all the vets in Eden Hollow for a meeting."

"Are we planning a Veterans Day weenie roast?" Lenny asked.

"I hope they're not going to roast *your* weenie, Len," Talia said. "They'd starve."

"I was under the impression my weenie did an admirable job of satisfying your voraciousness last night," Lenny said.

"I'm not complaining," Talia said. "You are very admirably satisfying."

"Far too much information," Miri said. "Get those gloves off and come with me, if you please."

"I like your sister-in-law when she's bossy," Talia said, and pulled on the ties of her gloves with her teeth to loosen them.

"Someone's gotta be in charge in the Horwitz family," Lenny said. "And no one wants that to be Frenchy. No offense, Miri."

"None taken," Miri said. "And I say that as the only person whom he actually doesn't boss around. He knows better than to try."

Gloves off, Lenny climbed out of the ring and put his hand on Miri's big belly. "You look like you're about to explode, sis," he said.

"I feel like it too," she said. "Hopefully, your niece or nephew will wait until after the meeting, though."

## Chapter Thirty-three

"How many of you have seen this stuff about 'Operation Supreme Flood for America' on the social media feeds and the emergency alerts?" Frenchy asked his fellow vets as they gathered in the back room of the camp office building, with Zev and Zadie Fischmann, the middle-aged couple who managed the grounds and operations at Eden Hollow.

"I think we've all seen it," said Rachel Cohen. She was twenty-five, petite, with a shrapnel scar down her left cheek. She had been a medic in the war and a paramedic in civilian life, but of course lately she was only allowed to serve in that capacity in the Jewish neighborhoods.

"Anyone know what it means?" Ethan Goldberg asked. He was also twenty-five and had been a schoolteacher until all the Jewish teachers had been fired. He'd been working with his fellow Jewish teachers to open up new schools in the Jewish neighborhoods for the coming school year, and even from Eden Hollow he spent several hours a day on Zoom calls and sending emails with his colleagues to prepare curriculum. He had an ugly scar on his left forearm where a bullet had gone in and out the other side.

"No one knows what it means," Levi Abramowitz said. "But it can't mean anything good." Levi was forty and stocky, with a buzz-cut. He was missing three fingers on his left hand from an exploding grenade during the war.

Despite that, he was widely regarded as the best auto mechanic in the city. He'd been relatively lucky in that his auto shop was already located in a traditionally Jewish neighborhood, so he didn't have to close it down and reopen when Jewish businesses were restricted, although he did lose at least half his clientele, who would no longer venture into Jewish neighborhoods to get their cars fixed.

"The rumor is they're going to wall off the Jewish neighborhoods and create ghettos," Sara Levy said. She was also about forty. She'd been in her thirties when called up for the war, already a successful practicing lawyer. She'd been made a lieutenant thanks to her degrees, but, of course, was never allowed to make captain any more than Frenchy and Miri were, on account of being Jewish. After the war she'd gone back to practicing law, but recently she'd been let go from her big law firm and had re-hung her shingle in Coventry Village, the same Jewish neighborhood where the Horwitz family lived. She was only allowed to serve Jewish clients. She had long red hair and a scar above her left eye from a Nazarene bayonet that fortunately glanced off her forehead instead of stabbing her in the eye, as intended.

"Really?" Bella Stein said. "Do they really want to be that obviously Nazi-imitative?" Like Lenny, she had been only seventeen when she'd been conscripted at the start of the war and was only twenty-four now. She was a graphic designer, and still did freelance work for non-Jewish firms, but only on the down low. She was short and wiry, and her muscular arms were covered with tattoos. The scar from the war on her neck, however, was not.

"I don't think they care about keeping up appearances anymore," said David Cohn. He was thirty-six, already a cop when he was conscripted as the war began. He was still a cop, but now assigned to the precinct in the Jewish neighborhood. He was tall and muscular and had a Star of David defiantly tattooed on his arm.

"What I hear, they're going to not only wall up the Jewish neighborhoods, but they're also going to consolidate them," said Izzy Friedman. "They're going to evict people from their homes in neighborhoods with nice houses and make them all cram into newly established 'Jewish Quarters' in the less desirable Jewish neighborhoods." Izzy was thirty, a freelance journalist, who, of course, could now only write for the unofficial online Jewish outlets based in Jewish communities, or for the foreign press under an assumed name. He wore glasses and had a prosthetic leg below his right knee thanks to a landmine.

Miri felt her heart sink. Was their neighborhood a desirable one or an undesirable one? Their house was old and not fancy, but it was big. Coventry Road was still a thriving commercial street. Maybe they wouldn't be expelled from their home, she hoped. Would they have to share it with strangers?

"Here's what I'm thinking," Frenchy said. "If Operation Supreme Flood for America turns out to be a worst-case scenario, we need to be prepared."

There was silence for a moment as everyone stared at Frenchy, no one daring to voice the question that was on the tip of all their tongues.

"Do you think it's a pogrom, Frenchy?" Rebecca Weiss asked. "Is that what you think they're planning?" She was twenty-six. She had been a combat medic, and was now a nurse – but of course, now only in the hospitals in Jewish neighborhoods. She was tall, had brown hair tied in a ponytail, and a scar on her cheek from a knife wound.

Frenchy shrugged. "I don't know," Frenchy admitted. "But if you remember back in the Before Times, when Hamas attacked the kibbutzim in 2023, they called that

'Operation Al Aksa Flood.' And one translation of 'Al Aksa' is 'supreme'."

"I thought it meant 'the furthest,' as in, 'the furthest mosque'," Aaron Schwartz said. He was twenty-eight and also had made lieutenant during the war. He wore glasses and walked with a limp from a gunshot wound. He was a software engineer and worked freelance from home so he could still unofficially work for non-Jewish firms . . . for half his usual fee.

"It means that, too," Frenchy said.

Sophie Cardoza, a twenty-nine-year-old social worker (confined now to Jewish neighborhoods only, of course), said, "but the Christian identity militia types hate Muslims, too." She had curly black hair and a scar from the war across her collarbone, visible above her crop top.

"They do hate Muslims, but they can be counted on to cheer for extremist groups of any sort when they kill Jews," Frenchy said. "And way back now, ever since 2023, they've been incorporating Hamas's rhetoric into their own as part of their effort to normalize antisemitism."

"At which they have succeeded beyond their wildest dreams," said Jacob Sterne. He was a thirty-five-year-old firefighter, now stationed, naturally, in one of the Jewish neighborhoods in the city. He had a shaven head, and he was big and muscular, with a scar from a war wound across his bare upper torso.

"Their wildest dreams and our worst nightmares," mumbled Ruth Levine. She was twenty-four, having been conscripted at seventeen like Lenny. She was an environmental activist or had been – now she was trying to figure out what she could be activist about without getting "disappeared," like the Horwitz parents. She had glasses and a nose ring and a scar across her cheek; unlike everyone else in the room, her scar was from a bar fight, however.

"Here's what I propose," Frenchy said. "We need to be ready to defend ourselves if it comes to that."

"Defend ourselves with what?" Sara asked.

"The camp has plenty of guns at the target range," Zadie said.

"For target shooting," David said. "I've got my service pistol, but that's not much up against a militia. Those guys pack heat, as the saying goes."

"I have guns," their cousin Rosa Lieberman said, suddenly.

"Cos?" Miri asked. "What are you talking about?"

"In the back of my van," she said. "I've got a few dozen AR-15s, Remington pump-action shotguns, a few sniper rifles, and a shitload of semi-automatic nine millimeters. Also, some bazookas."

"You have bazookas?" Miri asked.

"Only like half a dozen," Rosa said, mildly.

"Where did you get all that?" Frenchy asked.

Rosa shrugged. "I know a guy."

"*Why* do you have all that?" Miri asked.

"Well, ever since the war, you know, I like to be prepared," Rosa said.

Lenny was grinning ear to ear. "Cos, I love you," he said, and gave her a great big hug.

Frenchy thought it over. "Ok," he said. "We need to get those guns into the hands of everyone in this room."

"Not me," Zev said. "I'm a pacifist."

"I'm a pacifist too," Zadie said. "but I'm not stupid. I know how to shoot. I set up the range in Eden Hollow. I'll take a gun. Whatever you can spare."

Frenchy looked at Rosa. "There's nineteen of us," he said.

"I've got enough for everyone in this room to have an AR-15, several handguns, and either a shotgun or a sniper rifle," Rosa said. "And plenty of ammo, too."

"I don't need one," Zev said.

"Give him a pistol," Zadie said.

Zev shrugged. "I'll take a pistol," he said. "Just one. Ok, two. I'll be like Wyatt Earp."

"Let's discreetly take a few non-vets into our confidence and distribute some of the handguns to them as well," Miri said. "If this thing goes down the way we fear it might, we'll need all hands on deck for this.

"But let's otherwise keep this on the down low," Frenchy said. "I don't want to panic the civilians."

"Frenchy," Talia said. "We're all civilians, now."

Frenchy nodded. "Yeah, we are," he conceded. "But maybe not for much longer."

# Part Seven: The Deluge

**Seven years after the Collapse**

**The day of Operation Supreme Flood for America**

**The Day Eden Fell**

## I.

"A screaming comes across the sky."
Thomas Pynchon, *Gravity's Rainbow*

### **Frenchy:**

The rockets came at dawn, screaming across the sky as
Pynchon would have put it, slamming into the club house
and then the cafeteria.

The alarm began to blare from the speaker atop the
office building. That was Zadie and Zev, calling us to
action. The alarm had been installed years ago for tornado
warnings or in case of fire, so it was rarely used.

It was certainly loud enough.

I was up on the roof of our bungalow with Miri a second
later. We were each armed with an AR-15 and a pistol. I
also had a pump-action shotgun. Miri had the sniper rifle.

Miri is a really good sharp-shooter, one of the many
skills she learned during our five years of war and which
she undoubtedly would have preferred to forget.

We lay flat on the roof, our weapons aimed at the gate
to the camp. We dragged an inner tube to the roof with us,
so Miri didn't have to lie on her pregnant belly on the hard
roof. Instead, she positioned herself with her belly
suspended inside the inner tube.

At first, there was no one to shoot at; only rockets
screaming across the sky. One fell in the center of the
Great Lawn. Dirt billowed into the sky where it hit.

The next rocket hit the office building, silencing our
alarm.

I glanced behind me and saw the office building in
flames. I hoped Zadie and Zev had gotten out.

"Here they come," Miri said.

Several paragliders slid across the sky above the camp walls. The Nazarenes had also used paragliders, as well as Hamas on October 7, 2023, way back in the Before Times. It seemed to be a popular choice for Jew-haters.

The paraglider pilots each carried their own AR-15s, firing as they flew.

Miri took out the first one with a headshot. Red sprayed from his skull as his head snapped to the side. His glider plummeted to earth, as Miri took out the second one behind him.

A pick-up truck crashed through the gates, and I trained my weapon upon it. It had what looked like a Browning fifty cal mounted in the truck bed. Knowing the kill power of such a weapon, I found this alarming. I had no idea where they got a Browning fifty caliber. Even in this day and age, that type of weapon was supposed to be illegal for civilian use.

This raised the possibility that our attackers, although clearly dressed in civilian clothes or hunting attire or Army surplus camo, where not strictly speaking civilians.

I took aim and my first shot hit the man at the Browning in the chest, knocking him from the truck bed. My next shot took out the driver. The pick-up drove up an embankment and flipped onto its side.

Men and trucks were streaming through the gates now, and more paragliders were sailing over the walls. The rest of our improvised Maccabean fighting force were by now out on the rooftops of their own bungalows, shooting down the pilots and firing on the pick-ups and the gunmen.

We killed more men than got through, but some were getting through even so, scattering throughout the camp.

Zev and Zadie appeared on the lawn, firing on the gunmen as they streamed in. Zev had a pistol in each hand, Zadie an AR-15. About a dozen invaders fell before someone shot Zev and Zadie down.

There seemed to be no more paragliders, and the men nearest the gates were all down, bleeding into the dirt and grass. I was most concerned about the men who had scattered, especially if they had made it to cabins or bungalows that were not defended by one of the Eden Hollow Maccabees.

"Stay here," I said. "Shoot down anyone that comes through that gate or over that wall."

"Be careful," Miri said, just before she sighted an invader and shot him through the throat. The man went down, holding his throat, writhing on the ground.

"Owch," I said.

"I was aiming for his head," Miri said, sheepishly.

"Don't shed any tears for him," I said and kissed her before slinging the shotgun over one shoulder and securing my pistol in my shoulder holster as I slid off the roof and down to the ground, the semi-automatic rifle in my hands.

As I moved towards the undefended cabins, I could hear explosions coming from the direction of the beach and the lake.

I hoped that was our Maccabean forces, taking out any attackers coming by boat with the bazookas Rosa had provided.

If it was the attackers firing RPGs at our guys on the beach, that had the potential to be really bad.

II.

I had seen several invaders running down Yosef Trumpeldor Lane, so I followed.

I turned the corner onto the lane and stopped short when I saw two invaders, a man and a woman, at the Herskowitz family's cabin, tossing in a device through a broken window. There was a bang and a woosh and then flames licked the shattered glass.

I raised my rifle and shot the man in his temple. He dropped as his companion turned to me, raising her own AR-15. I fired, and my bullet tore through her throat and out the other side.

She looked shocked as she put her hand to her throat. Maybe she hadn't expected Eden Hollow to be defended or maybe it had never occurred to her that she could ever die.

Or maybe she had thought Jews were defenseless and passive and would never shoot back.

She sat down on the ground, blood seeping from between her fingers, a gurgling sound in her throat. She looked no older than me.

I shot her in the forehead so she wouldn't die slowly.

It was better than she deserved.

I could hear screaming and cries for help inside the Herskowitz home. I'd had the foresight to put on my steel-toe-tipped hiking boots, if nothing else except cargo shorts and my weaponry, and so I kicked open the front door, but the flames were already too strong. There was no way I was getting in, or anyone was getting out, through the front door.

As I ran around the back, I heard gunfire throughout the community. We had posted defenders strategically throughout Eden Hollow, and it appeared fire fights were breaking out everywhere as the invaders pushed deeper into the campground.

Around the back of the Herskowitz home, I found another invader, a grizzled man with a bushy beard wearing a camo t-shirt and shorts, lugging what appeared to be a World War Two vintage belt-fed Browning M1919, firing into the home. The belt dragged beside him, lurching bullet by bullet into the weapon and spewing out spent cartridges which littered the ground at his feet.

I noticed he was wearing knock-off Crocs, also camo-decorated.

The Browning M1919 was designed for two soldiers, one firing and the other feeding the belt. You sometimes see movies where a lone soldier wields the weapon without help, but you never see that in real life – or at least I never did during the war.

Bushy Beard Man was about to find out why.

He saw me and pivoted, aiming the Browning right at me, and pulled the trigger.

I thought for sure I was a dead man and felt my heart seize in my chest, but when nothing happened, I realized the belt feed had jammed.

Bushy Beard Man looked at his weapon, looked at me, dropped his weapon and pulled a nine-millimeter pistol.

I fired and my shot shattered his jaw, leaving it hanging from one side of his face.

I hadn't meant to do that. I was going for a clean kill.

It's hard to aim accurately during a firefight.

The force of the impact caused him to drop his pistol, but he appeared outraged by the whole thing, and pulled a knife from a harness around his chest and came at me.

I fired twice more and put him down with two rounds in his chest that burst out his back.

I turned to the house and kicked open the back door, already pockmarked with bullet holes. A woosh of flame leaped at me, driving me back.

I could still hear screams and cries for help from inside.

I rushed around the perimeter until I came to the bathroom window. The glass had been broken and Mrs.

Herskowitz was yelling through the hole it created.

They were smart to hide from the fire in the bathroom, but the window was too small for humans to fit anyone through.

"Stuff some towels through the window and move away," I commanded.

Mrs. Herskowitz did as instructed. I smashed out the rest of the glass with the butt of my rifle, laid the towel down on the jagged window frame, grasped it and pulled for all I was worth, bracing my foot against the wall for leverage.

A moment later, Jules and Artie appeared beside me. They wrapped their hands around the bottom of the window frame and pulled along with me.

"What are you doing here?" I grunted as we pulled.

"We came to help," Artie said.

"You were supposed to protect the kids."

"Miri is doing an excellent job of that," Jules said.

Just then, the window frame gave way and pulled from the wall, taking some of the wall with it, and leaving a wide space into the bathroom. It would be wrong to say the cabins were flimsy, but they were not built for winter use, and the walls tended to be on the thin side. In this case, that was a fortunate thing.

Mrs. Herskowitz handed us her kids, Hunter and Dylan, a boy and a girl, eight and ten, and then we helped Mrs. Herskowitz through. They were all coughing from smoke inhalation and had cuts on their feet from broken glass.

"Mr. Herskowitz?" I asked.

Between hacking coughs, Mrs. Herskowitz shook her head. Her eyes were red, from smoke or weeping or probably both.

I turned to Jules and Artie. "Get the Herskowitz family to the library, we've got triage set up there," I said. "Get our family in there as well. Go. Are you armed?"

They nodded and showed me the nine-millimeters I had

given them and which they now carried tucked into their shorts.

"Don't carry them like that or you'll shoot your *schmekels* off," I said. "Get moving. Shoot anyone who doesn't belong here, before they shoot you."

My little brothers were good shots and they'd had a lot of target practice at Eden Hollow.

They'd never actually shot an actual person, as far as I knew.

Then again, once upon a time, neither had I.

There's always a first time for everything.

III.

Several houses were on fire as I travelled down Yosef Trumpeldor Lane, but at least the families were already safe in the streets. There were bodies on the ground, AR-15s and shotguns beside them. I didn't recognize the corpses, so I assumed they were invaders.

I didn't see any more living invaders on Yosef Trumpeldor Lane. They must have moved onto the next streets.

I saw Jacob Sterne as he jammed a fresh clip into his weapon.

"Give me a report," I said.

"They've been working their way down the street, firing into houses, throwing grenades or homemade incendiary devices into people's homes," Jacob said. "We picked off most of them, but some got through."

"Escort these civilians to shelter in the library with the medical team," I said. "Then organize a firefighter team and get these fires out before the whole community goes up in flames."

No one had officially put me in charge, but since I had organized our defense, people treated me like I was.

The medical team was made up of Rebecca Weiss and Rachel Cohen, the only medical professionals in camp with combat experience, as well as Dr. Gabe Resnick and Dr. Lavonne Siegel, whom the vets had taken into our confidence. The library was a brick building, somewhat safer from fire than some of our other buildings in Eden Hollow.

Jacob nodded and led the displaced civilians along Yosef Trumpeldor Lane towards the library.

I could still hear gunfire.

I turned down Rose Schneiderman Road, where I found Lenny and Talia crouched behind a golf cart turned on its side, trading fire with a band of invaders further down the road. Talia had a sniper rifle; Lenny had an AR-15.

A golf cart doesn't provide much protection from semi-automatic weapon fire, but it provided more than the invaders had. They crouched, about a dozen of them, down the street, without anything to hide behind.

I knelt down beside Talia, took aim over the side of the sideways golf cart. I fired, and the face of the invader in my sights, a young man my age, disappeared in a splash of red. I pivoted my aim to the young woman beside him. She briefly glanced at her fallen comrade lying next to her. I fired and her head snapped back as the round struck her in the temple and burst out the opposite side.

There was ten of them left, and half were firing at us, and the other five were going down the street and firing into the cabins.

"You two concentrate your fire on the ones shooting at us, I'll focus on the ones attacking the cabins," I said.

Talia and Lenny both fired, and two more of the attackers fell.

I got an older, grizzled looking man with white stubble on his chin in my sights. He was firing an AR-15 into the Berger cabin. I fired and a hole ripped into one side of his ribcage and out the other.

I took aim at a middle-aged woman with Aryan Nation tattoos on her bare arms, who was jacking round after round into her shotgun and firing into the Appelbaum bungalow. Huge chunks of wood and glass burst into splinters with each blast. I fired and the top of her head exploded, and she fell motionless to the dirt.

Talia and Lenny had taken down two more shooters. Only one was left among those taking aim at us as we crouched behind the golf cart.

A young man was pulling the pin from a grenade as he prepared to toss it into the Cooperman's cabin. I shot him and he collapsed to his knees. The grenade exploded in his hand and set off the others he had strapped to his torso.

His comrade across the street from him was preparing to toss a grenade of her own into the Drucker's cabin. She was a young woman about his age, early twenties. She looked like a college student. The blast from his grenades set off those she had strapped to herself as well, and her torso was eviscerated into a cascade of red mist and chunks of meat. A look of surprise appeared on her face as her body disappeared, and then her disconnected head fell to the dirt, rolling beside her pair of Timberland boots which stood there, smoking.

Talia felled the last of the attackers shooting at us, and the last invader attacking the cabins, realizing it was hopeless, dropped his rifle and raised his hands in surrender.

He looked no older than eighteen. He wore a t-shirt that read "America First," and a pair of camo-decorated cargo shorts.

Talia shot him through the eye. He collapsed in a heap, the blood from his wound spreading in a circle and soaking into the dirt road.

IV.

For the next two hours, we fought block by block, pushing the invaders from street to street.

We joined up with small teams of defenders, who had been doing the same from different directions.

We finally pinned the invaders in the space we called the "Emma Lazarus Village Square," where several streets joined into a small park with a gazebo at its center. The invaders from each direction were pushed to the gazebo, where they tried to make a stand.

There were about twenty of them, and fourteen of us.

Lenny, Talia, and I were at the mouth of Emma Goldman Street.

I could see Rosa, Miri, Levi Abramowitz, and Ethan Goldberg at the mouth of Hannah Arendt Way.

Sara Levy, Bella Stein, Izzy Friedman, and David Cohn crouched at the corner of Clara Lemlich Drive.

Aaron Schwartz, Sophie Cardoza, and Ruth Levine were at the mouth of Pyotr Alexeyevich Kropotkin Street.

Rebecca and Rachel were presumably still in the library treating the wounded. Jacob was hopefully busy fighting fires throughout the community with volunteers he had gathered. Our contingent of non-veteran volunteers we had taken into our confidence and provided with weapons, such as Artie and Jules, had hopefully by now gathered the surviving civilians and taken them to safety in the library and the adjacent reading room, both of which were made of brick and were somewhat defensible.

Miri, Rosa, Talia, David, and Aaron were all armed with sniper rifles, and the rest of us laid down a steady barrage of rapid-fire semi-automatic rifle shots while they picked off the invaders one by one.

I was angry that Miri had risked not only her safety

but the safety of our unborn baby to join the firefight, but I had to admit I found the image of her, pregnant and wearing a sports bra and yoga shorts while firing a sniper rifle, strangely beautiful.

Five invaders were down within seconds.

I saw another pull the pin on his grenade. He wore a t-shirt that read "Camp Auschwitz" and a baseball cap that read "White Nation." He looked about forty, with big arms jutting out of his sleeveless t-shirt, an ample gut, and impressive Elvis sideburns.

Even with his big arms, I didn't think he could make the throw to the mouth of any of the streets that fed into the Village Square from that distance, but I wasn't going to take a chance. I aimed for his chest, and the row of grenades that hung there from a harness.

The grenades exploded and so did he. His body disappeared into a blur of red and gray liquescence. The explosion also killed six of the invaders around him.

They were now down to nine and we were still at fourteen.

But not for much longer.

A young man in camo fatigues and a scraggly red beard crouched with his AR-15 and fired a shot that hit Sara Levy in the forehead. Her head snapped back, and she went down. David, crouching beside her, glanced at his fallen comrade, and then returned fire, landing a headshot that dropped her killer.

A young woman with a swastika tattoo on her bicep and a shaved head got off a lucky shot from her hunting rifle that blew out Ethan Goldberg's chest. My heart stopped when I saw that, not only for Ethan, but for my cousin Rosa and my wife Miri, who were beside him, to say nothing of our baby inside Miri's belly.

Rosa and Miri both returned fire at the same time. The swastika-tattooed woman's shaved head exploded like a watermelon.

They were now down to seven and we were down to

twelve.

I took out a young man wearing a t-shirt that read "6MWE," which stands for "Six Million Wasn't Enough." Then I took out a middle-aged woman wearing a "Blood and Soil" t-shirt.

They were now down to five.

I ejected a clip and inserted a new one from the harness around my torso as the rest of the defenders continued to lay down a steady barrage.

By the time I again raised my rifle, they were down to three. But the next shot, fired by a middle-aged man with a white horseshoe mustache and a soul patch wielding an AR-15, drilled through Aaron Schwartz's chest.

Rosa took out horseshoe mustache man with a head shot.

The two surviving invaders dropped their weapons and raised their hands in surrender.

Rosa and Talia fired at the same time, hitting both of them in the forehead. The backs of their skulls burst in a mist of blood, brain, and bone, and they both crumpled to the ground.

## V.

There were still bursts of gunfire punctuating the morning air.

We split up into two person teams, and one three-person team, and went off in different directions to mop up and help Jacob fight fires.

"We don't know how many invaders are still at large," I said. "Stay frosty."

Rosa was with me. She walked up to me, a look on her face I'd never seen before. She'd experienced plenty of combat during the war and had seen the same brutality I had, so I knew it wasn't just the firefight itself that had put that expression on her face.

"You need to see what they did on Hannah Arendt Way, Frenchy," Rosa told me, barely above a whisper.

In the Orlofsky cabin on Hannah Arendt Way, Rosa led me into the kitchen. There, Michael and Golda Orlofsky sat upright against the kitchen wall, their feet and hands bound. They had both been shot in the head. Slowly congealing blood pooled around them.

Across from them, propped against the cabinets below the kitchen sink, their children, Shoshana, eleven, and Joel, six, sat with their hands and feet also bound. They too had been shot through the forehead.

The kitchen floor was a sea of thickly coagulating blood.

I'd seen blood and cruelty and death before, during the war.

But this was different.

I felt everything inside my stomach suddenly rush to get out. I ran to the front yard and vomited.

As I stood there bent over with my hands on my knees trying to regain my equilibrium, I felt Rosa's hand gently placed on my back.

"There's more," she whispered. "There's so much fucking more."

In front of the Koeman cabin, ten-year-old Kaylee lay on her back, her eyes wide and still and staring at the sky.

Her right arm had been severed clean off at the elbow, possibly with a machete.

"She was still alive when we found her," Rosa said, her voice cracking. "We tried to put on a tourniquet, but she'd lost too much blood."

At the Freundel cabin, Emmanuel Freundel, a sixteen-year-old, lay dead in the yard with his throat torn open by the garden hoe that still lay beside him.

Inside the Eckstein cabin, Hédi and Sima, a married couple, and their child, eight-year-old Dorrit, had been bound with wire, doused with gasoline, and set on fire. At least, I thought it was Hédi, Sima, and Dorrit. Their bodies were charred and blackened beyond recognition.

In the Rappaport cabin, four bodies were piled up in the small laundry room. Blood soaked the tile floor. The bodies appeared to be those of a man, a woman, and two preteen boys. They were presumably the bodies of Nate and Leora and their boys Amos and Sam. I couldn't tell for sure, because they were face down, and the blood obscured their features. I decided not to disturb the bodies, even though I knew a crime scene investigation was unlikely. It looked like all of their throats had been slit.

On the wall of the laundry room someone had fingerpainted in blood the words *"Kill All Zios."*

In the Yakobovich cabin, we found Tihila and her husband Noam tied with wire against the wall of the bedroom. On the bed, their daughter, Sapir, lay face down, with her legs splayed. All their throats had been slit.

"I think they probably raped her in front of her parents before killing them all," Rosa whispered.

I had been thinking the same thing, but it hurt more to hear it spoken out loud.

In the Idelson cabin, we found both parents, Doug and Jeremy, shot dead in the living room. We found their infant son Lev shot dead three times in his crib. He was still in his diapers. Their toddler, Ellie, about two-years-old, had been blackened and charred by fire.

In the back lawn outside the Barenboim cabin, the bodies of Harvey Barenboim and his fourteen-year-old son Reggie lay on their backs, decapitated, their blood soaking the grass.

The Mollie Steimer Communal Garden was strewn with body parts and viscera. A pile of unidentifiably charred bodies lay beside a rose bush. I think it was five bodies. It was hard to tell.

At the end of the street was a dumpster filled with charred body parts and bodies.

I would have thrown up again, but my stomach was empty.

The rest of me felt pretty empty, too.

## VI.

Out of two hundred and fifty people in Eden Hollow, sixty-five were killed. That's about twenty-six percent.

The explosions from the beach did indeed turn out to be our defenders taking out the invaders, which provided some small comfort. If the invaders from the lake had made it to shore, it's possible the death toll would have been much higher.

Back in the library where the wounded and the survivors had taken shelter, a news broadcast was on the radio.

There had been attacks on Jewish or Jewish-identified institutions and neighborhoods throughout the Sovereign Republic. The body count was coming in at around ten thousand so far, a not insubstantial number for the area between the Ohio and the Missouri Rivers, in which resided only an estimated eight-hundred-thousand Jews.

Given the ferocity of the attack on Eden Hollow, however, I expected that number to rise as more information came in.

Sure enough, the attack was called Operation Supreme Flood for America. The government denied any responsibility or foreknowledge, but there were many reports of the authorities standing aside and refusing to intervene to stop the violence.

A group that called itself the "Operation Supreme Flood for America Resistance Movement Steering Committee" issued a statement that was broadcast on all news outlets:

> *"Our heroic resistance proves that*
> *White Christian America will never sit*
> *idly while our people are colonized,*
> *brutalized, and ethnically cleansed by*

*the Zionist Occupied Government Entity. We uphold the right of White Christian America to resist colonialism, imperialism, and White Genocide, and to reclaim our land as our birthright by any means necessary. The Jews are responsible for the oppression of all Americans. There is only one solution: White Christian revolution. "*

The government issued decrees instituting emergency measures, which mostly involved evicting Jewish families from their homes in areas formerly designated for them and consolidating the Jewish population in a handful of neighborhoods they were now calling "Jewish Sectors." They said this was for our own safety.

The government further issued an order stripping Jews of their property, cash, and assets.

It was clearly time to put escape plans into effect.

Some of our wounded were in rough shape, but most were ambulatory.

Most of the parents who had been murdered had been murdered along with their kids. As terrible as this was, it meant we only had two kids in the community who had been orphaned – Billy Zucker, ten, and is sister Summer, eight, whose parents had been killed by a hand grenade thrown into a back room of their cabin in which the family was hiding. Billy had also lost an eye in the explosion. They were taken in by the Vogel family, who were cousins.

It was agreed that everyone should destroy or leave behind anything that could identify us as Jewish, including Magen David necklaces, Jewish-themed swimwear or t-shirts, and prayerbooks. We also agreed to burn our passports. Even books by Jewish authors like Saul Bellow, Michael Chabon, and Judy Blume were to be left behind. The plan was for everyone to head to the nearest border and try to cross it. For most of the members, that was to the East and into the United Democratic States of America. It was about three hours to that border, in Western PA, from Eden Hollow. The UDS of A wasn't accepting any refugees or immigrants, but there was hope they might make an exception for people who had family in the UDS of A, which many of us did. Getting across the border without a passport was going to be an almost impossible task but trying to cross the border *with* a passport that identified the bearer as Jewish was going to be infinitely worse.

A few people had who owned boats or had access to one planned to cross the lake into Canada. They offered to ferry across as many passengers as possible, and they had enough takers to guarantee their boats would be full. This was a risky proposition because the lake was heavily patrolled by SRNA Coast Guard, but if they managed to cross the international boundary lines, they would be theoretically safe on the other side. Canada wasn't keen on accepting refugees either, but it was widely believed that while they might not grant indefinite residency, they wouldn't turn anyone back, either.

No one was going south to the White Christian Confederacy of the Nazarene Nation, of course.

Everyone who had a dog tag issued later during the war – the ones without religious identification -- was advised to wear it openly. Just as the Sovereign Republic worshipped guns, God, and free enterprise, they worshipped the military. A dog tag without religious affiliation could prove useful in a hostile world.

Despite everything, some people were not going to try to cross the border. They had family back in the city or elsewhere in the Republic and they weren't going to leave without them. They would reunite with their families, move to the designated Jewish Sectors, if necessary, and hope for the best.

Of course, the Horwitz tribe had family, too -- our parents, whose whereabouts – and condition – were still unknown.

But there wasn't very much we could do about that right now.

The Horwitz family was going to try to make it to California and the Cooperative Commonwealth of Pacifica. It was a longer trip, but we still felt Miri's family in California presented our best hope of finding refuge. In addition, Rosa's parents also now resided in California. We probably had distant relatives in the UDS of A, but I had no idea who any of them were nor how to find them, and, in any case, none of them were close relatives like Miri's parents. I wished we'd taken her parents' up on their offer to take us in earlier. But that was before my parents had been disappeared, when we still had three music and record stores to run, and we thought things weren't going to get any worse.

Lesson learned.

Things can always get worse.

Between Rosa's stash and the guns used for target practice, there was plenty of weaponry in Eden Hollow, so we made sure every car had at least one firearm for their flight. Of all the precariousness involved in our journeys, this was by far the least dangerous aspect. The Sovereign Republic was a gun-lover's paradise, and permits were not even required to carry one.

Izzy Freidman documented the atrocities committed in Eden Hollow in graphic detail, both in print and in photographs he took on his phone. He uploaded everything he had to every independent and alternative

news outlet he knew of throughout not only the former
USA, but the world. He did the same with his social
media feeds.

All there was left to do was to bury the dead and
hope the world would care.

We buried the slaughtered members of Eden Hollow
in the Great Lawn, with armed lookouts posted around
the perimeter of the camp in case of a second wave of
invaders.

We left our slain attackers to rot in the streets where
they lay.

We didn't have a proper ordained Rabbi, but one of
our members, Harry Wannamaker, was a former
yeshiva boy, and he did the honors, presiding over as
formal a service as we could manage under the
circumstances.


Polly, Manny, Bertie, Miltie, Artie, Jules, and Lenny
tearfully kissed their summer romances goodbye. They
were all going off with their families, or to rejoin them
elsewhere. Jules and Artie offered to go with Adie and
Eden, but the women gently declined, not wishing for
any more families to be torn apart.

Eden was going to try to get to her family in Israel, a
dicey proposition made even more dicey as she had
already given up her Israeli dual citizenship, but
nevertheless one she felt she had to attempt.

The Horwitz family climbed into our Ford Transit.
Rosa joined us. She could have taken her own van, but
we figured it was better to ride together than to worry
about losing each other on the road.

We loaded up all of our belongings that didn't
identify us as Jews, including our musical instruments.
I wasn't sure what we were going to do in California
when we got there. Maybe we could get jobs in local
music stores. Or maybe we could make some money
playing music. We were all pretty good at that, even if

Artie was the only one who had gone to school for it.

It would take us about fifteen hours to get to Council Bluffs if we took minimal food and bathroom breaks. I thought we could make it.

Getting across the Missouri River into Nebraska and the Great Plains Agricultural Federation was going to be another matter entirely.

We took with us plenty of guns in case we encountered any trouble along the way.


"What do you think is going to be the official Jewish Sector back home?" Lenny asked. "You think our house will be in it?"

"If I were to guess, I'd say, yeah, maybe," Miri said. "I think they're going to consolidate all the Jews clustered in the eastern suburbs into our neighborhood, because it's already majority Jewish."

"But where are they going to fit all those people?" Artie asked.

"I think everyone's going to have to take in lodgers," Jules said.

"Single family homes will become multiple family homes," Miltie said.

"Sounds like a blast," Bertie said. "Of course, it also depends on how many homes were burned down in the Jewish neighborhoods."

"Or how many Jewish residents were killed," Manny said.

"Which might make it easier to shove everybody into one neighborhood, if there aren't as many of us left," Polly said. "Or harder, if there's not enough houses left that haven't been burned down."

We let that thought sink in and rode along in silence for a while.

"Hey, you know how God created nine hundred and ninety-four versions of the earth which he destroyed until he settled on this one?" Polly asked after about fifteen minutes, breaking the silence.

"What about it?" Manny replied.

"Well, one has to ask," Polly said. "After nine hundred and ninety-five tries --- is *this* world really the best *Hashem* could do?"

The question hung in the air as we continued north toward the junction of Interstate 80.

# Part Eight: Transit on the Mother Road

275

# Chapter Thirty-four

They made it six hours and just past Joliet before they pulled over into the Ronald Reagan Truck Stop for fuel and something to eat.

They had listened to the news on the radio, and it had been all bad.

The death toll had been raised to fifteen thousand -- and counting.

All Jewish "alien residents" – as they had all been newly designated -- had been ordered to report to their assigned "Jewish Sector." Those who failed to do so within seventy-two hours would have warrants issued for their apprehension, along with a bounty of one thousand dollars per fugitive Jew.

They had three days to get out of the Sovereign Republic before they became outlaws.

Frenchy had always thought the idea of being an outlaw sounded kind of romantic.

Now, it kind of sucked.

As Frenchy filled up the car, Polly asked, "can we go inside and scope out the eats?"

"Just make sure you don't say anything . . ." Frenchy looked around to make certain no one was within earshot. "Too *Jewy*."

"Thanks for the reminder, bro," Polly said, irritably. "Because I'm so fucking *stupid*."

As the mob of Horwitz siblings and their cousin Rosa filed into the rest stop, Miri joined Frenchy at the gas pump.

"How are you doing?" she asked.

"How *you* doin'?" Frenchy responded in a bad imitation of Joey from
*Friends*.

Miri glanced to the rest stop building. "How *they* doin'?"

Frenchy shrugged. "How's *anybody* doing?" he said. "You don't know your world is ending until it's too late."

"Did we wait too long?" Miri asked.

"Yeah," Frenchy admitted. "We did. That's on me. But we've got a bagful of cash – everything liquid I could get my hands on, plus most of Lenny's winnings since we got back from the war. All the broken republics still use old-fashioned US of A hard currency, so we're good there. And we'll have the profits from the sale of the store and the inventory, and maybe our home if it comes to that – the authorities might try to have that seized once they figure out that we're not coming back any time soon, but I transferred the deed to Jayson, so we'll see. Assuming Jayson can find a way to get the money to us, of course."

Frenchy finished gassing up the Ford and returned the pump handle to its cradle.

"You got the bag o' cash?" Miri asked.

"You think it's safer with me or locked in the van?" he asked.

"You packin'?"

Frenchy lifted up his Hard Rock Cafe t-shirt, revealing his nine-millimeter in a holster on his belt.

Miri lifted up her Queen of Hearts t-shirt and revealed her own nine-millimeter strapped to her belt.

Then with a grin she lifted up her shirt further and uncovered her big round belly. Then she lifted up her shirt even further and flashed him her big round bare breasts.

God, she was beautiful, Frenchy thought. He smiled, even as he hoped they hadn't been observed. He had an instinct to look around for onlookers, but he couldn't take his eyes off her.

Miri lowered her shirt and clothed both her nakedness and her weaponry.

Frenchy thought to himself, not without irony, that they lived in a world that outlawed public displays of nudity but not the public brandishing of guns.

"I think the bag o' cash is definitely safer on your person than locked in the van," Miri said.

## Chapter Thirty-five

Polly and Manny had found Ronald Reagan and Margaret Thatcher bobbleheads in the giftshop.

"Mr. Gorbachev, tear down this wall," Manny said, holding the bobblehead and moving it so that its head bobbled as he imitated the fortieth president of the former USA pretty convincingly, Polly thought.

"Oh my God, I had no idea you could do imitations!" Polly cried. "Do you have other hidden talents I don't know about?"

"I can write my name in the snow with my pee," Manny said.

"I've seen you do that already," Polly said, dismissively. "I mean something I don't know about."

"Do Thatcher," Manny said, handing her the Thatcher bobblehead.

"Oh, Ronnie, I do so want to give you a big sloppy kiss," Polly said in a high-pitched faux-English accent, moving the bobblehead as she spoke.

"You sound like one of the Monty Python guys when they play a lady," Manny said.

"Oh Ronnie, I do so want to nibble on your SPAM," Polly said in the same fake English Thatcher voice.

"You sound nothing like Thatcher," Manny said.

"Oh, Ronnie, do give me a kiss with your tongue so I can taste the SPAM in your mouth," Polly said in her Thatcher voice.

"Now, Maggie, I don't think Mommy would like that," Manny said in his Reagan voice.

"Why do you call your wifey 'Mommy,' Ronnie?" Polly/Thatcher said. "It's so infantilizing."

"Well, you know, she does change my diapers," Manny/Reagan said.

"Are you kids gonna buy those bobbleheads or what?" said the man behind the counter. He was about forty and looked as if he'd been born unhappy. He had a mustache, glasses, and a puffy face. He looked a little like Heinrich Himmler if Himmler had been a gas station attendant.

"Well, we have to try them out, sir," Polly said. "So, we know they work correctly."

"They're bobbleheads," the man said, irritably. "Their heads bobble. That's all they do. The rest of it is your own imagination."

"But we need to find out if their bobbling heads inspire our imaginations," Manny said.

"You kids from around here?" the man asked, giving them a hard stare. "We don't get a lot of imagination around these parts."

"Sure, we're from here," Polly said. "That's why we're at a truck stop on the interstate. Because that's where all the cool kids hang out."

"You'd be surprised," the man said. "Just don't bobble those heads with too much force. And watch your language. There's kids around here."

"We're kids around here," Manny said.

"There's actual fun-sized kids, I mean," the man said.

"My brother's weenie is fun-sized," Polly said. "Like one of those little candy bars at Halloween."

"Polly!" Manny protested. He turned to the man. "Please excuse my sister. She has deranged personality derangement syndrome."

"I think it's time for you kids to make your final purchases for the night," the man said.

"How much?" Polly said, holding up the Thatcher bobblehead.

"Fifty-five dollars each," the man said.

Polly's eyes widened in shock. "Is that based on average GDP during their administrations, or average unemployment?"

"Good night, kids," the man said. "Time for you to skedaddle."

"Good night, sir," Manny said, as they put the bobbleheads back on the shelf.

"Please send our regards to Mrs. Himmler," Polly said, as they waved goodbye and exited into the restaurant.

# Chapter Thirty-six

"How's your chicken and dumplings?" Julius asked Bertie.

"It tastes like glue," Bertie said, her mouth full. "It's good if you like glue."

"My fried chicken is excellent," Miltie said, as he chewed on a drumstick.

"Guys, Miltie is going to be farting all the way to Council Bluffs," Bertie said. She gave Miltie a serious look. "Fried food makes you fart."

"Everything makes *you* fart," Miltie said.

"That's not true," Bertie said. "Pretty girls don't fart."

"That's what I say!" Polly exclaimed. She turned to Manny. "Isn't that what I say?"

"That's what you say, but that doesn't make it true," Manny replied.

"Polly knows," Bertie said. "Pretty girls don't fart and if they do fart it smells like lavender."

"Your farts smell like gorilla feet," Miltie said.

"Your farts smell like Limburger cheese," Bertie said.

Polly and Manny both laughed.

Rose got up from the table and walked out of the restaurant.

After a moment, Miri got up as well.

"Excuse me for a second," Miri said, adding, "don't

let them take away my chicken pot pie."

"Were they offended by our fart jokes?" Bertie said, worried.

"I don't think it's your fart jokes, Bertie," Frenchy said.

Miri found Rosa standing in the parking lot, her body wracked with heaving sobs, so intense she was almost hyperventilating. Her face, usually fair-skinned and freckled, was bright red. She looked like her head was about to explode.

Miri took her in her arms and held her. Rosa wept into Miri's shoulder.

"I can't stand it," Rosa blurted between violently gasping and bawling. "I can't stand it. I keep seeing it. I can't unsee it."

"I know," Miri whispered into her ear as she stroked her hair. "None of us can."

Rosa wept with renewed vigor.

Rosa had always been the most ebullient, boundaryless, joyful person Miri had ever known. The war had changed her – made her more serious and more thoughtful – but not that much. And she'd seen things during the war, as they all had – terrible things.

But the things they'd seen at Eden Hollow during "Operation Supreme Flood for America" – that was something else.

Miri knew exactly how Rosa felt. Miri felt the same way. She was just managing to tamp it down better than Rosa was. Miri imagined at some point she would break as well.

Rosa's body went limp, and Miri eased the two of them down to the curb, where they sat. Rosa flopped into Miri's arms.

A few people getting out of their cars looked over at them, and then hurried quickly away.

Miri knew Rosa's kind of sorrow.

There was nothing to do but wait until the weeping passed.

## Chapter Thirty-seven

Lenny was at a restroom urinal when the guy next to him, a tall man with a red beard, a beer belly, and arms as wide as telephone poles, looked down at him and said, "you're cut."

Lenny was confused. "Where?" he said.

"I mean you're circumcised," the man said. His voice was gravelly from too many cigarettes and too much whiskey. Lenny could smell both of them on his clothes and breath even over the smell of piss and disinfectant.

"Why're you looking at my wiener, dude?" Lenny asked.

"You a Jew?" he asked.

"About twenty-five percent of American guys are circumcised, bruh," Lenny said.

"Mostly Jews," the man said. "Or Muslims."

"Two-point five percent of Americans are Jewish," Lenny said. "About one percent are Muslim. You do the math."

"But what's the percentage in the Sovereign Republic?"

"I look like a statistician to you, buddy?" Lenny said. "It's a lot less than twenty-five percent, I can tell you that."

"You don't see a lot of circumcisions around these parts," the man said, not without menace in his tone.

"You spend way too much time looking at and thinking about other men's dicks," Lenny said, as he gave his own a shake and flushed the urinal.

"What are you implying?" the man said.

Lenny stepped away from the urinal, his *schmekel* still hanging out of his pants. "You want to take a good look to satisfy your curiosity, mister?" he said. "You want to do a scientific comparison of length and girth?"

The man's face turned redder than his beard. He quickly finished his business and hurried to the exit.

"Don't forget to flush," Lenny called after him. "And for the love of God, wash your fucking hands."

Outside the restaurant, Frenchy stood over Miri, who sat on the sidewalk holding Rosa, who was crumpled in her arms and sniffling.

"I got your left-over chicken pot pie," Frenchy said, holding up a doggie bag. "And your chicken and waffles, Rosa."

Rosa sniffled. "Did you get us dessert?" she said through a stuffy nose and hoarse voice.

Frenchy held up four more doggie bags. "I wasn't sure what you guys wanted, so I got you both double chocolate fudge Coca-Cola cake and peach cobbler," he said.

There was silence for a moment.

"Oh my God, cousin, I love you so much," Rosa said, sitting upright and wiping the tears from her cheeks.

"That goes double for me," Miri said. "Double chocolate fudge Coca-Cola cake, that is."

"I got plastic forks," Frenchy said. "Let's hit the road. We can eat in the car."

"What's this 'we'?" Rosa said. "You're not getting any of my cobbler."

## Chapter Thirty-eight

When they reached the van, Miri's heart seized when she saw the Sovereign Republic Homeland Security uniformed patrol officer standing beside a huge man with a red beard waiting for them.

"That's the guy," Red Beard said pointing at Lenny.

"Identification, please," the officer said. He was not as tall as Red Beard, but he was as tall as Frenchy. He wore a crisp uniform and black boots. He had a shiny black belt and a shiny holster in which rested a very large pistol.

"What's this about, officer?" Frenchy said, as he handed the cop his driver's license.

"Identification," the officer repeated.

Everyone handed him a driver's license. Polly and Manny handed him their school IDs.

"Passports?" the officer said.

"We don't need passports to travel domestically, do we?" Miri asked.

The officer looked at her with cold, expressionless eyes and held up her license as if to confirm she was the same person on the card. "That's a little convenient, don't you think?" he said.

"What's convenient?" Julius asked.

"A driver's license doesn't indicate your racial identity in the Sovereign Republic," the officer said.

"How is that relevant?" Artie asked.

"What kind of a name is Horwitz?" the officer said.

"It's German," Frenchy said. "It's the German pronunciation of the Bohemian Czech town of *Hořovice*."

"So, you guys aren't Jewish?" the cop asked.

There was silence for a moment as the question hung in the air.

Miri felt her heart go from seizing to sinking. She saw Frenchy and Lenny's fingers twitch and wondered if they were going to go for their weapons. She felt her own fingers twitch as well.

Miri glanced at Rosa. Her cousin-in-law was standing stock-still, her hands at her sides. No twitching. Staring at the cop.

Miri thought if violence erupted, it would be Rosa who drew first.

"I don't understand the question, sir," Frenchy asked.

"Is this about my wiener?" Lenny said.

The cop looked at him, stone-faced. "Sir?"

"Why aren't you interrogating that guy for staring at wieners in the rest room?" Lenny said, pointing at the Red Beard.

The cop turned to the Red Beard. "Is that what this is about?" the cop said. "Were you staring at wieners in the rest room?"

"He's circumcised," Red Beard said.

"Twenty-five percent of American men are circumcised," Bertie said.

"What's the percentage of men in the Sovereign Republic who are circumcised, though?" Red Beard said.

"I don't think they've compiled those statistics, yet," Manny said.

Frenchy held up his dog tags. "What's the percentage of folks with one of these?" he said. "Have you got one?" he asked Red Beard. He turned to the cop. "Have you?"

Lenny, Miri, and Rosa held up their own dog tags as

well for the cops and Red Beard to see.

The cop slowly looked at each dog tag in turn.

"If I run your licenses what's it going to tell me about your racial and religious classification?" he asked.

Everyone was silent again.

"It's not going to tell you anything," Rosa said. "Because driver's licenses aren't part of any database that tells you the driver's racial and religious classification. The only way to look that up is with our passport, which we are not required to travel with unless we are crossing borders."

"They're Jews," Red Beard whispered to the cop. "You know they are."

"It's not illegal to be a Jew," the cop said, as he handed back the driver's license. "It is illegal to be Jews who aren't heading to their designated Jewish Sector in the next forty-eight hours. I don't know where you came from or why you're here, but right now you need to be heading back to your addresses in Ohio. That means when you pull out of here, I need to see your van heading east, or else we're going to have to investigate this matter further. Am I making sense, or do I need to say it in Yiddish?"

"Do you speak Yiddish?" Polly asked.

"I don't speak Yiddish," the cop said. "You have forty-eight hours to report to your assigned Jewish Sector. Drive safely." He turned to Red Beard. "And you stop checking out wieners in the rest room."

"I was doing my patriotic duty," Red Beard grumbled.

"Forty-eight hours," the cop repeated, as he walked away with Red Beard.

Everyone stood there for a moment in silence, taking in this new development.

"You know," Polly said, "before the Maccabee revolt, some Hellenized Jews reversed their circumcisions."

"How do you even do that?" Manny asked.

"I'm not sure, Polly said. "But I bet it hurts."

Miri opened the side door to the van. "Climb in, kids," she said.

"Which direction?" Lenny said.

"East, I guess," Frenchy said.

"Back to Ohio?" Miri asked.

"Back to Chicago," Frenchy said. "Then south on Old Route 66."

Route 66, decommissioned in 1985, had been recommissioned about five years before the Collapse and the subsequent war in a nostalgic bid to try to unite a fractured America through a nostalgic reminder of shared history of roadside kitsch.

The bid at cultural re-unification had failed, but the highway remained.

"That'll be a longer trip," Miri said. "And we'll have to cross different borders."

"Maybe 66 is less heavily patrolled than I-80," Frenchy said. "Besides, I've always wanted to see the Cadillac Ranch in Amarillo."

As they pulled out onto I-80, now heading east, Miri connected her smart phone to the van stereo and played Bruce Springsteen's song "Cadillac Ranch."

## VII.

### **Frenchy:**

Driving through the night, we made it to Joplin, Missouri in ten hours on Old Route 66, making minimal pitstops for bathroom breaks.

Polly tried to make us stop at Ted Drewes Frozen Custard, but they had already closed for the night.

We finally pulled over to the Great Biscuit restaurant in Joplin, which was just opening for breakfast.

We sat around a big round table in the corner, and I picked up a couple of newspapers at the counter as well as a few local brochures to look for a place to stay while we figured out how to get over the border into Kansas and the Great Plains Agricultural Federation for eleven miles until Old Route 66 jogged into Oklahoma and the Free Republic of the Southwest.

I felt a little nauseated from all that driving and the lack of sleep, but I also felt ravenously hungry. I ordered the "Bigger Big Breakfast:" two eggs over easy, a sausage patty, three bacon strips, a smoked ham steak, potatoes, and a buttermilk biscuit with sausage gravy.

Miri, always a more sensible person than me, ordered two eggs, scrambled, with bacon and a buttermilk biscuit.

Polly ordered the "Bonut:" buttermilk biscuits dipped in French toast batter and fried, tossed in powdered sugar, topped with strawberries and bananas.

Lenny ordered the Three Car Pile Up, which was a giant pancake topped with eggs scrambled with sausage, bacon, mushrooms, peppers, onions, cheddar, and potatoes, served with hash browns and two buttermilk biscuits with sausage gravy.

Bertie ordered two eggs scrambled with a side of sausage patties and a biscuit.

Julius ordered corned beef hash and scrambled eggs

with a biscuit.

Artie ordered French toast with eggs and bacon.

Miltie ordered country fried steak and eggs with sausage gravy.

Manny ordered a bacon and cheddar omelet.

Rosa, for some reason, ordered chicken and waffles, the same thing she had eaten for dinner the night before.

I was getting a little worried about Rosa.

We all drank coffee, even Polly and Manny, despite my half-hearted protestations. The coffee was hot and strong. As I drank, I scanned the newspapers.

The death toll in the Supreme Flood for America was now estimated at around thirty thousand, with reports still coming in. Almost every Jewish-identified building in the Republic – synagogues, community centers, summer camps, museums, fraternal organizations, libraries – had been gutted by fire. Private homes had been set ablaze as well. It wasn't quite clear to me how widespread the arson against private homes had been, but every Jewish neighborhood had been attacked by arsonists to some degree.

The food arrived. I'd lost my appetite, but I picked at my food while I read the papers and drank my coffee.

I didn't share what I'd read. The rest of the family was enjoying their breakfast and engaged in robust conversation, mostly about how good the biscuits were. Miri put her hand on my arm and gave me a supportive squeeze. Sitting beside me, she could see the headlines.

In the local papers, I read that the one local synagogue in Joplin, which had stood for one hundred years, was now only cinders.

Everyone finished their meals except for me. I threw mine in a box and hoped wherever we stayed would have a fridge and a microwave. I could probably feed the entire family for a week on my leftovers alone.

## VIII.

We decided to stay at Tivoli Courts, an old -fashioned motor court just outside Joplin that had been closed after Route 66 was decommissioned but restored and reopened after the road had been recommissioned.

Most of the cabins were small, for a maximum of four people, but we were lucky that the one larger cabin in the motor court was vacant. Miri and I had a room together. Rosa, Polly, and Bertie had a room with three twin beds. Artie, Jules, Manny, and Miltie shared a room with two bunkbeds and a trundle bed upon which Lenny insisted he'd be just fine – it couldn't be more uncomfortable than a foxhole, he reasoned. We parked the Ford Transit in the driveway alongside the cabin and trundled in, every one of us exhausted.

There was a living room/dining room area, and a kitchenette. Sure enough, there was a fridge and a microwave. There was even an oven and stovetop. Everything was in vintage or faux-vintage (I suspected faux) decor to evoke the glory days of the Mother Road. There was a "Missouri Route 66" road sign on the wall. There was a Burma Shave series of signs that read "Hinky Dinky" "Parley Voo" "Cheer Up Face" "The War is Thru" . . . "Burma Shave."

If only that was true, I thought. If only the war was really through.

In the living room area, there was a large couch and a faux-vintage art deco television. The kitchen was likewise equipped with faux-vintage art deco appliances. There was even a washer and drier in a small laundry room (more of a laundry closet, but even so). Outside, there was a swimming pool for motor court guests to use.

I reminded everyone not to wear any Jewish themed swimwear if they wanted to use the motor court pool. Polly said that was the only kind of swimsuits any of them owned and anyway they had left them all behind at Eden Hollow. She asked if they could swim nude. I told her only if they could reverse her brothers' circumcision. She said she'd work on it. Manny went pale. I assumed she was joking, but just in case, I clarified that nude swimming in the motor court pool was not allowed, regardless. Nor was speaking Yiddish in public. This was not a meeting of the Eden Hollow Anarcho-Naturist Youth Brigade, after all.

If we had to stay here for a while, it was suitable enough, if we could buy some nondescript swimsuits somewhere. But I wanted to be over that border and out of the Sovereign Republic before the deadline to report to our designated "Jewish Sector" had arrived.

I stuffed my leftovers in the fridge. Rosa disappeared into her room. Artie, Lenny, and Jules disappeared into theirs. The four teenage Horwitz siblings plopped themselves down on the couch and immediately began arguing over who controlled the remote.

I schlepped into the master bedroom, dog tired.

The room consisted of a dresser, a king-size bed, and a small writing desk placed at a window. I could hear water running, and then I saw Miri standing naked in a doorway.

"Our bedroom has its own bathroom," she said, her hands on her big belly. "Let's take a bath."

She looked haggard and bedraggled, her hair an uncombed mess, deep purplish rings under her eyes.

She never looked more beautiful, I thought.


After that long drive, sitting in that hot water with Miri leaning against me, my arms wrapped around her, resting on her tummy, was the best thing ever.

"You know, other people know how to drive," Miri said, gently admonishing. "we can take turns."

"I wanted to get here quick," I said.

"You mean you wanted to be in control."

"Well, yeah," I admitted. "That too."

"You don't have to be in control all the time," Miri said.

"I feel like if I'm not," I said, "I'll just fall apart."

## IX.

We retired to the bed, and I drifted off for a bit lying with Miri in my arms, side by side. But all of a sudden, I was seized with panic and my eyes snapped open.

I was momentarily confused and disoriented. Light was still shining in through the curtains. I judged I hadn't been asleep for long. I checked my phone. I'd been asleep for about twenty minutes.

I was still dog-tired, but now my heart was slamming into my ribcage. I gently extricated myself from Miri's limbs and sat on the side of the bed, looking at my feet.

Then I stood up and got dressed.

On my way out, I again looked at Miri, lying there sleeping naked, the blankets tangled up in her arms, her leg thrown over them. I took a moment to appreciate her physique, her magnificently ample *tush*, the swooping curves of her body, her beautifully enlarged bosom and pregnant belly. Her gorgeously curly hair, her round cheeks, her delicate chin. I wanted to kiss her, but I was afraid of waking her up.

I went out into the living room.

The four teens were fast asleep with their heads back on the couch, the TV blasting news reports. I gently extracted the remote from Polly's grip without disturbing her slumber.

I looked at the TV and watched the crawl. The death toll of Operation Supreme Flood for America had reached fifty thousand. The deadline for Jews to report to their assigned sectors was ticking away in a digitized countdown in the corner of the screen.

On the screen flashed clips of fires in Jewish neighborhoods throughout the Republic. One zipped by and I thought I saw a street in Coventry Village. I wondered if our store on Coventry Road had been set ablaze. I wondered if our house on Balfour Court had been.

There were also reports of Jews stopped trying to cross the borders at Interstate 80 in both directions, as well as trying to flee to Canada by boat across the lake.

I thought of all the people we knew from Eden Hollow who had set out to make those very trips. I hoped against hope none of them were among those detained, even as I knew that was likely too much to hope for.

I clicked off the TV and quietly placed the remote on the coffee table before heading out the door.


I pulled into the Shady Knoll Manufactured Housing Community about fifteen minutes later. I followed the signs along treelined lanes until I found Thirteen Primrose Place. It was a nice unit, with a wooden deck, and flower beds with colorful flowers. I went to the door and rang the bell.

A shirtless White man wearing a baseball cap with the logo for the Joplin Blasters, a defunct minor league baseball team, appeared at the door. His right arm had been replaced by a prosthetic that was attached by a black strap which ran from his shoulder across his torso.

"Motherfucker," Hank "Gunner" Günther said. "Of all the trailer parks in all the Ozarks, you had to walk into mine."

"Glad to see you, too, Gunner," I said.

"Who is it, hon?" came a voice from within the mobile home.

"You better see for yourself," Gunner replied.

After a moment, Gillian "Gillie" Gilroy appeared, wearing a t-shirt with the logo for the Joplin Crusaders, a semi-professional football team with the Central States Football League.

"Well, I'll be fucked back, front, and sideways," Gillie said when she saw me.

"Hi, Sarge," I said, pleasantly surprised. "I hadn't expected to find you here."

This was true. I had no idea that Gillie and Gunner

were keeping house together. A more unlikely pair I could not imagine – a Black ex-soldier and an unrepentant White racist. Other than the alliteration of their nicknames and their missing limbs, I could not think of anything they had in common.

Except of course for the war.

Which I guess can change a person.

Even a person like Gunner.

Gillie gave me a powerful hug with her one arm, and I embraced her back with both of mine.

"I had not expected you to show up unannounced," Gillie said.

"Aren't you supposed to be headed to a Jewish Sector?" Gunner asked.

"We've got a day or so before anyone realizes we're no shows," I said.

Gillie and Gunner were both silent for a moment as they looked at me.

Then they looked at each other.

Then they both nodded.

Then they looked back at me.

"Well, you better come in," Gillie said. "Let's talk about finding a way to get you across the border."

## X.

A week later – well past the deadline to report to our designated Jewish Sector – we pulled up to the border checkpoint from Missouri to Kansas, and from the Sovereign Republic to the Great Plains Agricultural Federation.

We each had with us forged passports that identified us as White Lutherans of German descent. The passports used our real names but created new identities for us. We had also switched out our license plates. In case anyone ran them, we were assured, they'd back up our new identities.

We also had forged work papers: we were now a travelling family of musicians who specialized in American folk music, heading out to tour the Free Republic of the Southwest.

For some reason, Johnny Cash's song "The One On the Right Is On the Left," about a folk group with irreconcilable political differences among themselves, kept playing in my mind.

We also had two new passengers, also with forged passports.

One of them was Lucy Fischer. She was ten. The other was her little brother, Max, who was eight.

They had been orphaned in Operation Supreme Flood for America.

Gillie and Gunner had taken them in, but they wanted the Horwitz family to take them with us to get them out of the Sovereign Republic and find somewhere relatively safer. That had been their only condition for helping us with the passports.

By the time we drove up to the border, Polly had taken the Fischer siblings under her wing and was distracting them by teaching them harmony for Taylor Swift songs.

Gillie and Gunner hadn't done the forging themselves.

They didn't have that particular skill set. But they knew who did. Which I thought they might. That's why I had reached out to them for help in the first place.

Actually, that's why I reached out to Gunner, and I'd thought he would be a tougher nut to crack than he turned out to be.

With Gillie at his side, Gunner was a different person.

A better one.

Or at least he was trying to be.

Even so, I had to pay the forger – Gillie and Gunner couldn't get the job done for free and didn't have the cash themselves; nor would I have expected them to bear the cost. Those passports and work papers hadn't been cheap. My bag of money was significantly lighter than it had been before. And this was after the "family and friends" discount Gillie and Gunner had negotiated for us.


"Horwitz, Lieberman, and Fischer?" the Sovereign Republic Homeland Security Border Protection Officer said, as he examined our passports. "And you're Lutherans?"

We had kept our real names so they would match our driver's licenses. Max and Lucy, of course, didn't have driver's licenses, but we kept their real names anyway to make it easier to remember.

"We get this a lot," I said. "These are good German family names. A lot of Jewish names are just repurposed German names. There was even a Nazi official named Rosenberg, can you believe that? Alfred Ernst Rosenberg, look him up. Anyway, it leads to confusion. But we're all descended from good Lutheran German stock, all the way."

The Border Protection Officer lowered the sunglasses on his face. He looked about thirty years old, with dark hair and a strong chin. His border patrol uniform looked like an old-fashioned State Trooper uniform, with a wide-brimmed hat instead of a cap. The name on his badge read "Morgan."

"If you're Lutheran and musical and all that, I assume you can sing some Lutheran hymns?" he asked.

"Are you Lutheran, Officer Morgan?" I asked.

He shook his head. "I'm an Ozark Evangelical," he said.

"Well, we can just as easily sing something you might be more familiar with," I said.

And I began to sing "Down to the River to Pray."

My entire family immediately joined in. Even Lucy and Max knew the song and sang along.

Silly man, I thought. You thought a band of travelling Jewish-American folk musicians wouldn't know any traditional gospel songs?

The song goes like this:

> *As I went down to the river to pray,*
> *Studying about that good old way,*
> *And who shall wear the starry crown,*
> *Good Lord, show me the way.*
>
> *O sisters, let's go down, let's go down, let's go down,*
> *O sisters, let's go down,*
> *Down to the river to pray*

And then it repeats, exactly the same but switching out "sisters" for 'brothers," then "fathers," then "mothers," and, finally, "sinners." In our version, the last line swaps out "starry crown" for "robe and crown."

We sang the whole thing, with Polly, Rosa, Miri, and Bertie providing some gorgeous alto and soprano harmony.

We had, of course, learned the song from the version Alison Krauss sings on the *O Brother Where Art Thou?* soundtrack. But the Border Protection Officer didn't know that. Or, if he did, he was suitably moved by our rendition, nonetheless. By the time we finished, he was wiping a tear from the corner of his eye. So were the other border agents standing within earshot.

Officer Morgan handed us back our papers. "Go right on through," he said. "And good luck to you on your tour."

I saluted and drove on.

About a hundred feet on, after a sign that read "Welcome to Kansas and the Great Plains Agricultural Federation" we pulled into another border checkpoint.

"Passports, please," the woman said who came to my window. She was uniformed, but less militaristically than the Sovereign Republic Homeland Security Border Protection Officer. She wore a light blue shirt, black pants with a yellow stripe down the seam, and a light blue cap. She had a name tag that read "Blake." "She looked more like an old-fashioned milk delivery person than a border guard.

I handed her our passports and work papers.

She scanned the work papers. "You're headed to the Free Republic of the Southwest?" she asked.

"Yes, Officer Blake," I said.

"Border Supervisor Blake," she corrected me. "We're not a bunch of swinging dicks like your guys on the other side of the border."

"Well, they're not exactly *my* guys, but that sure is good to know," I said.

"You've only got thirteen point two miles in Kansas on Route 66 before you reach the border, all of it in Cherokee County," she said. "Enjoy your stay with us. We don't care what religion or race you are, as long as you don't scare the horses or molest the cattle."

"We don't do much cattle molestation where we're from," I assured her.

"You should know there's not a lot of law enforcement in these parts," she said. "We've got one of those 'constitutional sheriffs' who think the county, not the Federation, is the ultimate authority. Basically, what that means is that he doesn't enforce the law unless he feels like it. Since most of the highway bandits around here are his militia buds, he gives them wide latitude. Much too wide if you ask me. Or if you ask anyone who isn't a dipshit."

"How many highway bandits are there in Cherokee County?" I asked, the worry seeping into my voice.

She handed back our passports and papers. "Don't stop for anything outside of the designated tourist attractions until you're in Oklahoma."

"How's the law enforcement in Oklahoma?" I asked.

"Not great," she admitted. "They also have funny ideas about freedom, you ask me."

"'Freedom is not constituted primarily of privileges but of responsibilities'," I said. "Albert Camus said that."

"Whoever *that* is," she said. "We believe in responsibility in the Federation, too. Problem is, we don't have the manpower to manage the ones who don't. Like the Sheriff of Cherokee County. So, watch yourselves. I take it you're armed?"

I hesitated.

"Don't worry, we practice 2nd Amendment purity in the Great Plains Agricultural Federation," she said.

"We're armed," I admitted. "Every one of us, except the two little ones."

"They're allowed to carry, too," Border Supervisor Blake informed me.

"Good to know," I said, although I was flummoxed as to what kind of firearm a ten-year-old and an eight-year-old could safely carry.

"Well, lock and load, that'd be my advice," she said. "God bless and God speed."

It sounded like we were going to need it.

## XI.

Everything was fine until we got to the Brush Creek Rainbow Bridge.

We'd passed through Galena, the site of some pretty nasty labor troubles back in the thirties. Polly, who had spent the week in the cabin reading up on what to expect on our trip, pointed out "Cars on the Route," which used to be a gas station, and still had vintage gas pumps outside. Now it was a welcome center, and souvenir and sandwich shop. The kids screeched with excitement when they saw Tow Tater, a bedecked tow truck that was the inspiration for Tow Mater in the animated movie *Cars*. They begged me to stop so they could take a picture, but I demurred. I was anxious to get through the 13.2 miles of Cherokee County as quickly as possible. Polly led the kids in a rendition of the song "Route 66" (the version from the movie) to distract them from their disappointment. Lucy and Max knew all the words by heart.

My heart broke for those kids, but my heart also melted to see Polly suddenly take on seriously this new role of responsibility and nurture to these two traumatized children.

We went through Galena, a picturesque town packed with historic buildings, and onto Riverton, where we passed Nelson's Old Riverton Store, a colorful snack and souvenir shop.

Then we got to the bridge.

The Brush Creek Rainbow Bridge is the last surviving Marsh Rainbow Bridge on Route 66. It's a narrow concrete and steel truss design with two elegant arches on either side, painted white. It's only one lane, so motorists have to take turns crossing it from different directions.

As we pulled up to the bridge, a gaggle of four men

and two women, all of them in camo fatigues and carrying semi-automatic rifles, stood in our way. I hoped against hope they were officials assigned to direct traffic flow in both directions over the bridge, but I sort of didn't think so.

I pulled to a stop and rolled down my window. A man with a salt-and-pepper beard who looked like an extra in a post-apocalypse movie approached.

"You folks from out of town?" he asked, nicely enough.

"Yes sir," I said. "We're heading to the FRS."

"Always happy to host travelers through Cherokee county," he said. "You folks want to know a little history of the Rainbow Bridge?"

"We'd love to, but we're on a tight schedule," I said.

The man nodded understandingly. "I hear you, I hear you," he said. "Well, go right on through. As soon as we take care of the toll."

Of course, there would be a toll, I thought. This guy and his gang are bridge trolls.

"Guidebook didn't mention the toll," I said.

"It's for upkeep and whatnot," the man said, casually. "After all, it's a historic bridge."

"It sure is a beauty," I said.

The man looked admiringly at the Rainbow Bridge. "It sure is," he said. He turned back to me. "What we got here? Ten travelers?"

"You charge by traveler instead of by vehicle?" I asked.

The man ignored my question. "I count twelve. But we discount for minors. That's everyone under fourteen. So, that'll be one thousand."

I blinked as if I'd been slapped in the face. "Dollars?"

"Each," he said. "Five hundred each for the kids. That'll make it an even ten."

"Thousand?" I asked.

"Dollars," he replied.

I scratched my head. "Ten thousand dollars to cross a bridge?"

"It's a historic bridge."

I calculated how much money we'd have left if I paid this guy ten thousand dollars to cross a bridge.

It wasn't enough.

"You take checks?" I asked.

"Cash only," he said. He looked inside the Transit. "And your girls."

"Pardon?"

"Not the little one," he said. "Just the two teens."

"What do you want our girls for?" I asked.

The man grinned and slipped the rifle from his shoulder. "You know what we want them for."

That was when the top of his head exploded.

## XII.

"Down!" I cried. "Down on the floor, now!"

Shots were flying through the air. A headlight and our side mirror were both shattered.

Everyone got down on the floor of the van while I tumbled out the passenger side door, my pistol already in my hand.

Miri was already out, leaning over the hood, her pistol out.

It was she who had shot the toll man's brains out. An executive decision.

When her family is threatened, Miri doesn't fuck around.

Rosa and Lenny tumbled out as well, AR-15s in their hands. I crouched beside Miri. Steadying my weapon on the hood of the Transit, I shot one of the toll trolls in the face.

Lenny and Rosa came around the back of the van, fearless, and fired off shot after shot in quick succession. Two of the bridge trolls fell, shot through the chest.

I could hear bullets *thunk* into the side of the van and *crack* into the windscreen. The passenger side window by my head shattered. I fired again and shot a bridge troll in the throat. He dropped his gun, put his hands to his throat, and gurgled, choking on his own blood as he collapsed.

Miri shot one of the women, the bullet drilling a hole in her forehead.

The last guy started to run across the bridge away from us.

Rosa shot him in the back. He went down and didn't get up.

I stuck my head inside the van. "Is anyone hurt?" I demanded.

"Define hurt," Polly said, still lying on the floor with Lucy and Max.

"Any bullet holes?" I clarified.

Artie sat up and brushed glass off his shirt. So did Jules. Bertie sat up and brushed glass out of her hair.

One by one, Manny, Miltie, Polly, Max, and Lucy sat up and reported none of them had been hit by bullets and had managed to avoid getting broken window glass in their eyes.

They were all Ok, more or less. But of course, they were all traumatized, or retraumatized, especially the kids. Especially Lucy and Max.

"Ok," I said. "Let's roll."


We dragged the bodies out of our way and drove across the bridge.

Rosa finished off the bridge toll who had been shot in the throat, and was still alive, if only just.

Driving at top speed, we sped past Fort Blair, which had been attacked by Quantrill's Raiders in 1863. We passed the historic Phillips 66, a 1939 gas station restored to its original appearance and repurposed into a visitors' center. We drove through Baxter Springs and its vintage storefronts and murals depicting local history.

We finally reached the border. It couldn't have been more than a few minutes, but it felt like hours.

Polly held Lucy and Max tightly in either arm, softly singing them Taylor Swift songs, encouraging them to remain calm. They sniffled in the backseat but managed to tamp down the terror they were undoubtedly feeling as we pulled up to the checkpoint.

The Great Plains Agricultural Federation Border Supervisor, a young man in glasses with a wispy mustache, glanced at our papers and waved us through.

As we approached the checkpoint into the Free Republic of the Southwest a hundred yards further down the road, I could hear sirens, distant but getting louder as they approached.

The Free Republic border guard who took our papers was a Native American woman with a round face and straight, dark, lustrous hair. "Welcome to the Semi-Autonomous Quapaw Tribal Nation of the Free Republic of the Southwest," she said. She looked up into the distance as she became aware of the increasing volume of the siren. "You folks have any trouble along the way?"

"There was some confusion over a toll," I said. "And human trafficking."

She nodded, as if she understood all too well. "Go right on through," she said. "Don't worry, no Jayhawk 'constitutional sheriff' is going to chase anyone into the Quapaw Nation." She nodded to a machine gun nest atop a building off the side of the road, in which a young man, also Native American, manned a fifty caliber Browning. "About twenty minutes down Route 66 near the town of Miami there's a body and glass shop called 'Classy Chassis.' They can fix up the damage to your vehicle. Tell them Ardina Good Eagle sent you."

A sheriff's car was bouncing down the road towards us. Ardina Good Eagle waved us through. She nodded to the machine gunner, who fired a blast into the engine block of the sheriff's vehicle.

The Crown Vic came to a shuddering stop, steam pouring through the hood. The sheriff stepped out, angry as a nest of wasps, and whipped off his sunglasses for emphasis.

"God damnit, Ardina!" he shouted. "How many Cherokee County Sheriff vehicles does that make it now?"

"Howdy, Sheriff," Ardina Good Eagle said. "Welcome to the Semi-Autonomous Quapaw Tribal Nation of the Free Republic of the Southwest. Where're you going in such a hurry?"

# Chapter Thirty-nine

At Classy Chassis a buxom Native woman in her fifties looked over their car and said "I can fix it up for you in about five days. Got to order some parts. You folks got somewhere to stay? Spring River Cabins is nearby. They got a lodge you can rent with enough room for all of you. Or you can stay in one of the casino motels."

"I like the idea of a casino," Lenny said.

"The lodge sounds fine," Frenchy said.

"Vetoed again," Lenny said with a sad face. "Lodge it is."

"Tell 'em Luisa Difficult Woman sent you," the woman said. "Why'n't you drive up there and unload your things, then come back here? My husband can give you a ride back to the lodge."

"You don't have to do that," Frenchy said. "I can take an Uber or something."

"Don't insult our hospitality," Luisa Difficult Woman said, pleasantly enough. "We try to be neighborly around here."

"Well, I surely appreciate it," Frenchy said.

Situated on a bluff in the woods, the lodge was rustic and homey, with quilted bedspreads and Quapaw blankets and weavings hung on the wall. It had a kitchen and several bathrooms. It had beds everywhere, including in the living room area, but at least there were enough for them all. It had a wooden deck overlooking the river.

They unloaded all the gear, including their instruments. Somehow, the instruments had survived the shoot-out, although there were several dents in Artie's harp caused by bullets.

Then Miri and Frenchy went grocery shopping. After the groceries were unloaded, Frenchy drove the Ford back to the Classy Chassis.

Polly took Lucy and Max out on the deck. Despite the summer heat, there was a coolness in the shade of the woods and from the cool river water flowing by.

"People seem nice here," Lucy said. "Maybe we can stay here."

"Maybe," Polly said. "I don't know. Maybe they're so nice because they know we're just passing through. Frenchy and Miri still think California's our best option."

"Will Mom be in California?" Max said. He was having a hard time accepting the death of his parents.

Polly didn't know how to answer him.

Trying to distract Max, she pulled a travel brochure she had picked up in the auto shop out of her back pocket. "Hey, once the car is fixed, you guys want to stay here?" she said. She laid the brochure on the patio table and flattened out its crumbled pages. "It's called 'The Blue Swallow.' It's a vintage motel."

"What's a 'vintage' motel?" Max asked.

"It's an old-fashioned motel," Polly said.

"Why don't they call it that?"

"I don't know," Polly admitted. "But look. It's got one hundred percent refrigerated air."

"What's that mean?" Lucy said.

"That's just a fancy way of saying it's air-conditioned."

"Why don't they just say that?" Max said.

"They think the fancy way of saying it is more vintage," Polly explained. "Look, each room has its own garage so we can park right next to our room. And each room is decked out with vintage furniture and appliances."

"There's that word again," Max said. He was cheering up a little. The brochure was filled with colorful photographs that seemed to take his mind off things.

"Look at the TV!" Lucy said, pointing to a photograph of an old-fashioned TV in a wooden cabinet.

"Why do they put the TV in a box?" Max asked. "Is that vintage?"

"That's how TVs used to look," Polly said. "They used to look like furniture. And look at that." She pointed to a photograph of a boxy thing with a big dial on the front. "Know what that is?"

"No, but I bet it's vintage," Max said.

Polly laughed. "You're right about that, it is vintage. It's a vintage radio."

"You can really listen to the radio on that thing?" Lucy asked.

"I mean, I think you can," Polly said. "I think everything works. It's not just for show."

"But it's also for show," Lucy said.

"Well, sure," Polly said. "That's the whole vintage aspect. Look at this." She pointed to another picture. "You know what this is?"

"Another radio?" Max asked.

"It's a phone," Polly said. It was a picture of a big, black, rotary dial phone.

"That looks nothing like a phone," Lucy said.

"That's what phones used to look like," Polly said. "And you know what else? You couldn't even listen to music or watch movies or play games on them. All you could do was make phone calls."

"What about text?" Lucy asked.

"Not even text."

"Things must have been so boring back when it was vintage," Max said.

"Well, to us it probably would be," Polly said. "But to folks back then, everything here was state-of-the-art. You know what 'state-of-the-art' means? It means brand new. Oh, look here." She pointed at another photograph. "That's a vintage refrigerator. And that's a vintage stove."

"They look like space-ships," Max said. The appliances were decked out with sleek chrome adornments.

"That was the idea," Polly said. "Everybody made things look like spaceships then to show how brand new everything was."

"Why is The Blue Swallow all vintage now?" Lucy asked.

"Well, this road we're on, Route 66," Polly said, "they used to call it 'The Mother Road.' That's because it was one of the first roads to connect so much of America. This was back when America was one country, of course. Back in the Before Times. Before it got split up into a bunch of broken places. Way before you guys were born. Route 66 opened in 1926 when they started the first Federal highway system, and if you think about it – cars had only been around in big numbers for a little while then, since 1908 when Henry Ford made the first Model T factory. So, that's eighteen years. My brother Artie is only a little older than eighteen. Think about that. Before then, they didn't have any road that could take you all over the country. Just trains on railroad tracks. But then with Route 66, all of a sudden, they did have a road that connected America – or at least Chicago to Santa Monica. And when people started to travel Route 66, folks along the way made a whole bunch of crazy attractions and places to stay to entertain people, because it was a long trip – over two thousand miles. And cars were slower then. So, roads like Route 66, they united the United States – they helped make us one nation instead of just a bunch of different places inside the same country."

Max and Lucy furrowed their brows while they thought that over.

"Then why didn't we stay that way?" Max asked. "Why didn't we stay just one nation?"

Polly took a deep breath and let it out slowly. The question felt painful, and it hurt to try to think of an answer for it.

"The truth is, Max," she said, "I'm not sure anyone really knows."

# Chapter Forty

When Frenchy arrived back at the lodge, Polly, Manny, Lucy, and Max were busy playing with a garden hose out front, spraying each other with water. Polly and Manny had on the non-descript swimsuits they had bought at a Target so they could swim in Tivoli Courts pool as they waited for their forged papers. Lucy and Max, who evidently had lost any swimsuits they once owned in the pogrom that killed their parents, played in shorts and t-shirts.

Frenchy made a mental note to buy them both swimsuits once they got their transportation running again.

On the deck, Rosa stood, looking into the distance, a haunted expression on her face. She stood there completely naked and seemingly oblivious to her surroundings.

Frenchy wondered for a moment if Rosa was trying to re-start the Eden Hollow Anarcho-Naturist Youth Brigade. Rosa now wore the scars of her wartime service on her body -- as did Frenchy, Miri, and Lenny.

But Frenchy quickly decided this was something other than an effort to revive the Youth Brigade.

"There's a natural sandy beach area on the river down that hill," said Samuel, Luisa Difficult Woman's husband, when they pulled up to the lodge and he observed Frenchy's family, both the kids and Rosa. "If you all want to go swimming, that's the spot. Current's gentle, so you should be Ok, and you don't get a lot of folks this far upriver, you can expect some privacy."

Frenchy thanked him and climbed up the stairs to the deck. He went to Rosa and stood beside her.

"Cos?" he said. "You Ok?"

Rose continued to stare into the distance.

"You want to help me make dinner?" Frenchy asked.

Rosa turned to him. "Sure," she said, with none of her usually brightness. "I'd like that very much."

Frenchy put his hand gently on her arm, led her into the house, and they started to make dinner.

They spent five days in the lodge, walking the trails, skipping rocks on the stream. Miri and Frenchy did most of the cooking, which was a little bit like feeding an army. In the evenings, they played music and sang songs together. Max and Lucy were already talented singers. Polly taught them both how to play ukulele.

On several occasions, Frenchy found Rosa standing naked on the deck, staring out into space. He wanted to ask her what she was looking at in her mind's eye, but he thought that she probably didn't want to tell him.

He asked his siblings to keep one eye on Rosa at all times. He was getting a little concerned.

When their van was ready, Luisa Difficult Woman delivered it to the lodge, with her husband following in a tow truck with the Classy Chassis logo on the side. Frenchy and Miri paid them and invited them to stay for dinner. He promised to get the family to dress for the occasion, but Luisa Difficult Woman insisted that would not be necessary.

It was taco night, and Luisa Difficult Woman joked

that Frenchy made respectable tacos for a White guy.

Polly thought how ironic it was that in the space of about twenty-five miles the Horwitz family had gone from not-White to White again.

The next morning, they resumed their journey.

In Catoosa, they drove past the famous Blue Whale wooden structure which had been restored and now served as a roadside attraction and swimming platform. Lucy and Max went bananas and wanted to swim, but Frenchy was insistent on not stopping until Amarillo.

As they drove through Tulsa, Polly thought about the Tulsa race massacre of 1921. That event had been scrubbed from their school curriculum, but her parents had told her about it, and the Horwitz family had books on the subject in their home library.

The massacre had destroyed Tulsa's "Black Wall Street," and destroyed the prosperity of Tulsa's thriving Black community. There had been similar massacres throughout the country during the early 1920s. So, Operation Supreme Flood for America was not unique in American history. It was just that the targets of attacks like that shifted from time to time.

In Oklahoma City, just past the "Golden Driller," a statue of a roughneck standing beside an oil derrick, they drove by a new statue – one of Timothy McVeigh, the late-20th century terrorist. A sign read:

**Timothy McVeigh**
**Hero of the Free Republic**
**Striking the First Blow Against**
**The Zionist Occupied Government Entity**
**April 19, 1995**
**"Independence Day"**

McVeigh had also been scrubbed from her school's history curriculum, but Polly knew about him from her parents and from the books they kept on their library shelves. April 19, 1995 was the day McVeigh blew up the Alfred P. Murrah Federal Building in Oklahoma City. It wasn't totally clear to Polly how a mass murderer like McVeigh, who had killed one hundred and sixty-eight people, including nineteen children in a day care center, had become a hero in the same town where he had committed that atrocity. She supposed the extremist libertarian anti-government sentiment in the Free Republic was strong enough that a guy like him was now considered a liberator instead of a villain.

Polly also knew that McVeigh had been inspired in his act of terror by the book *The Turner Diaries*, which depicted with celebratory enthusiasm the mass murder of Jews and non-Whites.

So, maybe not everyone was so nice in Oklahoma after all.

Four hours later, they pulled into the parking lot at the Lone Star Republic Steak Ranch and Saloon in Amarillo, Texas.

"My name's Sally and I'll be your server today," said the nice waitress in a spotless red, white, and blue uniform as she approached to take their order. She looked about forty and Polly thought she seemed like she had been born waitressing at the Lone Star Republic Steak Ranch and Saloon. "Where you folks from?"

"We're from the Sovereign Republic," Frenchy said.

"My oh my, but I heard you folks been having a mess of trouble up there lately," she said. Her expression took on a troubled caste. "I seen some things I can't unsee on the interwebs."

So, Izzy Friedman's reports had gotten out, Polly thought. Frenchy had told Polly all about it but refused to let her see the pictures. It was good the truth was out, but Polly doubted it would make much difference.

"It seemed like a good time to take a road trip," Miri said. "Show the youngsters some of America on Old Route 66."

"Well, you folks enjoy yourselves," she said. "Here in Potter County, we don't care what religion you practice, as long as you don't spook the Texas Longhorns."

"The livestock or the football team?" Polly asked.

The waitress Sally smiled. "Why ain't you just a peach?" she said. "I suppose don't spook either one just to be safe. And take care when y'all get to Deaf Smith county. They got one of them 'constitutional sheriffs' there, which means he can enforce the law any old way he sees fit. If you stick to the speed limit going through there you should be Ok. And there ain't no speed limit in Deaf Smith. Can I get you folks a round of drinks?"

"Sweet tea all around, I think, mostly," Frenchy said. "Unsweetened for me."

"Unsweetened for me as well," Miri added.

"I'll have a Texas Amber Ale," Lenny said.

"You folks need a minute for your lunch orders?" Sally asked.

"What's this I hear about a seventy-two-ounce steak challenge?" Lenny asked.

"Well, now, you got one hour to eat a baked potato, shrimp cocktail, dinner salad, a dinner roll, and a seventy-two-ounce steak," Sally said. "If you can finish it all in an hour, the meal is free. But you gotta eat it all, not just the steak."

"I can do that," Lenny said.

"I don't want to be stuck in a van with you farting all the way to Tucumcari," Julius said.

"I don't fart," Lenny said.

"You sure do," Artie said. "You fart like a skunk ape after a meal at White Castle."

"I'll have the steak sandwich," Lenny said, his fighting spirit draining away.

"He'll have unsweetened iced tea instead of a beer, too," said Frenchy to Sally. "He might need to take a turn at the wheel."

"Ain't no freedom in the Free Republic when you travel with my brother, Sally," Lenny said, handing her the menu. "Unsweetened iced tea it is."

The rest of the family ordered steak and chicken quesadillas, cheeseburgers, chicken strips, buffalo burgers, steak sandwiches, and plentiful sides of fried pickles. Max ordered the Roy Rogers – four steak fingers with cream gravy -- from the kid menu, and Lucy ordered the Annie Oakley grilled cheese sandwich on Texas toast.

"You think we have to worry about Deaf Smith's sheriff?" Rosa asked.

"Not as long as we keep to the speed limit," Lenny said.

"And if he pulls us over, we'll tell him we're Lutheran," Miri said.

"That's our story," Julius said. "And we're sticking to it."

"All the way to California," Artie said.

# Chapter Forty-one

Outside of Amarillo they stopped at the Cadillac Ranch.

Polly thought the display, ten vintage, tail-finned Cadillacs planted nose-first in the ground and covered in graffiti, looked more like a junk yard turned on its side than anything else. The guidebook said the Cadillacs were planted in sequential order, with models ranging from 1949 to 1963. Polly couldn't tell one from the other, though. She didn't know from Cadillacs.

"It looks like Stonehenge," Max said.

"The cars are set at the same angle as the Giza pyramids," Lucy said. She must have got that from the same guidebook, Polly thought.

Polly had brought her ukulele, and equipped Max and Lucy with one each in addition. They had been working on this song together for a while.

"Ready?" Polly said. "And a-one, and a-two, and a-three!"

Polly, Max, and Lucy launched into Springsteen's song "Cadillac Ranch." Frenchy, Miri, and Artie seemed delighted. Everyone else seemed moderately amused.

Soon, the entire Horwitz clan and Rosa were singing along.

There were only three other tourists nearby, but

they stopped to listen and seemed to enjoy themselves. Two of them applauded when the performance finished.

One of them glared at them.

He was a young man about Frenchy's age, with a buzz cut, long sideburns, and a t-shirt that read "Impeach Earl Warren."

Polly wondered if he even knew who the long-dead Earl Warren had been.

"Why you singin' that Zio song?" the young man asked, taking a toothpick out of his mouth.

Frenchy looked at him in silence for a long time. Polly surmised her oldest brother was deciding if fight or flight was the best course of action.

"We're Lutheran," Lucy said.

"And Springsteen's not Jewish," Bertie said.

"With a name like that?" the young man said.

"A common misperception," Rosa offered.

"It's actually a Dutch name," Artie said. "His family came from Holland when America was still a Dutch colony. His ancestor John Springsteen fought in the War of Independence against the British."

"And we're Lutheran," Lucy repeated.

"Not from around here?" the young man said.

Lenny stepped forward. "You got something you need to get off your chest, buddy?" he asked, pugnaciously.

Frenchy put a hand on Lenny's shoulder to restrain him.

Polly was pretty sure Lenny could take this guy, but she wasn't sure getting into a fist fight at the Cadillac Ranch was the best way to lay low on their way to California.

The girl standing beside the guy put her own hand on the guy's shoulder. She looked barely older than Bertie. She was short and blonde and had a pretty, moon-shaped face with big eyes that made her look like a blonde Bettie Boop.

"Come on Billy," she said. "Why you gotta get all up in other people's business all a' the time?"

"I was just curious is all," Billy said, seeming to relax. He nodded at the Horwitz family. "You folks have a nice day." He put the toothpick back between his teeth.

Billy and Betty Boop wandered off, arm-in-arm, gazing at the Cadillacs.

The third person, a man of about thirty with the same haircut as Billy but also a goatee, said to them, "I apologize for my brother. He's had a few too many Red-Bulls today."

"It'll happen," Frenchy said. "Lenny here's had a few to many ice teas."

Billy's brother nodded understandingly and rejoined Billy and Betty Boop.

"That's what they call Texas hospitality," Miltie said.

"Maybe he's not from Potter County," Manny said.

"Maybe he's from Deaf Smith," Julius suggested.

"Let's hit the road, Horwitz family singers," Frenchy said. "No sleep 'till Tucumcari."

## Chapter Forty-two

In Deaf Smith County, they began to see signs on service stations and motels that read "No Blacks, Mexicans, Indians, Dogs, or Jews."

That's the thing about libertarians, Polly thought. They won't pass laws against Jews, but they won't pass laws preventing anyone from discriminating against them, either.

"Good thing we filled up the gas tank," Frenchy said.

"I hope no one has to pee," Lenny said.

"I have to pee," Bertie said.

"I've had to pee since Amarillo, and your nephew spends all day pressing against my bladder," Miri said. "Hold it until New Mexico."

Just before they reached New Mexico and the town of Glenrio just over the border, they were stopped at a checkpoint.

A deputy sheriff with a badge in the shape of the Texas Lone Star and a nameplate that read "Wallis" stepped to the driver side window. He was tall and rangy, with a strong jaw and a pair of mirrored sunglasses that hid his eyes. He had a big revolver on his hip. Polly didn't know from guns, but she thought it might have been a 44. Magnum, like the kind Clint Eastwood used in the *Dirty Harry* movies.

Polly liked *Magnum Force* the best of all the *Dirty Harry* movies. She thought that was the one that held up best.

"Passports," the deputy said, gruffly.

Frenchy handed him their passports. "I didn't think there were border checks within the Free Republic," he said.

"We do things our own way here in Deaf Smith," the deputy said. He slid the glasses down his nose, revealing icy blue eyes. "You have a problem with that?"

Polly saw Lenny stiffen in the seat in front of her and saw his arm move, ever so slightly.

She assumed he was putting his hand on his pistol. She crossed her fingers and gritted her teeth, hoping Lenny wouldn't escalate things.

"No problem here, Deputy Wallis," Frenchy said, pleasantly.

The deputy looked over their passports.

"You folks aware there's a bounty out on fugitive Jews from the Sovereign Republic?" the deputy asked.

Polly felt her heart freeze in her chest.

"We don't know anything about that," Frenchy said. "You guys enforce Sovereign Republic bounties here in Deaf Smith?"

"We do what we have to," the deputy said, vaguely.

"Well, in any case, as you can see from our passports, we're Lutheran," Frenchy said.

"We can sing you a Lutheran hymn," Bertie said. "If I can pee, first."

"I can do better, I think," Polly said, as a notion seized her. She grabbed her ukulele and began to play and sing "I'm A Good Old Rebel."

The song was an old post-Civil War song from the point of view of an unreformed, treasonous former Confederate soldier. It was a disgusting song, shocking

in its unrepentant anti-reconstructionist ideology,
although it had a catchy tune:

> *O I'm a good ol' rebel,*
> *Now that's just what I am.*
> *For this "fair land of freedom"*
> *I do not care a damn.*
> *I'm glad I fought against her,*
> *I only wish we'd won,*
> *And I don't ask no pardon*
> *For anything I done.*
>
> *I hates the Yankees nation*
> *And everything they do,*
> *I hates the Declaration,*
> *Of Independence, too.*
> *I hates the glorious Union -*
> *'Tis dripping with our blood -*
> *I hates their striped banner,*
> *I fit it all I could*
>
> *I hates the Constitution,*
> *This great republic too,*
> *I hates the Freedmans' Buro*
> *In uniforms of blue.*
> *I hates the nasty eagle,*
> *With all his braggs and fuss,*
> *The lyin' thievin' Yankees,*
> *I hates 'em wuss and wuss.*
>
> *I rode with Robert E. Lee*
> *For three year near about,*
> *Got wounded in four places*
> *And starved at Point Lookout*
> *I cached the rheumatism*
> *A' campin' in the snow,*

*But I killed a chance o' Yankees*
*And I'd like to kill some mo'.*

*Three hundred thousand Yankees*
*Is stiff in Southern dust,*
*We got three hundred thousand*
*Before they conquered us.*
*They died of Southern fever*
*And Southern steel and shot,*
*I wish they was three million*
*Instead of what we got.*

*I can't take up my musket*
*And fight 'em now no more,*
*But I ain't going to love 'em,*
*Now that is sarten sure,*
*And I don't want no pardon*
*For what I was and am.*
*I won't be reconstructed,*
*And I do not give a damn.*

*O I'm a good old rebel,*
*Now that's just what I am.*
*For this "fair land of freedom"*
*I do not care a damn.*
*I'm glad I fought against it,*
*I only wish we'd won,*
*And I ain't asked no pardon*
*For anything I done.*

*I ain't asked no pardon*
*For anything I done*

When Polly finished, there was silence all around for a moment as the song hung in the air.

The deputy cleared his throat.

"You folks drive safe now," he said, his voice cracking, choked with emotion, as he handed back the passports.

Frenchy waved amiably as they drove past the checkpoint and over the border into Glenrio, a former ghost town that had revived with the restoration of Route 66.

"Where'd you learn that song, Polly?" Miri asked once they had crossed.

"Mom and Dad have an old CD in their collection, *Songs of the Civil War*," Polly said. "Hoyt Axton sings it. He also sings 'The Yellow Rose of Texas'."

"Oh!" Bertie said. "I love *that* song!"

Bertie began to sing, and they all joined in, even Max and Lucy, who somehow knew the song:

> *There's a yellow Rose in Texas*
> *That I am gonna see*
> *Nobody else could miss her*
> *Not half as much as me*
> *She cried so when I left her*
> *It like to broke my heart,*
> *And if I ever find her*
> *We never more will part*
>
> *She's the sweetest little rosebud*
> *That Texas ever knew*
> *Her eyes are bright as diamonds*
> *They sparkle like the dew*
> *You may talk about your Clementine*
> *And sing of Rosa Lee*
> *But the yellow Rose of Texas*
> *Is the only girl for me*
>
> *Where the Rio Grande is flowing*
> *And the starry skies are bright*

*She walks along the river*
*In the quiet summer night*
*I know that she remembers*
*When we parted long ago*
*I promised that I'd return*
*And not to leave her so*

*She's the sweetest little rosebud*
*That Texas ever knew*
*Her eyes are bright as diamonds*
*And sparkle like the dew*
*You may talk about your Clementine*
*And sing of Rosa Lee*
*But the yellow Rose of Texas*
*Is the only girl for me*

*Now I'm going back to find her*
*For my heart is full of woe*
*We'll do the things together*
*We did so long ago*
*We'll play the banjo gaily*
*She'll love me like before*
*And the yellow Rose of Texas*
*shall be mine forever more*

*She's the sweetest little rosebud*
*That Texas ever knew*
*Her eyes are bright as diamonds*
*And sparkle like the dew*
*You may talk about your Clementine*
*And sing of Rosa Lee*
*But the yellow Rose of Texas*
*Is the only girl for me*

"Can I pee now?" Bertie asked, as Frenchy pulled into a service station in Glenrio.

"I second that emotion," Miri said to Frenchy. "Your kid has been tap-dancing on my bladder since Wildorado."

# Chapter Forty-three

Tucumcari boasted of two thousand motel rooms, and not one, as far as they could see, denied entry to Blacks, Mexicans, dogs, or Jews.

They had to book several rooms at the Blue Swallow to accommodate them all. Max and Lucy asked to sleep in the same room as Polly.

Max and Lucy were excited by the room's vintage décor. After watching some television on the vintage set, they joined the family for dinner at nearby Del's Restaurant, which had a plastic cow atop its sign and served really good Mexican food.

When it came time to retire, Max and Lucy crawled into Polly's bed with her, rather than sleep in their own.

Polly was Ok with that. These kids had been through a lot.

Of course, so had they all. But at least Polly was a little older than Max and Lucy, and maybe could handle it better.

Not much better.

But maybe a little.

They got a good night's sleep in Tucumcari. After a hearty breakfast at Kix on 66, they hit the road once again.

They had seven hundred and five miles and ten hours and twenty minutes, give or take, to California.

After six hours and one bathroom and refueling break in Albuquerque, passing through high desert by Nine Mile Hill, through a landscape of red, black, purple, and brown, through the valley of the Rio Puerto, crossing the river over a steel bridge and into the Laguna Indian Reservation, driving by tall mesas, crossing the San Jose river and into the town of Laguna, passing an old Spanish mission, over the Continental Divide, and twenty-six miles past the neon heart of Gallup, they crossed the border into Arizona.

Polly recognized the scenery from the movie *The Grapes of Wrath*, directed by John Ford and starring Henry Fonda. It looked almost the same now except in color instead of black and white, but with the same powerful red sandstone cliffs alongside the road. A sign identified this stretch as the Will Rogers Highway, which Polly thought was interesting, since Will Rogers was politically liberal, and the Free Republic of the Southwest was definitely not.

The scenery was also different from the movie in that the road over the border was lined with gas stations and garish tourist shops, which had not existed when the Joads crossed this same stretch of highway.

They stopped for lunch in Lupton at the Route 66 Railway Café. A sign above the counter inside read, "Be Nice or Leave."

This was much preferable to "No Blacks, Mexicans, Dogs, or Jews," Polly thought.

They passed Petrified Forest Republic Park and the Painted Desert. At Holbrook, Max and Lucy proclaimed their desire to sleep in a teepee as they passed the Wigwam Village, but Polly explained to them they were hoping to make it all the way across Arizona and into California before they stopped for the night.

They passed the Geronimo Trading Post and later the Jackrabbit Trading Post near Joseph City. The route gave way to high desert grassy hardpan and creviced arroyos. Polly was glad for the Transit's air conditioning.

They passed the ruins of the town of Two Guns, where there once had been a zoo.

They passed through Winslow, and everyone began to spontaneously sing "Take it Easy" by the Eagles. As they sang, Polly wondered on which corner Jackson Browne and Glenn Frey had been standing when they saw the girl in the flatbed Ford.

Beyond Winslow, they passed the ruins of the Twin Arrows Trading post, with giant plastic arrows still marking the spot, and later went by Meteor City, resisting another outcry from Max and Lucy to stop and see the meteors. The landscape gave way to pine forest as the road hugged the old Santa Fe railroad tracks.

They went by Winona and took a bathroom and refueling break at Flagstaff, then continued their journey alongside more pines in the Coconino National Forest. At the foot of the Bill Williams Mountain, they passed through the town of Williams. They ignored the signs to take the Grand Canyon Railway to see one of the natural wonders of the world and kept going. Polly wished they could have taken that ride, which was on an old steam train. She resented the world for the danger and inhospitality that forced them to keep going.

They passed through the dazzling Route 66 kitsch of Seligman, and stopped for a dinner break at Kingman, about an hour from the border.

Polly noticed something that disturbed her as they entered Kingman, however. The sign welcoming them said Kingman was the seat of Arpaio County. She had thought it was Mohave County. She realized the county must have been renamed for Joe Arpaio, who had called himself "America's Toughest Sheriff." Polly didn't know much about him, since he was at best a minor figure in American history, but she remembered he had been emblematic of a hardline anti-immigrant philosophy and had also been a convicted criminal for, among other things, racial profiling, abuse of prisoners, and using the power of his office to target political opponents and reporters.

They ate at Rutherford's 66 Family Diner, then drove through Kingman, past the beautiful scrub and rocky landscape of the Sacramento Valley and up the steep grade of the Black Mountains. They drove through the former gold mining town of Oatman, where wild burros roamed the streets.

The road ran through yucca, mesquite, and greasewood, to the Colorado River Valley.

When they arrived at the river crossing into California, they discovered the border was closed until morning. So, they drove north to the outskirts of Bullhead City, until they found the Sunrise Motel, where they booked rooms for the night.

Polly was again joined by Max and Lucy, who crawled into bed with her. They fell asleep watching a movie called *Raising Arizona* on television. Polly thought the movie was pretty funny, but even she fell asleep before the end.

XIII.

## Frenchy:

"The border opens at six in the morning," I said, as Miri and I lay together in the queen-sized bed in our room at the Sunrise Motel. "We'll be there right when it opens. We'll find somewhere to eat in Needles."

"If we're going to apply for asylum at the border, we should eat before we cross," Miri said. "There's a lot of paperwork involved, and it could take a while before we're processed."

"Ok," I said. "Does the motel offer a continental breakfast?"

"This place?" Miri said. The motel was clean, but definitely no frills. "I doubt they have coffee."

I thought it over. "I'll get up earlier than everyone else and get some breakfast to go at that joint across the street," I said. "We can eat on the way. It's about half an hour to the crossing. That should be enough time."

We watched a little TV before going to bed. *Raising Arizona* was on one of the channels, which is a great movie, but I was anxious to get some news.

The death toll of the Supreme Flood for America had now exceeded one hundred thousand. Photos and footage had gotten out and the massacre was being condemned by the United Democratic States, the Great Plains Agricultural Federation, and the Mountain States Federation.

The White Christian Confederacy of the Nazarene Nation praised the killing spree effusively.

Perhaps most disturbingly, the Free Republic and the Cooperative Commonwealth were both conspicuous in their silence.

At four in the morning, I woke up, showered, dressed,

and went across the street to The Burrito Barn, which was just a shack on the side of the road with a take-out window and picnic tables set in the shade of an awning. It was already hot in the Mohave at five in the morning when the joint opened.

I ordered breakfast burritos and coffee for the adults, juice for the kids. They put the food in a paper bag and the drinks in two oversized cardboard drink carriers with handles. I could just barely manage it all.

As I turned to cross the road, I saw half a dozen men in the parking lot.

Polly, Max, and Lucy were with them, still in their pajamas. The men were leading them, with hands on their shoulders, to a black van.

I didn't know what was going on, but it didn't look promising.

All my instincts ripped into overdrive. I dropped the food and coffee in the road and began to run towards the men and their van, drawing the pistol on my belt from under my t-shirt, holding it two handed in front of me as I dodged traffic. Cars screeched to a halt as I ran in front of them, their horns blaring. But at least they stopped. With all the rugged individualism around those parts, one never knew.

A man with his hand on Polly's shoulder saw me and smiled as I neared. Calmly, he cut his head to his right hand, showing me his own pistol, which he casually pointed at Polly's back.

I slowed down, but I continued in his direction, keeping my gun trained on him.

"That's far enough, soldier," the man said, in a calm, even voice.

He looked about thirty. His hair was cut short, and he wore neatly trimmed sideburns. He wore a grey t-shirt without any logo. He wore polished cowboy boots that poked out beneath the cuffs on his jeans.

The rest of his crew wore the same outfit, more or less,

like a uniform of sorts. Beside him was a red-haired man with a baseball cap supplementing his wardrobe. Probably a good idea, given the relentless Mohave sun and his fair, freckled skin. He looked younger, I thought, maybe early twenties. He held a pistol with one hand, pointed at Max. He held Max's hand in the other, in an almost fatherly manner.

Beside him, a large man with his chest and arms bulging out of his grey t-shirt stood with a hand on Lucy's shoulder and another wrapped around a thirty-eight-caliber revolver that almost disappeared into his meaty hand. He was bald on top but wore a horseshoe mustache on his face and a soul patch on his chin. He wore no hat, and his shiny bald pate glistened in the sun.

Next to him, a small, muscular woman of about thirty with hair cut as short as her comrades' and a tear-drop tattoo on her face stood with a huge revolver, a Ruger Super Redhawk, all out of proportion to her compact frame. Her arms rippled with tightly coiled muscles, like a diamondback ready to strike.

If it came to it, I thought, I'd kill her second, right after I took out their leader.

Whoever that was.

In front of the van stood two more of this child-napping commando team. One was a tall, gangly guy with a scraggly mustache and a cigarette in the corner of his mouth, whom I took to be the driver. He held a cut-down shotgun outfitted with a pistol grip. Beside him stood an equally tall and gangly woman, also with close-cropped hair, hers blond. She held a snubbed nose thirty-eight.

I was trying to figure out who their leader was, so I'd know who to shoot first.

I was leaning toward the guy who had spoken initially.

## XIV.

"I've got papers authorizing me to take the Horwitz family into custody, but I'm assuming you don't really care about that, do you?" said the guy who had spoken first, pressing his pistol into Polly's shoulder.

He was definitely the leader, I thought, and he'd be the first one I killed if it came to that.

"Who are you?" I asked, politely enough. I didn't think I could avoid bloodshed in this situation, but I felt I should try. I was seriously outnumbered, and I wasn't sure I could take them all out with sufficient rapidity, so a peaceful solution was optimal . . . if unlikely.

"All we want to do is exercise our legal responsibility to bring you back to the Sovereign Republic," the man said.

"You have no legal authority here," I said.

"Want us to call the Sheriff and ask him what he thinks about that?" the man said, with a smirk. "You willing to test that proposition with the constitutional sheriff of Arpaio County?"

"You let those children go and drive away from here and we can act like this never happened," I said.

"I've got a better idea," he said. "Why don't you gather your tribe and come to us, unarmed, in five minutes and we can get on with this? You know how this is going to end, right? There's no way this works out in your favor unless you cooperate."

"You want money?" I said. "I can get you money."

"Whatever you own is mine already, Mr. Horwitz," he said. "I need you to see that so we can get through this as easily as possible."

"I'm not making this easy for you no matter what, cowboy," I said.

The man sighed. "I wish you wouldn't take that attitude," he said.

Polly bent her leg at the knee and kicked him in the shin as she spun and grabbed his gun-hand.

Polly wasn't a fighter, but we all had been trained in self-defense, even the youngest ones. She twisted his hand with both of hers wrapped around his fist.

I saw the look of pain on the man's face as Polly's strength had surprised him.

This was going to end one of two ways. He was going to drop the pistol, or he was going to kill Polly.

I decided for a third option.

I shot him in the forehead.

He grunted as the bullet punched through the back of his skull and splattered brain, bone, and blood in a grey and red mist behind him. The glass from a van window behind him shattered.

I spun and fired two more rounds in quick succession. The first one left a hole where the red-haired man's face had been. He dropped into a tangle of limbs onto the parking lot, as the second round punched through the big man's mouth and out the back of his head. He fell like a tree, and I felt a tremor in the pavement under my feet when he landed.

I hadn't yet killed the woman with the tear-drop tattoo and the Ruger Super Redhawk. I'd decided my first shots had to be aimed at the kidnappers who held guns to the kids. But I knew this put me in a bad spot.

I dropped to one knee as Polly grabbed Max and Lucy and pulled them both to the pavement.

Sure enough, the woman with the tear-drop tattoo was raising her Ruger at me. I raised mine in response, but my heart froze as I realized I might be too late.

Then I heard two snaps of pistol fire behind me, and the tear-drop tattooed woman's eyes bulged as a bullet caught her in the throat. At the same moment, a round struck the gangly driver in the chest. His cut-down clattered on the cement as he slid down the van's exterior and came to a stop in a sitting position. The life went out of his eyes even as the cigarette continued to smolder in the corner of his mouth.

The blond woman stood there, glancing at her fallen comrades, unsure of her next move.

I shot her in the chest and saved her the trouble of having to decide.

Miri and Rosa appeared beside me, their nine-millimeters in their hands. Lenny was right behind them, also armed.

Rosa was nude, as she had been that time on the deck at the lodge, and she had the same distant, haunted look in her eyes, but all I really cared about at that moment was that she was armed and that she fired her gun in the right direction.

"That was some good shooting and quick-thinking ladies," Lenny said. "I wasn't even out the door when you made those shots."

The tear-drop tattoo woman was the only one of the kidnappers still alive. She held her throat and gurgled, choking on her own blood.

Rosa went to her, looked down at her, and kicked her Ruger Super Redhawk away from her with her bare feet . It clattered as it spun out of sight beneath the black van.

Then Rosa shot the tear-drop tattoo woman twice more, once in the chest and once through her tear-drop tattoo.

The tear-drop tattoo woman stopped gurgling.

Artie and Jules had joined us by now, also armed. Manny, Miltie, and Bertie followed.

"Oh," Bertie said, looking at the carnage. "That is *so* gross."

Polly held tightly to Max and Lucy, who were clearly traumatized, but too terrified to cry.

"Rosa, you better at least put on some shoes," Lenny said. "There's broken glass all over the place."

Miri turned to me. "We need to get across that fucking border, now," she said.

I looked at our breakfast and coffee, lying in the road,

as a pick-up truck went by and ran it all over.

"Maybe they'll at least give us coffee while they process our application," I said, hopefully.

## XV.

We sped the twenty-five minutes to the border, then slowed down as we approached, to do our best to look like model citizens.

I handed the border guard our passports.

"You guys enjoy your stay in the Free Republic?" asked the border guard. She was a woman of about thirty, with auburn hair. She wore a simple uniform of a tan shirt and dark pants with a gun on her hip and a rifle on her shoulder. She had a wide-brimmed hat, like a park ranger, and wore dark glasses.

"Sure did," I said. "Especially the Lone Star Steak Ranch House in Amarillo."

"You folks try the seventy-two-ounce steak challenge?" she asked, as she looked through our passports.

"I wanted to, but my siblings said it would make me fart all the way to Arizona," Lenny chimed in from behind me.

The border guard laughed, continuing to peruse the passports. "You know," she said, "there's been reports of bounty hunters going after Zios escaping from the Sovereign Republic."

"I hadn't heard that," I said. "Well, we're no bounty hunters."

She looked at me and slipped her dark glasses down her nose. She had green eyes. "Yeah, I don't make y'all for bounty hunters."

"We're not Jewish either," I said.

"We're Lutheran," Max called out from the back seat.

"Says so right on our passports," I said.

"Yeah, well, we don't put people's religions on their passports here in the Free Republic," she said. "That's just disgusting. 'Course, we're not big fans of the Zionists, either. But that's not the same thing."

I wanted to ask her if she was sure of that, but all I did

was nod.

"Surely is a shame what happened up in your neck of the woods," she continued. "Last I heard, the dead numbered close to a hundred and fifty thousand."

"That sure is a lot of dead folks," I said, feeling my heart race and my stomach roil. I hadn't yet heard this revised figure.

"Sure is," she said, sadly, and pushed her dark glasses back up her nose and handed me back the passports. "Well, you folks drive safe, now. Come and visit us again real soon."

"We sure will," I said, as I put the car in gear and waved goodbye.

We crossed the Old Trails Bridge, which had been returned to use as a highway bridge when Route 66 reopened. It was the same bridge the Joad family used to cross into California in *The Grapes of Wrath*.

"This is where the Joads almost tipped over," Polly said, recalling that scene from the movie.

"You think we can finally get B'nai Mitzvah-ed in California?" Manny asked.

"You think they'll give us refuge in California?" Miltie asked.

"They have to," Miri said. "They've got an open-door policy for asylum seekers. Plus, my parents live here, which means I have a right to resettle here and you all have a right to come with me, because you're all my family."

"Even me?" Max asked.

"Even me?" Lucy asked.

Miri smiled sadly. "Including you guys," she said. "You guys are part of our family now."

We were silent for a moment.

"Maybe I can finish my music studies," Artie said.

"Maybe I can be like Billy Joel and get a job as a piano man somewhere," Lenny said. "Playing for real-estate novelists."

"I would support you in that more than if you take up boxing again," Jules said. "Boxing is for dummies."

"That's why I do it," Lenny said. "It's perfect for me."

"You said it, not me," Jules said.

"Maybe we can go back to school," Bertie said. "I always wanted to grow up to be a high school graduate."

"We have schools in California," Miri assured her.

"With girls' lacrosse?"

"Definitely."

"You know what I was thinking?" Polly said.

"No Polly, none of us are mind-readers," Manny said.

"I was thinking, you know how God is supposed to have made and destroyed nine hundred and seventy-four worlds before he finally settled on one? And how, like, I thought he should have kept trying because our world kinda sucks?"

"Ok," Bertie said. "What about it?"

"Well, what if that story isn't totally right?" Polly said. "What if God didn't destroy the previous worlds, just set them aside? And what if our world isn't the last try? What if our world is just one of the failed efforts, and that's why our world is such a broken one?"

Everyone was silent for a second thinking that over.

"So, where do we find this more perfect world where we're supposed to live?" Rosa asked. "California?"

Bertie shrugged. "Maybe," she said. "California's worked out all right for the Jews before. You know Hollywood and all that. Even if they're sour on the Zionists."

I could hear sirens distantly as I pulled up to the border guard on the California side.

"Welcome to the Cooperative Commonwealth of Pacifica," she said. She looked about forty, with blond hair, and a uniform similar to the border guard on the Arizona side, right down to the park ranger hat, the dark glasses, the pistol at her side, and the rifle on her shoulder.

"Thanks," I said. "We'd like to apply for asylum."

The border guard lowered her sunglasses and scrutinized me. "You folks on the run from all that craziness in the Sovereign Republic?"

The sound of the sirens was getting louder.

"We are," I said. "Among other things."

The border guard looked into the distance, towards the sound of the sirens.

"I don't know who is after you, but they're not crossing into the Cooperative Commonwealth," she said, slipping her rifle off her shoulder. She pointed behind her. "You see that building about a hundred yards down that way? You pull over there and tell them what you told me. You'll have a shit ton of paperwork, but they'll take care of you. Hope you had breakfast already."

"We tried," I said. "But we were interrupted."

She looked at me, pityingly. "Well, maybe they can get you all coffee and donuts or something."

The siren was even louder now.

"Cash! Suri!" she called. "Get over here! We're expecting a visit from the Arpaio County Sheriff."

Two additional border guards, an older man and a younger woman, stepped from a booth just beyond the bridge, slinging their own rifles off their shoulders. They were dressed in the same uniform as their comrade.

"I hope we haven't started a war," I said.

"This happens all the time," she said. "They come up here, we tell them to go back, they stomp their feet. It's just for show. Those 'constitutional sheriff' types are just a bunch of swinging dicks." She looked at me again. "You folks have a nice day now."

"Thank you," I said. "We will."

I drove past her toward the building she had pointed out, an old brick house at the side of the road.

Miri fiddled with her smart phone and played Elvis Presley's version of Chuck Berry's song "Promised Land" through the Ford's stereo.

Everyone began to sing along.

We pulled over to the building and I put the Transit into park.

I waited until the song was over before turning off the engine.

"I hear they don't exactly love Jews in the Commonwealth," Manny said.

"But maybe they don't totally hate us, either," Polly said.

I nodded and opened the door and stepped outside. One by one, the Horwitz siblings, my cousin Rosa, my wife Miri, and Lucy and Max climbed out of the van.

"Let's go inside and find out," I said.

# Part Nine: World 974 – The Insalubrious Promised Land

## XVI.

The room where they reviewed our asylum application wasn't exactly inviting, but at least it was clean. The furniture looked new. The lighting was simple industrial neon, like a classroom, but at least it worked. The walls were of the same red brick as the exterior of the building, which seemed to somehow keep the room relatively cool against the heat of Needles, California.

While we were filling out our paperwork, a news crawl on the TV in the waiting room informed us that the death toll of Jews or presumed Jews from Operation Supreme Flood for America had now reached two hundred thousand.

Our application officer, a woman in her thirties with dark hair pulled back on her head, a drab tunic not unlike the kind worn in China after the revolution, and a name badge that read "Brooks," took Miri and me into an interview room and then while we sat there, took her time reviewing the paperwork that we'd spent hours filling out for each member of our family – me, my wife Miri, my brothers Lenny, Jules, Artie, Miltie, and Manny, my sisters Polly and Bertie, and the kids we'd taken under our wing after their parents were murdered, Max and Lucy. Although the wait was excruciating, I took it as a good sign that she bothered to review it so thoroughly.

"Well," she said, finally, looking up at us as she took off her reading glasses. "On the face of it, you appear to have a strong application."

"We hoped after the pogroms in the Sovereign Republic, you'd see it that way," I said.

Brooks held up a finger as if to stop me. "We don't use the term 'pogrom'," she said.

This confused me.

Miri said, "what else would you call a coordinated attack against Jews from the Ohio to the Missouri Rivers and from the Great Lates to the border of Tennessee? A dance party?"

Miri's sarcasm alarmed me. I worried it would not help our cause. But, unlike the rest of us, she'd been born in California, before it became the Cooperative Commonwealth, and as such had a citizenship claim that could not be disputed. So, she probably felt a little more leeway to call them out on their bullshit.

"The word 'pogrom' suggests a special status conferred upon Jewish victims of this kind of violence," Brooks said. "But such violence isn't special, unfortunately, and to suggest it is puts Jewish claims of persecution above those of genuinely marginalized groups."

"What are you talking about?" Miri said, her anger rising. She put her hands on her pregnant belly – she was by now just past her due date – her face twisted with emotion. Her voice quavered when she next spoke. "Two hundred thousand Jews were just murdered in the Sovereign Republic out of a population of eight hundred thousand. That's a quarter of the Jews in Ohio, West Virginia, Kentucky, Illinois, Missouri, Michigan, Wisconsin, Minnesota, Iowa, and Western Pennsylvania combined. My family barely escaped with our lives. That's not *marginalized* enough for you?"

"I don't mean to minimize what happened," Brooks said.

"Excuse me," Miri countered. "But I think you do."

"In any case, the problem we have here is that under Commonwealth law, Jews are excluded from refugee status, regardless of the circumstances," Brooks explained.

Miri and I both sat there for a moment in utter silent bafflement.

"Agent Brooks," I began.

Brooks held up a hand. "'Citizen Brooks', if you please," she said. She smiled. "We're all 'Citizen' here in the Commonwealth."

"How lovely," Miri grumbled. "All citizens but for the Jews."

Brooks frowned. "Native born Jews are full citizens, the same as everyone else." She smiled at Miri. "That includes you, Citizen Bernstein."

"Horwitz," Miri said.

"The Commonwealth does not recognize the practice of a woman taking her spouse's name."

Miri resoundingly slapped her palm against her forehead. "So, I'm a citizen, but not my husband?"

"Your husband and his siblings are a different matter, yes."

"Why?"

"White Jews are historically and today the oppressors of all subjugated peoples," Brooks said.

" *White* Jews?" Miri scoffed. "In the Sovereign Republic, we stopped being *White* years ago."

"European Ashkanormative Jews are descended from Khazar converts and have no middle-eastern genetic heritage whatsoever," Brooks said.

Miri wobbled to her feet, one hand on her belly, the other pointing at

Citizen Brooks with Semitic vehemence. "That is a lie! That is a racist, antisemitic lie!"

"Cooperative Commonwealth policy is scrupulously anti-racist," Brooks insisted.

"Except when it comes to the Jews!" Miri shouted.

"Antisemitism is not racism," Brooks said. "It is objectionable, of course, but it is not racism, because Jews are not a race."

"Being Jewish is not a choice, Citizen Brooks," Miri said through clenched teeth. "It is something we are born to."

"It is a religion," Brooks said. "Religion is a choice."

"It is a religion, a culture, a nation, a people, and, more to the point where racism comes into play, an *ethnicity*," Miri snarled. "Test my DNA if you don't believe me."

"In any event, Cooperative Commonwealth policy is

scrupulously not antisemitic," Brooks said.

"My head is going to explode!" Miri declared. "You don't get to be *not* antisemitic by just *saying* you're not antisemitic! You have to actually *be* not antisemitic!"

"Citizen Bernstein, you are free to go anywhere you like," Brooks said. "Back to your parents if you wish. Mr. Horwitz – "

"Not 'Citizen' Horwitz?" Miri demanded.

"He's not a citizen."

"He's not a citizen in the Sovereign Republic, either."

"We are not the Sovereign Republic."

"Really, Citizen Brooks?" Miri said. "From my perspective, the only modification is that you couch your antisemitism in a different style of rhetoric."

"Citizen Liebermann is free to join her parents, who are citizens of the Commonwealth," Brooks said. "Mr. Horwitz and his siblings will have to be deported."

Miri turned pale. "You can't send them back to the Sovereign Republic."

"They will be escorted to the border."

"The Free Republic of the Southwest is only marginally better."

"Where they go from there is up to them."

"Where they go? There is nowhere *to* go! Don't you get that?"

"This hearing is concluded," Brooks said.

"I'm not leaving my husband," Miri said.

"You are free to stay or go as you please."

"You're a fucking fuckety fucker, Citizen Brooks," Miri declared.

"Thank you for your time," Brooks replied.

Liquid suddenly gushed out of Miri's sundress and onto the floor, soaking her sneakers.

Miri put her hand on her belly. "Oh shit," she said.

"Oh shit," I repeated.

"Oh shit," Brooks agreed.

Miri looked at me, wide-eyed.

"My water broke," she said.

## XVII.

Miri gave birth to a healthy baby girl.

We considered naming her for my mother, who along with my father had been "disappeared" and not heard from since.

But in the Ashkenazi tradition, babies are usually named after deceased, not living, family members. Although I had, by now, come to fear the worst for my parents, to name our daughter after my mother at this point felt like giving up the last vestige of hope; accordingly, we named her Emma Golda Horwitz, after our favorite female Jewish anarchist, Emma Goldman, and our favorite female Israeli Prime Minister, Golda Meir.

To their credit, the border officials did not send us to some ramshackle refugee clinic, but to a proper hospital with a proper maternity ward. It wasn't pretty, but it was clean and well equipped, and the staff was excellent.

I was sitting in Miri's room, sunshine streaming in through the window, as my wife breast-fed our daughter, when Citizen Brooks walked in.

"Mazel Tov," she said.

I was as surprised by her congratulations as much as by the fact that she knew the Yiddish and Hebrew phrase.

"Are you here to inspect my episiotomy?" Miri asked, scornfully.

"No, but now that you mention it, I suppose it's good that you had a girl," Brooks said. "Since genital mutilation is outlawed in the Commonwealth."

It took me a second to catch up with that. "By which you mean, circumcision, I assume?" I asked. "Does this apply to your Muslim residents as well?"

Brooks ignored the question. "In any case I have some good news for you," she said. "As the proud parents of a brand-new citizen of the Commonwealth, you are now both legally entitled to stay, along with the rest of your family."

Miri frowned. "That's why you were so eager to get us back across the border in a hurry," she said. "You were afraid of our anchor baby."

"What about Max and Lucy?" I asked.

"Under the circumstances, as their de facto guardians, they are now considered your common-law adoptees, and you are entitled to keep them."

"Keep them?" Miri said. "They're children, not *tchotchkes.*"

"All we need for you is to fill out some paperwork," Brooks said. She started handing me papers. "We have forms to turn over all your cash, assets, and property to the Commonwealth –"

"All of it?" I interrupted.

Brooks looked up at me as if confused. "We are the *Cooperative* Commonwealth, after all."

"Sounds more like highway robbery than cooperation," Miri said.

"We need to keep our musical instruments," I said.

Brooks looked at me in bewilderment for a moment. "Well, since you're all musicians, the Commonwealth will of course provide you with instruments to practice your trade."

"We need *our* instruments," I insisted.

Brooks considered the notion. "I think that can be arranged," she said. "The state can loan you back the instruments on a permanent basis."

"How kind of you," Miri said, not at all sincerely.

"And, of course, the same will apply to your vehicle," Brooks said. "Your clothing will be confiscated, and you will all be provided with the standard citizen's tunic."

The "citizen's tunic" appeared to be the all-purpose civilian uniform that Brooks wore, and which apparently was mandatory attire for Commonwealth citizens. It was drab and deeply unstylish, but high fashion was hardly my primary concern.

"Anything else?" Miri said, irritably, as she switched

Emma to her left breast from her right.

"Just the standard denunciation of the colonial settler White supremacist Zionist ideology," Brooks said.

Miri and I were both silent for a moment, staring at her dumbfounded.

"Do you mean we're to denounce Political Zionism, Practical Zionism, Synthetic Zionism, Labor Zionism, Liberal Zionism, Revisionist Zionism, Religious Zionism, Revolutionary Zionism, or Reform Zionism?" Miri asked.

"Those distinctions are meaningless," Brooks said.

"They most certainly are not," Miri insisted. "You may find them inconvenient, but that does not make them meaningless."

Brooks furrowed her brow. "Are you refusing to sign the standard denunciation?"

"Do you ask any non-Jews to sign such a document?" Miri asked.

"Why would we?"

"The form is a violation of the Commonwealth's own constitution, which requires equal protection under the law," Miri said. "You cannot demand this of Jews if you do not demand it of gentiles."

"But it only applies to Jews."

"Which violates the equal protection statute."

Brooks was silent as she contemplated the dilemma.

"I can take this to the asylum committee and have them review it," she said. "But in the meantime, you'll have to reside in a displaced persons municipality."

"You mean an open-air prison?" Miri said.

"No," Brooks said. "That's what your people constructed for Gaza."

This enraged Miri. "*Our people?*" she shouted. "Blaming American Jews for the actions of a government not their own in another country is antisemitism 101. You're blatantly admitting you don't view Jews as equal citizens, as you are required to do under the law. Do you use the racist term 'Zios' as well?"

"We do not use that term, but it is not a racist term, because Jews are not a race and it refers to Zionists, not Jews," Citizen Brooks said.

"Your declaration for us to sign literally conflates all Jews and all Zionists," Miri said. "Which was KKK Grand Dragon David Duke's intent when he popularized the word back in the day. The term 'Zio' is racist as hell, and you know it."

"You and your daughter are free to join your parents or go anywhere you like in the Commonwealth," Brooks repeated. "The rest of you will have to reside in the displaced persons municipality."

"Unless we sign the declaration?" I asked.

"Signing the declaration would certainly improve your overall situation, but, no, you'd have to go to the displaced persons municipality regardless," Brooks said. "As non-citizens without refugee status but father to a citizen, you and your family cannot be deported from the Commonwealth but may only reside in a displaced persons municipality. Only Citizen Bernstein and your daughter are free to go where they like, as well as your cousin because she has citizen parents living in the Commonwealth, as they became naturalized before the restrictions of refugee status became codified."

"By which you mean *Jewish* refugee status," Miri said.

"Be that as it may," Brooks said.

"I'm not going anywhere without my husband and our family," Miri insisted.

"I can arrange for you to join them in the displaced persons municipality," Brooks said, gathering up her paperwork and hurrying towards the door. "Thank you for your time."

## XVIII.

"I didn't know you cared about Zionism so much," I said.

"It's not the Zionism," Miri said, softly, so softly I knew she was really, really furious. There's nothing scarier than Miri in her quiet fury. "I'd feel the same way if they told me to denounce Johnny Cash."

"Johnny Cash I might have a problem denouncing," I said. "Otherwise, I couldn't care less what dog and pony show I have to put on to keep our family safe."

"It's the principle of the thing ."

"I'm willing to compromise principles for refuge," I said.

"I'm not," Miri said. "This is the land where I was born."

"I want both Jews and Palestinians to live in peace, security, and self-determination in their historical mutual homeland as well as everywhere else in the world, the same thing I want for everybody – including us," I said. "Does that make me a Zionist? I don't even know what they mean by Zionist."

"They mean 'Jew' when they say 'Zionist,' Frenchy. But we have a right to live here no matter what they say or what they mean by it."

"They don't seem to feel that way."

"Fuck them."

I took a deep breath. "Ok," I said. "Fuck them."

"I'm going to fight them on this, Frenchy, I'm going to fight them to my last breath. As a citizen of the Commonwealth, I have a right to petition a court of law for redress."

"You sure the courts aren't fixed?"

"I'll keep fighting them until we find one that isn't," Miri said.

I knew better than to argue.

"I hear the refugee camps are nice in the

Commonwealth," I said.

## XIX.

"Nice" might have been too strong a word but I guess we could have done worse.

The displaced persons settlement was located near Santa Barbara, so at least the weather was agreeable, an improvement over the Japanese internment camps in California during World War Two, which were in general located in places in which the weather was less amenable.

The houses were simple and no frills, but solidly built, pre-fab houses on concrete-slab foundations. They were built for families, so at least we weren't forced into dorms or barracks. They weren't large, so Artie, Jules, and Miltie shared one room, Bertie and Rosa (who, like Miri, had refused to sign the denunciation and had opted to stay with us rather than reunite with her parents) shared another, and Polly, Manny, Max, and Lucy shared another. Miri and I and baby Emma shared another. Each house had its own toilet facilities, although shower, laundry, kitchen, and eating facilities were communal. Meals were eaten in a community dining room. The residents prepared their own meals, but the government provided the food, which was not always kosher. The Horwitz family doesn't keep kosher, but I suspected with so many Jews, some of the others in the camp would, or try to.

We were not all Jews in the camp, but most of us were. We were mostly secular or Reconstructionist or Reform or Conservative or otherwise non-Orthodox , but there were definitely some *Haredim* as well. It was my understanding that some of our non-Jewish fellow inmates were common criminals or "political criminals." It wasn't clear to me what constituted a political crime in the Commonwealth. I was a little nervous to find out.

The streets were unpaved, but the camp was laid out like a proper town, on a grid system. The streets were numbered, and the avenues were named Noam Chomsky

Boulevard, Hugo Chavez Avenue, Robert Mugabe Concourse, Yasser Arafat Way, Maximilien François Marie Isidore de Robespierre Concourse, Che Guevara Thoroughfare, and Ilich Ramírez Sánchez Drive. In the middle of it all was an avenue simply called Main Street that included a commissary, a library, a dining hall, a post office, and a community center.

There were schools for grades K through 12. There was a large grassy park with a gazebo and picnic tables. There was a sports center with basketball and tennis courts, a soccer field, a running track, and a community swimming pool.

The swimming pool had a sign indicating that only naked, mixed gender swimming was allowed. There was some kind of confusing language about how this supposedly facilitated "gender equality." The same was true of the showers.

People could avoid the swimming pool, of course, if they were uncomfortable with the arrangements, but the showers were another matter. That was likely a big problem for the *Haredim*.

Not so much for the Horwitz family. Those of us who served in the war had experienced far worse. Polly and Rosa even celebrated the reformation of the Eden Hollow Anarcho-Naturist Youth Brigade.

There were no churches, synagogues, mosques, or other houses of worship.

We turned in all our property and clothing, but we were allowed to keep our musical instruments as long as we promised to play one free concert a week for the residents. We were supplied with the same drab "citizen" tunics as Citizen Brooks had worn.

I found it an odd thing that the most fashionable clothing in the Commonwealth so far had been worn by the border guards.

"Do you think we can finally get our B'nai Mitzvahs,

now?" Polly asked me. bouncing on the balls of her feet, as we stood outside our new home after settling in. The freshly painted door behind us gleamed in the sunlight. I could hear the faint sound of children playing in the nearby park and smell blooming flowers from the window boxes in every house.

"Religious services are not allowed in the Commonwealth," said a woman of about forty as she approached. She was tall and had dark hair streaked with gray pulled back on her head. She had a surprisingly youthful, even cherubic, rounded face. She wore the same drab, genderless tunic we all wore. "I'm Rabbi Zelensky."

I shook her hand. "It must be a drag being a Rabbi when you're not allowed to conduct religious services," I said.

"We have a work-around," Rabbi Zelensky said. "We insist they are cultural celebrations. The Commonwealth has a strict policy of non-interference in cultural celebrations."

"So, we can get our B'nai Mitzvahs, finally?" Polly asked.

"I think we can work something out," the Rabbi said.

"How do you find things here?" I asked, staring past the streets at the high walls topped with barbed wire that penned us in.

"See those guard towers?" the Rabbi said, pointing at the towers that lined the walls at regular intervals. "The guards atop them are armed with radios, but no weapons. If we attempt an unauthorized exit, they will alert the authorities, but won't try to stop us."

"So, we can escape if we want to," I said.

"We can," Rabbi Zelensky agreed. "But the police would soon intercept us and bring us back here. And besides, where would we go? We'd be fugitives in the Commonwealth. Compared to the Before Times, this place stinks. Compared to everywhere else now?" She shrugged. "We could do worse."

"That's always been my hope for the future," Polly said,

wistfully. "That we could do worse."

I turned to the Rabbi. "How do we address you?" I asked. "Are we allowed to call you Rabbi? Or is it only 'citizen'?"

"We're not considered citizens, so you don't have to call me 'citizen'," Rabbi Zelensky said. "But technically, I'm not allowed to serve as a Rabbi, either. I can use 'Morah' since that's simply the feminine for 'teacher' in Hebrew. But everyone just calls me 'Sarah'."

"Pleased to meet you, Sarah," I said.

"Welcome to the 'Cooperative Commonwealth of Pacifica Displaced Persons Temporary Settlement Area'," Sarah said. "We call it the 'Green Acres Gulag'."

A crackly loudspeaker suddenly erupted into a garbled announcement.

"Dinner is served," Sarah said. "Hope you don't keep kosher, because that's not an option."

"We don't," I said.

"But it'd be nice to have the choice," Polly grumbled.

One by one, the rest of the family – which now officially included Max and Lucy -- filed out of our assigned house.

"Sarah, this is the gang," I said. "Gang, this is Rabbi Sarah."

I'd decided to say "fuck all" to the rules and call her "rabbi." Besides, "rabbi" can also be translated as "teacher."

After everyone introduced themselves, Manny asked, "what now?"

"Now," I said. "We eat. Tomorrow . . ." I shrugged. "We'll see."

And with Rabbi Sarah leading the way, we marched off to the communal dining hall on Main Street for our first meal in our new – and hopefully, temporary -- home.

It was better than being murdered in our beds back in the Sovereign Republic.

But that wasn't a terribly high bar.

I couldn't imagine living the rest of our lives here. I

certainly couldn't imagine raising Emma here.

I was still optimistic enough to believe we wouldn't have to.

Maybe we could even hold out hope that our parents were still alive and that one day we would be reunited with them.

Maybe, just maybe, despite present circumstances and all available evidence to the contrary, we could hope for a future that would be better than "it could be worse."

On balance, there were crazier things to hope for.

## The End

# A Note on Eden Hollow

Although the Eden Hollow Health and Nature Outdoor Recreation Association Family Bungalow Community, where the Horwitz family are lifetime members, is fictional, the history and philosophy of its founding is not without precedent. A vegan, anarcho-naturist community really was founded by Yiddish-speaking refugees from the Lower East Side in 1917 in New Jersey:

> **Portnoy, E. (2024, March 12). *The Naked Vegan Tolstoy of the Lower East Side.* Tablet Magazine.**
> https://www.tabletmag.com/sections/history/articles/the-naked-vegan-tolstoy-of-the-lower-east-side

# About the Author

Peter Ullian is the author of the Amazon-bestselling collection, *Pulp & Circumstance,* as well as the novella *The Why & the Yes or A Quarantine with a View* and the post-apocalypse cli-fi novel, *The Last Electric House*, all of which are published by Swamp Angel Press.

He is also the author of the Science Fiction & Fantasy Poetry Association's Rhysling Award-nominated poem "Nixon's Planet," subsequently included in the SFPA's 2019 anthology. His short story, "The Vietnamization of Centauri V," was published in the DAW Books anthology *Star Colonies.* His Amazon Short, "To Repair the World," received over 200 five-star reader reviews. Peter is also the author of the short stories "The Sun Sets on the Hall of Justice," published in the anthology *Crimeucopia -- Say What Now?* from Murderous Ink Press; "Ribbons and Tin" and "Owen's Blood," both published in *Cemetery Dance Magazine*; and "The Ballad of Beeve Wellington," "Apprehending Mr. Howard," and "Dreaming of Pesach with the Last Bandito," all published in *Frontier Tales Magazine.*

Peter has written screenplays for major and independent film studios, such as Paramount, Hollywood Pictures, and Zeal Pictures. Peter also served as the 2019-2020 Poet Laureate of Beacon, New York. His poetry is published in anthologies and periodicals; in the chapbook *Secret Histories and Exobiologies* from Poet's Haven; and in the full-length anthology *The Fevered Dream-Crimes of Pulp Fiction Poets and Other Love Stories* from Autumn Lion Music Publishing. His poetry has been nominated for the Pushcart Prize.

Additionally, Peter's work for the stage has been

produced off-Broadway, regionally, and internationally, and directed by such major theatre artists as Harold Prince, David Esbjornson, and Lynne Taylor-Corbett. Publications of his plays include *Big Bossman* and *The Triumphant Return of Blackbird* Flynt (Broadway Play Publishing), *New American Century & Fair City* and *Pan-American* (NoPassport Press), and *Valhalla Correctional,* included in the anthology *When the Promise Was Broken: Short Plays Inspired by the Songs of Bruce Springsteen* (Smith & Krauss). His other theatrical work includes *Flight of the Lawnchair Man, Eliot Ness in Cleveland, Hester Street Hideaway – a Lower East Side Love Story,* and *Signs of Life.* He has received numerous awards for his dramatic writing including the Roger L Stevens Award from the Kennedy Center/Fund for New American Plays and production grants from the National Endowment for the Arts and the New York Foundation for the Arts.